Times of Distress

A Story of Unswerving Faith and Commitment

Gerard Charles Wilson

Gerard Charles Wilson Publisher

Times of Distress

A Story of Unswerving Faith and Commitment

Sixties Series Book 1

Copyright © 2020 Revised 2025 Gerard Charles Wilson

Gerard Charles Wilson Publisher

Mount Martha VIC

Australia

Email: gerard.wilson1@bigpond.com

ISBN 978 1 876262 34 1 paperback

ISBN 978 1 876262 33 4 ebook

Cover Illustration by dr_evil istock

Dedication

To those dedicated nuns, brothers, and priests who gave me an excellent
education and a love of reading

Contents

Chapter 1

War threatens

JOS VAN ENGELEN'S teacher saw more in him than the typical tall, sandy-haired 17-year-old walking the streets of most Dutch towns. His classmates found him dull, with his nose stuck in books rather than sharing their adolescent fun. Meneer Dijksma, on the other hand, detected a sharp mind and a sympathetic spirit under that misunderstood reserve. He was so impressed that, though Protestant, he could not help favouring the local parish priest with his opinion when he came across him on market day.

'That boy has an aptitude for learning, Father Schoonhoven. Have you seen that?'

'Yes, indeed, Meneer Dijksma—the father's influence, no doubt.'

'It's not my business to say these things, but I thought he might interest you.'

'Your disinterested opinion is appreciated, Meneer.'

Besides Jos's keen intellect, Fr. Schoonhoven admired his strength of character and catechetical knowledge. He asked Simon van Engelen if his son showed any signs of a vocation.

'I don't know what exactly those signs could be. That's rather your province, Father.'

'You have no objection, Meneer van Engelen, if I initiate a process of discernment?'

'Of course not, but I think Jos is the one to ask.'

Young Jos had not thought much about it, but was happy to submit. Fr. Schoonhoven, refusing to let the chance slip, began a period of spiritual reflection. At the end of six months, after final exams, Jos waved to his bemused family huddled on the station platform and departed the unspoiled medieval town of Middelburg with its famous Gothic town hall. He was on his way to the seminary of the Wounded Heart of Jesus near Breda in the Province of Noord-Brabant. His brother Frans, four years younger, also showing an aptitude for learning, felt obliged to follow his admired older brother. After two years of heroic struggle, Frans found it was not for him. With a consoling pat on his brother's shoulder and a sympathetic grimace, he said farewell and returned to Middelburg, where his father enrolled him in a notarial course.

Jos persevered and was ordained in 1936 at twenty-four. His superiors wanted to send him to Rome, but Fr. Jos begged to go to the missions. He had become a priest to spread the Good News, not go stale, giving the same lectures year after year to baffled philosophy students. The superior general, Fr. Albers, relented, but with the warning, he might review his decision. He could not afford to waste the academic talents of one of his priests. And so, instead of enjoying the delights of papal Rome, Fr. Jos found himself in the sunny, sweaty town of Lae on the northern coast of Papua New Guinea.

With four daughters still at home, Frans's parents' decision to send him to Rotterdam for his studies meant strict economies. No one complained. Frans's sisters were eager to help their clever, outspoken brother realise his talents. Frans, determined to acquit himself of the privilege, breezed through the course with distinction, fulfilled the required administrative steps and returned to Middelburg to set up a practice. He remained at home, avoiding commitments, so he could contribute to the household's running and repay his parents and sisters for their generosity. But events disturbed his plans. In 1939, no one could ignore the signs of war. The Nazi invasion of Poland brought a declaration from Great Britain and France on 3 September. Mobilisation had begun. A British expeditionary force crossed the Channel.

Through the war preparations, everywhere evident in the Low Countries, life continued undisturbed in Middelburg. Frans and his father, a government official at the Abbey, the seat of Zeeland's provincial government, discussed contingency plans. Once overrun, the former island of Walcheren, on which the towns of Vlissingen and the provincial capital Middelburg were, was likely to become a pivotal defensive position against retaliation from across the Channel. Vlissingen stared across the North Sea at the Thames Estuary. Troops were stationed at Zanddijk on Walcheren and Bath in Zuid-Beveland. They had no expectations of Germanic goodwill once the Nazis had Walcheren in their hands. However, they were confident that, given the Nazis could not ignore the Dutch people's racial origins, not much of the town's administration would change. That meant Simon van Engelen would be safe. But Frans?

'You don't think I'm going to sit on my hands, do you, once the barking *Mof* have infested the place?'

'I don't want you doing anything wasteful,' said his father. 'It'll serve no purpose. We must plan how to deal with an occupation without grovelling.'

'There are ways without running into the street with guns.'

'We will resist, but with judgment.'

Early March 1940, in the bitter cold of the evening, a snow-blown shadow lugging two suitcases appeared in the family's front doorway. Relieved of his bags and after many handshakes and hugs, Fr Jos sat down with his bemused family and a cup of hot chocolate.

'I received an unexpected summons eight months ago to return to the motherhouse—'

'What for?' came a chorus before he could continue.

'And why didn't you tell us?' said his father.

'The reasons were vague. The superior general, who appeared happy with my work, said new circumstances required my return. He would explain once I was here. I had instructions to wear civilian clothes, as you see, and not to speak with anyone about it. I don't know why. In fact, I was to leave all trace of religion behind in New Guinea.'

'Goodness,' said his mother. 'And in the middle of winter. Why?'

'He didn't explain. Not about anything. He told me to burn the letter. Very unlike the usually bland superior general.'

'How on earth did you get here?'

'Boat to England, and a private boat to Vlissingen. I spent some time in London before setting out four days ago. I can't talk about the delay in London.'

'Why not?' said Frans.

'Been told to keep my mouth shut.'

There were several moments of staring surprise.

'What happens now?' said Frans, posing the question in each's eyes.

'My strict instructions were to contact the superior general, personally, I mean, by phone, as soon as I arrived here in Middelburg.'

'I'll arrange it,' said his father.

'London has changed arrangements, Pappa. I'd like you to ring for me if you don't mind. I don't want to leave the house unless I must. I'll tell you what to say.'

'Of course, my boy.'

'Why all the secrecy, Jos?' said Ada, the eldest of the four sisters.

Jos hesitated. 'I can't say, and I must ask you not to repeat this conversation.'

Mevrouw van Engelen made up a bed in the attic. When Frans deposited his brother's bags on the bed, he said, 'Okay, cut the nonsense, Jos. What's going on, and what's with these heavy bags?'

'Calm down, younger brother. I need your confidence—and help.'

The summons to return to the motherhouse and his delay in London, followed by a private boat to Vlissingen, were two different things. He could tell Frans nothing more about the summons because he knew nothing, but he could talk about London—in confidence.

'After clearing customs, I went to the order's house in London to arrange the earliest passage to Oostende. The next morning, a man from the British government turned up, asking if I would oblige by accompanying him to a meeting, a polite request I obviously could not refuse. He would not say what it was about. But I wasn't to worry. It turned out to be a meeting with people from British intelligence. One was Dutch, a military man. They had learned I was a priest on my way home to Middelburg, and I could speak English. In brief, they wanted me to help if the Germans occupied Holland, which they considered imminent. Well, it wasn't so much a request as an order. Very polite, of course. Very British.'

'What do they want you to do? Why you? And where do I fit in?'

'As a priest, I had a good cover. Two transmitters are in my bags. They want one working out of Walcheren and one elsewhere in Holland, wherever seemed most effective.'

'If you want me to work one, fine.'

'I have to set one up here as soon as possible to ensure no problems. We'll leave the other until we can decide where to use it—or where they want me to use it.'

'Let's do it, brother.'

'But I don't want Mamma and Pappa involved in any way. They must not know anything. Not a thing. They are not even to suspect anything.'

'I'll be on tiptoes.'

'I've been through an extensive briefing on this—operating a clandestine transmitter, intelligence gathering, spycraft, etc. I'll run through it all with you.'

'As I say, let's do it.'

'Remember, I will maintain my role as a priest, as a cover, and as a priest.'

'Understood.'

The following morning, Jos visited the little-known Augustinus House in Middelburg to arrange to say Mass while he stayed. Afterwards, he proceeded to Frans's office. They were soon in contact with London. Now that they had established a connection, the transmitter would sleep until needed. Jos spent the rest of the day tutoring Frans in intelligence gathering, coding, and operating the transmitter. Simon van Engelen returned from work with the news Fr. Albers would come to Middelburg the following day.

'Was that all?'

'Yes, nothing else besides polite questions about the family's health. He didn't even mention the war declaration, not that there's much war going on. He seemed unaware of the oddity of your unexplained arrival and his coming alone to this out-of-the-way town.'

When the superior general arrived the following morning, his expression showed something was preoccupying him, even if it was not the circumstances' oddity. After the required polite conversation and coffee, Fr. Albers asked to be excused. Mevrouw van Engelen offered the lounge room for private discussions, but Fr. Albers would not hear of it. Instead, they would seek a suitable place in town to talk. As it turned out, he drove to nearby Vlissingen and parked on the Boulevard overlooking the North Sea and the entrance to the River Schelde. Military preparations were everywhere.

'Come, let's walk,' he said, wrapping his coat around him against the icy wind.

They walked awhile, dodging soldiers and military activity, before he spoke.

'You know, of course, about the writings of Pope Pius X against modernism and its influence in the Church.' Jos nodded. 'Among his targets was liberalism, the idea of freedom based on a naturalist or materialist view of the world. The Church was not against freedom as such, but the idea of freedom without any objective moral restraint. The fight continues, as it has always done long before the modern rationalistic theories.' Jos nodded again. 'You must also be aware of the recent encyclicals against communism.'

'Yes, both of exceptional clarity.'

'Precisely. To be blunt, I perceive signs, even though vague, not of the naturalistic theories, but the influence of dialectical materialism among the seminary's teaching staff.'

'I was never aware of it.'

'That was four years ago. Things have changed. I'm saying there's a hint. And I'm far from sure about it. Talk of oppressive capitalism and the oppressed working class is not necessarily an indicator. No, that's not it. The sympathetic reference to German philosophy, notably Hegelian dialectics and a related form of social analysis, has disturbed me. As you know, I wanted to send you to Rome for further studies in philosophy, but gave in to your wish to go to the mission territories.'

'I have always been grateful, Father.'

'I'm afraid, Fr Jos, you and your skills are needed. During your training, you were the only one to pay attention to German philosophy, particularly Immanuel Kant and Georg Hegel. I trust you have not lost interest?'

'No, no, I have an abiding interest.'

'Good. If your parents are agreeable, you will stay here until I send for you. A week or so.'

'Yes, of course, they will be happy to have me.' He hesitated. 'Why, may I ask, has there been such secrecy?'

'I'm cautious precisely because I'm not sure of my suspicions,' Fr. Albers said, looking around and fidgeting as if his mind was not entirely with his words. 'Second, I don't want to appear inordinately concerned about communism. You understand the fascists and Nazis have been critical of communism. I want to avoid any unpleasant associations.' He paused. 'Third, there is the tactic of entryism, as you may know, where a group infiltrates an organisation to manipulate it in a particular direction. The followers of Leon Trotsky favour this tactic. You do know what I am talking about?'

'Yes, yes, I'm aware. Trotsky was not shy about it.'

'Good. The possibility of subversion is all the more reason to be careful. It could draw the accusation of a conspiratorial mentality, which may feed the resistance I'm facing.'

'Resistance?'

'I don't want to discuss that now. The possibility of a Marxist agenda is more important. There's a lot more to this than I can say. My connections with people in Rome, you know. I will leave it at that—at least for the time being. Keep this conversation to yourself unless I say otherwise.'

'I'm under your direction.'

'Good. When you arrive in a week or so, people will know you have returned for a break, after which you will pursue your doctoral studies, which were interrupted by your work in the missions. Many remember your academic ability. Along with your studies, you will be responsible for organising a course as a counterpoint to Hegelian ideas, to his dialectic. It will be under my strict supervision. That will relieve you of having to play a double role.' The superior general was about to turn to walk back to the c ar.

'Father, there's another matter that I must tell you about.'

'Oh?' Fr. Albers glanced around him again.

They walked on while Fr. Jos spoke of his meeting with British intelligence and undercover operations training.

'*Goede Hemel!*' said Fr. Albers, stopping. 'They're very presumptuous. Don't they understand your duties as a priest?'

'They didn't seem to care.'

'How do you feel about it?'

'Well, in a way, they gave me no choice. The matter had the highest priority. It seemed Dutch intelligence had a crucial role in it. I had a national duty. So, it was difficult for me to refuse. I did not want to refuse, considering what was at stake.'

'Why you? There must be dozens of Dutchmen in England, far more experienced in military and intelligence matters.'

'I have an excellent disguise as a cleric. My proficiency in English. My hometown of Middelburg. They had obviously done their homework. They seemed to know everything about me.'

'That would not have been difficult. And your vow of obedience?'

Jos hesitated, looking out over the peaking, windblown waters of the Schelde. By this time, they had reached the end of the Boulevard from where they could see Breskens on the Zeeuws-Vlaanderen shore opposite.

'These are the scenes of my childhood. So often, Frans and I bicycled from Middelburg to spend the day on the beach here. The trip on the ferry to Breskens was a special treat. That all this, our way of life, would fall into the hands of the Nazis is an unbearable thought.'

'How bearable is breaking the vow of obedience?'

'Also difficult.'

'You don't want me to force a choice.'

'Perhaps it is a weakness, but, no, I don't.'

'Have you thought you might be underestimating me?'

'I ask forgiveness if I have.'

'Let's walk.'

They walked back to the car in silence, the icy, watery wind from the sea blowing against their faces. Fr. Albers clutched the wheel and said nothing on the drive to Middelburg as if Jos had disappeared. When they pulled up outside the Van Engelen house, he sat, staring ahead. Jos waited.

'I will see you back at the motherhouse. Please give my respects to your parents. Tell them I can't linger in Middelburg. And bring your transmitter with you, suitably hidden.' He leaned over and took Jos's hand. 'Go now, lad. The moral cause has a higher priority than a legalistic understanding of the vow of obedience. There's no dilemma for you. I know more about this than I have said, at least about the wider picture.'

Jos spent the rest of his stay speculating with Frans and his father about what might result from a German move against the British and French forces in France. The Dutch government's declaration of neutrality would not halt the invasion of Holland. It was foolish to think it would. Hitler would regard such a declaration with contempt. They discussed a range of contingency plans if the Germans seized Walcheren, a strategic corner of the country at the mouth of the river Schelde, which flowed to the even more strategic Antwerp harbour.

Ten days later, after a message from Fr. Albers, Jos took the train to Breda, where someone from the motherhouse would pick him up. As the train drew away from the platform in Middelburg and Frans's figure disappeared in the curve of the tracks, he wondered if he would see his brother again. It was an uncharacteristic thought. He was not generally fatalistic, but the combination of circumstances filled him with foreboding. His feelings did not deceive him. The Germans invaded Holland on 10 May and pushed through to the coast, but met fierce resistance on the outskirts of the urban areas. Frustrated by the unexpected resistance and to induce surrender, Hitler ordered the carpet bombing of Rotterdam on the fourteenth. It was a warning to other Dutch cities. The Dutch forces capitulated on the fifteenth. The dogged resistance, however, gave Queen Wilhelmina and her ministers a chance to flee to London, where they set up a government in exile.

THE PROVINCE of Zeeland did not join the rest of Holland. Reinforced by French troops, they resisted the advance of the German army. The authorities evacuated women and children from Middelburg. Mevrouw van Engelen and her daughters went to family in Zuid-Beveland. The Germans overran the Bath and Zanddijk positions and pushed through to the Sloedam causeway that connected Walcheren with Zuid-Beveland. From there, they began an artillery bombardment of the city centre. On 17 May, reconnaissance planes circled Middelburg. Bombers later came in wave after wave to complete the destruction of the constant shelling. Almost the entire centre of Middelburg, made up of splendid medieval and Dutch Renaissance buildings, was prey to the bombing. Frans and his father watched from their house on the town's outskirts as the smoke billowed into the air, carried away by a robust wind.

'What the bombs and artillery don't destroy,' remarked Simon, his voice barely heard above the roar of war, 'the fire will with the help of this perverse wind.'

'The low water level in the canals because of the drought won't help either.'

'I think we should stay here and await our fate.'

They did not have to wait long. Middelburg had been made an example, and the remaining Dutch forces surrendered. The French troops who had regrouped in Vlissingen made it across the Schelde to Zeeuws-Vlaanderen after a courageous holding action led by Brigade General Marcel Deslaurens, who died in the fighting. Simon van Englen was right. The

artillery and the aerial bombing had been the match to light the confla-
gration. When the smoke had cleared, the horrible destruction of most
of the ancient part of Middelburg's town centre became visible. Around
six hundred houses and public buildings lay in ruins. Perhaps worse, the
town's documents and records going back a thousand years disappeared
in the flames. To ensure the maximum destruction, the German command
forbade anyone from going near the smouldering ruins for forty days. One
bright note was that the early evacuation order meant only twenty-two
people perished.

The Germans' first task was to secure the occupation. They commandeered whatever buildings they considered necessary. Those included
schools, halls, and other public buildings. Apart from the military tasks,
the German administrator, Commissioner Willi K.H. Munzer, ordered
Zeeland's population to go about business as usual. This generous allowance was Germany's concession to their Dutch cousins. Whatever the
graciousness of Commissioner Munzer, who took up residence with his
family in the elegant country house *Der Boede* and requisitioned the
desirable address 6-8 Dam for his office, the Germans were a trial. They
disrupted daily living and the running of businesses in every way. Simon van Engelen was right about his middle-level clerical position in the
municipal administration remaining unaffected. He reported to his work
daily, obeying his superiors, who took their orders from Commissioner
Munzer. Munzer surrounded himself with the despised collaborators of
the Dutch National Socialist Movement (the NSB-ers), to whom he gave
plum positions.

Frans continued his work as a notary, not that there was much work. The
lack of work suited him. After Jos's departure, he prepared for the occupation. He was in regular contact with his friends and business acquain-
tances, subtly sounding them out about a German invasion. He made up
a list of those most critical of the occupation. With them, he became more
open. Eventually, he focused on three who shared his readiness to resist the
Nazis. To his surprise, they were not among his closest friends.

During this time, he reviewed all the information Jos had given and the
instructions to work the transmitter. He swatted on the code until he was
confident with its use. Two weeks after the capitulation and the Nazis had
settled in, he secured a commitment from his friends and began operations.
He formed a cell, hiding the identity of each from the others. He drummed

into them the absolute need for secrecy, encouraging the thought that only he and each friend were in it together. The revelation of the transmitter and the function of each as a watcher deterred none.

He followed Jos's strict instructions about evading the German detection units. The transmissions must be short. He must keep on the move and have the watcher in a strategic position. As he got more proficient, he transmitted more often. The lesson of not keeping to the rules became apparent. An underground press lost no time in setting up. Flyers and pamphlets appeared, damning the Germans and encouraging resistance. The price for incaution was summary execution. A few were incautious and shot on the spot. The few transmitters flouting the rules suffered the same fate. The Germans were not stupid.

By exercising utmost caution, Frans and his cell continued to escape detection. He fed much military information to London, including details passed on by his father. He took his success as a warning. Never let your guard down. Eighteen months later, an obstacle arose to hamper his activity. The Germans summoned able-bodied men between sixteen and forty-five to report for work in the German factories. Frans and his friends went into hiding. It made things more difficult. A network of safe houses, his knowledge of the Walcheren countryside, and his unfailing caution kept him and his friends alive.

Simon van Engelen also took care while gathering information that issued from Munzer's office on Dam Square. He kept his head down, but his eyes and ears were receptive to anything interesting. Only once was he neglectful. On 24 March 1942, having arrived at work, he heard the German command had ordered Middelburg's Jews to assemble in Stationstraat. Saying nothing to his work colleagues, he hastened the short distance to find Middelburg's Jewish community gathered with bags, rucksacks, and whatever else they could carry. These people were part of his community: tailors, shopkeepers, business owners of all sorts, people with whom he had regular contact. Doctor Weyl, known to many in the town, stood on the far side of the group. He acknowledged Simon's furtive wave but stayed where he was. Simon sidled over to Meneer Kramer, nearest to him, whose menswear shop he patronised for its elegant style and taste.

'What's happening, Meneer?' he whispered, glancing at the nearby German soldier.

'We've been ordered to Amsterdam.'

'What for?'

'I don't know exactly, but it can't be good whatever it is.'

The German soldier waved his rifle, and Simon stepped away.

'Godspeed.'

The Jewish businessman nodded. Simon van Englen hastened back to his office, turning to glance once more. Later, he heard that a crowd had grown. When the time came, there was some momentary jostling as the crowd moved to accompany an integral part of Middelburg's community to the station. The German soldiers, taken unaware, acted quickly with swinging rifles to drive the crowd back. Undeterred, the crowd silently followed to the station and waited until the train departed. Frans relayed the information to London.

Chapter 2

Renewed friendship

FR. JOS STARED through the misted window as the early morning train rattled through the dripping fields, along the waterways, the rows of poplars, over the bridges, and past small villages with their church steeples dominating the rural scene. The lowering grey clouds and the drizzle sent his mind back to the sun, heat, and humidity he had left behind in Lae. Would he ever see it again? He had hoped before leaving Lae that his return to Holland would be short, a sort of sabbatical, a holiday from the burden he willingly took on. It wouldn't be. For one thing, the coming war would keep him in Holland. Then, there were his new duties and the superior general's suspicions about the staff. No, even if Fr. Albers's fears were groundless, he was stuck in Holland for the moment.

He opened his breviary to read his daily office. But he could not concentrate. So much crowded his mind. Spy on his brother priests? It presented a dilemma. He had never played a deceptive role. Deception and false behaviour were abhorrent to him. Fr. Albers had arranged his duties so he would not have to be false. Well, not openly. But his reports on his teaching and that of others with whom he collaborated would amount to intelligence reports, would they not? These thoughts occupied his mind until the train pulled into the station in Breda. He was surprised to see Fr. Albers on the platform, staring at the ground in front of him. He didn't look up until the train stopped, and Jos stepped onto the wet platform holding his two bags.

'Here, let me take one of those,' said Fr. Albers, glancing around in the same distracted way Jos had observed in Vlissingen.

'You didn't have to pick me up, Father.'

'Yes, I did, actually. Come on, let's get out of the cold.'

French soldiers were in the streets, some acknowledging the priests as they walked by. Jos glanced at his superior as the car pulled out from the curb. He waited for him to speak, curious about the unusual decision to come instead of one of the lay brothers.

'Have you had any thoughts about our conversation?' said Fr. Albers, frowning and pursing his lips.

'Not really. Perhaps only that I might be spying on my brother priests.'

'Yes, I thought that would still bother you.'

They drove on in silence for a few minutes before Fr. Albers spoke.

'I've explained, haven't I? I've arranged your duties so they come under my direct supervision. I'll be telling you what to do.' He tapped the steering wheel. 'That should relieve you of any thought of complicity.'

'Yes, I understand, Father, but—'

'When you consider what's at stake here, spying should not conflict you,' Fr. Albers continued with a sharp glance. 'You don't know what's on in the background—and you mustn't know for the moment. I have no choice. I'm forced. Think well on this: covert action is justified when the enemy follows a plan of subversion.'

'Enemy?'

'Well, what would you say about a person, even persons, who enter the priesthood to corrupt his fellow priests? To destroy the priesthood. I don't have to tell you that the priesthood is the great bulwark against the many attempts to destroy the Church.'

'It's a hellish thing to do. But do you really suspect such an evil plan in our fraternity? Priests with heretical motivations have always existed. The Church authorities dealt with them.'

'I'm talking about something quite different.'

'You mean Marxist subversion.'

'Yes, but reflect, Fr. Jos. There is something more.' The superior general paused as if struggling to find the words. 'How would you corrupt the priesthood other than by spreading ideas harmful to the faith?'

'I'm not sure what you're getting at. I suppose you mean particular actions as opposed to ideas.'

'Of the three vows—poverty, chastity, and obedience—which appears to be most difficult to live for a priest?'

'Most people would say chastity. But the authorities look on such transgressions as moral failings, don't they? And they deal with the clergy according to the seriousness of their actions.'

Fr. Albers rubbed his chin, glanced out the window, and tapped the steering wheel.

'You're assuming transgressions of the vow of chastity are about a priest's behaviour with one of his female parishioners, as regrettably happens.'

Jos frowned and glanced at his superior. 'You're alluding to other behaviour?'

'The Church is not keen to talk about it for obvious reasons, but in the long history of the Church, it has caused grave problems.'

'Isn't the approach the same? Disciplinary action.'

'This is different. It's no longer a simple question of transgression. On the contrary, normalising all sexual relations is an integral part of the Marxist agenda in undermining the family, which the Communists see as the capitalist order's basis.

'Normalising all sexual relations?' said Jos, looking askance at his superior.

'The communists' logic about the family and sexual relations was clear to those who thought about it.'

By this time, they had entered the seminary grounds, passed the lush green lawns and neatly tended gardens, and were about to pull up at the main building's entrance.

'But what's this got to do directly with the influence of Marxist ideas among the teaching staff?' said Jos. 'Surely, you don't think ...?

Fr. Albers did not budge. He grasped the steering wheel, twisting it to the left and right.

'Well ... we'll talk about it later. But consider. How easy would it be for such a priest to go about unnoticed among his confreres?'

'Still, that does not mean he will give in to his inclinations, does it? It's the same for every priest, isn't it? We must discipline ourselves.'

'What if an ideological intruder's sole purpose is to seduce a young seminarian for ideological purposes?'

'I hardly know what to say.'

'It's not as far-fetched as you imagine. There have been reports in the American Church.'

Fr. Albers alighted and went to the boot. Jos followed and took the bags handed to him. A lay brother arrived to wait on the superior general.

'We'll talk more when you have settled in,' said Fr. Albers, and turning to the lay brother, 'Please show Fr. Jos to his room.'

The talkative lay brother took one of the bags and led Jos to the priests' quarters on the upper floor.

'That's heavy,' said Br Lucas, placing the bag on the floor. 'What did you bring from missions—carvings of some sort?'

'Well, yes, and books and things,' said Jos, annoyed with himself for giving the lay brother the bag with the transmitter. 'Thank you for your help.' He hoped he did not sound evasive, though he spoke the truth about the books.

'The Angelus is at twelve and lunch at twelve-thirty,' said Br Lucas, satisfied with the explanation. 'You know where the refectory is?'

'Yes, thank you, Brother.'

Fr. Jos looked around his new accommodation. It pleased him to be in a room overlooking the front gardens and the long tree-lined avenue leading from the public road. Although spartan, the room was comfortable with a wardrobe, desk, chair, and bookshelf. A crucifix hung above his desk. It was all he needed. He unpacked his clothes, the transmitter, and the few books he had brought from Lae. The transmitter went into the wardrobe, awaiting discussions with the superior general. He sat by the window and contemplated the scene. There was still an hour to wait before chapel. From his present observation, nothing had changed since his departure four years earlier—not that anything should change. The routine and its purpose were set years ago.

Shortly before twelve, he left for the chapel on the ground floor. A gathering bustle of subdued voices and scuffing of feet on the polished floors accompanied him as the junior seminary classes broke up and headed to the chapel. The smaller classes of those in priestly formation, those in their years of philosophy and theology, were more subdued. Jos knelt in a back pew with the teaching staff and the lay brothers. There were looks of surprise and friendly glimpses. The rector of the junior seminary led in the Angelus, after which the rosary followed. The recitation of the familiar prayers was comforting and reassuring. It was a communal comfort he missed in Lae. He noticed one change, though. The numbers were larger in all sectors—more junior seminarians, more in priestly training, more

teaching staff, and more lay brothers. At the finish of prayers, Fr. Albers beckoned him.

'I'll announce your arrival at lunch. Stay with me.'

Jos was shown to a seat beside the superior general in the refectory. On the other side of Fr. Albers were the junior and the senior seminary's rectors, Fathers Koeman and van Rossem. Fr. Koeman nodded with a welcoming smile. Dr. van Rossem acknowledged him with a slight bow and a scowl. Fr. Bart Timmermans, a former classmate and a dear friend, was on his other side. He was there next to him for a purpose, Jos thought. After grace, Fr. Albers asked for the attention of the refectory.

'My dear brothers, on your behalf, I welcome Fr. Jos van Engelen, who has been in the missions in Papua New Guinea these last four years. You of the junior seminary will not know him, although he may be familiar to you from mission reports. Some of the teaching staff will remember him for his impressive academic record. Fr. Jos chose to go to the mission territories instead of pursuing further studies in Rome. He has been called home to take up the studies he had postponed. His duties will be in the philosophy department for the next year before he proceeds to Rome for doctoral studies. Under my supervision, he will put together a new course, a critical introduction to modern philosophy, as a counterpoint to our established Thomistic course. This task will be essential to his preparation for his doctoral studies. In honour of Fr. van Engelen, I suspend the rule of silence for this meal. Reader, please stand down. *Deo Gratias.*'

There were bemused expressions on some faces while the junior seminarians took advantage of the suspension and broke into noisy chatter.

'Now you know what you'll be doing, Fr. Jos,' said the superior general out of the side of his mouth. 'Sorry to break it in this way. I had my reasons.' He turned to Dr. van Rossem, who showed no inclination to moderate his scowling. 'You won't have any trouble adjusting to Fr. Jos's program, will you, Father?'

'It will take a bit of reorganising, Dr Albers, but I suppose it won't be too disruptive. The Germans will be more disruptive.'

'Well, I can't wait on the pleasure of the Germans. I had to act when the opportunity became available in Rome.'

The superior general and Dr van Rossem went on to speculate about the Nazi's intentions.

'I had no idea you were returning,' said Fr. Bart, who had started his teaching duties just as Jos boarded the boat for Papua and New Guinea. 'I'm surprised Dr Albers summoned you home during the present upheaval without telling anyone. Such behaviour is not like our superior general.'

'I had no warning, either. But we're here to obey.'

'Some of us are—at least some of us are conscious of that vow.'

'Oh?' said Jos, not missing the pointed comment.

'I think you'll find changes in your absence,' said Bart, lowering his voice. He glanced past the superior general at Dr van Rossem. 'We'll be working together, I expect.'

'What are you teaching?'

'The basics of Thomistic realism—you know, the theory of being and theory of knowledge. It's for the first-year students.'

'Oh?' Jos remembered Bart as a competent, honest student who showed a traditional understanding of classical realism.

'What? What are you thinking?'

'I am yet to discuss the course details with Dr Albers,' said Jos, aware he sounded guarded, 'but you're right. It seems we'll be working closely together.'

'Have you decided on the content for this course?' Bart gave Jos a searching look, which Jos did not miss. Besides the proposed course, some worry seemed behind Bart's cautious inquiry.

'Well, not in detail, but a basic coverage would include Enlightenment philosophers like Descartes, the British empiricists, especially David Hume, Immanuel Kant, and some introductory Hegel. The critical part would be searching for those theories' weaknesses and investigating whether classical realism provides an adequate answer. That is quite a substantial course. Indeed, there may not be time for Hegel's abstruse works. But, on the other hand,' said Jos, talking more to himself than his friend, 'one must understand Hegel to understand Marx's metaphysics with which some academics seem infatuated.'

'Well, indeed,' said Bart, raising his eyebrows.

'It's what one would expect under the heading of an introduction to modern philosophy,' said Jos, not understanding Bart's reaction.

Bart glanced to the side. 'I mean what you say about Marxist metaphysics.'

'What about it? You'll have to explain.'

'About infatuation,' said Bart, glancing at Fr. Albers, still discussing the Nazi's next moves with Frs. van Rossem and Koeman.

'What did the British say, Fr. Jos, about the Germans?' said the superior general, breaking in on their conversation. He turned to Frs. Van Rossem and Koeman, 'Fr. Jos was in London before coming across to Holland.'

Jos hesitated, not knowing what Fr. Albers had told them. He leaned forward and said, 'They seemed to think the Germans were on the point of engaging the British and French in France.'

'Well, that doesn't add anything,' said Van Rossem. 'We can work that out too.'

The abruptness and scowling indicated a surprising change in Fr. van Rossem. He had been one of Jos's philosophy lecturers. His rigour and precision in argument had been a significant influence.

'But it helps to hear even the passing views of the British,' continued Fr. Albers. 'We know they're planning for conflict.'

'The comments were the views of a small number,' said Jos, aiming to divert the conversation. He did not want to lie, nor did he want to risk saying something incautious. The lessons of British intelligence still sounded in his head. Whether by design or chance, Fr. Albers took the spotlight away from him by offering suggestions about the Germans' next move. Van Rossem took no further notice of him.

'We'll talk about it later,' whispered Bart when he saw Fr. Albers had engaged Frs. van Rossem and Koeman.

'There's something to talk about?' Jos could not help asking.

'There is always something to talk about,' said Bart with studied irony. 'Now, let me hear about your experiences in the missions. I can't imagine the difference in the cultural environment. You must have experienced a huge cultural shock.'

'I'm suffering as much cultural shock now,' Jos said with a smile.

Chapter 3

Surveillance plans

AFTER LUNCH, Fr. Albers left Jos to continue his acclimatisation. There will be adjustments to make, he said, despite his familiarity with the buildings and location. Nosy around and relax. Indeed, the chance to settle and relax was welcome. The lunchtime conversations were full of tension, and reasons for Fr. Albers's apparent preoccupation were emerging. Something was going on. Bart's reactions suggested it, too. Still, did Bart's and the superior general's have the same background? It seemed so. Anyhow, he would take advantage of the free time to nosy around, as the superior general put it. The trim lawns and the gardens in their winter slumber relaxed him, as did the unchanged surroundings. The three-story main building containing the splendid chapel, now nearly a century old, was as bold and solid as ever. On the sound of the bell for afternoon tea, he made his way to the staff common room.

Bart joined him as he poured his tea and took some biscuits, but any conversation had to wait. No sooner had they sat down than staff, those known and unknown to Jos, paraded before him, some welcoming, some just polite, and a few with a hint of irony about the course he would give. It reminded him how clergy could sometimes be rude without being open about it. Two priests, senior in appearance and manner, were among the first to approach. They remained standing with their teacups held in front of them, from which they sipped as they spoke.

'Well,' said Fr. Wouter Muller, head of the philosophy department, 'this was a surprise, young Jos. We thought we had lost your superior academic ability to the missions.'

'Did the glories of Rome change your mind?' said Fr. Aart Goedkoop, tilting his head.

'Dr. Albers warned he would likely call me home to continue my studies. I would have preferred to stay in New Guinea.'

'And your ambitions to spread the Gospel have thus been thwarted,' said Muller.

'I was happy with my work in the missions.'

'What about the nitty-gritty of your course? Does Fr. Timmermans see any conflict with his lessons?' continued Muller, nodding at Bart. 'At this stage, nobody has consulted me.'

'Fr. Albers has not discussed the details with me,' said Jos, 'but I imagine I would include Descartes and the British empiricists in an introductory course on modern philosophy, as well as Kant and perhaps Hegel with reference to Marx's dialectic.'

'As far as Marx?' said Goedkoop, rounding his lips and glancing at his colleague.

'Just as far as the materialist dialectic to show how Hegel's dialectic was manipulated to arrive at a materialist version rather than idealist.'

'That's a substantial course, it seems to me,' said Muller, holding his cup to his lips and taking an emphatic sip. 'Are you up to it? I mean, you've been in the jungle these last four years.'

'Lae is not quite the jungle. It's one of the biggest settlements along the coast.'

'Still, the point remains,' said Goedkoop. 'You would be more than a bit rusty.'

'There is always time for relaxation. I was warned not to wear myself out. That would serve no one. Reading was my relaxation.'

'Struggling through the *Critique of Pure Reason* as relaxation?' said Muller, smirking at Goedkoop.

'Nevertheless.'

At that moment, Fr. Albers entered the common room, looking around. He came to them.

'Ah, Fr. Muller, I was hoping to catch you before you spoke to Fr. Jos,' he said as if he had been running. He still wore that harassed appearance.

'No need now, Father,' said Muller, looking down his nose. 'Fr. Jos has just described his course.'

'I didn't mean the course,' said the superior general. 'That's straight-forward, isn't it? Descartes, the British empiricists, Kant, and so on. No, I wanted to discuss aligning Fr. Jos's course with Fr. Timmerman's—make one complement the other. We can do it when you're ready. No great hurry at this point. It'll be a few weeks before he can start.'

'That long?' said Muller, his frown deepening. 'The second semester has already begun.'

'Fr. Jos needs time to settle in—prepare the course—and I need time to discuss his doctoral thesis and establish a research program. Perhaps we can shorten it. Are you available to discuss it tomorrow morning? I'm sorry I have left it until now.'

'With such a brilliant academic record, I'm sure young Jos will need only a week. I will check my timetable and advise you later.'

'Good. Fr. Jos, please see me in my office when you're ready—say, in 20 minutes.'

With that, the superior general hurried off, his head bent a little forward.

'He's constantly in a hurry these days,' said Goedkoop, watching the door shut.

'You would think he was hatching some sort of dark plan,' said Muller, smiling. Not giving his colleague a chance to reply, he turned to Jos. 'I'll see you after discussing the timetable with Fr. Albers. We need to put some precision to your plan. You'll have to postpone pursuing your Roman dream for a day or two.'

'Yes, of course, Father.'

Muller turned and, saying nothing more, walked off with Goedkoop in his wake.

'They're not happy.'

'No, it would seem so,' said Jos to encourage Bart.

'It does seem strange that the superior general has sprung it on them. If I heard nothing about your recall, it seems Frs. Muller and Goedkoop hadn't either. That's not like Fr. Albers, as I say.'

Jos hesitated. He had to be careful not to betray Fr. Albers's confidence. Nor did he want to be dishonest.

'The recall came with no detail other than the instruction to be careful. I heard about the course after I arrived.'

'Careful? Why?'

'Fr. Albers didn't explain, but I suspected the growing troubles were the reason. Religious are always visible—and not always liked, as you know. At least, that's what occurred to me as soon as I arrived in London. War preparations were everywhere, just as here. I now suspect another reason.'

Bart seemed to ponder this information. Jos took the chance to divert the conversation. 'What did you mean about disobedience?'

The question caused Bart to ponder further. He glanced around him. Several staff members approached with their best wishes, and he remained thoughtful during the brief exchange. Other staff arrived. When there was a lull in the greetings, he said, 'Perhaps I was flippant. Perhaps heads of departments and senior lecturers cannot be disobedient. Perhaps they only have honest disagreements.' There was a fleeting, ironic smile. 'Fr. Goedkoop, with the support of Dr van Rossem and Fr. Muller, seems intent on highlighting the plight of the working class under capitalism. The emphasis is on capitalism as a system—as an evil system. He does this in class and general conversation, exploiting Pope Leo's encyclical on the working class to its fullest. Dr van Rossem and Fr. Muller's support is not open, but it's clear they approve of his agitation.'

'Agitation?'

'Yes, that's what it looks like.' He paused. 'Have you noticed a change in Dr van Rossem?'

'Yes, he is not as relaxed as he used to be. He appeared a little testy in his conversation with Dr Albers.'

'I'd call it irascible. He closely monitors my lecture program, criticising me for perceived faults in explanation. He is good enough not to do it in front of students. Anyhow, Dr Albers has warned that any discussion about the working class's plight should be mindful of socialism's utter inability to alleviate workers' suffering. The proof was the communist states. He insisted on a correct explanation of Leo XIII's encyclical, a close reading of the encyclicals on communism, and a firm understanding of the principles of solidarity and subsidiarity. But that hasn't deterred Goedkoop, who seems somewhat fixated on the subject. Here in the common room, I once ventured to say that advances in technology and production processes were raising living standards despite some people's miserable circumstances. The role of the state should be to set limits on economic activity. Well, it was like I hurled a bomb among the cups and saucers. My ignorance couldn't be measured, as far as Goedkoop was concerned. And how could I take the side of the fat cigar-smoking factory owners against the poor? What sort of talk was that from a Catholic priest? I soon shut up.'

'Didn't you get support?'

'No, our colleagues didn't want the nuisance, were too afraid to say anything, or agreed with the denunciation of rampant capitalism. As if I favour rampant capitalism.'

'Was it the imagined excuse for the oppression of the working class that lit Goedkoop's wick? Was it the actual reason? I don't remember any fascination with socialism when he taught me. He was straight up and down in his teaching of Church history.'

'I don't know. There's something else, though. While Goedkoop is open about his preoccupation with the working class and his antipathy for business owners making huge profits, a theme or a thread, if I can call it that, runs below the surface of the general discourse.'

He stopped and looked into the air as if ordering his thoughts.

'Yes, what do you think it is?' said Jos to encourage him,

'Let me put it this way, for want of a clearer formulation. It's like there's a loss of confidence in the philosophical defence of key dogma, that our teaching is inadequate in explaining modern life.'

'Modernism?'

'Yes, but not exactly of the liberal, materialistic sort. It's something else.' He paused. 'We have a bright student in his second year of philosophy, Hans de Jonge, with a keen interest in the liturgy. He makes much of the weaknesses in classical realism—what he perceives as the weaknesses. He jumps from those criticisms—he does it in subtle ways—to the cultural problems of the present Latin liturgy, that is, its incompatibility with modern life and with the cultures of non-European lands. He influences his fellow students.'

'A liturgical movement has, for some years, entertained these sorts of ideas. It's not big, as far as I'm aware. Stuff for intellectuals.'

'Yes, I know. But this is different. De Jonge gives the impression he sees a connection between our European-based liturgy and the capitalist order.'

'Really?' said Jos. 'Bart, how much do you know about Marxism?'

'Just the basics.'

'Does economic base, production relations, and superstructure mean anything to you?'

'Vaguely.'

Jos looked at his watch. It was past the twenty-minute mark.

'I must be going,' he said, getting to his feet. 'I'm late. We'll continue this conversation later. Let's keep it to ourselves.'

'I have no choice if I know what's good for me,' said Bart, with his boyish smile.

FR. ALBERS sat at his desk, frowning at a document in his hand, when Jos arrived at the open door.

'Come in,' he called when Jos knocked. He rose, slipped the document into his desk drawer, and locked it. 'Before you sit down, you had better fetch you-know-what. We should set that up. Make it as unobtrusive as possible. Put your coat over it or something.'

'Actually, it looks like a case.'

'All the better.'

Jos wondered on his way to fetch the transmitter if he should hide it. Would he stand out carrying an unfamiliar case? He could wrap it in his jumper or coat. No, that would attract attention. He would carry it, hoping nobody would be interested enough to stop him. To his frustration, he passed Fr. Muller and two of his staff in the corridor. They were deep in conversation and did not notice him until he was abreast of them. He saw out of the corner of his eye that Muller had stopped. He hurried on, hoping Muller would not call him back. At the corridor's end, he turned and glanced back. Muller was lingering with his eyes on him.

'I passed Fr. Muller in the corridor,' he said after arriving at Fr. Albers' office. 'He stopped and turned, but I carried on.'

'I wouldn't worry. If he asks you about it, say you had brought something back from New Guinea for me. Nothing unusual about a case.'

'As it happens,' said Jos, 'I did bring a few carvings for you.'

'There you go. Thanks, lad. You can fetch them later.' He closed the door, opened it again, glanced up and down the corridor, then shut it. 'Now, let's get that thing operating. It will be needed. The Germans are ready to pounce.'

Jos explained the workings of the transmitter and gave a quick demonstration by contacting London. London acknowledged without delay, and Jos shut it down. Fr. Albers made notes. Jos then ran through a covert agent's procedures, emphasising the need to keep the contact via the transmitter as short as possible and keep on the move. The Germans would have mobile detection units. It would be fatal to make careless mistakes. He stressed the grave warnings he had received during his London training, not that he gave any detail of his London briefing, and Fr. Albers was wise enough to know he should not inquire.

'Because I must keep on the move, I can't work from the seminary. It would be disastrous if the Nazis locked onto this place.'

'I understand. What do you suggest?'

'We're in a rural area, which I am used to. I propose reconnoitring the area to find suitable places. Is there a way I can do this without arousing the interest of the seminary population or the farm people?'

Fr. Albers walked to the window overlooking the front gardens and the fields beyond. He gazed into the distance over the flat landscape with its lines of poplars, where his mind seemed to become lost. Jos had the impression his thoughts had passed to another matter.

'For a start,' said Albers, turning abruptly, 'you can go for walks in the neighbourhood.' He came back to his desk and contemplated the transmitter. 'That's normal recreation for us, as you know,' he continued, looking up. 'The distance you cover is limited, of course. But there are other options. Some farms supply us with produce. You could be one of our contacts with them. We also have relations with the outlying parishes for whom we sometimes supply a priest for Mass. That will take you even further afield. So, I suggest you start a walking routine. I will arrange contact with the farms and the parishes.'

Jos was happy with the arrangements. Without taking a breath, the superior general outlined Jos's program for the next week. First, he was to spend time in the library thinking about his doctoral thesis and checking what research material was available.

'Have you got any ideas?'

'Unless you have a research area in mind, I thought I might investigate the epistemological development in David Hume's, Immanuel Kant's, and Georg Hegel's theories and assess how they made up for the perceived deficiencies in the realism of Christian Aristotelianism.'

'You have thought about it, I see.'

'The issues of the Enlightenment's theory of knowledge, or rather various theories of knowledge, have always fascinated me. It is a coincidence you have asked me to give a course on the subject.'

'Perhaps not such a coincidence,' said Albers, opening his hands and smiling. 'You were under my supervision for eight years.' He paused as if to emphasise its significance. 'Now, good, that's settled. I want you to draw up a preliminary reading program and submit it to me by the end of the week. I will inform Fr. Muller of my directions.' That was the signal that the meeting had ended. Fr. Albers's mind appeared to have already shifted elsewhere. The distracted look returned.

'I would like to put the transmitter in an accessible place on the ground floor, so I don't draw attention to it,' said Jos, rising and closing the lid of the case.

Fr. Albers's mind was brought back.

'Yes, of course, let me think about it. Leave it here for the night. I will inform you tomorrow.'

The following morning, after breakfast, Jos repaired to the library to check the availability of the texts. Only one copy of the texts on which he would lecture was available. He would have to arrange equal access. He made a rough plan for a two-semester course, covering two of the four philosophers in each. At ten o'clock, he made his way to Fr. Muller's office. Muller was busy with Van Rossem and had him stand in the corridor for around fifteen minutes. When Van Rossem emerged, he scowled at him.

'I hope you have a clear idea of what you will teach in a course imposed without notice.'

'Yes, Dr van Rossem,' said Jos, 'the course fits my abiding interest in epistemology—'

'Yes, yes, of course, I remember. You don't have to tell me.' Van Rossem waved his hand. 'Make sure an outline is with me by the end of the week.' He walked off, still scowling.

Muller spent the next half-hour drilling Jos about the course he had sketched. He listened and perused Jos's jotted outline, expressionless.

'Very good, young man,' he said, to Jos's surprise. 'I want you to know I support this course. It's about time our students had some notion of Hegel's dialectics. Your basic program is fine, but I want you to reorganise it, emphasising Hegel's thought. You can cover Descartes', Hume's, and Kant's main arguments in the first semester and devote the second semester to Hegel, referring to the three when required. I trust you can do that?'

'Yes, of course, Father,' said Jos, pleased with the suggestion. He had intended to focus on Hegel and his dialectic in his thesis. 'The clarity of

Descartes' and Hume's arguments lends them to summary. Kant is more difficult, particularly the "Transcendental Deduction," but I will do my best to convey the thrust of his ideas.'

'I'm impressed, young Jos,' said Muller, leaning back, 'but you were always a committed student, especially in philosophy. I wonder that you had the time in the missions.'

'I caught the philosophical bug when I read St Augustine's Confessions. That great saint's preoccupation with the nature of truth. It's in my mind no matter what I'm doing.'

Muller's lips broke into a small, thin smile, and he nodded. After lunch, Jos sought his trusted friend.

'Do you want to walk?' he whispered, sidling up to Bart and dodging the pushing junior seminarians as they emerged from the refectory. 'We have an hour before classes.' So, they set off down the main drive, intending to take the path along a narrow waterway towards the nearest village. It had been one of their favourite walks in the neighbourhood before ordination.

'How did you go?' said Bart before Jos could speak.

'Van Rossem behaved as if I were still his student. Muller was a little better, surprisingly affable after his terse manner yesterday.'

'Hmmm,' was all Bart could say as he turned to Jos. The irony was written over his face.

'I have an agreement on the course's form,' said Jos, leaving questions about Bart's penchant for irony for later. 'I have to align my course with your classes on realist metaphysics. I suggest we discuss it lesson by lesson.'

'Great idea. We'll need to sit somewhere quiet.'

'On Saturday morning, in the library, after I have submitted my final program to Muller and have it passed by Van Rossem. We shouldn't be disturbed. With Muller's unexpected support for the semester on Hegel's dialectics, we can be quite open about it.'

'Why unexpected?'

It was the question Jos was hoping for.

'Hegel's thought, to be blunt, is totally incompatible with the realist theory of being and knowledge that supports Catholic doctrine. One would have thought the senior lecturer in philosophy would show more reserve. The idea that doctrine undergoes a dialectical development from age to age is seductive, wouldn't you think?'

'To those whose minds are hyperactive?'

'Anyone in mind?'

'Fishing?'

'You're either quick or suspicious,' said Jos. It did not matter that Bart was onto him. His question took him where he wanted.

'Quick, I prefer. Yes, Hans de Jonge is a candidate. It seems to me he would eat up a semester on Hegelian dialectics, as you describe it. And, yes, Muller has been encouraging him.' Bart stopped and took Jos by the arm. They were about to cross a little wooden bridge over the waterway. The low-hanging branches of a massive oak tree sheltered them. 'We were good friends during our training, weren't we, Jos? We were completely honest about our vocation and hopes for the future.'

'Yes, we were, Bart. I always valued your friendship and support.'

'Let's be honest. There is a hint of purpose in what you're doing and whatever Dr Albers has organised for you. Maybe others don't notice. But I know you well. And the change in the superior general's behaviour seems to be connected. What's it about? You can trust me.'

'Come on. Let's keep walking,' said Jos. 'I don't want to attract attention.'

They crossed the bridge and continued along the path towards the village whose church spire rose above the grey slate roofs.

'There is something, but I can't tell you. At least, I can't tell you more than you've latched onto. I have a task to carry out.'

Bart was silent until they reached the first line of the village houses.

'Let me summarise what I have noticed,' he said as they stopped to turn back towards the seminary. 'You turn up unannounced to take up doctoral studies and give lessons in philosophy. The superior general has personally organised it all, apparently without consulting the seminary rector and head of the philosophy department, both of whom seem put out. You've constructed a course analysing ideas incompatible with Church teaching but with the apparent purpose of counteracting those ideas.'

'Is it all so obvious?'

'No, I would say not to most. Nobody else seems to see anything out of the ordinary. Most know about your academic ability and interests. Nobody is surprised you're taking up doctoral studies. And most know of the antagonisms Van Rossem arouses. People are too busy to notice, anyhow. Finally, Dr Albers's behaviour over the last year has sometimes been odd.'

'He seems distracted, as if his mind is not quite with you when talking, as if he has other things on his mind.'

'You don't know what it is?' said Bart.

'No, not with any clarity.'

'But you can confirm the rest.'

'Cleverly manoeuvred,' said Jos. 'Yes, I can confirm your observations, but I don't want to say more.'

They walked on in silence until they reached the front gates of the seminary.

'Let me repeat,' said Bart, 'you can trust me—absolutely. I won't pressure you and will act with discretion.'

'I appreciate that. If I can or need to tell you more, I will.'

'I have a feeling you will—I mean, need to tell me more. There's evil abroad.'

In the following weeks, Jos put the plans into operation. He settled on a course program, submitted it to Van Rossem and Muller for approval, and conferred with Bart about a series of philosophical counterpoints. Bart could not have been more pleased with the intellectual challenge. Strangely, Fr. Albers, who had been so insistent about supervising the course, remained at arm's length. He did not mention the course until two weeks later, and then only asked about it in general terms, and with his mind not entirely on his questions. Arranging Jos's contact with the farms and the outlying parishes seemed a prior interest.

'I want you to cycle to these farms and introduce yourself,' he said, handing him a note in the staff common room. 'This liaison is your particular job while you are with us. You need to keep up some pastoral activity. Any questions?'

With a furtive glance around him, Jos took the note, surprised that Fr. Albers was so open about it.

'No, Father.'

'Good. On Sunday, you will say Mass at Steenhoop, a little village about fifteen kilometres from here. You can take your bike. Make sure you leave early enough.'

Fr. Albers did not linger. Jos watched him go.

'You're having a busy time,' said Bart, who had been speaking with Jos before the superior general intervened.

'Fr. Albers does not want me to stay idle.'

'Is that all?'

'You weren't going to pressure me.' But before Bart could answer, 'I'm going to organise bike rides for whoever among the juniors wants to join me. That's a recreation option for them. It will be weekly. That's also part of my pastoral duties. You can help supervise.'

'Count me in. I need the exercise.'

Jos settled into a busy routine that no one interrupted or seemed interested in. Besides the bike rides and the trips to the farms and outlying parishes, he kept up a routine of walks after classes. Besides Bart, seminarians and staff from the junior seminary joined him, all of whom enjoyed the exercise and the fellowship. He took a map on which he made marks and notes. On the bike rides, he was more particular about his notations. Again, no one seemed to think this was worth commenting about—except for Bart.

'Are you going to tell me why you're doing this?' he said one afternoon. The group had kept up a solid pace, cycling north of the seminary along out-of-the-way routes and through small villages, covering around thirty kilometres with the Moerdijk Bridge over the Maas now in sight. They had stopped in a small village square. Except for Jos, who added to his notes, the others sat or stood around, grateful for a breather.

'I want to know where we're going and where the most pleasant and interesting outings are.'

'Is that all?'

'What more could there be?' said Jos, recognising he had asked a silly question.

'I can only speculate.'

'Well, don't waste your energy. We've got a lot of distance to cover before we return to the seminary.' He gave an unobtrusive wink, which Bart understood.

'Tell me the fruits of your speculation,' said Jos the next day, Sunday, when he and Bart were strolling alone in the grounds after lunch.

'You must trust me, Jos, if we pursue this conversation. Can you do that? There's no point otherwise.'

'I realise that. Come on, what have you made of everything?'

'The purpose of the new course is clear enough,' said Bart. 'It's to counter the uncritical slide in the philosophical department to incompatible theories and their insidious influence.'

'I could hardly put it better,' said Jos, thinking if he had drawn that conclusion, others might have too.

'Nobody is discussing it openly,' said Bart, as if he had read Jos's thoughts. 'The only talk is about the course itself, not about a hidden or not-so-hidden purpose. It's something new and interesting. I think you'll have inquiries from the senior seminarians. I'm thinking of Hans de Jonge and his little group.'

'All right. Anything else?'

'Your bike rides. We've been all around the district, east towards Tilburg, north to the Moerdijk Bridge, and west to Roosendaal. But not south. Why and what are all the notes for? You're surely not making tourist notes. To be blunt, it looks like intelligence gathering.'

'You're not giving in to fantasy, are you?' said Jos with a sharp look.

'Come on, Jos. You can do better than that.' Bart gave him a friendly nudge.

'Yes, I suppose I could. If I have your absolute confidence, I'll give you the full story, but before I do, you must consider that what I say might ultimately put you in danger—big danger.'

'That bad? Well, slap me with the unedited version.'

'You must promise absolute secrecy.'

'You've got it.'

Jos gave almost the unedited version, interrupted only by a variety of noises from Bart, who listened with his head down as they walked between the vegetable gardens at the rear of the property. He only held back what exactly a covert agent did. That would come when Bart decided he was fully in.

'I thought it might be some sort of intelligence activity,' said Bart in awe. 'But I could not have guessed how deep you were in it. So, the British are convinced the Germans will invade Holland?'

'Not just the British. Our government thinks so, too—at least, some in our government.'

They walked back in silence to the main building, Fr. Bart to go to his next class and Jos to the library.

'Think about it, Bart,' said Jos as they reached the point where they would go their separate ways. 'Involvement is fraught with danger.'

Bart turned to go to his class but stopped after a few paces.

'I'm in,' he called to Jos, who was already on his way to the library. Jos turned to signal his pleasure. At that moment, Muller walked by, also to go to the library. Muller glanced back at Bart.

'Your course seems to have roused a lot of interest,' he said as they entered the library. 'It's something new. It breaks the drudgery of the scholastic philosophy we've had drummed into us for so long. Well done.'

Jos sat at a library table holding a copy of David Hume's *A Treatise of Human Nature*, pondering Muller's words. Was he to take Muller's words at face value, that his course was interesting, a little intellectual food to balance the bland diet of realist philosophy with which they were sated? Or was there something more, something sinister, as Dr Albers suspected? It suddenly occurred to him that the superior general might be off target in suspecting a Marxist influence. Perhaps Hegel's dialectic, the idea of a constantly evolving truth, was the stronger influence.

He sought an interview with Fr. Albers, who for once seemed not to understand Jos's distinction. Or he was too distracted to concentrate. He was brief in his assessment. Fr. Bart's and his work in integrating their two courses were to his satisfaction. Fr. Jos was not to worry—just continue what he was doing. He kept a close eye on things, even though he might not look particularly engaged. The news that Bart had become involved concerned him more. Jos said he could not avoid an explanation when Fr. Bart began asking questions. Besides, he needed a backup for the actual covert activity and operating the transmitter.

'Yes, I understand,' said Fr. Albers. 'You and Fr. Timmermans were good friends. You could not have a more trusted backup. I assume he understands the dangers. Carry on, then. But I don't want him talking to me about it. He must have contact only with you.'

'Thank you, Father. I will make sure he knows.'

Chapter 4

Signs of conflict

JOS'S ROUTINE was well established as they passed into April. The finer weather made the bike rides more enjoyable and encouraged more seminarians to join them. Now his notated maps assumed a use he had not foreseen. Some, unfamiliar with Noord-Brabant's rural scene, wanted to return to the more interesting villages. Jos's maps let him know when and where they had visited a particular village. All this suited his hidden purpose, which was not to record Noord-Brabant's pretty villages for the seminarians' benefit but to establish networks not only along roads and lanes but across the fields. If he had to move quickly and undetected, he must know where he was going and where best to avoid a detection unit restricted to the established ways.

On one outing, Hans de Jonge and two classmates joined the group without warning. Jos was surprised. Their unfit and fastidious appearance did not signal them as sporting types. So, it was unsurprising when they complained about the pace after twenty minutes, forcing Jos to stop more often than he wished.

'It's not a race, is it?' said De Jonge, draped over the handlebars when they had stopped once again.

The overdone puffing of his two friends supported the question.

'No, it's not a race,' said Jos. 'You should think more about your fitness.'

'We're too slow,' said Bart. 'We need to keep the speed up. Otherwise, we won't see all we want to visit this afternoon. Okay? And it's Father van Engelen, Meneer de Jonge, please.'

'Sorry, I'm a little out of breath,' said De Jonge, frowning and not showing much contrition—or respect.

'I think you should reflect before joining us again,' said Jos. 'It's unfair to those who want to see something of Brabant besides having the exercise. Exercise is important for a clear mind.'

A frown and a disagreeable nod were the only responses, other than the increased effort to keep up with the group. Despite the extra exertion, they kept falling behind. Jos struggled to maintain his patience, more so because he thought it was half-hearted. A glance at Bart showed he, too, had trouble suppressing his annoyance.

'I think you should wait here for us,' said Jos when the group stopped at a small, picturesque village. 'We won't see everything at this pace. You'll be comfortable here. We'll collect you on the way back.'

'No, no,' said De Jonge, whose red, perspiring face was suddenly animated. 'I promise we'll make more effort to keep up. I want to see all the places on your list.' His disgruntled friends, surprised at De Jonge's eagerness, showed no sign of wanting to go on.

'Well, all right,' said Jos after reflecting. 'I'll give you another chance, but you must keep up.'

De Jonge did make an extra effort, at times pulling faces and whispering to his friends. Jos had to be satisfied. It would be unfair to press them anymore. Besides, they would see most of the sights he had on his list at an increased pace. But he did wonder why De Jonge did not take up his offer to wait for the group on their return. His wish to go on seemed perverse. There was something else, too. De Jonge closely watched what he was doing whenever they stopped. What possible interest could the senior seminarian have in his itinerary and notes? His friends were bored stiff. Jos hid his awareness of De Jonge's interest while keeping him under close observation. De Jonge's attention did not diminish, though he and his friends were ready to drop when they returned to the seminary late that afternoon. To Jos's amazement, De Jonge turned up the following week, now without his friends.

'Are you sure you want to go with us?' said Bart, looking him up and down. 'Have you recovered from last week's ride? If this is your way of indulging in self-mortification, please spare us. Try something else with less exhibition.'

'We will not wait for you this time,' said Jos, barely hiding his amusement at Bart's sarcasm. 'If you can't keep up, we'll have to leave you behind. Understood?'

'Yes, all right, I know,' said De Jonge, unable to stop his lower lip curling.

Again, he did his best to keep up. Again, he paid close attention to Jos's paperwork until they returned to the seminary, where he scarcely had enough energy to put his bike away. Jos was intrigued. What was motivating De Jonge?

'Did you notice De Jonge's interest in my maps and notes?' he said to Bart the following day after lunch.

'No, not more than the others, but to be honest, I wasn't paying attention. Lagging behind the group was irritating enough. Why would he have an interest anyhow? Then, again, his perverse insistence on going on the ride when it was obvious he hated it is no more explicable.'

Jos did not take it any further, realising Bart's innocent comment suggested there was indeed an explanation for the purposefulness of De Jonge's contradictory behaviour. The two bike rides were like all the others—along rural byways and through small villages. Everyone took his note-taking to be for tourist purposes. Nothing out of the ordinary. Was there something special or different in those two bike rides? There was. They encountered military activity when on the main thoroughfares. The first trip had been north towards the Moerdijk Bridge, a crucial strategic point for invaders, and Fortress Holland's entrance. There were signs of the Dutch military everywhere. The second was east towards Tilburg. French troops were stationed east of Breda, and the Dutch army was entrenched along a major defence line west of Tilburg. What was De Jonge's interest in the military—if it was that? And why wouldn't he have said so? The answer to those questions was elusive. Hans de Jonge did not go on another bike ride.

Jos's interest in the senior seminarian increased when De Jonge received permission to attend his classes on the Enlightenment philosophers. In contrast to his lack of interest in physical activity, De Jonge was all attention. He joined the class when Jos began his survey of Scottish philosopher David Hume's empiricism, in which De Jonge showed a keen interest. He sat at the back of the class, scribbling notes and occasionally asking for clarification of difficult points. With glee, he brought up Hume's arguments for destroying the principle of causality, showing that he was reading ahead of the first-year seminarians.

'The clarity of Hume's writing and his surprising counter-intuitive conclusions are a very seductive combination,' warned Jos. 'His arguments are not watertight.'

'What philosophers are?' said De Jonge, smirking.

'Context is important. You should compare Hume's work with the classical realism of the scholastics and—'

'I do,' De Jonge interrupted, continuing to smirk.

'Then you would do well to analyse them carefully and not skip like lambs in a lush meadow with arguments that have the appeal of novelty.'

De Jonge bowed his head but hardly altered or tried to hide his smirk, causing Jos more irritation than he usually succumbed to. De Jonge never intervened in class again, keeping his head down and concentrating on his notetaking. Fr. Jos wondered about the change. It was as if someone had told him to pull his head in. He had noticed De Jonge and his friends often in conversation with Fr. Muller outside of class and sometimes with Dr. van Rossem. Was he unnecessarily suspicious and drawing links that were not there? What special interest could Muller and Van Rossem have in the day-to-day conduct of his classes? They had copies of the course program.

TOWARDS the end of April, Fr. Albers seemed to snap out of his distraction. He had been talking with Jos in a general way about Holland's military preparations, which had begun in August the previous year when Germany's increasing belligerence became a worry. Now he was clear and focused. A series of confidential meetings followed with Jos, during which he explained what he knew of Holland's military preparations while referring to a large map he had laid out on his desk. He said that the Dutch government had long been in a state of total unpreparedness for war. Scandalous. Now they were suffering under the delusion that Holland could declare itself neutral. The delusion was especially acute when it was common knowledge that the Dutch armed forces lacked training, officers, and equipment.

'Absurdly enough,' he said in frustration, 'Holland has military equipment on order with the Germans.' He tapped the map several times. 'When the Germans attack, they will run straight through the Dutch defence lines.' He laid his finger on the map and traced a line along the eastern border with Germany. His finger then followed another route through the middle of the country from the IJssel Lake to the south. 'Take it from me: they are going to attack.'

'Do you know that for sure?'

'Yes, I have trustworthy information. I can't tell you where it originated, but it is sound. In a few weeks, maybe earlier, the Germans will launch an all-out attack on the British and French positions. When they do that, they will neutralise the Dutch territory, which makes sense from a defensive perspective. The government had the choice of joining with the British and French, forming a strong defensive line, but, showing a perversity approaching insanity, they knocked back the offer.'

'You are sure about this?' Jos repeated, bending over the map to examine the defence lines the superior general had traced.

'As sure as I can be,' said Fr. Albers. 'But that's not our concern. Now, look here closely.' He put his finger on the line through the middle of the country. 'This is the so-called Grebbel Defence Line joining the Peel-Raam Defence Line down to the Belgian border. The Germans will crash over the border and head for the Moerdijk Bridge. It's critical to take that bridge. That means, I speculate, they will come along this route.' He drew his finger from Gennep on the German border directly west through 's-Hertogenbosch and along a major road to the bridge over the Maas. 'They may be held up here at the Peel-Raam Defence Line.' He again tapped the map. 'But they'll quickly break through and pass close by us, to the north. Now, what does that mean?'

'I'm not sure,' said Jos, hesitating in the face of the superior general's fervour.

'They didn't say anything in London?'

'No, they concentrated on my spy training.'

'There you are,' said Fr. Albers, patting Jos's arm.

'I'm not quite sure what you're getting at, Father.'

'They gave you a second transmitter because they knew you would be resident not far from the Moerdijk Bridge, the entrance to Fortress Holland, the country's last stand. We're close to a critical crossroads. They've put you in the thick of it, expecting much from you.'

'I see what you mean,' said Jos, bending over the map to survey the Moerdijk area.

'There's also this,' the superior general continued. 'We're also near the crossroad to the southeast.' He traced a route southwest from the Moerdijk Bridge through Roosendaal, Bergen op Zoom, Middelburg, to Vlissingen on the coast of Walcheren. 'The Germans will send a force to take your part of the woods as soon as possible. They need to secure Walcheren and the entrance to the Schelde.'

'Where my brother Frans has the other transmitter,' said Jos, staring at the marked map.

'Precisely. We must pray that he is prudent in its use.'

'I'm confident he knows what's at stake.'

'It's not only the Germans he has to fear,' he said, slapping his desk. 'It's also our fellow citizens.'

'No, I can't believe there's that risk,' said Jos, shaking his head. 'The Dutch Nazis are very visible, my father said.'

'Beware, lad, beware. You can trust very few people during these diabolical times.'

'I will be careful,' said Jos, backing off. He had not seen the superior general's face so animated.

'Good. It's time for us to review your preparations.'

'If I may say so, Father,' said Jos to divert the conversation from an unpleasant subject, 'this seems to have been on your mind for a while.'

'Yes, lad, but don't ask questions. Very dangerous. After this meeting, we'll talk only when it's absolutely necessary. We must avoid the impression that we are meeting for a purpose other than your class duties and studies. No, no questions. Come on, sit down,' he said, pointing to the armchair near his bookshelf. 'I want you to tell me what you've organised. Everything. Time is pressing.'

Jos spent the next hour running over his past month's activities, isolating four networks through back roads and lanes he could take if pursued. Besides the back roads, he had isolated routes across farmland that joined the networks. He would not alert the farms' owners if he had to take them. The ditches would offer cover.

'Now that I know where the detection units may come from and the possible placement of troops, I can refine the networks,' he said, finishing.

'Very good. Well done. You seem to have covered most contingencies.' That distracted expression suddenly returned, and Fr. Albers did not speak for a while. Jos waited. And just as suddenly, he broke out of it, resuming his spirited manner.

'The farmers know you—I have had good reports—and most of the surrounding parish priests know you—again, good reports.' He waved his hand to silence any retort. 'There are several farms you can absolutely trust, not that you should distrust the others. I know these people would give their lives for their faith, for good over evil. It's the same with the outlying parishes. You can bet your life on two.' He scribbled names on a piece of paper. 'I want you to memorise these names and then burn the paper—no, memorise them within the next twenty-four hours and then give it back to me. Understood? Any questions?'

Jos understood and, for the moment, had no questions. No doubt, some would occur over the next few days. The vital questions would come when the Germans had overrun Holland and set up camp in the vicinity. But would it all go as the superior general speculated? He was pretty sure of himself. Jos suspected Fr. Albers had not told him everything, only that which involved him directly, enough to carry out his covert tasks without getting into unnecessary danger. He would have to wait to find out whether his suspicions were reliable.

The horrible notion flashed through his mind that the superior general was playing a double game, that everything he told him was a hoax, and that he was manipulating him for nefarious purposes. No, it could not be, and he felt ashamed of having entertained such melodramatic suspicions. It was entirely out of character, but then he had never known the superior general so distracted, even to be a little—it should not enter his head—even a little unbalanced. As if to encourage these devilish thoughts, the superior general disappeared for three days.

'Have you any idea where Fr. Albers has gone?' said Muller, trying to sound casual during the morning break on the second day of his disappearance.

'No, Father,' said Jos innocently. 'The superior general does not keep me abreast of his agenda.' He regretted at once the mildly sarcastic retort.

'Doesn't he just?' said Muller. A sneer was on the edge of his lips. 'You seem to spend a lot of time with him these days.'

'I cannot compare,' said Jos, trying to sound conciliatory.

'Just attending to your duties?'

'Yes, Father.'

'You're a model for the rest of us,' said Muller, walking off.

'I would be careful of getting on Muller's bad side,' said Bart. 'He has a sneaky way of getting back at you.'

'Things are a lot sharper than before I departed for Lae. Have you noticed, Bart?'

'Yes, they are, and I'm not entirely sure why. There is a subtle but persistent—what shall I call it—a persistent disagreeableness running through the community. No, it's not quite that. I need another word.'

'Don't worry. I get the idea. When did it start?'

'About a year ago—perhaps longer.'

'About the same time as the change in Fr. Albers?' suggested Jos.

'Yes, I suppose so. Do you see a connection?'

'It could be coincidental.' But he did not think so.

The next time he saw him, the superior general was chatting with Muller and Van Rossem in the common room after the day's classes. It seemed like a friendly chat over a cup of tea. They left together without acknowledging Jos and Bart, who sat in their usual places. A few minutes later, Muller returned.

'Fr. Albers wants to know how your classes are going,' he said to Jos. 'Please leave a report at my office after dinner.'

'Yes, Father. Did you discover the whereabouts of the superior general?'

'Don't be impertinent, Father van Engelen,' said Muller, turning on his heels.

'I warned you not to annoy him,' said Bart, smiling.

'I'm surprised at my boldness. Perhaps it's getting to me, too.'

Jos considered that possibility later when writing the report. It was not like him to be sarcastic or impertinent without reason, though impertinent was slightly overstated in this case. But he had been a bit impish. What had brought it on? Was the creeping sharpness in the community of priests infecting him? Or was the concentration on the secular activity of preparing for a military invasion suppressing his religious life? As was usual, he said Mass every morning, kept up his reading of the divine office, and set aside time in the chapel for his daily rosary, also as usual. No, despite his focus on his covert preparations, he was always mindful of his priesthood. He decided at length that it was the seminary atmosphere and would take steps to correct his behaviour. When he knocked on Fr. Muller's door with his report, Muller opened to reveal Dr. van Rossem lounging in an armchair, glass in hand, and scowling.

'Come in, Father,' said Muller. He grabbed the report Jos was about to hand him.

Jos, surprised at the invitation, entered and stood at attention. Muller remained standing while he perused the report. Dr. van Rossem said nothing.

'Good, very good,' said Muller, laying the report on his desk. 'You seem to keep to your undertaking despite your heavy sporting schedule.' He picked up a glass from his desk and sat opposite Dr. van Rossem in an armchair. 'I don't remember your being so sportive.'

'I was instructed to keep fit before I left for the missions. Recreation was essential for the mind and body.'

'Admirable,' said Muller, with a glance at Van Rossem, who was observing Jos. 'Your recreation here has been vigorous.'

'Others wanted to see the sights in the vicinity.' Jos was now aware they were fishing, for whatever reason, and before he could stop himself, he added, 'I recommend you join us for the exhilaration of touring beautiful Noord-Brabant.'

'This is another change in you,' said Muller. 'The sun and the idyll of the tropics have loosened some strings.'

'My apologies if I sounded inappropriately light-hearted,' said Jos, quickly correcting himself. 'The bike rides in the neighbourhood were most enjoyable both for their exercise and the tour of the Brabant countryside.'

'I hear you make an excellent tour operator,' said Van Rossem.

'Those on the rides seemed happy to leave the organising to me.'

'Which you gladly did,' said Muller.

'Yes, Father, I enjoyed it.'

'You were always well organised, I remember well,' said Van Rossem, as if this was a deficit.

'Thank you, Father.'

'You might organise bicycle tours around Rome when you leave us for the eternal city,' said Muller.

'I would enjoy the opportunity.'

'You can go now, Fr. van Engelen,' said Muller. 'I will hand your report to Dr Albers with my approval.'

'Thank you, Father,' said Jos. He glanced at Van Rossem, who, a little hunched, sat regarding him darkly from under his bushy eyebrows.

As he walked along the corridor to his room, he wondered about Muller's trenchant manner and Van Rossem's antagonism. What was motivating them? It was usual for the senior priests to test the younger priests' pride. A little humiliation was good for the soul. But Frs. van Rossem and Muller seemed motivated by more than lessons in humility. It occurred to him that Fr. Koeman, the junior seminary rector, polite and correct to a point, seemed not to belong to Fr. Muller's little club. Hans de Jonge and his two classmates were more often with Muller. Before he reached his room, a breathless junior seminarian caught up with him to say Dr Albers wished to see him.

'We have to prepare for action,' said Fr. Albers, looking up and down the corridor before he closed his door. 'Things are hotting up. The transmitter has stayed here in my room to avoid accidental discovery. It's time to shift it to operational status. I have made a place for it in the shed where we keep tools and agricultural equipment. There's a small cupboard out of the way in a corner. You know where I mean?'

'Yes, I know the shed,' said Fr. Jos, understanding from the urgency in Fr. Albers's voice that he was deadly serious. 'You have been alerted?'

'Don't worry about that.' He took the transmitter from his cupboard and laid it on his desk. 'Make contact with London and tell them we're ready.'

'Tell them we're ready?'

'Do as I say. No questions.'

Jos made contact and signalled the message. He had an immediate response.

'Ask them if they have any specific instructions.'

Jos did so and received instructions to maintain operational status.

'Anything else?' he said, understanding that Fr. Albers intended to direct him from now on.

'No, break contact and take the transmitter to the storeroom. And be careful to do it unobtrusively. Go by the corridors and stairs where there is the least traffic. Here's the key to the cupboard. Remember, you're now in operational mode.'

'Yes, Father,' said Jos, taking the key. 'You think the Germans are on the point of attack?'

'Yes, any day now. I will announce that the junior seminarians are to return home. I want you to organise them. Make a plan and give it to me in the next few days.'

'Yes, of course.' He hesitated. 'You have no doubt the Germans will invade Holland?'

'No doubt whatsoever. Foolish people in this land of ours still fantasise that the Nazis will bypass us and concentrate their military on the French and British positions. The defence of our peace-loving folk is in the hands of a few brave, undeluded people.'

Two days later, on 3 May, Fr. Albers addressed the seminary population at a special assembly. There were gasps as he announced the junior seminarians were to return home and await further direction. This was a sensible precaution, he explained. Fr. van Engelen would coordinate a staggered departure. In the meantime, the teaching staff were to round off their lesson schedule and prepare a home study program. The arrangements would, of course, be temporary. It depended on the Germans for what the seminary did next. In the event of an invasion, the junior seminarians were safer under the care of their parents.

'This is absurd talk,' muttered Dr van Rossem.

Jos glanced at Fr. Muller beside Dr. van Rossem. He was stony-faced. The rest of the teaching staff looked bemused. Dr van Rossem, with Fr. Muller in his wake, hurriedly followed the superior general out of the hall. Late in the afternoon, Jos caught up with Bart in the common room, buzzing with conversation.

'I suppose you knew about all this?' said Bart.

'Yes, he had discussed it with me. Actually, I was told. There was no discussion.'

'It seems from the reaction that Fr. Albers discussed it with nobody.' Fr. Bart pointed to Frs. van Rossem, Muller, and Goedkoop in their exclusive place on the other side of the room. Fr. Goedkoop was gesturing while the other two listened with thunderous expressions. 'They're clearly not happy with the command.'

'It had to be so, even if they weren't told. What did they expect, anyhow? Their reaction is strange.'

'Have you any idea why Fr. Albers didn't take them into his confidence?'

'Well, what can I say?' said Jos, opening his hands.

'Well, not much, I suppose, but you have information none of us has.'

'Let's meet after dinner. I want to avoid giving the impression we're in a factional discussion.'

He was about to get up when Van Rossem and his companions rose, put their cups on the sideboard, and turned to walk out. Muller stopped when they were abreast of them.

'You seem to be the superior general's snowy-haired boy,' he said with a mocking smile.

'I don't know what you mean, Father.'

'Don't you just?' The smile broadened.

'No.'

'Admirable innocence—or unswerving loyalty.'

He walked on with his frowning companions without saying anything or looking back.

'What disagreeable heads,' said Bart. 'They seem to imagine you have something to do with Fr. Albers's decisions.'

'Total nonsense, of course. The superior general is acting on his own information.' He rose. 'I'll see you after dinner.'

Bart was waiting out of the light when Jos appeared from the main entrance.

'Sorry, some teachers detained me—about the return home of the juniors.'

'Any problems?' said Bart as they set off down the drive, merging with the dark as they moved out of the scant light from the entrance.

'No, no, they're fine with the general arrangements. Just a few details to deal with.'

'You're not getting the same reaction from the Muller faction?'

'No,' said Jos, reflecting. 'I had not yet compared the reactions. But you're right. It's significant.'

'There's a pattern to the Muller faction's reactions. It looks like there's a purpose, too.'

'What do you think it is?' said Jos, testing his friend.

'If I put together all the odd changes of the last year or so,' said Bart, 'I would conclude they have a purpose incompatible with how things have been done here.'

'Any idea of the purpose?'

'What's been the change here? I would say the underlying thread of critical thought, as I suggested with Goedkoop. That directs their purpose.'

'That makes sense,' said Jos to encourage him.

'That's the only thing that occurs to me. One thing is sure. They're on a different course.'

'It aroused the superior general's interest.'

'It's the reason he has dragged you home?'

'Give the man a prize.'

They stopped by the front gates at the end of the long avenue and turned to look back at the building, whose faint outline in the dark, cloudy night made it look like a monster with irregular, gleaming eyes.

'If Fr. Albers wished to be discreet about his suspicions,' said Bart, 'he has failed. If I have twigged to his actions, others are likely to have, too.'

Jos hesitated. 'It's time to give you the rest of the story—about my part in it all and what I want you to do.'

'I'm all ears.'

With Bart following, Jos went beyond the gates and walked along the road until he stopped at a tall poplar, the first of a long line. He turned again to look back at the seminary complex of buildings. Further along the road, the lights flickered faintly through the oaks on the outskirts of the nearby village. Sheltered by the poplar, he elaborated on his meeting with British intelligence, his spy training, and working the transmitters.

'Good lord,' said Bart. 'And Fr. Albers is in all this?'

'It's better I keep to what you and I do. If you are with me, I must instruct you in covert operations in enemy-occupied territory. There's a lot to it.'

'I'm with you,' said Bart, taking hold of Jos's arm and shaking it. 'This'll be a change from talking about potency and actuality.'

Jos spent the next half-hour covering the basics of covert action, coding, operating the transmitter, and the critical watcher's role.

'We must return now. We don't want our absence noticed. The next thing is the practical exercise. We'll do this late on Sunday evening. Get some rest in the meantime. It will be a long night.'

Later that evening, he approached Fr. Albers as he left the chapel.

'I need money for clothing. As a cover, I will visit my farm contact near Breda tomorrow morning.'

'How much?'

'Enough for two sets of clothing.'

'Come to my office at nine tomorrow.'

The following morning, Jos cycled to his farm contact, where he drank coffee served with apple tart while discussing the seminary's needs. Afterwards, he cycled to Breda, where he bought dark clothing suitable for night operations in the wet and cold. He was back at the seminary shortly before the morning classes had finished. At half-past one, he and Bart were on the main drive waiting for anyone who wished to join them for the afternoon walk. Two junior school seminarians turned up. They wanted to enjoy their last walk before leaving to return home the next day.

'We have a small group this afternoon,' said Jos, welcoming them.

As they were about to set off, Hans de Jonge appeared.

'Are you coming with us?' said Bart.

'I'm allowed to, aren't I?'

'Of course you are,' said Jos.

'Didn't you have enough with the last bike ride?' said Bart.

'A walk is different. Besides, I need the exercise.'

'Well, keep up.'

Jos could no longer doubt Hans de Jonge had a purpose in joining them—and it had nothing to do with exercise and enjoying the rural surroundings. No, he was there to check on him, but not for himself. His sullen, resentful expression said it was for someone else. Why else would he engage in an activity he so obviously disliked? He had to be under the instruction of Muller and his faction. For what purpose? Why did they want to know what he was doing on the walks and the bike rides? The ready answer was for some sinister purpose. He could hardly believe it. Knowledge of his mapping had nothing obvious to do with setting up a course to counter the Marxist ideas that were vaguely spoken about, even if Fr. Albers's suspicions were correct. Unless ... He would keep De Jonge under observation.

Ten minutes into the walk, Jos stopped, unfolded his map, and made a show of looking at it and then at the fields on his right. De Jonge had begun the walk in a sullen mood but brightened as he engaged the two schoolboys in animated conversation. He kept speaking when Jos stopped, but when aware they had stopped, he halted in mid-sentence and glanced at the map. When Jos resumed the walk, De Jonge continued chatting with the schoolboys, pretending to have no interest in the map.

At length, Jos broke up the exclusive conversation. It was not difficult. The boys were weary of De Jonge's enthusiastic discussion of the Latin liturgy's faults, much of which was beyond their understanding, and were relieved when Jos drew their attention to the sights. When they stopped at the next village, Jos and Bart took them on a tour of the old church. De Jonge sat on a bench in the village square, making no effort to hide his boredom. When the walk resumed, one of the boys asked Jos about his experience in the missions. Jos had much to relate when not talking about the sights they passed. De Jonge's sullen, unresponsive mood returned. When they arrived back at the seminary, he left them saying nothing. He makes a very poor spy, Jos thought, watching him march through the first available doorway.

'What do you make of De Jonge's joining us today for an activity he clearly loathes?' he said during the break after dinner.

'I have no explanation for such perverse behaviour,' said Bart. 'He's a rather perverse fellow generally. And an irritant in class.'

Jos related his suspicions.

'Good heavens! Are you sure?'

'I've given you the details. Doesn't it all fit?'

'It's too mad to contemplate,' said Bart, his mouth open. 'If you're right, he's spying on you on behalf of the Muller faction. To state the obvious, they have interests opposed to yours and Fr. Albers'.'

'I didn't want to draw that conclusion.'

Bart remained silent, staring ahead of him. 'I'm trying to ward off an episode of paranoia,' he said at last.

'Let's attend only to the concrete details.'

'Then the conclusion is irresistible,' said Bart, sighing. 'What sort of a mad world has the seminary become?'

'It confirms my suspicion that Fr. Albers knows far more about this business than he is saying,' said Jos. 'We won't resist the conclusion, but we won't act on it as certain. We must stay supremely cautious and accept we're on our own in this. When the Nazis are among us, a false move will mean the end.'

'You don't suppose Muller supports the *Mof*, do you?' said Bart.

'No, not that.'

Bart stared at Jos, his lips moving slightly. 'Don't tell me what you're thinking. It's too horrible.'

'Just remember, we can't trust anyone. Come to my room later when everyone has retired. I've got some things for you.'

The agricultural shed was among some utility buildings at the rear of the main building and hidden by a hedge. Shortly after midnight, Jos, carrying the transmitter, wheeled his bike out. A moment later, Bart appeared, his beanie pulled down to his eyes and his scarf wrapped around his neck and c hin.

'Do I look the part?' he said.

'Perfect. I can hardly make you out. The moon is cooperating. Grab your bike, and we'll be off.'

They wheeled their bikes in silence to the public road. They looked back at the main building, shrouded in darkness. Not a sign of life.

'Okay,' whispered Jos. 'This is it—our first dummy run. Are you ready? We'll go as far as the Moerdijk Bridge, at least to a point where we would surveil the forces in control of the bridge. Then we will pick a place to transmit.'

'Show the way.'

'No talking unless it's necessary.'

'Roger,' said Bart with a laugh.

'Don't laugh. This is serious.'

'I know. It's so serious I can't help laughing.'

'Then laugh without making a noise,' whispered Jos, riding off.

'Roger and out.'

With Bart following close behind, Jos rode through a network of by-roads, tracks, and laneways for around forty minutes until he stopped at the Zwaluwsedijk. From that point on the dyke, they could see the Moerdijk Bridge over Hollands Diep about a half-mile downstream on the Maas.

'Glad to see you had no trouble following,' said Jos.

'I had paid dutiful attention.'

'We don't have to be closer to see military activity on the bridge,' said Jos, staring into the misty darkness.

'It would help if you had binoculars.'

'Yes, it would. Okay, the next step.'

They rode back the way they had come for around twenty minutes. Jos stopped on a track that crossed the fields of an isolated farm. He prepared the transmitter and sent an alert. An answer came after a few minutes. He signalled it was a test run and signed off.

'Come on,' said Jos, packing up the transmitter. 'We both have an early Mass. We can't let our little jaunt sap our attention.'

'Little jaunt!'

They arrived back at the seminary at two-thirty. After lunch that day, Monday, 4 May, Jos fell in with Fr. Albers as he walked to his office.

'I need more money,' he said, now without ceremony.

'How much?' said the superior general without slackening his pace.

'For equipment.' He listed the items.

'Write it down and bring me the list in half an hour to my office,' said Fr. Albers, signalling an end to the exchange.

Jos brought the list as bidden, preparing to receive a thick envelope. But Fr. Albers took the list and told him to return that evening after nine o'clock.

'You'll find all you need in the shed,' said the superior general when Fr. Jos had returned. 'It's packed in boxes. Don't worry. I fetched it myself. Nobody saw what I was doing.'

'Thank you, Father.'

'Prepare yourself. The fruit has ripened to bursting.'

'Do you know something?'

'Just prepare yourself, young man. You are on the point of sliding into hell.'

IT WAS not an image that thrilled Jos, perhaps too melodramatic, but the meaning struck home. He would quicken his preparations. He made a tour of the farm contacts, discreetly sounding them out about the Nazis and the possibility of invasion. They were all typically blunt in their views, but one stood out for the vigour of his denunciation and his deploring of the government's lack of preparation.

'They've lost their heads,' said old farmer Vos in his thick dialect, 'if they think Nazi jackboots won't be trampling over our floors before long.'

It was enough for Jos to risk it. Would farmer Vos mind if he kept some camping equipment with him for a while? Farmer Vos looked at him, surprised at the request, and then seemed to understand.

'Of course, lad—I mean young Father—bring what you want here. It'll be safe. You can trust the wife and me.'

'Thank you, Meneer Vos,' said Jos, deciding to say no more. Farmer Vos had no questions, but he did have a request.

'It's spring, Father. Would you mind blessing the animals?'

'No, of course not, Meneer. I will do so on my next visit.'

'Can't you do it now—a short one?'

'No, Meneer Vos. It is a particular ritual and must be done correctly.'

'Of course, lad—I mean Father—I'll be ready.' He clapped Jos on the back. 'And remember, you can trust me with your life.'

Jos ferried the camping equipment piecemeal to farmer Vos, who, in the spirit of things, stowed it in an out-of-the-way place in his barn. He seemed to see no need for questions. Jos made two more midnight excursions, west towards 's-Hertogenbosch and southwest towards Roosendaal, but without Bart. By Sunday evening, he felt he had done as much as possible in the present circumstances. It was now waiting to see what the Nazis would do.

'Have you heard any comment about me?' he said when he and Bart took their customary walk after dinner on Sunday evening.

'No, not a thing.'

'Have you noticed how agitated the superior general seems these last few days?'

'No, I didn't. Is he?'

'Yes, he knows something,' said Jos.

'Where's he getting his information, then?'

'I have no idea. He's keeping it close to his chest. We're on the eve of big events, I conclude.'

Chapter 5

Covert operations

ON MONDAY, 10 May, the seminary awoke to the hum of aircraft flying north of them towards the coast. At breakfast, Fr. Albers announced the Germans had invaded Holland without a declaration of war. One could assume they had launched an all-out assault on the Allied forces in Holland, Belgium, and France. At lunch, there was more news. Planes had bombed the airfields around Rotterdam and Den Haag and landed paratroopers. There would be prayers in the chapel at 2 o'clock.

'The strategy seems clear,' said Jos when he and Bart sat in the community room after lunch. 'They've struck straight at the heart of government. They'll cut off the blood supply by capturing the strategic bridges over the Maas and Rhine. I'd be surprised if their thick jackboots weren't already trampling over the Moerdijk Bridge. We'll see anyhow.'

'What do you mean?'

'It's not a rehearsal any longer. Coming?'

'Of course.'

'Utmost care, remember.'

Late that evening, Jos, with Bart following, took a direct route to the Maas, confident the invading German army would take a few days to join the paratroopers. He was right. The road from 's-Hertogenbosch was deserted. He was also right about the German paratroopers.

'They're there,' he said, lowering his binoculars. 'Let's get as close as we can.' He hesitated. 'No, you stay here, Bart. There's no point in endangering both of us. You need to keep the transmitter safe. Retreat to the hedge around that farm.' He pointed to a small farmhouse further along the road towards the village of Lage Zwaluwe. 'If I'm not back in an hour, you'll know I've been stupid.'

He did not risk walking along the road beside the dyke, although there was barely any light from the new moon. A route across the fields gave him more cover. It was slow going because he had to skirt around the farm between him and the bridge while looking out for the hidden water-filled ditches. He joined the road just before the railway line, cautiously made his way under the railway bridge, and took cover in a bushy area near the water. He dared not go any further. He was close enough. The German soldiers had already set up a fortification on the south side of the bridge with several on guard. It was as he had surmised. They were waiting for the invading columns to link with them.

'Come on,' he said when he joined Bart, who was near the road peering at the bridge. 'We'll wait until we're among the fields before we transmit.'

They crossed the 's-Hertogenbosch road and were among the fields before stopping.

'You must take more care, Bart,' said Jos as he set up the transmitter. 'Your back was unprotected. What if I had been a German soldier reconnoitring the area?'

'Cut it out. I checked the area.'

'Just be careful.'

Jos made contact, transmitted a brief message about the paratroopers' placement, and shut down the link.

'Come on. Let's get back. It's later than I had wished,' he said, mounting his bike. 'And I won't assume there's no detection unit operating from the bridge.'

'Jawohl, mein Kommandant.'

While Jos was devesting after Mass, the superior general came by with the request to see him at his office late in the afternoon. He arrived to find Fr. Albers sitting glumly at his desk and staring into space.

'Shut the door and sit down,' he said, coming to. 'Any news?'

'The German paratroopers have control of the Moerdijk bridge.'

'I assumed. Anything else?'

'No. I would expect a few days delay before the major invasion force links with them, granted our forces cannot hold them.'

'It will be less than that, I fear,' said Fr. Albers, tapping his desk. 'The news is vague, but I have the impression the Germans are running over our defences. The French in our area seem immobile. I can only guess that it's all a bit disorganised. The French forces will probably fall back towards the Belgian border to maintain their defence line.'

That evening in the community room, he announced the Germans had broken through the Peel defence line, and the French forces were staying put below Tilburg.

'Things are falling apart,' said Bart.

'It seems so.'

'What can we do?'

'You're going to do nothing.'

'And you?'

'I'm thinking.'

On his way from the room, the superior general commented, 'The French will hightail it to the Belgian border. Mark my words.' He was gone before Jos could answer.

The following day, 12 May, Jos waited until classes resumed before taking off towards the north. Again, he kept to the byways. He did not want to run into a forward panzer group reconnoitring the area, and he did not want to be in the way of the French forces if they decided to move north from Breda. Before noon, he arrived at the main route from 's-Hertogenbosch and took up a position among bushes at a safe distance from the road. Around mid-afternoon, he heard the rumble of heavy military vehicles.

He watched spellbound as the Nazi invasion column lumbered by. The proud, confident, determined expression on the officers was expected. But how, Jos wondered, did the rank-and-file soldiers feel? They were young men, most not much younger than him, with clear, fresh faces. Did they understand, really, what they were doing? Were they prepared to shoot him without hesitating and leave him lying in his blood if he broke cover and approached the column? It was likely, he admitted. The Nazi propaganda had been so powerful and pervasive that those young men were reduced to killing machines bereft of all feelings for those not belonging to the correct political club. He waited until the column had passed out of sight before he made a move.

'The evacuation of Breda has taken place,' said Fr. Albers when Jos had returned. 'It's chaotic. Madness. What did they expect with 50,000 civilians fleeing south to escape the war?'

'What's to be done?'

'We can't do anything other than hope they don't get caught up in the retreating French soldiers if they fall back.'

Late that evening, he and Bart cycled to one of their chosen spots in the fields to transmit his observations. The following morning after Mass, Fr. Albers asked Jos to join him in his office.

'The invading column reached the Moerdijk Bridge late yesterday afternoon,' said Fr. Albers helplessly. 'They are facing brave opposition, but it's just a question of time. The French forces are falling back to the Belgian border. A contingent of the Germans will go after them, of course. I assume there's a rout also in the north. It's all over for us.'

'It would seem so.'

'I don't want you going out anymore at night. The Germans will be everywhere in the coming days. Wait until they've settled in.'

The mood in the seminary was sombre. The community followed their routine, subdued and in silence. In the evening, Fr. Albers announced the royal family had left for England. The Dutch government had also left to form a government in exile. The news was greeted in silence. At 11 o'clock, the superior general knocked on Jos's door.

'The Germans have gone after the retreating French,' he said, pushing his way in, 'and the people fleeing have been caught in the fire. There are casualties.'

'And Breda?'

'The Germans have left it alone, as I thought they would.'

'Then we must do something.'

'What?'

'We must go and urge as many as possible to come back. Spread the message. Walking would take more than five hours to get to Zundert, nearly 20 kilometres away. I imagine few would be much beyond Zundert at this time.'

'All right, but make sure you go dressed as a religious.'

Jos and Bart took a network of byways to skirt around Breda but ran into a company of soldiers just before Rijsbergen at about one in the morning.

'Slow down and take it easy,' Jos said.

The first soldiers turned their rifles on the pair but lowered them when the priests drew near.

'Go back,' said a sergeant.

'Yes, yes,' said Jos in German, 'but we want to urge our compatriots to return to Breda.'

'Go back,' repeated the sergeant.

'The refugees need our help, would you please ...'

The company's major heard the exchange and approached.

'What's going on?' he said, flashing his torch. 'All civilians must return ...' He stopped when he saw the clerical collars.

'Greetings, Major. We would like your permission to go and urge our people to return to Breda.'

The major contemplated the request. 'You have 12 hours. Official steps are underway to bring your people back. You'll only get in the way after that.'

'Thank you, Major. God bless you.'

'Thank you, Father,' said the major. 'Now go.'

'A very obliging German soldier,' said Bart when they were out of earshot.

'Indeed.'

Their search for the refugees was haphazard because, by this time, the column of refugees on foot had scattered, many taking refuge in surrounding farms. The priests tracked down as many as possible and spread the message that it was safe to return to Breda. Going further south would risk becoming caught in the battle between the French and the advancing German army. Besides, the battle for Holland was over. The refugees received the message hesitantly, many staying put. The noise of the fighting and the overflying planes was receding south. At midday, Jos decided to return to the seminary. Not much else could be done. North of Zundert, they came across a group of people resting in the grass beside the road. Children and old people were among them. What did they intend to do? The answer was a tentative plan to continue their way south.

'You'll walk into danger,' said Jos. 'You must return to Breda. It's completely safe. The German planes have not touched it.'

There were doubtful looks and silence.

'How do we know you're not NSB-ers?' said an elderly man lying in the grass.

'What purpose, Meneer, would we have as NSB-ers in getting you bombed?'

'It's a trap.'

'No, Meneer, it's not a trap. What would we be as priests if we were leading you into a trap?' This point seemed to be well taken. 'We'll walk with you. Come on. It's not more than a few hours' walk to Breda.'

'It'll take more than that,' said the man. 'Why do you suppose we've only come this far?'

The elderly man, a handicapped woman, and a couple of very young children had delayed the group. Jos suggested that the man and the woman take their bikes, and he and Bart could take turns carrying the children. This suggestion was a breakthrough. The group got itself together and set off. As they approached Rijsbergen, they ran into the same company of German soldiers. Jos calmed the group, some of whom emitted sounds of terror.

'Thank you again, Major,' he said with a frightened child on his shoulders as they trooped past.

'Steps have already begun to bring your people back. Our personnel are helping,' said the major with a formal nod.

'God bless you.'

The major nodded without saying anything. Late in the afternoon, they came into view of Breda, whose intact sight cheered the group. Jos and Bart ensured the old people and the children arrived home safely and then returned to the seminary, arriving late in the evening. Fr. Albers expressed relief that they had safely carried out their mission.

'Go to the refectory. The cook has put aside food for you. After dinner, you are excused. Go to your rooms and get some rest. You must be exhausted.'

After lunch the next day, Fr. Albers announced the German air force had launched a raid on Rotterdam, laying waste the inner city. This attack was a barbarous action and a sign that there were no limits to what the Nazis would do. He expected the army to capitulate within twenty-four hours. The following day, the fifteenth, the news of the surrender came through. Only the French in Zeeland, with flimsy fortifications in Zuid-Beveland and Walcheren, were holding out.

'They don't have a chance,' said Fr. Albers after he had summoned Jos. 'It'll take a couple of days to mop them up. The Nazis will probably use the same strategy of bombing the population into submission. I hope and pray your family won't be casualties.'

'I'm sure my father will take the family to relations outside the town.'

'Fortunately, they've had a warning. Now, about you. I want you to continue your routine of visiting the farms and outlying parishes. You know where you're going. Always make sure your religious clothing is visible. Don't do anything suspicious. You can make notes when you return.'

'Yes, of course. I agree to proceed with caution.'

'And no transmitting for at least a couple of weeks. I expect we'll receive a visit shortly.'

Fr. Albers was right. The commandant appointed to the area south of the Maas turned up with a protective entourage and an SS officer. He summoned the senior priests, Frs. Albers, van Rossem, Muller, and Koeman. The meeting did not last long. The commandant told them they had nothing to fear as long as they cooperated and stuck strictly to their religious duties. He would be back when things were more settled. Fr. Albers warned the seminary population to be careful and do as the commandant instructed. They should not be overly concerned, provided the Nazis did not interfere with their religious duties. Everyone must wait and see how the occupation turned out.

'My first duty was to allay fears,' he told Jos later. 'The seminary must continue to carry out its role of preparing young men for the priesthood. Stability must be maintained. But some of us, those competent, prepared, and willing, have a duty to resist. I include you, you understand.'

'I understand and am willing. Are there others besides Bart and me?'

'I know nothing about Fr. Timmermans,' said Fr. Albers, wagging his finger. 'And you deal only with me. Understood?'

'Yes, Father.'

'Good. Carry on as you have been until we discuss extending your activity.'

Jos continued teaching and visiting the client farms amid the seminary's sombre, subdued atmosphere. Van Rossem and Muller had nothing to say to him other than on matters concerned with his teaching. The sly, sarcastic comments stopped. Indeed, they paid little attention to him compared with the previous weeks when they seemed to have a constant eye on him.

Chapter 6

Betrayal

ON A SATURDAY evening, three weeks later, Fr. Albers called Fr. Jos to his office after dinner, saying he had an urgent plea, a phone call, requesting a priest to say Mass at one of the outlying parishes. Fr. Janssen, the parish priest, was sick.

'I want you to slip out and say nothing to anyone. Here, take some money.' He pressed an envelope into Jos's hand.

'Why do I need money?'

'Just take it. No arguments. You never know. Now, get going. Make sure you take warm clothing and a change of clothes. The weather may turn bad, and Fr. Janssen might want you to stay a day for other things.'

Jos posed no more questions, taking it as an example of Fr. Albers's odd behaviour. He collected his things, put them in a rucksack, and slipped out of the building. He was about to wheel his bike out of the shed when he felt the urge to check the transmitter. He unlocked the cupboard and felt around. Yes, it was there, as he expected. He locked the cupboard and went on his way. Deciding it was safer, despite thinking there was no danger, he rode by a network of byways to the parish. It took nearly an hour to arrive at the presbytery. The parish priest opened the door, surprised to see him.

'Fr. Albers said you needed me for Mass tomorrow.'

'What? Are you sure? Have you got the right parish?'

The phone rang. Fr. Janssen left to answer it while Jos waited in the front parlour, holding his rucksack.

'You've got an urgent message not to return to the seminary,' said Fr. Janssen when he returned.

'From whom?'

'He didn't say. He gave the message and hung up.'

Jos sank into a nearby chair, still holding his rucksack and trying to fathom what it meant.

'I must leave,' he said, rising. 'You'll be in danger if I stay.'

'Why?'

'If the Germans turn up, say you've seen no one. It would be safer for you. I'm sure nobody saw me arrive. I'll get going.'

More than an hour later, Jos approached farmer Vos's farm. He lingered in sight of the farm, surveying the surroundings. It was too dark to see more than the farmhouse's outline and the light from the lounge room. He put his bike against a poplar and covered the rest of the way on foot. A dog started barking as he walked up the drive. There was movement from within.

'Who's there?' said farmer Vos, opening the door and calling the dog.

'It's me,' said Jos as he walked into the light from the open door.

'*Goede Hemel*! Young Father! What are you doing here?'

'May I come in?' said Jos, eager to get out of sight.

'Of course, Father,' said Mevrouw Vos, who had come to the door.

Jos said he had been on an errand when he received a mysterious order not to return to the seminary. He suspected trouble.

'Wait while I ring them,' said farmer Vos.

'No, don't! It could put you in danger.'

Farmer Vos understood. Jos asked if he could stay the night. The next day, he would try to find out what was going on, if anything, at the seminary.

'I have a better idea,' said farmer Vos. 'We'll go to Mass there as usual and sniff around. If you're in danger, you should stay out of sight.'

Jos agreed, fetched his bike, and settled down for the night in the attic. The following morning, the farmer and his wife left at their usual time but returned a half-hour later.

'German soldiers stopped us at the entrance and told us to go home,' said farmer Vos. 'They pointed their rifles at us when we asked why.'

'My God,' said Jos, falling into an armchair. 'What has happened?'

'Wait while I contact a few people.'

He made a few calls. Nobody knew anything. After midday, he received a call saying people had heard gunshots near the seminary. Jos sat with his head in his hands.

'Don't imagine the worst, Father,' said Mevrouw Vos, patting him on the shoulder. 'Wait until we know what's happened.'

Late in the afternoon, the news came that two priests had been shot as spies. The Nazis were making it clear that the penalty for espionage was instant death.

'How could it be? I don't understand.'

'Can you think of any reason at all for this?' said Mevrouw Vos.

Jos turned to her and was about to speak but stopped. 'No, you're in danger if I stay. I don't know what's happened or why, but I'm sure you'll be in danger if I stay. The Germans are likely looking for me.'

'No, lad, we're in this together,' said farmer Vos. 'I had an idea of what your business was. Get your camping equipment from the barn. We're going to set you up somewhere in the fields. For the moment.'

'Thank you, Meneer Vos, but you'll be in danger. I don't want it on my conscience if you, too, become entangled.'

'I told you, lad, don't worry. We're with you against these evil people. Now, come on. Time is critical.'

'Would you please try and find out who the priests were?'

'Of course, but I'm sure you already know.'

Farmer Vos attached a trailer to his tractor, threw in the camping equipment with picks and shovels, and told Jos to get in and lie down. He laid a sheet of canvas over him when he was settled. The tractor trundled over the fields to a clump of trees, part of a line of poplars. They spent an hour digging a ditch in which they set up the tent and organised the rest of the equipment.

'Many thanks, Meneer Vos,' said Jos when they had finished. 'I couldn't be safer for the moment. I don't know how long ...'

'Don't worry, Father. We'll do all we can to keep you safe for as long as it takes. Come to the farmhouse after dark. Mother Vos will have some tucker for you.'

Jos watched the tractor slowly trundle its way to the barn beside the farmhouse. No sooner had Farmer Vos emerged from the barn than a military truck packed with soldiers swung into the drive. Farmer Vos, unseen, entered the house through the back door while the soldiers jumped from the truck and fanned out. The officer approached the front door, where Meneer and Mevrouw Vos greeted him. Jos watched helplessly, his stomach in knots, as the search continued for a half-hour. The couple waved them away when the officer decided he had seen enough.

Jos sat on his camping stool and stared at the ground before him. What had he done? What mistakes had he made? He reviewed his past month's activities to isolate possible errors through inattention. He had been as cautious as possible—so he thought. But there were two dead. It could only be Fr. Albers and his dear friend Bart. Nobody else. Had his enthusiasm and commitment to the task blinded him to fundamental mistakes? He put his head in his hands and sat there until dark, his thoughts compulsively on Bart's bullet-riddled body. Fr. Albers knew what he was getting into. He was prepared. But Bart? He had taken to the task with youth's innocence and sense of adventure. He should have prevented him from taking part. These thoughts turned over and over in his mind until he decided he should honour farmer Vos's invitation to eat.

'I imagine it won't surprise you to hear the priests shot were Frs. Albers and Timmermans,' said farmer Vos when they were at the table.

'No, it does not.'

'Don't be too upset, lad. It's war. People die in war.'

'I know. Do you know the circumstances?'

Farmer Vos hesitated. 'You should finish your meal first.'

Jos put down his knife and fork. 'No, tell me.'

'A contingent of soldiers burst into the main building and found the two priests with a transmitter.'

'Where?'

'That's as much as we know.'

'No, it's not possible.'

'That's what we've been told—from a reliable source.'

Jos took up his knife and fork and resumed eating while Meneer and Mevrouw Vos regarded him with sympathy.

'There's been betrayal,' he said when he had finished eating. 'Thank you, Mevrouw, for dinner.' He rose.

'Who?'

'I can't say with certainty. Besides, I don't want you involved. It's too dangerous. The Germans have not finished with me. I must get away as soon as possible.'

'Don't rush it, Father.'

'I won't.'

Jos stumbled back to his tent and collapsed on the sleeping bag. He remained there paralysed for the next few days, except for meals at the farmhouse. He had promised Mevrouw Vos he would eat. His mind was full to bursting with questions, grief, and blame. He could not see how anyone could have penetrated his activities. He had been so careful. Nor did he believe Bart had been careless, despite his enthusiasm. Then, there was Muller's criticism and interest in him and De Jonge's unexpected attention to his maps. But that surely was not enough. The horrible conclusion he and Bart had drawn came back to him about Muller and Van Rossem's possible motives in getting rid of obstacles to changes in the priests' training. He could hardly think it likely they would resort to such diabolical measures. No, no, it was unimaginable. He could not believe it. Who then, and what for?

He pondered Fr. Albers's sending him away on a bogus errand that evening. Why was he so incautious if he had a hint of what might happen? And why were he and Bart operating the transmitter when he didn't want any contact with him? It did not make sense. None of it made sense. But two priests were dead, those committed to resisting the Nazis, one of whom was determined to stop Marxism's influence in the seminary. It occurred to him that Fr. Albers's activities could be far more extensive than he had considered. He knew so much of what was happening, far more than the surrounding evidence suggested. Perhaps there were more profound and remote reasons to eliminate Fr. Albers that drew Bart in as collateral damage—and himself had he been present that evening. Did that account for the bogus mission Fr. Albers sent him on? That did not explain why he sent him without Bart. He could just as easily have sent Bart on a similar errand. No, Bart must have been unforeseen collateral damage.

Still, he could not stay lying on his back in his tent, staring blankly at the seams in the canvas. He must rouse himself, even if it was only to remember the continual danger in which his presence placed the farming couple. No, he must leave as soon as possible. He must make plans. He sat on the stool, now staring at the freshly ploughed fields glowing in the early spring sun. The occasional pheasant roamed over the dirt, picking here and there, and the odd hare with its peculiar gait hopped in random directions. The birds singing and fluttering in the trees were a soothing accompaniment. These manifestations of the natural surroundings helped him to relax and focus on his predicament. By evening, he had made decisions. His thoughts turned to the envelope of money the superior general had pushed into his hands. He had not yet opened it. To his surprise, he counted 200 guilders. A generous sum. That was fortunate. Again, he had to wonder about it.

'Have you heard any more from the seminary?' he asked that evening while sitting at the table.

'The Germans are still stopping people from entering the seminary grounds,' said farmer Vos. 'I heard a funeral undertaker in Breda took charge of the bodies. They have buried them in rough graves on the seminary's grounds. The new rector has promised the commandant he would not make a fuss about them.'

'A fuss?'

'That's what I heard. I assume he is cooperating so as not to endanger anyone else.'

'I suppose so,' said Jos, considering for a moment the idea that the rector's first thought was of the welfare of the seminary's population. He assumed Van Rossem had taken charge. He did not voice his scepticism, attributing the best motives until the evidence showed otherwise.

'We'll go to the seminary for Mass, as usual, tomorrow,' said Mevrouw Vos, placing a plate of roast beef and steaming vegetables in front of him.

'That will give us a good idea of what the *Mof* are doing about this,' said farmer Vos.

'Yes, I agree. But even if they give the appearance of letting it rest, I still think they will be looking for me. They're not stupid—at least not in a military sense. So, I must leave as soon as I can.'

'What do you have in mind?'

'No, I won't say. The less you know, the better. I would like you to do something for me.'

'Just say so, lad.'

'I want some old clothes, farm labourer's clothes, and a bike repair kit. I need a bigger rucksack in which I can put my sleeping bag. That's all the camping equipment I'm taking with me. I've got money to pay for it.'

'Keep it, Father,' said Mevrouw Vos. 'You'll be needing it.'

'Thank you, Mevrouw. But there is something else. Do you have red wine?'

'Never drink the stuff,' said farmer Vos.

'We'll get some,' said Mevrouw Vos.

'And ordinary bread made from flour and water. It need not be unleavened. Just ordinary bread will do.'

'I will bake some tonight.'

'Finally, you're likely to get another visit from the Germans. They're banking on my being incautious eventually, as well as those they presume are hiding me. Prepare for another sudden raid.'

As Jos approached the barn the following evening, he heard a slight noise, like something scraping on the cobblestone path around the barn. He was already in a crouch but dropped flat on the uneven grass. He waited, listening. There was nothing more. He crawled to the side door. Once inside, he asked for the curtains to be drawn.

'I heard something near the barn.'

'What?' said farmer Vos.

'I don't know. An indistinct scraping.'

'It's probably some little animal or bird. We get them.'

Jos was not so sure, but he did not argue. There were other matters to discuss. First, what happened when they went to Mass?

'Nothing,' said Mevrouw Vos. 'There were no soldiers. Mass was said as if nothing had occurred. The only difference was that no priests appeared to speak to us after Mass. Nobody waited to chat. Everyone wanted to get away as quickly as possible. I don't blame them.'

'I'm very uneasy,' said Jos. 'I have a terrible feeling that something's hanging over us.'

'What?' said farmer Vos.

'Yes, I must go. I won't delay more than another night. I'll pack things up and leave after midnight tomorrow. I suggest you fetch the camping gear as soon as possible and erase all the signs that I have been there. I will say Mass after dinner and then return to my tent to prepare.'

'You're not letting things get the better of you, Father?'

'No, Meneer, I'm not. Besides, I can't stand the thought of the danger here.'

On leaving, he waited at the barn door until the farming couple had settled down. He crouched and listened. He crawled away from the barn and towards the fence of the adjacent field. He listened again. A noise. He stiffened. He crawled back to the barn. There was a scuffling of feet. He hastened after the disappearing footfalls as quietly as possible. When he reached the front, he saw a dark figure crouching in the ditch running along the roadside. He waited. A half-hour passed before the figure emerged from the ditch, took a bike from behind the nearest poplar, and cycled off towards Breda. The seminary was in the other direction. Who was it? Was it the Germans on the lookout for him? It seemed an odd way of doing things because whoever it was must have known he would flee if he saw someone spying on him. Surely, he had some sort of backup he could call in immediately. Nobody came.

Jos hastened back to his camping site and packed up the tent. He carried it to the barn and put it in a corner without attempting to hide it. He returned to the site and packed his rucksack with what he meant to take. A half-hour had passed, and still no raid. He returned to the house, entering through the barn. The couple was surprised to see him.

'I'm going. I caught someone spying on us.'

'No,' said Mevrouw.

'They've taken off, pedalled furiously in the direction of Breda. But I'm not sure it was the Germans.'

'Then, who?'

'I don't know. But whoever it was, they're after something. I'll take the bread and wine if you don't mind.'

'Of course, but you can wait another ten minutes while I pack some food for you.'

When he was ready to go, Mevrouw Vos took him in her arms.

'Go with our prayers, Father, and look after yourself.'

'Yes, lad,' said the old farmer, 'look after yourself. You have our constant prayers.'

'Thank you both very much. I hardly have words to express my gratitude.' He took the farmer's gnarled, calloused hand and shook it. 'The tent's in the barn, Meneer. There are just a few things among the trees to clear away.'

A vehicle swung into the drive and skidded to a stop. The sound of heavy boots trampling over the cobblestones reached them.

'Quick,' said farmer Vos, 'in the attic.'

Jos grabbed his rucksack and scrambled up the steep stairs into the attic two floors up. He felt around to find somewhere to hide. There was a pile of wooden boxes in the corner. He crouched behind them, out of breath. A loud, peremptory voice speaking German penetrated the attic, after which he heard the softer voices of the farming couple. Then there was silence.

Next, cautious footsteps on the creaking attic stairs. They stopped at the top. The beam of a torch flashed around the attic. Steps approached the boxes. They flew aside.

'You!' said the major, pointing his pistol.

Jos stood up with his hands, protecting his eyes from the powerful beam. He didn't speak, waiting helplessly. The major lowered the torch so Jos could look him in the face. It seemed an eternity before the major spoke again.

'You have twelve hours.'

'Thank you, Major. God bless you.'

The major walked to the top of the stairs.

'Watch your back,' he said, turning around.

Jos breathed a sigh of relief after the major had called his soldiers together and departed. When he came down the stairs, the farming couple looked at him in wonder. Jos told of his connection with the German army officer.

'Not all humanity is lost in war,' he said to finish.

'May God reward him for his act of mercy,' said Mevrouw Vos.

'Yes, indeed. But now I really must depart. Time is pressing.'

In the stillness of the moist rural air, he set off. He slowed as he approached the seminary building complex squatting in the dark. There was just one light on in the monster. Who could that be? He detected movement on the avenue leading to the front entrance. He stopped and strained to see who or what it was. In the scant light from the one room, he made out what looked like a figure wheeling a bike. But it had disappeared before he could be sure of what he saw. If he were right that it was someone wheeling a bike, it could not have been the same person who cycled furiously away from the Vos farm earlier. Surely not. Perhaps he had gone in the direction of Breda to mislead him and then doubled back. No, he would have arrived back at the seminary long before now. Or maybe not. Perhaps he had waited long enough to ensure the deception.

Was there another way? There was. But it was a great distance around and only covered by a fit cyclist within that time. He knew no one at the seminary with that level of sporting prowess. Certainly not De Jonge or his friends. He rode on, unable to reconcile what he saw with the person who had spied on him. On the straight evidence, it was a German spy, the one who alerted the major. But that did not ring true, either. By taking the most out-of-the-way lanes and byways, he arrived at Fr. Janssen's presbytery.

Placing his bike out of sight, he crept in the shade along the house to the back door. After a few insistent knocks, the bleary-eyed priest opened.

'Who is there?' asked Fr. Janssen, holding the door ajar.

'It's me, Fr. van Engelen. Would you please let me in?'

The priest opened the door, staring. 'Yes, yes, come in. What's going on?' he said, leading Jos into the parlour.

'Please don't turn on the light. Have the Germans been here?'

'No.'

'Thank heavens. Can I stay the day so I can rest? I will be gone by late evening.'

'What's going on? Why are you here?'

'It's better you know as little as possible, but I need your help. I would like you to write a brief letter of introduction for me, just confirming I'm a priest.'

Fr. Janssen looked doubtful but agreed to the request. After Jos refused further attention, the priest showed him to the guest room. When the housekeeper arrived in the morning, Fr. Janssen put her off, saying he had visits to make and would not be at home the whole day, which the house-keeper readily accepted. Jos slept most of the day, and when he awoke, he pored over his map, marking a line of parishes on a roundabout route north. He had one further request of Fr. Janssen before he left. Would he ring Meneer and Mevrouw Vos and ask if anyone had visited during the day? He did so, and after some hesitation, Mevrouw Vos said no one had called. Jos was relieved.

He set off after eleven o'clock and cycled through the night. At the next parish, he showed his letter and was welcomed without any questions. At his asking, the parish priest wrote a letter of introduction. Jos disposed of Fr. Janssen's letter. And so, Jos made his way on a roundabout route to Amsterdam, where he arrived two weeks later, exhausted, dishevelled, unshaven, and unwashed. In the last parish, Amstelveen, just south of Amsterdam, the parish priest took one look at him before putting him in a shed out of sight in the back garden. Two hours later, several men arrived in a truck with farm produce in the back. They installed him, his rucksack, and his bike among the potatoes, carrots, and beets and drove into Amsterdam, letting him and his bike out in the city centre. They mentioned an address and how to find it, and then disappeared into the traffic around Dam Square.

Chapter 7

Resistance

FR. JOS LOOKED around, staggering from fatigue. He quickly righted himself against the bike. There were German soldiers everywhere, but they had the swagger of the vanquisher. They chatted, lounged about, and verbally accosted whatever pretty girl chanced to pass. A dirty, unshaven beggar was not worth a glance. He saw what he had to find—the Damstraat sign. He wheeled the bike as unobtrusively as he could along Damstraat to Oudezijds Achterburgwal, a street running along a canal, the sort of canal people spoke about when they discussed their visit to Amsterdam. His instructions were to cross the bridge and turn up the other side of the canal. His destination was a narrow street near Nieuwmarkt Square. He found the house, relieved it had all been without undue anxiety. His fear was of getting lost in the maze of streets or that the haze of his fatigue would misdirect him. He leaned the bike against the wall and knocked on the weather-worn door. No sound for what seemed a long time. Then, some faint shuffling and whispering behind the door. The door opened to a little crack. Slowly, an eye appeared in the crack. A female eye.

'Fr. Hoekstra sent me, Mevrouw,' Jos hastened to say to the wary eye. 'I'm a Catholic priest.'

The door opened a trifle more to reveal two female eyes. Two suspicious male eyes appeared above them. They were examining him. Jos could not wait while they made up their minds.

'Excuse me, I need to ...,' He leaned against the door and attempted to sit on the doorstep. They instinctively resisted, leaving him to sink to the footpath and roll over on his side.

'Help him in—quickly,' said the man opening the door. 'Leave the bike for the moment.'

Jos felt himself grabbed weakly by four hands, and he gathered the strength to stand up. They pushed him inside and shut the door.

'Come to the lounge room,' said the elderly woman, supporting him on one side while the elderly man took his other arm.

'Who did you say you were?' said the man, taking Jos's rucksack before they eased him onto the couch.

'I'm sorry, Meneer,' said Jos, taking a breath. 'I'm afraid I was at the end of my reserves. I've been on the road for the last two weeks ... Fr. Jos van Engelen.'

'Where from?'

'I'm from—' Jos stopped. 'I can't tell you. It may put you in danger.'

The two glanced at each other.

'Why did Fr. Hoekstra send you to us?'

'He said you'd know.'

They glanced at each other again.

'We're sorry, Fr. van Engelen. We can't be too careful. Jeroen and Sophie de Vries.'

'I understand, Meneer and Mevrouw de Vries. No apology necessary.'

'You need some rest, Father,' said Mevrouw de Vries, putting her hand lightly on his shoulder. 'Just sit there for the moment. I will make a pot of tea and prepare something to eat.'

'Thank you, Mevrouw,' said Jos, leaning back and closing his eyes.

Despite being thirsty and hungry, he resisted falling asleep until he had eaten. Mevrouw hastily made the tea and prepared slices of bread with cheese. Jos finished his tea, bread, and cheese and was prepared to sit back and doze, but Mevrouw de Vries had not finished. She gave him a change of clothes and took him to the laundry, where there was a towel, a face washer, soap, and a bucket of water. He did not expect a bathroom in such a house.

'You can clean yourself up and then put on these clothes. Meneer de Vries is around the same height, but a little fuller. They will do for the moment. I will take your clothes and wash them. When you finish washing, you'll find a room at the back of the house where you can sleep without being disturbed.'

'Thank you, Mevrouw. I appreciate your care.'

'You're welcome, Father. My husband has gone to consult—. He says not to venture outside, not that I have to tell you.'

Jos was pleased to find the back room overlooking a small lawn and garden. It even had a little afternoon sun. Strange to find such an oasis in the dark, narrow streets of Amsterdam. When he awoke, it was dark. He felt unusually refreshed, considering the demands he had put on his body over the two weeks. He went to the lounge room, where he found the elderly couple sitting and chatting.

'The rest and a wash have done you a lot of good, Father,' said Meneer de Vries.

'You are young and fit enough to recover quickly,' said his wife.

'Thank you, Mevrouw, but I am conscious of my imposition and cost. I have some money ... but have you any news for me? I must resolve where I can stay and what I can do. I don't want to put you in danger.'

'Don't worry about us, young Father,' said Meneer de Vries. 'You'll have to be patient. I have made inquiries. I await a response.'

'From whom?'

'You must understand, Father, the situation we're all in. You must stay here for the moment and not leave the house.'

'Yes, of course. I understand.' He looked around at the darkly furnished room, exhaling the breath of the previous century. He hesitated. 'I would like to say Mass. I have not attended to that duty in over two weeks.'

'You can say Mass here, Father. Just tell us what you need,' said Mevrouw de Vries.

A week later, in the morning, Jos came from his room at the back of the house to find a young woman, untidily dressed, sloppily groomed, hair everywhere, no makeup, and around his age, sitting in the lounge room with the elderly couple.

'We'll leave you to talk with Femke,' said Meneer de Vries, rising.

'We'll return early afternoon,' said Mevrouw de Vries, also rising. 'That will be enough time, Femke?'

'Yes, Mevrouw, thank you,' said the young woman in a manner that belied her appearance.

The couple departed, leaving a bemused Jos facing the untidy, ill-groomed, hair-everywhere young woman.

'Sit down, Father,' said Femke. 'We need to have a chat.'

'Of course, Juffrouw, Mevrouw ...?' said Jos, sitting in the single lounge chair.

'Please call me Femke,' said the confident young woman, resuming her seat on the couch. 'You will know me as Femke. Now, tell me how you arrived here and why exactly. Please be honest with me and tell me everything. It will be for your protection. We can only assume there is something irregular about the arrival of a young priest here in Amsterdam, worn-out, dirty, and speaking with a slight regional accent. It's not Brabants nor Limburgs. Perhaps Zeeuws?'

'Correct, Juffrouw. I was born in Middelburg,' said Jos, understanding that Femke's appearance was a cover. 'Just as your accent is not typically Amsterdam, which one would expect from your appearance.'

'Just Femke, please, no Juffrouw. And, yes, I am not originally from Amsterdam.' She smiled. 'I assure you I can speak Amsterdams as well as any local servant girl. These circumstances do not require it. But your perception tells me much about you already. Now let's begin.'

Jos's espionage training suggested Femke was a member of some sort of covert group, likely engaged in counterintelligence against the German occupation. He sat back, crossed his legs, and began relating his training with British intelligence, moved on to his actions at the seminary, and ended with his flight to Amsterdam after the execution of Frs. Albers and Bart. Femke continually interrupted him with questions, sometimes urgent, and requests to be more specific. When he finished more than an hour later, Femke stared at him, blinking.

'You did not expect such a story?' said Jos. He could not help being amused by Femke's unguarded reaction.

'I expected you had some trouble with the Nazis, but nothing like this.' She stared into space, put her hand to her mouth and ran her index finger over a moist bottom lip. 'I need time to digest it all. I will make a cup of tea.' She rose and absently left the lounge room.

Reviewing the meeting and the conversation, Jos was now convinced that Femke was part of a covert operation. Putting a fence around her meant the group realised the importance of isolating its members. He expected he would meet nobody else in the group. Femke would finish her interview, go away, and consult before the next move.

'Can you really operate a transmitter?' she said, putting the tray with the teapot, cups, and a plate of biscuits on the coffee table.

'Yes. It was a crucial part of my training. As I said, the plan was for me to pass on intelligence about the German military activity. It later appeared, though they said nothing, that they had chosen me because of the vicinity of the seminary. At least, that was an important reason. It seems to be at a switch point for military operations.'

'Indeed,' said Femke vaguely as she poured the tea.

'May I ask something, Juff ... Femke?'

'Yes ... what ...?' said Femke, coming to herself. 'No, not really ... well, you can ask, but you may not get an answer.' She handed him a cup and a saucer with two biscuits on it.

'You are obviously part of a resistance group,' he said, taking the cup, saucer and biscuits. 'I must say it has formed quickly. British intelligence expected it, though perhaps not as quickly. Have other groups formed?'

She hesitated and then shook her head.

'I still have some questions for you,' she said, sitting down with her cup. No biscuits.

'May I make an observation before we go on?' said Jos.

'Just an observation?'

'I quickly realised your appearance is a cover. Your manner and intelligent expression, especially in your—if I may say it—in your eyes, give you away.'

She stared at him again. She blushed. 'Thank you, but I—'

'It's not meant to be a compliment, Femke. Take it as a compliment, if you wish, but it's rather a warning.'

'Well ..., I have adjusted to your company ....' Her poise had slipped a little.

'Are you Catholic?

She hesitated again. 'Yes.'

'It's a Catholic group?'

'Yes, but that's as far as I'm saying.'

'It's enough. I don't have any more questions—as yet.'

'Good.' She changed her posture as if reorganising her thoughts. 'Now, about the route you took to Amsterdam from the Vos's farm, I would like you to give me as much detail as you can remember. Please.'

Femke showed tenacious interest in his roundabout route to Amsterdam and could hardly exhaust her stock of questions. How did he choose the route? How did he escape the German patrols? How did the parish priests react? What did he do about food? Where did he sleep? And so it went on for another hour.

'You're not taking notes,' said Jos when Femke paused. 'I understand why, but are you sure you can remember it all?'

'Yes, in a word.'

'You have practised?'

'Just a few more questions, and we're done.'

'And then you will go away, consult with your superior, decide how to use me and then come back again.' He smiled. She could not help smiling in return.

'Yes, I suppose one should accept you are familiar with covert operations. In fact, you are ahead of most of us. Nevertheless, Father, you know how important it is to guard identities and maintain a disconnection between the people involved.'

'Yes, I do. You have my cooperation.'

She asked a few more questions and then rose.

'I will return as soon as possible. You know you must not leave the house.'

'I will stay put; I promise.' He looked up at her. 'Let me suggest you call me by my name. It's best to get used to it. It may prove fatal if we slip in public. And we are around the same age.'

'Thank you, Jos. I was going to suggest that. How old are you?'

'Twenty-eight.' He rose.

'So am I. You have estimated correctly despite my appearance.'

'That's another warning about disguise. It must be convincing. You have not been doing this for very long.'

'No, and point taken. I will make some adjustments.' She picked up her bag, the only thing she had brought, and threw it over her shoulder.

'Can you bring me a supply of Communion wafers and wine for Mass?' Femke nodded. 'Also, something to read. All my books are at the seminary.'

'What, for instance?'

'Preferably books on philosophy—Aquinas, Augustine, Hegel, Marx. It's my academic discipline.'

She raised one eyebrow and tilted her head. 'I'll see what I can do.'

'Thank you, Femke. I would appreciate it.'

The front door was heard creaking open. Femke waited for the elderly couple to appear.

'You have finished, have you?' said Mevrouw de Vries, all smiles and solicitation.

'Your timing is perfect, Mevrouw,' said Femke. 'I will see myself to the door. Thank you and goodbye. Goodbye, Meneer de Vries.'

'A very precise and well-organised young woman,' said Meneer de Vries after the door had creaked shut.

'What do you know about her?' Jos dared to ask.

'We've never seen her before.'

'Who did you consult, then, to bring her here?'

'Can't say.'

A FEW days later, Jos again found Femke in the lounge room when he arrived for morning tea. Two books and a package were beside her on the couch.

'Goedemorgen, Femke. I did not expect to see you so soon.'

'Goedemorgen, Father. I have the basic needs for your Mass and some books. I understand you may not have enough to occupy yourself while confined.'

He took the two books Femke held out to him and sat down. 'One on Hegel and the other on Thomistic philosophy,' he murmured. 'You surprise me, Femke.'

'They were among your requests.'

'They would not have been easy to find. You must have access to a good bookshop or library.'

'You can count yourself fortunate they were available from whatever source I happened to find.' She turned to Mevrouw de Vries. 'Do you mind, Mevrouw, if I have a private chat with Father? These houses usually have a back garden. And then I'll be gone.'

'But won't you stay for coffee first?'

'No, I must not stay any longer than necessary. Thank you, all the same.'

'Then I will prepare coffee for you and Father in the back garden. It would be unfair to deprive Father of his coffee and biscuit.'

'All right, Mevrouw,' said Femke with a smile, a charming smile Jos noticed. He also noticed she was not as untidy or ill-groomed as on the previous visit, and her hair had been clipped. The rebellious curls and strands had gone. She had taken his comments seriously. The gap between her speech and appearance was suitably narrowed.

'We found confirmation of your story about the execution of the two priests,' said Femke after they were seated at the small, unsteady garden table. 'There was a report in an Amsterdam newspaper warning that immediate death followed for those engaged in sabotage. There was nothing about the priests other than their location—Breda.'

'I'm not surprised,' said Jos. 'Of course, it's totally false that Fathers Albers and Timmermans were engaged in sabotage.'

'There's more. Breda Command believes a third person was involved, and that person is now on the run. It warns that death also awaits those harbouring a saboteur. They know who he is, and it's only a question of time before they track him down.'

'That makes Meneer and Mevrouw de Vries more vulnerable.'

'They know. They know the risks, and they are willing to accept them.'

'But am I willing to put them in such grave danger?'

'How would the Germans know that it's you who is on the run?' she said, ignoring his question.

Mevrouw de Vries arrived with coffee and biscuits. She did not say anything, only put the coffee and biscuits on the table and departed, giving them a warm smile and Jos a pat on the back.

'Two ways,' Jos continued, 'either from those now in charge of the seminary or a German major I came across during the evacuation of Breda.'

'What German major?'

Jos had not included his meeting with the German officer in his account of his escape to Amsterdam. He now did so.

'Good heavens,' said Femke. 'Not all is lost among those sad people.'

He repeated the major's warning about watching his back, which confirmed his heavy suspicion that someone in the seminary had likely betrayed him and Fathers Albers and Timmermans. Femke was not interested. Other matters took priority.

'What matters—what could be more serious than the fatal betrayal in a Catholic seminary?'

'Stay with me, Jos. I want to concentrate on how you managed to make your way from Breda to Amsterdam without starving, collapsing from exhaustion, or losing your way. It's more than a hundred kilometres.'

'I've already told you. And I was on the point of exhaustion when I arrived.'

'But you arrived. No, Jos, there's more to it. What did you do that others could not or would not do?'

'Why this concentration on how I arrived in Amsterdam?'

'Concentrate, Jos.' She held her hand up as a sign that he should block out all other thoughts. 'What gave you an advantage over someone like me? I'm fit. I have exercise. I walk. I ride a bike. But I doubt I would have lasted more than a few days. The Germans would have picked me up in no time, exhausted and disoriented.'

Jos examined the fresh, open, intelligent face, bending forward and appealing to him. There was something about that face he could not pinpoint.

'I can see you're a city person—with a good education.'

She shook her head. 'Go on.'

'Despite growing up in Middelburg, the capital of Zeeland, I'm really a country person. Zeeland is very rural. I breathe and exhale the country air. My brother and I spent many hours hiking or riding around Zeeland on both sides of the Schelde River. I know how to find my way around the countryside. You get a feeling for the different types of roads, where they lead, and why settlements are in particular places. The geography of an area tells one lots. The geography of Zeeland is thousands of years old. I can tell you why some towns are where they are and not elsewhere. Perhaps that's the difference—at least a difference with city-bred folk.'

'Yes, perhaps it is,' she mused while contemplating him. 'Did you ever lose your way?'

'I would call it taking a wrong turn, but I found the right way after a while.'

'How?'

'As I said, the geography of an area ... but I didn't stray too often because the parish priests usually gave me reliable directions. There were farmers I could ask, too, and people I encountered.'

'What about food?'

'The parish priests gave me enough. But, again, there were also the farms. You see, I took roads away from the main arteries into the farming areas. Farmers are helpful people. I can also milk a cow,' he added playfully.

Femke stood and ambled to the garden's back boundary, obviously turning over the answers to her questions in her mind. Jos watched her, intrigued, as much by her as by her questions. This was a very different sort of woman. Utterly focused. But where precisely was she going with her questions? He thought he could provide pastoral care to Catholics in some way or another. No doubt, the Germans would pick on Catholics. If there was a resistance already arising in Amsterdam—and Femke was the proof there was—he could help train people in the ways of espionage. But all these questions about how he managed to make it to Amsterdam—he could not see a connection.

'You say you mapped the district around Breda,' she said, returning to her seat at the garden table and taking up the cup of coffee she had ignored.

'Not only Breda. I went east to Tilburg, southwest to Roosendaal, and north to the Moerdijk Bridge. I followed the people fleeing Breda south to Zundert near the Belgian border. To safely transmit, I had to know how to outrun the German detection units. British intelligence stressed that I should not underestimate the Germans. They were a clever folk. Of course, I knew that, having taken German and German culture in my school studies.'

Femke fell silent, sipping her coffee. Jos waited. She was debating how to proceed. What would be the next bundle of questions? Hopefully, they would be about working a transmitter. But who would have a transmitter?

'That's it for the moment, Jos,' she said suddenly, putting her cup on the table and standing. 'I'll be back.'

'When?'

'I don't know. Be patient.'

'You can't give me a clue when and the point of your questions?'

'I thought there would be clues enough by now.'

'No, there's not.'

'That pleases me.'

'Don't speak in riddles. Why?'

'Be patient, Fr. Jos.' She mounted the short flight of stairs and disappeared inside, leaving him staring after her.

Another two weeks elapsed before Jos again found Femke cosily sitting in the lounge room with a cup of coffee, chatting with the elderly couple.

'Goeiemorgen, Father Jos,' she said with a waggish smile.

'Goeiemorgen, Femke,' said Jos, taking a seat. 'I hope you have news for me. I can bear being cooped up, especially with books to distract me, but I would like to be doing something useful.'

'I will make coffee for you and Father,' said Mevrouw de Vries, 'and then Jeroen and I will take a walk into the city centre.'

Femke waited until coffee and biscuits were put before Jos, and the couple left the house.

'Now, Jos, I've got something for you to do, you'll be pleased to hear. You are now a labourer working with a farm produce supplier. You board here with Meneer and Mevrouw de Vries. Here are your papers.' She drew papers from her bag and put them on the coffee table before him, nudging the identity card forward. 'Your name is Ruud Volkerts. Ruud Volkerts is a real person or has been a real person. He is now dead. His death has not been registered. The farm produce supplier is an actual company. You will have little to do with them. That may change, however.'

'What will I be doing, then?' he said, examining the papers. There were ration cards among them. 'What's the point of having the identity of a dead labourer working for a company I will have little to do with?'

'I want you to make a clandestine trip back to Breda,' said Femke, typically ignoring Jos's questions, 'along the same route you came to Amsterdam by and then on to Zundert, avoiding the Germans.'

'Whatever for?'

'You can't think why?'

'No, the mad idea behind it is beyond my imagination.'

'Yes, it is indeed mad—and dangerous.'

'All right, stop talking in riddles and give me the full story.'

'The full story is that you will make the trip and take someone with you.'

'What!'

'Your task is to smuggle a person to Zundert. In Zundert, you will hand that person over.'

'Who? To whom? For what purpose?'

'No, at this point, you are only to know what the task is. Let me say your success may turn out to be supremely important. If you get caught, it will mean torture and death. What I need now from you is a commitment.'

'You want me to do something that risks my life for an unknown purpose with someone I don't know?'

'Yes, in brief.'

'Has it got anything to do with my priesthood?'

She thought a moment. 'Only in the sense that it will be a supreme act of charity.'

Jos searched her face. Illumination suddenly came. How slow he had been.

'When?'

'As soon as you're ready. It's urgent. Can you be ready within the week or so? I will make all the arrangements—a change of clothes, bikes, provisions, maps.'

'Yes, all right, I commit. I'll be ready.

'Thank you, Jos. Now write down the towns or villages of all the parishes you visited.' She took a folded sheet of paper and a pencil from her bag and laid them on the coffee table. 'Write "lovely" beside the name where the parish priest was helpful, "messy" where he was moderately helpful and "not worth visiting" where he showed reluctance.'

'I think I could rely on all if pushed,' he said when he had completed the list. 'Fear was the motivation, not an unwillingness to help.'

'Friday over a week, at five o'clock, when the traffic is heavy around Dam Square,' she said with a typical shake of her head, 'be at Damstraat where you were dropped off. The same truck will slow down so you can slip into the cabin. Wear the labourer's clothes you've been wearing—not that you have a choice, of course. Leave without saying anything to Meneer and Mevrouw De Vries. They know nothing about this, nor should you ever let anything slip about it. All right?'

'Understood. It's important to provide warm, waterproof clothes. Whoever it is may not be used to Holland's wet and cold.'

'All is arranged. You will receive further instructions.'

'When?'

'You will know when you receive them.'

Chapter 8

The first operation

JOS APPROACHED the appointed spot in Damstraat five minutes before the arranged time. He held back, pretending to browse along the shops. At precisely five, he hurried forward as the truck turned from Rokin towards Damstraat. Barely slowing, the driver leaned over and swung the door open. Jos grabbed the handle and eased himself in. He looked around to see if they had alerted the soldiers hanging around Dam Square. They hadn't. He was about to utter a greeting, but the driver looked ahead with a slight shake of his head. They made their way through a labyrinth of dark, narrow streets, the slime of centuries dripping down the walls, before coming onto a main road. After half an hour, they reached the outskirts of Amstelveen, south of Amsterdam, where the driver came alongside open fields. He slowed beside a cluster of trees.

'Say "nice evening for a walk" in English. Now get out. I can't stop.'

Jos opened the door and jumped out, expecting that he would take a tumble, but managed to stay upright after a few stumbles. He looked around. Nobody. He walked up and down beside the cluster of trees for several minutes when a figure crept from behind the trees. 'Oh, no,' he murmured. A rather plump late middle-aged man of dignified bearing, dressed incongruously in labourer's clothes and a cap, approached with caution.

'A nice evening for a walk,' said Jos.

'Thank heavens I have the right person,' said the man in an upper-class English accent that told Jos bike riding would not have been a regular pastime. 'I'm Bishop Eliott from London ... Oh, I'm sorry, I'm not supposed to tell you that, am I?'

'No harm done, Your Excellency,' said Jos, frowning at his shiny dress shoes. 'But please keep to the instructions and don't speak to anyone we come across. I'm Jos. I will be leading you.'

'Thank you, young man. I'm relieved to hear you speak good, clear English. I'm in your hands.'

'How much do you know, Excellency, about this action?'

'Only that your guidance is a stage in getting me out of Europe.'

'You know we will be travelling mostly through the night and avoiding populated areas?' His suspicions were now confirmed. Femke's plans were to establish a clandestine route out of Holland for people like Bishop Eliott.

'If I didn't, I understand now.'

'Have you ridden a bike before?'

'Of course,' he scoffed. 'I was a keen bike rider in my youth, including my time at the seminary.'

'Good,' said Jos, relieved but still doubtful. 'Now show me the bikes and provisions.'

The bikes, parked behind the closest trees, had saddle bags with clothes, a small quantity of food and drink, and a map. His rucksack was there, too. He put the map into the bag and slung it over his back. There was a note from Femke.

'Bishop Eliott was caught in Amsterdam when the Germans invaded. For several reasons, he can't stay. He must go. He does not speak a word of Dutch. His unfamiliarity with Holland and his lack of fitness will be an extra burden, as you have undoubtedly seen. I will endeavour to warn your contacts before you arrive in their area. You will have to manage if I can't get you a list of contacts between Breda and Zundert. Your Zundert contact will be at the northern entrance. Be there at 5 p.m. I will be more specific in due course. The same greeting. The rest is up to you. Destroy this note. May God's blessings go with you. You will be in my prayers until you return. Femke.'

He reread it, ripped it into pieces, and stuffed the remnants in his pocket. He would discard them at an appropriate place. It was the first time, he mused, that Femke exhibited some emotion about their enterprise. He had seen she was far from a cold, unresponsive person, but until then, she had been strictly business-like.

'Are you ready, Excellency?' he said to the bishop, waiting patiently for his instructions.

'As ready as I ever can be, young man. You will, of course, remember I could be fitter for such an exercise.'

'One moment,' said Jos, again noticing the shiny dress shoes. 'Take off your shoes.'

'Take off my shoes?'

'Yes, Excellency. Didn't they give you more suitable shoes?'

'Yes, well ... they were so miserable ... and what difference ...?'

'You're meant to appear as a farm labourer, Excellency. Now take them— Wait, I'll help you.' He knelt, untied the laces, and removed each shoe while the bishop steadied himself with his hand on Jos's back. He took the shoes to the roadside, vigorously rubbed them in a rough, gravelly patch of dirt, then jumped up and down on them.

'Good gracious, young man, do you realise how much those shoes cost?' the bishop said when Jos returned.

'Are they worth more than your life?' said Jos, wondering why Femke chose such an unsuitable candidate for the first run of her plan. There must indeed be something about this bishop that necessitated his direct removal from Holland.

'I suppose not.'

'We will go at a leisurely pace with frequent stops during the first week while you get used to the exertion,' said Jos when he had returned the bishop's dirty, battered dress shoes to his feet. 'It is more important, though, to keep your wits about you. Be prepared for the unexpected appearance of German patrols. Ditches run along country roads. Be ready to dive into one.'

'Can you imagine me diving?' joked the bishop, oddly forgetting the ruination of his expensive, elegant shoes.

Jos was happy with the cheerful, optimistic mood. The bishop would need to maintain that spirit over the following days. As they were riding into the summer months, the light of July evenings lasted until 10 o'clock. It allowed them to make good progress and stay out of the way of the German soldiers. The cheerful start, however, did not last longer than the second day. The bishop began to struggle, not only with the exertion but with the route Jos took. To his surprise, the frequent stops to check his bearings and the seemingly endless turns around the expansive flat fields affected the bishop's increasingly frail state of mind.

'We seemed to be going around in circles,' he puffed when Jos stopped yet again at a crossroads to check his bearings. 'I'm becoming disoriented.'

'If you allow me, Excellency, I urge you to relax and not think about it. Leave it to me. You knew bringing you to the Belgian border might take three weeks. Your first task is to relax and save your strength.'

'Yes, of course, Jos. Excuse me. But how do you know what you're doing? How do you know we aren't really lost?' Fear and uncertainty passed over his face.

'I grew up in the country. I am familiar with the organisation of Dutch roads. Most importantly, I successfully negotiated this route recently. Trust me.'

'Sorry, young man. I must admit this is a long way from my comfortable bishop's office at the Cathedral. I'll try to do better.'

It was no good. The rest stops became more frequent, and the bishop's face more drawn and paler. In the second week, he lay prostrate in the grass, emitting a low moan whenever they stopped. Jos encouraged him to keep going. Each day, they were making progress. Each day, they were approaching their destination where he would have a chance to rest. But Jos said that for encouragement. He did not know if Femke had organised a rest break at Zundert. He would certainly need it. Things were looking grim, so grim that Jos did not dare to take him into the villages to collect provisions and possible messages from the parish priest. He left him out of sight, lying flat in a field with instructions not to stand up while he hurried to complete his errand. Fortunately, there were no hitches—but no messages.

Towards the end of the second week, they arrived without mishap at an out-of-the-way punt that would take them across the river Maas. That was the least likely place to find a German patrol, Jos had calculated. Bishop Eliott hung over his handlebars, gasping, while they waited with a few locals to board the punt that had just docked. The bishop glanced behind him and froze. He slumped and toppled to the ground with the bike ending on top of him. The locals gathered around him. One removed the bike. Jos looked back and saw a small German patrol on the road along the river looking at them. He bent down. 'Don't say a word.' He hailed the German soldiers.

'Could you help us with my sick uncle?' he said in broken German to the two soldiers who answered his call. 'I need to take him home to my aunt over the river. He's a bit heavy for me.'

The young soldiers took a lingering look at Jos, the bishop, and the farming folk.

'Come on,' said one, 'Let's get this dirty fat country bumpkin on the punt. It will be today's good deed.'

'*Danke sehr, Danke sehr,*' said Jos, bowing when they had deposited the bishop on the punt, where he flopped to the floor. The locals looked suspiciously at him. 'I can't thank you enough. My aunt thanks you, too.'

The soldiers nodded, waved their hands, and returned to the group on the road.

'We don't know what you're up to,' said one of the men in a heavy regional accent, 'but we'll help where we can.'

'Thank you, Meneer. I do indeed need some help. Are the Germans—?'

'Don't worry about the *Mof*. You won't see them around here for the rest of the day.'

'We need some shelter for a while ... a shed or something ... out of the way. We won't stay more than a day or so.'

'Follow me,' said the man holding Jos's bike.

Jos helped the bishop onto his bike, whispering, 'Don't say anything,' and pushed him along after the man while his two companions helped to steady the bike.

It wasn't long before they came in sight of farm buildings. They left the road and took a track across the fields to a hay shed behind the farmhouse.

'You'll be right here,' said the man. 'Nobody, except us, will know you're here. I will fetch some food and drink.'

'I can't express enough gratitude—'

'No thanks necessary. We don't know what you're doing and don't want to know.' His two companions nodded. 'But whatever it is, it takes a lot of courage. We can see your friend is not Dutch.'

'Thank you again.'

Jos made a bed of hay as far inside the shed as possible and helped the bishop to become comfortable. The bishop lapsed into a state of unconsciousness. A groan came from him now and then as Jos contemplated his options. There weren't many. He could not extend their stay in the hay shed. He had promised to move so as not to endanger the farming folk.

Second, he could not count on the German soldiers remaining oblivious to whom they had helped. It was necessary to move, but he must also find a place where the bishop could recuperate for several days. The only place that came to mind was the Vos farm. That was probably two days away on the bishop's present rate. There was an advantage in coming into an area he knew well. He knew where to halt safely out of the way of the German patrols. That was his only option. And he could count on Meneer and Mevrouw Vos. The bishop slept through the night until late the following day.

'I'm a dratted nuisance, aren't I?' he groaned, struggling to prop himself up on one elbow.

'You've had a good rest,' said Jos. 'Now, have something to eat and drink before we plan our next move. There's a bucket of water and a cloth to clean yourself up.'

'You haven't given up on me, then?' said the bishop, sitting upright and seeing the bowl of bread and a cup of water to his side.

'We won't give up, Excellency.'

The bishop grabbed the bowl and gobbled down the bread, after which he drank the cup empty.

'I know we are not to discuss this action, Excellency,' said Jos while the bishop cleaned his face and neck, 'but I can't help wondering why you, when you are, to be honest, quite unfit for it. You need not respond if you don't wish.'

The bishop remained silent for a while, looking wearily around him.

'You really are quite a determined young man, Jos, fully conscious of your duty.' The bishop focused his eyes on him. 'I understand why they chose you for this hazardous operation. You are unfaltering.' He held up his hand to stop a response. 'To answer your question, I know too much. It was necessary to get me out of Europe. We did not expect the Germans to invade so soon. We thought I would have more time. The carpet-bombing of Rotterdam locked me up in an environment where I was entirely unsuited to pursue the business—I won't say any more.' He waved his hand dismissively and then contemplated Jos. 'Have you ever thought of a vocation to the priesthood? The Church needs young men like you.'

'We?' said Jos, with a hint of a smile.

'I'll leave you to speculate.'

'I have said too much and broken my own rules,' said Jos with a wry smile. 'Do you think you are ready to resume our journey? You don't have a choice, actually.'

'Help me up, young man.' The bishop held out his hand, and Jos pulled him unsteadily to his feet. He placed his hand on Jos's shoulder. 'Now kneel down.' Jos sank to his knees with the bishop's hand still on his shoulder. 'May Our Lord and His Blessed Mother bless and preserve you.' He raised his hand and made the sign of the cross, '*Benedicat tibi Dominus et custodiat te.*'

'Thank you, Excellency.'

'I'm ready when you are.'

Two men from the previous day arrived, wheeling their bikes.

'Where are you going? I mean, what direction?' said the man who had shown them to the shed. He handed over a bag. 'Here's some food to keep you going.'

'To Breda—the west side of Breda. I know the way from north of Breda.'

'We will ride ahead of you on the best route to avoid the German patrols. We'll give a warning if we see anything suspicious.'

'Are you sure?' said Jos. 'I don't want to put you in danger. To be frank, you risk your life if you get caught with us.'

'We'll be okay. Piet will go ahead of me, and I will go ahead of you. I'm Hans, by the way.'

'Our hearty thanks, Piet and Hans, but keep in mind our pace will be slow, and we might have to stop now and then.'

'I'll do my best,' whispered the bishop, understanding. He earned an admonishing shake of the head from Jos.

The plan worked well. They had to retrace their way only once, and the bishop required no more than two rest stops during the night. As the sun rose, Jos called to his scouts.

'Wait to the side, Excellency, and don't say anything.' Jos waited until the scouts drew up beside him. 'We'll be right from here, *Heren*. Many thanks again.'

'It is the least we can do when we see what you are doing,' said Hans. 'We wish we could do more.'

Jos hesitated. 'May I call on you again, perhaps sometime in the future?'

Farmer Hans's expression suggested he understood. 'In the same circumstances?'

'Perhaps,' said Jos. He was placing great trust in the unknown farmer.

'You can trust me,' said Hans, seeing Jos's caution. 'If there's a next time, go straight to the shed and leave a pile of hay outside that can be seen from the farmhouse.'

The two farmers went on their way, and Jos headed to a cluster of poplars he knew from his previous explorations. There was shelter there, and they were out of view of anyone happening along that secluded rural way.

'Make yourself comfortable, Excellency, and take a long rest. We are not far from our immediate destination, and I don't want to stop again.'

The bishop meekly followed Jos's directions and lay in the grass. Within a few minutes, he was sleeping soundly. Jos, too, settled down for a rest. In the early afternoon, the bishop awoke and looked around as if trying to discover where he was.

'You've had a good sleep, Excellency,' said Jos, sitting against the trunk of a poplar. 'Have something to eat and prepare to leave in an hour or so.'

The bishop took the bread and cheese Jos had laid out for him and ate silently. He seemed to be turning things over in his mind.

'Do you want to hear more about my activities in Amsterdam, Jos?' he said. 'I can see you're still puzzled why such a man as I, seemingly unsuited for espionage, was sent precisely to do that—spy, I mean—and why getting me out of Holland is so important.'

'I confess I am curious. It is against our instructions, though.'

'Blow the instructions.'

'Well, Excellency, I can't overrule a bishop.'

Bishop Eliott laughed. 'Nobody has ordered me around so much and in such a peremptory manner since my seminary days.' He held up his hand. 'I know, Jos, you're just doing your job. Well, I came to Amsterdam to take part in a meeting about ecumenism—'

'But the Church has spoken against ecumenism,' said Jos before he could stop himself.

'Now that gives something of yourself away,' said the bishop with a knowing look. 'Who but an educated Catholic would know the Church's views on ecumenism?'

'Please go on, Excellency.'

'There's no change to the Church's stance on a syncretic type of ecumenism,' continued the bishop, with a playful look, 'but some of us think we should know what the different ecumenical groups are thinking. We should know how sincere they are about resolving doctrinal differences. We know, for example, that the Marxists have infiltrated some groups to undermine Christianity in general and the Catholic Church in particular. The Soviet Union is pumping money into them. Then there's Freemasonry. Of course, there are Freemasons and Freemasons. For the truly enlightened Freemason, though, Enlightenment reasoning is central to Freemasonry. Are you with me, Jos?'

'Yes, of course, Excellency. As you say, an educated Catholic would know about these things, even if superficially.'

Jos was surprised by the bishop's sudden animation. He had risen above his exhaustion, the effort bringing a layer of perspiration to his forehead and temples.

'Good. But note well. I have said the truly initiated. What could I mean?'

'You must tell me, Excellency.'

'Despite Freemasonry's boast that reason is the final tribunal, not religion or tradition, it has a range of steps or thresholds to perfect enlightenment. A member must demonstrate that he can penetrate the barriers and arrive at this perfected knowledge. It's not open to everyone.'

'Gnosticism,' said Jos, suspecting the bishop was testing him.

'Aha!' said the bishop, pointing. His face was flushed from the exertion. 'You are a strange spy, Jos. You are clearly up to your neck in counter-intelligence, but you show you know something about the occult and esotericism. 'Who are you, Jos?'

'We've been instructed to keep our conversation to what's necessary. There are good reasons for this, as you are aware. I must confess my curiosity got the better of me when I should have resisted.'

'I wasn't just satisfying your curiosity. I think you know that. As a counterintelligence agent, you should know about my spying activities—as meagre as they are—compared to yours.'

'True,' said Jos, reflecting unguardedly. 'Perhaps Femke should have—' He stopped.

'Who's Femke?'

'Just someone connected with—never mind. Who is overseeing your removal? We have come this far. Perhaps you can tell me what you know. It may fatally influence my decisions.'

Jos was aware he was fishing for other connections. He could not resist.

'To be truthful, I'm not sure,' said the bishop, leaning back. 'With the Rotterdam bombing and my isolation in Holland, the danger became immediately obvious—to others as well as me. The local bishop told me to keep low until something could be worked out. I twiddled my thumbs for a week. Then, a priest knocked on my apartment door late at night. He was in clericals. He didn't say who he was, and I had never seen him before. He was Dutch—his accent, you know. He told me to get ready immediately, to take only what was necessary. He left without giving me a chance to ask questions. I packed and waited.

'At two o'clock in the morning, there was another knock. A thickset man, most of his face hidden by a scarf, pushed past and grabbed my bags. "Follow. Don't talk," he mumbled in a thick accent. He took me to an old, broken-down truck parked in a side street. He signalled to keep out of sight. It seemed like we drove for hours, with me crouching, but it was only an hour or so. We ended up at a farmhouse way out in the country. I was given farming clothes and left in the charge of a robust woman who could not speak English. But she made delicious meals as robust as she.

'There I stayed, crushed by boredom, until some weeks later when the same unknown priest turned up late at night, but now in civies. He was on a bike. Be ready, he said. I would be smuggled out of Holland. I could take nothing—only the clothes I wore. The same truck arrived mid-afternoon the next day. The same gruff man checked to ensure I followed instructions and then brought me to where you found me. I had to wait for two hours behind those poplars.'

'He missed your precious shoes.'

'But you didn't. Now, does that help? I imagine it does.'

'Yes, it does,' Jos mused. 'A resistance ...'

'Yes, Jos, you can say it. An organised resistance is developing.'

'Yes, but ours is a Catholic resistance, I note.'

'There will be others. The Dutch Communist Party appears to be going into action.

'That's in character. People must be careful not to become tools in their grander plans.'

'Once again, Jos, you give yourself away.'

'Do I?' said Jos innocently.

'Yes, and you have exhausted me. I need another half-hour.' He lay back in the grass and closed his eyes. He was soon emitting a dull, choking snore.

Jos contemplated the prostrate prelate. He was showing signs of recovery. He had lost much weight, though he could still lose more. A week's rest at the Vos's should make him fit enough to cover the last leg to Zundert. His mind turned to the ecumenical gathering. He was aware of the ideological attempts to exploit the sincere desire of many Christians to end the division. The Communists' tactical rhetoric about oppressors and oppressed was well known to the hierarchy, as was Freemasonry's deceptive rhetoric about the brotherhood of man. One should by now be capable of distinguishing Marx and the Enlightenment rationalists from Christian Aristotelianism. The Church had issued condemnations. But the mention of Gnosticism in Freemasonry had sparked his interest. How would that work in an ecumenical gathering? How would the idea of penetrating the deceptive curtain of existence to a special inner knowledge help in reconciling doctrine?

'We have been neglecting our prayers, Jos,' said the bishop when he awoke after a half-hour. 'We will say the rosary before we continue.' He took his rosary beads from his pocket.

'Disobeying instructions again,' commented Jos.

'There are limits, young man. What difference would a string of beads make to the Nazis?'

'All right, but we'll say the prayers as we ride along. We don't want two scruffy labourers seen kneeling in the fields saying prayers. That would indeed attract attention.'

The bishop acquiesced, and they resumed their way along isolated country roads that gave the impression the world around them was uninhabited. They made excellent progress along the backroads Jos knew well, partly because the bishop now did not need as many rests. At two o'clock in the morning, they came abreast of the seminary of the Wounded Heart of Jesus. Jos glided to a stop, running his eyes over the buildings lit by a quarter moon. The memories flowed back, Bart among them. No lights were on, and the complex of buildings seemed even more like a monster crouching menacingly in fields around it.

'Why are we stopping here?' said the bishop, missing Jos's interest in the seminary.

'I think we'll take a rest here. We are not far from our destination. You can have a rest.'

The bishop had nothing to add, and they rode on until the seminary was just behind them. Jos stopped near some poplars. The bishop used to Jos's ways, dismounted, lay in the grass, and promptly fell asleep. Five minutes later, Jos rose and, in a crouch, slowly made his way across the fields to the main seminary building. It was against his better judgment because his actions would surely be pointless. He skirted around to the shed where he had kept his bike and the transmitter. He had to be careful now that he did not make a noise. He felt around the door for the handle. Relieved there was no lock, he gradually pushed it open, hoping to avoid the creak it usually made. The door creaked, and he stopped, looking around. He heard a movement somewhere. Then, footsteps that sounded like boots on a dirt path. He could not gauge exactly where they came from. He must do what he came for, however unwise it was. He pushed the door open, entered and felt around for the cupboard that housed the transmitter. The door was missing, and the cabinet was empty. He could feel that the door had been ripped from its hinges.

He quickly shut the shed door, still not avoiding a short creak, and fled across the lawn to the grassy fields. He fell to the ground when he heard a door open. He caught the flash of a torch. He continued to crawl away, glancing at where the light was coming from. He stopped and pressed himself into the grass as he caught sight of two figures who had come from the back of the building, where the seminarians' rooms were.

He could not discern who they were as they walked along the shaded wall of the building. They came into the scant moonlight. A German soldier and, if he weren't mistaken, Hans de Jonge in his dressing gown. He looked around for a car. There it was—a German staff car parked among the trees at the back of the building. What were the Germans doing so late at night at the seminary? And what role did De Jonge play in the midnight meeting? Then Muller appeared fully dressed. They consulted for a moment. Muller, gesturing De Jonge and the soldier to stay put, made his way along the building and disappeared behind the trees and utility buildings, among which was the tool shed. A few seconds later, he reappeared and casually walked to join De Jonge. Signalling the soldier to stand back, he consulted with De Jonge again. Then, all three disappeared around the back. Jos crept back to the bishop, who he found sleeping blissfully in the grass.

'Come on, we must move on,' said Jos, shaking the bishop.

'What ...? said the bishop, blinking. 'Why the change?'

'On reflection, we should continue to our destination while it's still night.'

The bishop did as he was told while Jos contemplated his decision. He was in a bind. He had made a mistake out of his eagerness that may prove disastrous. It was possible that once aroused, the Germans would organise a search. They would likely be captured. If he went for shelter at the Vos's, he might put them in danger. Lights flashed from the direction of the seminary. Jos signalled to the bishop to stay put. A minute later, the staff car passed them, going towards Breda. Jos made out a driver and a sole passenger in the back.

'What on earth is a Nazi staff car doing here at this time of the night?' said the bishop.

'Who knows? We are close to Breda, where the area command is.'

'Shouldn't we then stay put?'

'No, it's best we get off the road while we have the cover of the dark.'

The bishop acquiesced again and meekly followed Jos as he set off for the Vos's. They found the farmhouse in darkness.

'Stay here, off the road,' said Jos. He expected the dog would bark, rousing the farmer, but would shut up when he sniffed who it was. So it happened.

'Who's there?' said farmer Vos, opening the front door and patting his docile dog. 'Lad, is that you?' The heavy Brabants dialect reassuringly filled the still country air.

'Yes, Meneer Vos, can I come in?'

'*Goede Hemel*, Father, what are you doing here looking like that? Yes, quick, come in.'

Jos had not had a shave or haircut since he left that fatal night, and his clothes were only a degree above rags.

Meneer and Mevrouw,' he said, as the farmer's wife appeared in her dressing gown, 'I haven't got time to explain, but you have relations in Breda if I remember correctly.'

'My brother,' said Mevrouw Vos.

'Could you go there as soon as you can pack and stay until late tomorrow?'

'Yes, but if you are in danger,' said Meneer Vos, 'we won't desert you.'

'You will help best by doing what I ask. My plan is the best chance for my survival.' The farming couple nodded their acquiescence. 'Now, I have a religious with me who does not speak a word of Dutch. I'm smuggling him out of Holland, out of the hands of the Nazis. I'll fetch him, but I ask you not to address me as "Father". He does not know I am a priest, and it is absolutely crucial for future action that he does not know. Call me Jos or whatever you're comfortable with.'

'What have you got yourself into, lad?' said farmer Vos, showing some understanding, 'if you hadn't risked your life enough already. Why would anyone know you're here? I can roughly guess.'

Jos found the bishop at attention, holding both bikes and curiously peering around at the fields in the approaching dawn light.

'Come on, Excellency. We have a safe shelter here with Meneer and Mevrouw Vos. You won't find a kinder couple with such immovable faith. I thought it best to tell them what I am doing. They would guess, I think. They know you're a religious, but I haven't said what. I'll see how that plays out. Like farmers Piet and Hans, they'll soon see you're not an ordinary priest. The clothes won't hide it from these down-to-earth people.'

'I am continually in awe of you, young man,' said the bishop, patting him on the shoulder. 'Your organisational powers in such critical changing circumstances are astounding. If we get through all this and peace comes, I want you to contact me in London.'

Jos was right. The farming couple's eyes widened while Jos introduced the bishop as a Catholic religious and explained their needs for about a week. The bishop, despite his tatty labourer's clothes, did not help. He stood tall, dignified and straight, in all his bishopric elegance, his three-week beard adding to his dignified bearing. The couple quickly got over their bemused reaction and went into hospitality mode. Coffee was offered, which the bishop gratefully accepted, and he was shown to the most comfortable chair in the lounge room. When Mevrouw Vos had attended to the bishop's sustenance, she repaired to the attic to arrange the accommodation. To Jos's silent amusement, Farmer Vos attempted conversation and a posture he thought he owed to a man of such bearing. The bishop knew his diplomacy and steered his conversation through Jos to farming matters. But he could not pretend indefinitely.

'You'll have to take over, Jos,' he said. 'I can't keep this up for much longer.'

'This gentleman,' said Farmer Vos, before Jos could say anything, 'has never been around a cow in his life. I can't respond much longer to polite but ignorant comments. What's more, he is no ordinary religious as you describe him. It's best, lad, that you tell us what he is exactly so we can pay him proper respect—and not look foolish.'

'As a rule, we must say as little as possible about us, but you're right, Meneer, my apologies,' said Jos as the bishop looked from one to the other. 'In these circumstances, we should be completely open.'

He revealed that the farming couple was accommodating a bishop from London, but they should not fuss about him. The request was hardly out of his mouth when Meneer Vos stood and bowed solemnly before the bewildered bishop.

'What do I call him?' said the Brabants farmer from the side of his mouth.

'I had to tell him you were a bishop, Excellency,' he said quickly to the bishop and then to Meneer Vos, 'the correct title is Your Excellency. But Meneer Vos, please don't make a fuss. The circumstances don't require it, and His Excellency doesn't want it.'

'Tell him not to make a fuss,' said the bishop. 'It's not necessary, and it's better in the circumstances.'

'Meneer the Bishop, Your Excellency,' said farmer Vos, ignoring the requests. 'We are honoured to have you stay with us.' He bowed again with great solemnity. 'We are ready to supply your every need.' He bowed again, this time lower.

'You'll have to indulge him, Excellency. These are ordinary people who have great respect for the clergy.'

'Not always with justice, alas,' said the bishop drily. He gave the farmer a warm smile.

'Mevrouw Vos,' said farmer Vos to his wife, who at that moment appeared at the bottom of the stairs, 'we have a bishop staying with us. You must say, Excellency, when you address him.'

'What ...?' said Mevrouw Vos, who took the news much better than her husband. 'A bishop? How ...?'

Jos intervened to explain again that the bishop did not need and did not want special treatment. He was deeply grateful for their hospitality. All the bishop needed now was a place to rest. Because the farming couple would never entirely be at ease in the presence of such clerical grandeur, Jos sent the bishop to the attic to rest.

'I've explained you need to rest,' said Jos.

'I've guessed it, Jos. You have been seconded from the Dutch government's diplomatic corps for this work.' The bishop smiled and rose from his comfortable lounge chair. 'Am I warm?'

'No comment,' said Jos, responding fittingly to the bishop's jesting.

Chapter 9

Bishop Eliott

Now that the bishop was safely installed in the attic, Jos was eager to see the farming couple depart. A raiding party could turn up at any time if suspicions had grown. Whose suspicions—the Germans' or Muller's, he thought? To try his patience in difficult and dangerous circumstances, Mevrouw Vos would not budge before she had prepared food for two days, which included an apple tart, especially for him. She went about her task with a minimum of urgency. After she was finally satisfied that her high standards of hospitality had been met, she climbed into the truck's cabin with her cheery husband, and they departed among a flurry of waves, hay and other farming fragments flying from the empty tray. Jos returned to the lounge room, where he sat wearily on the couch.

He lay down and rested his head on a large, quilted cushion. He, too, needed a rest. Soon, visions of the collapse of his failed covert operation came back to shake his efforts to rest. Bart's cruel, unjust, unwarranted death possessed his mind. Innocent, optimistic Bart, who would surely have made an excellent pastoral priest once he shook off the academic role he really wasn't suited to—why him? Why did he let Bart become involved when it wasn't necessary? So, again, the same questions tormented Jos until the tears trickled down his cheeks. Near midday, Jos was roused by heavy steps on the stairs.

'They're very steep stairs for an overweight cleric like me,' the bishop commented when he entered the lounge room. 'Are you all right?' He looked searchingly at Jos.

'I'm fine,' said Jos, sitting up. 'I needed a rest, too.'

'Yes, indeed, I should not forget you're not Superman, although you sometimes give that impression.'

'Superman!' laughed Jos. 'Far from it. I'm glad you're here. I need to prepare you for some possible drama. Mr and Mrs Vos have gone to relations in Breda to be out of the way.'

'Out of the way of what?' said the bishop, looking around. 'Something happened, didn't it, during that last stop, though I can't imagine what? And it has put us in unexpected danger.'

Jos hesitated. 'Let's just concentrate on the core problem. There's a chance the Germans will raid this house. We must prepare for it.'

'All right. I won't ask questions. But you have left me with a bigger puzzle.'

'There's no time to think about puzzles, Excellency. We must prepare. We'll have something to eat first. It's best to get that out of the way.'

After a lunch of bread, butter and cheese, Jos and the bishop returned to the attic, where they packed up the two camping beds and took the bed linen to the chest of drawers. The bishop then helped Jos arrange the same boxes and cartons into a hiding place, sounder than before, with an extra layer of concealment for the bishop. If Jos was discovered, he could emerge without the bishop having to move. He would only be discovered if it were suspected that two people were hiding. But Muller or the Germans would have no reason to think there was more than one person at the shed if they thought someone was there at all. Jos thought the bishop was safe.

'If there is a raid and we are discovered, you must let me do the talking. Don't say a word. As an Englishman, you will be considered a spy and executed.'

'You can speak German, too?'

'It's not unusual for an educated Dutchman to speak German. The two languages are close, you know.'

That's something more for me to think about.'

'Don't waste your energy, Excellency. Now, we must prepare. Perhaps we can say a rosary for our deliverance.'

'Your English is not book English,' said the bishop when they had returned to the lounge room. 'You've been in an English-speaking environment. But where?'

'Shall we begin with the Joyful Mysteries, Excellency?'

By the time they had finished the whole fifteen decades of the rosary, it was late afternoon. Jos had a feeling the raid, if it happened, would be before dark. So, they returned to the attic to wait. A half-hour later, they heard a vehicle changing down gears in the deathly still country air.

'Right, this is it, Excellency. Take your place, and don't speak or move.'

There was a knock at the front door. Silence. The door opened, and footsteps—not more than two people—were heard walking around.

'Sergeant,' said a voice in German, 'there's no one here. Get your men to fan out around the house and the fields. Make sure you check the barn. I'll check the upper floors.'

'Yes, Major,' said the sergeant sharply.

'What's he saying?' said the bishop.

'Shoosh. He's coming up here to check.'

Footsteps sounded on the two flights of stairs. They did not stop on the second floor but proceeded to the attic, halting at the top of the stairs as if the space were being surveyed. They moved around the attic space, stopping several times, and then came towards them. Several boxes were moved away.

'You,' said the major, lowering his pistol. 'For some undefined reason, I had an idea it could be you.' Jos quickly rose and stepped forward. 'What a state you're in,' he added. What are you doing, Fr. van Engelen? Why would you be back here?'

Jos had not been able to think of a good reason until the major's question.

'I want to know who betrayed me.'

The major frowned and looked around. 'Really?' He saw the camping beds stacked against the wall at the other end of the attic. 'Move away into the middle of the room.' He waved with his pistol. He strolled over to the beds, moved them around, inspected them, and came back to Jos. 'Stay there, and don't move.' He walked towards the boxes with his pistol raised.

'There are no guns here, Major. You're in no danger.' The major kept on walking.

'Wait, Major.' Jos could see Femke's whole enterprise collapsing. The major stopped, his pistol directed at the boxes. 'I am guiding an English bishop out of Holland.' It was best to come clean. It was his best chance. 'The bishop has nothing to do with the military. He was in Holland for Church purposes. Please do not address me as Father. It is important for the enterprise that he does not know I'm a priest.'

'For the enterprise?' The major approached the boxes and removed those hiding the bishop. 'Raise your hands, Excellency, and stand up—slowly,' he said in English, motioning with his pistol. Bishop Eliott did as he was told, his hands raised and his face pale, but managing to maintain his dignity. The major waved him to stand next to Jos. 'This is a little more than helping your frightened fellow citizens back to Breda, Meneer.' He patted the bishop down and stood back.

'I suppose it is,' said Jos.

'What am I to do, particularly as you appear to be conducting an ongoing operation?'

'It's the first time,' said Jos. 'The bishop is a special case.'

'But there will be others.'

'Yes, I expect there will be. It depends on the success of this run.'

'I don't know whether I should admire your bravery or dismiss you as mad.'

'It doesn't matter which as long as you let us continue.'

The major contemplated the priest and the bishop.

'You must be gone by tomorrow night.' He hesitated. 'Will this be a fixed route?'

'Yes, Major,' said Jos, thinking he understood the question's motive.

'All right. Tell Mevrouw Vos I have taken some food from the kitchen for the sergeant. I will settle with her in due course.'

Of course, Major, thank you. May God bless you.'

'Major,' called Bishop Eliott as the German officer turned to go. The major stopped. 'May I give you a blessing? The major hesitated again, a look of surprise replacing his usually tightly controlled expression. He nodded. The bishop approached him slowly with his hands held out. 'May I?' he said, indicating he wanted to lay his hand on his shoulder. The major nodded. 'May Our Lord and His Blessed Mother bless and preserve you.' He made the sign of the cross. *'Benedicat tibi Dominus et custodiat te.'*

'Thank you, Excellency.'

The major disappeared, hurrying down the stairs. Shortly after, an exchange between the major and his sergeant drifted up the stairs. Within minutes, the truck and the Germans had gone.

'God be praised,' said the bishop, breathing a huge sigh. 'You are under God's protection, it seems.'

'We are fortunate to have come across a Catholic officer with a conscience,' said Jos. 'He is risking his life.'

'Just fortunate?'

Jos did not have time to consider more than the last stage of his exhausting journey. Zundert was twenty to twenty-five kilometres away, and he was now entering new territory. Except for one reconnoitring trip from the seminary and the main roads he negotiated while pursuing the people evacuating Breda, he was unfamiliar with the road network. He sent Bishop Eliott to rest in the attic and studied the map Femke had provided. He remembered some of the isolated byways he had passed searching for the fleeing people. Connecting these with other isolated roads on the map, he established a route he thought would evade German patrols or roadblocks.

A more serious issue was the contact point and the time stipulated. He had not heard clarification from Femke as he had expected. Which northern entrance to Zundert was the right one? There were several. After studying the map, he decided the entrance Femke meant would be on Bredaseweg. That made sense because it was the route from Breda to Zundert via Rijsbergen. But are we talking about things making sense, thought Jos? Was that too easy? In the end, he decided on an intersection on Bredaseweg where the road entered the village.

But the time was all wrong. It would have been better to meet early in the morning. Now they would have to find somewhere to settle for the entire day after riding through the night. But he had to accept things as they were, not as he wished. To make things worse, he felt the strain of the last few weeks. It was like he had not stopped since leaving the seminary. Rest was needed. He returned to the attic and flopped onto the camping bed beside the bishop. The bishop was snoring regularly. Thankfully, he was recovering.

'You've had a good long sleep,' said the bishop when Jos appeared in the lounge room. 'It's no wonder. You must be exhausted. Can you make a cup of tea? I don't dare touch Mrs Vos's kitchen.'

Jos prepared a cup of tea with bread, butter, cheese, and ham and returned to the lounge room.

'Eat well, Excellency. Mevrouw Vos has left plenty for us, and you may not get another chance for a full meal.'

'You were thinking, no doubt, that I no longer have the layers of fat to sustain me.'

'I wasn't, but it is evident you've lost much weight. That's good. You still have a long way to go; the less weight you carry, the better.'

'Ever the practical man, Jos, even in response to a little humour. Your mind does not rest, does it?'

'Do you know where you're going after Holland?' Jos had already asked, but asked again in case the bishop had forgotten in the haste and tension of being ejected from Holland.

'No, I told you. I have no idea. Do you?'

'I imagine you will go as far as neutral Spain before taking a ship back to London.'

'Spain! No.'

'The trip will become less fraught, I imagine, as you progress through France and Spain. The Germans can't be everywhere in France and not at all in Spain.'

Silence followed while they relished their last supper.

'I hadn't finished telling you about the ecumenical conference I attended,' said the bishop with a self-satisfied expression as he put his plate and cup on the coffee table. 'Are you still interested?'

'I hadn't forgotten, and I'm still interested.'

'You're a mystery man, Jos, and for some reason I can't pinpoint, I think what I am about to tell you will be useful in the end.'

'You ended with the assumption I knew something about the occult and esotericism. I know something about Gnosticism, but almost nothing about the occult and esotericism. How does all that relate to ecumenism?'

'The occult is an umbrella term for many ways of thought that have to do with the hidden content of the mind and spirit. They involve secret practices that aim to manipulate invisible forces to achieve practical outcomes. We are talking about immanence as opposed to transcendence. The practitioners of magic seek to connect with the god within and become gods themselves. Esotericism comes under the heading of the occult.'

'I see the relation with Gnosticism but ecumenism ...?'

'Are you familiar with those Protestant groups that reject the Catholic Church and its teaching, believing they can connect through the Holy Spirit with the God of the Gospels?'

'Pentecostalism. I know little about that Protestant movement, but I see your connection. You are suggesting, I take it, that occultists can hide behind a Pentecostalist mentality to undermine Christianity.'

'Exactly—the Catholic Church in particular. It's literally diabolical behaviour under the guidance of a multitude of demons.'

'And you detected among—?'

'Not directly. Nobody was exhibiting clear signs of the occult, but there was an air, now and again, among some members of the conference. And another thing,' he continued, holding up his hand to stay comment, 'did you know that occultism has permeated German society since the beginning of the twentieth century?'

'No, but ... are you sure that—?'

'Absolutely,' said the bishop, continually talking over Jos and pointing, 'and you had better believe that the occult has deeply influenced some of the demented leaders of Nazism, including Hitler himself. People are missing the strong influence of the occult on Himmler, Goering, Hess, and Goebbels. They're infatuated with Nordic and Germanic myth, Teutonic knights—and the rest. Can you imagine these lunatics wandering around in flowing white robes with a crimson cross on the front?'

'No. You can't be serious.'

'You had better believe it because subjection to the occult often ends in possession—diabolical possession.' A layer of perspiration had returned to the bishop's forehead and temples.

'These days, a priest must be aware of the possibility of possession in someone diagnosed with a psychological illness. It's the exorcist that must be called rather than the psychiatrist or the men in white coats.' The bishop sat back, his animated explanation drawing on his low reserves of energy.

'It's hard to believe,' said Jos, keen to end the conversation. The bishop should not expend his energy on secondary matters.

'I don't know why I had this urge to talk to you about the occult and possession,' said the bishop, his voice dropping to just above a murmur. 'It's more the terrain of the priest than the spy, although you are an odd spy, Jos, as I have said. You come across in the long run as an academic, but how you have come to do the work so masterfully as a counterintelligence operative beats me.'

'There's no time to think about it, Excellency. You need to rest. The next stage, though short, might be the most hazardous.'

'Let me repeat my invitation to contact me in London when all this is over and we have both survived. Now, I will leave you to rest.'

Jos watched the bishop trudge wearily up the stairs. It was indeed odd that he had spoken about matters directly of interest to him as a priest, but had at no time thought he might be just such a person. He did not follow the bishop to the attic but remained in the lounge on the couch to rest. The farming couple arrived home late in the afternoon. They seemed unsurprised by the major's visit.

'You couldn't resist sneaking around the seminary, could you, lad?' said farmer Vos.

'That's about it,' said Jos with a shrug. 'I still can't get Bart out of my mind. It seems so unfair, and I feel so guilty. There is something evil about it all—even diabolical. How ...?' The bishop's brief words about the occult echoed through his mind.

'We understand,' said Mevrouw Vos, rising from her chair. She patted his shoulder and caressed his neck like he was family. 'It's not your fault, Father ... I mean Jos.' She glanced around. 'I'll have a look to see what the major took—not that it matters in the circumstances.'

'We'll leave around midnight,' said Jos, shaking the thought of Bart's murder from his mind. 'If all goes well, I'll return around the same time—if I may.'

'You're always welcome,' said farmer Vos. 'We will cooperate with your plans. You intend to do this again, don't you?'

'It's perilous, Meneer.' There was no point in beating around the bush. 'You'll be shot as a spy if caught.'

'Then we'll die in a good cause—as the saints did.'

'Only the apple tart is missing from the cellar,' said Mevrouw Vos, returning.

'Now that's going too far,' cried farmer Vos, wagging his finger. 'You make sure, wife, that you charge him good.' He laughed heartily, and his wife asked him to shush.

JOS AND the bishop set off at around 2 a.m. and rode with only one break to Bredaseweg and stopped about a kilometre up the road from the entrance to Zundert. The route was even more roundabout than before. To Jos's relief, the bishop kept up the pace and seemed not to notice the many dizzying turns. It was ironic that he had become accustomed to his routine just when they were at the end of this first sector.

'Wait here,' said Jos, dismounting. He swung around at the sound of a heavy motor. 'Quick, off the road and lie down.'

They flung themselves and their bikes into a ditch running along the road. A troop carrier with a dozen soldiers, coming out of the dawn light, sped past. Jos raised his head. The troop carrier stopped at the intersection. The soldiers tumbled out and set up a roadblock. Jos watched for two hours while the soldiers let most go by, only stopping a few. What were they doing? How long would they stay there? They dare not move away with their bikes for fear of being seen as the land around was dead flat. They could not lie there all day. He had to have a closer look.

'Stay here, Excellency, and for heaven's sake, don't move—especially not stand up.'

The bishop was out to it, pleasantly snoring. Just as well, thought Jos. He crawled away from the road until he came behind a farmhouse on a side road. Several more farmhouses hid him until he could approach Bredaseweg at about 200 risky metres from the intersection. He glanced up the road. There were a few locals at work in the fields. They seemed unbothered by the Germans. The bishop remained out of sight. At this proximity, he still could not guess why the Germans had set up a roadblock and how long they would stay. They looked very relaxed about it, whatever it was. Indeed, they seemed more interested in chatting than inspecting the people they stopped.

He stayed for half an hour, gazing at the roadblock, turning over in his mind his options. Then, without any urgency, the soldiers packed up, mounted the troop carrier, and headed up the way they had come. Jos relaxed but could not stop a gasp as the vehicle slowed around where the bishop was lying. Several soldiers jumped down from the vehicle and stood around while one approached a local in the field. There was a short exchange after which the soldiers remounted, and the troop carrier continued its way. Jos waited until the soldiers had disappeared before standing. Pondering, he strolled to where he had left the bishop. He stopped dead, horrified to see just one bike in the ditch. The bishop and his bike were gone. He looked around, walking up and down to ensure he had not wandered off. He felt sick. To lose the bishop after all they had endured was crushing. He approached the farmer in the field.

'Meneer, have you seen an oldish man with a beard wandering around here? His hair is almost white. He had a bike.'

'No, Meneer, I have seen no one. I've been too busy to notice.'

'Why did the Germans stop?'

The farmer stopped his work and stood straight. 'Why do you want to know?' he said suspiciously.

'They may have seen him.'

'Then you should ask them.' He returned to his work, a signal that he did not want to be bothered anymore.

Jos left his bike in the ditch and ambled a kilometre up Bredaseweg, openly now, because he was confident the Germans would not appear for a while. But nothing. He strolled back to the side street he had taken to escape the soldiers' notice, but again, nothing. Nobody he spoke to had seen an older man with a beard and white hair wheeling a bike. He dared not be too open with his questions. After an hour of fruitless searching, he sat in the ditch to make sure the bishop had not just wandered off without attending to the time. After all, they were due to meet their contact at 5 p.m. Perhaps he had met someone and was having a fine old chat? The bishop was a sociable prelate. But in the end, he had to face reality. For some inexplicable reason, the bishop had gone missing. So, after an hour, he gave up and headed back to the Vos farm. Without the bishop to hold him up or restrict his route, he rode the shortish route, only skirting around Rijsbergen. He arrived during the afternoon, where he related to the surprised farming couple the disastrous outcome of his trip.

'There's something fishy about that,' said farmer Vos. 'Someone just doesn't disappear into thin air.'

'But I searched everywhere, Meneer. There wasn't time for him to get far. I was no more than a half-hour away from him.'

'Still stinks,' said the farmer.

'Are you sure the Germans didn't pick him up?' said Mevrouw Vos. 'You might have been mistaken.'

'Yes, they were in full view all the time. I would have seen them take the bishop and his bike. This is an unmitigated disaster.' He let himself drop onto the lounge room couch. 'It shows how fraught and dangerous such an operation can be. It raises questions about its usefulness.'

'Don't be despairing, Father,' said Mevrouw Vos. 'I have some good news. The major came this morning with his sergeant. He apologised for taking the apple tart and paid me twice as much as it was worth. He said the sergeant liked it so much that he wanted to order another, which he would share with his soldier mates. Of course, he would pay for it.'

'That's generous of him,' said Jos, thinking it was not good news.

'He gave me a list of vegetables he wanted to order for his kitchen.'

'You should be careful,' said Jos, 'not to get involved with the Germans, as friendly as the major has been.'

'Yes, of course,' said farmer Vos. 'No intention. Show him the list, wife.'

'What should I see?' said Jos, looking briefly at the list of vegetables.

'Turn it over, lad.'

Jos turned it over to see 'AMS' above a series of small circles in an irregular pattern running down the paper. He studied it closely.

'Does it make sense?'

'I think it does.'

'I suspected a message,' said farmer Vos triumphantly.

'But I need to test it on the return trip. As far as that goes, I must depart as soon as possible.'

'No, lad, you must take a rest. It would be foolish to risk things because of exhaustion.'

'Yes, Father,' said Mevrouw Vos, 'you're looking tired. A couple of days won't make a difference.'

Jos gave in to being fussed over and set off two days later, loaded with food and a clean change of clothes. He kept to his route but made good progress over familiar ground without the drag of an unfit prelate. He took time to assess the safety of his stops. Not all the parish priests were comfortable with risk, though they did not hesitate to provide provisions and a place to spend the night if necessary. He noted those who showed full commitment. At the same time, he tried to check if the circles on the major's vegetable list were military encampments or stations. This was risky because it sometimes took him close to built-up areas. He needed confirmation of a small number to be sure, which he had. It seemed the major had rightly guessed he would travel down to the right of Utrecht and head to the left of Den Bosch to go to Breda. Less than two weeks later, he arrived at the Amstelveen parish in a better state than on the previous trip. He cleaned up before the same truck took him and his bike into Amsterdam. They dropped him off on Rembrandt Square, from where he took the backstreets to the De Vries house.

Chapter 10

Fr Jos's flock

JOS DREADED his meeting with Femke. How could he tell her the mission had been a failure after all her meticulous planning? The smile on Femke's usual business-like face made it more difficult when she turned up three days later. Meneer and Mevrouw de Vries departed after a friendly greeting.

'Glad to see you returned safe and sound,' she said, taking a seat in the lounge room. 'But you do look tired, very worn. You will rest for the next two weeks. You must fully recuperate before we can consider another operation.'

'I'm sorry to spoil your joyful mood, Femke. I have shocking news which may torpedo any such plan.'

'Do you?' she said mischievously.

'It sounds stupid—and it is deplorably stupid—but I'm afraid I lost Bishop Eliott at the last moment. It's as simple as that.'

'I won't tease you, Jos, though I am tempted. You didn't lose him. He made the contact safely, or rather, they scooped him safely out of the ditch where he was peacefully snoozing.'

'How ... how do you know? I checked everywhere. I saw nothing. How did they do it?'

'It is enough to know Bishop Eliott is safe and on his way through France. Traversing Belgium was easier than Holland. But I can tell you one thing. He left something on or in your bike to let you know he was safely picked up.'

'What?'

'I have no idea. You must look for yourself.'

'Wait here.'

He could not delay finding what he had missed. He hastened to the laundry where his bike was parked. Nothing on the frame or wheels. He searched through the saddlebags. Something was jammed into the bottom corner of one. He drew out the bishop's rosary beads. He smiled to himself. It must have taken a supreme effort for the unhurried prelate to pull his rosary out of his pocket and push it into the corner of the saddle bag.

'He left his rosary beads in one of the bags on my bike,' he said, holding up the rosary when he returned to the still-amused Femke. 'I didn't think to look. Such quick action was unlike His Excellency. It will teach me to expect the unexpected.'

'Yes, it is always prudent to expect the unforeseen,' said Femke, whose expression said her mind had moved to more serious matters. She picked up her bag, getting ready to go. 'I'll arrange for the bike to be collected.'

'You have been the most unforeseen development for me this year,' commented Jos.

Femke looked at him, surprise her first reaction, a searching frown the second.

'I thought we agreed it's best not to know anything about the other,' she said.

'You mean nothing about you. You now know plenty about me.'

'It's the same. You know it's important to keep agents shielded.'

'At least I did not get an impatient shake of the head this time,' he said with an ironic smile.

'You're not flirting with me, Father van Engelen, are you?'

'Flirting?' said Jos, raising his hands. 'I don't know what that is. The only females I've mixed with are my younger sisters. They have little in common with their serious older brother. They were not a good object to exercise the art of flirting on. No, I can't help sometimes being amused by your undeviating, determined manner. I mean it in good spirit, though. We spend so much time together. Naturally, that encourages some familiarity. But you're safe with me, Femke.'

'Just as well,' she said with mock seriousness.

'Because you're married?'

'Nice try, Father. I hope you give up shortly. You're wasting your time. Now I must go. I'll see you in two weeks. Prepare yourself for a thorough debriefing.'

'The more you hide, the more I can't help wondering who you are?'

'Bishop Eliott said the same about you.'

'All right, Femke,' he laughed, 'I will desist. By the way, the bishop had much to say in whatever message you received from him.'

'It was word of mouth.'

'Your network is extensive.'

'Goodbye, Jos. See you in a couple of weeks. Make sure you get a good rest. You are pivotal in our operation.'

'Our operation? I can't help wondering who "we" is,' said Jos before she could make a move. 'It's at least Catholic. Bishop Eliott gave too much away for you to deny it.'

'The sociable prelate was an acceptable risk. Besides, it is not much to give away to a tight-lipped priest.'

'I assume nobody will tell him that a priest was his guide. That would indeed risk compromising the operation—if it continues.'

'No need to worry. Only two people know.'

'Really, how do you manage that?'

'An unreflective few know that someone went to check on an exhausted priest staying with an elderly couple. Only two fully know the rest.'

Femke was standing next to Jos, who was a good deal taller. Unself-consciously, he looked down at her, admiration for her cleverness in his eyes.

'This is all your inspiration, isn't it?' he said, not noticing the slight change in colour. 'You're the one who came up with this idea, right?'

She hesitated as if working out how to respond. 'Extreme situations call for extreme measures,' she said as she walked to the front door. 'It forces one to concentrate. It was fortuitous that you unexpectedly arrived on the scene.'

'Providential, perhaps?' he said, following.

'That's what we believe as Catholics. Now, Father van Engelen, an end to this familiar purposeless manner of chatting, I must go. Next time, we concentrate on the job at hand. Right?'

'Of course, Femke, sorry to have detained you.'

Jos returned to the lounge room, where he sat reflecting on their conversation. He and Femke worked so closely and intensely together that a little familiarity was inevitable. His admiration for her organisational ability only added to the familiarity. But there was nothing in it. As he said, she was safe with him. His vows were under no threat. He thought that would have been obvious. Why, then, was she so quick to warn him about flirting?

Flirting? He had no idea how to do that. Who Femke was intrigued him more than ever.

FEMKE returned three weeks later.

'We have a lot to get through,' she said after Mevrouw de Vries had prepared tea with biscuits, and the couple left for the morning.

'I'm all attention.'

'You look much better,' she said, arranging her papers on her lap. 'You needed the rest. How do you feel? Will it take about three weeks to recover from such a trip?'

'Bishop Eliott would be more demanding than a younger, fitter person.'

'Good, that gives me an idea of how to space the operations.'

'So you have another operation?' She shook her head. 'So, we're back to shaking our head at questions we don't want to answer?'

'Please, Jos ... You know there are things I can't go into until the time is right. There are things I cannot talk about. Full stop. Stop being tedious.'

'Sorry, Femke. I will behave myself.'

She looked up at him from the paper she was consulting and gave him a smile. 'Now, can we continue without the side issues?'

'Of course, Femke. Sorry to be flippant. Being locked up causes uncharacteristic behaviour. Ordinarily, I am a boring academic sort of person.'

Well, that gives me the cue for the first point. I understand the discomfort of being cooped up. I have organised work for you at a fruit and vegetable stall at the Albert Cuyp market for a few days each week. It's all arranged. Just introduce yourself to the stall manager. He knows you're coming and won't ask any questions. Based on your information, I assume you won't have trouble helping at such a stall.'

'No, I imagine not. Middelburg has a well-known market on its town square. And I am familiar with country produce.'

'Good, now let's cover your trip to Zundert and back.'

As he expected, Femke was unrelenting in her questions about the Eliott operation, all of which he strove to answer with the desired accuracy. He left out the German major's and farmer Vos's connections. He did not want to run the risk of compromising either. Naturally, he would not speak of his stupidity in prowling around the seminary of the Wounded Heart of Jesus. What the seminary leadership did with the German command in Breda had no relevance to Femke's plans.

'Well,' said Femke, sitting back when he had finished, 'you have really pulled off an amazing feat. Quite exceptional.'

'Thank you, Femke. I had a few things in my favour.'

'Indeed, that's the point. You have been noticed, I must tell you, though I shouldn't.'

'By whom?'

'Completing the task has shown that it could be done—with the right person and the proper planning.'

'I hope those who noticed know the idea and the planning were yours. I simply carried it out.'

'Not simply carried it out. Without the ability to carry it out, the idea was useless.' She collected her papers, pushed them into her bag, and stood. 'All right, Jos, it's time for me to go. Meneer and Mevrouw will be back any moment.'

'There's one last thing. I have a sketch of possible German military placements along my route.' He handed her a redrawn sketch of the major's vegetable list, showing the towns.

'How did you manage this?' she said wide-eyed after studying it. Jos shook his head. 'Oh, I see; you have a connection you don't want to reveal?' Jos shook his head. 'Do you enjoy teasing me, Father van Engelen?'

'Is that what I'm doing?'

'It appears to be either teasing or flirting, both hardly proper in a priest.'

'I told you, Femke, I have no idea what flirting is. But you obviously do because you use the word. No doubt you have had your experiences.'

Femke could not suppress a smile. 'All right, I hope this connection bears fruit. I won't ask about it again, trusting you know what you're doing. As for your teasing, I will excuse it as an aberration due to the circumstances.'

'I'm just being friendly with someone I work with. Your stiffness has had that effect.'

'My stiffness?'

'That's what it looks like.'

'I'm mortified.'

'You know the remedy.'

The front door was heard opening.

'Goodbye, Jos.'

'When will I see you again?'

'There will be something. I will contact you when I have clearer signs. Be patient. In the meantime, maintain your fitness. Winter will be a different proposition. Hello, Mevrouw and Meneer; I'm just leaving.'

JOS HAD been saying Mass at a makeshift altar in the De Vries lounge room. His sole intention was to attend to his priestly duties. Meneer and Mevrouw were free to attend as they wished. No pressure. He understood daily Mass might be too much. But he was wrong. The elderly couple attended each Mass. They arranged their activities so that nothing disturbed them or Jos in this essential daily activity. The Mass was at 7 a.m., which meant the table, missal, cruets, and chalice were packed up and put away before Femke arrived, usually after 9 a.m. A worrying change came, however. Within a week of Jos's return, a second elderly couple turned up for Mass. Then a third, and a fourth. By the end of the second week, five couples were attending daily Mass. The arrivals began around 6 a.m., so he could hear confessions before Mass.

'I'm becoming anxious, Meneer and Mevrouw De Vries,' said Jos. 'So many people coming at such an early hour may attract attention. It could be dangerous. The Nazis are not exactly endeared to Catholics.'

'That's why they're here,' Father,' said Mevrouw. 'They're afraid to go out. They don't have to go far to come here, and they know they're safe.'

'We must anticipate possible German intervention.'

'Why would old people, some struggling on walking sticks, attract attention?' said Meneer De Vries. 'Many old people live around here. It's an old part of Amsterdam. And why would the Germans worry about old people attending Mass?'

Jos was not convinced. For one thing, Meneer De Vries was overlooking his double role as priest and labourer. The Germans would not swallow that. He must organise things so that the Mass appeared like some sort of prayer and Bible meeting.

How big is your attic, Meneer? Perhaps we can use that space. If the Nazis come calling, we will have time to pack everything away and pretend we are having a prayer meeting.'

'Of course, Father, there is space enough,' said Mevrouw de Vries. 'We'll have our very own little chapel, "Our dear Lord in the Attic."'

Mevrouw was referring to the famous clandestine chapel of the same name during the Reformation, when the Dutch authorities proscribed everything Catholic. With as much enthusiasm as their aging bodies allowed, she and her husband threw themselves into clearing out all that was not needed for Mass and installed the chairs and the small table that functioned as an altar. Father's requirements for Mass—vestments alb and stole, cruets for water and wine, and a simple, unadorned chalice, all supplied by Femke—were housed in an old cupboard permanently stationed t here.

'Excellent, Mevrouw,' said Jos, acknowledging the old lady's leading role in reorganising the Mass location. 'We will have time to readjust even if the Germans barge in. I hope everyone can climb the two flights of stairs.'

'We'll help those with difficulties,' said Meneer cheerfully. 'We can offer up any discomfort as reparation for our sins.'

'That's the Catholic spirit, Meneer.'

The regulars greeted the new arrangements with full cooperation. News of the Mass spread by word of mouth. The result was an increase in attendees, single as well as couples, to around twenty old people. Not all attended daily Mass, but most were present for their Sunday obligation. Jos was delighted his Mass was growing into a cosy little parish. He wondered what Femke would think of this unexpected development. He suspected it would not fit into her vision for him. Femke stayed away longer than usual. As fate would have it, she arrived much earlier than expected, around mid-November, to find the De Vries lounge room filled with old people enjoying coffee and biscuits and a jolly chat.

'What's going on, Mevrouw?' she said after being warmly greeted by Mevrouw De Vries. She shot a worried look at Jos, who came to join her.

'Let me explain, Mevrouw De Vries,' he said before that friendly old lady had a chance to explain.

Mevrouw was all too willing to hand the task over to Jos and returned to ensure her guests were comfortable. Jos led Femke upstairs to the attic, where he explained the developments.

'This is more than the private Mass I understood you wanted to offer,' she said, looking around at the chairs.

'It was a natural development I, like you, did not foresee. And I can't say I am not pleased. It's precisely what I became a priest for—to say Mass for the faithful, provide the sacraments, and offer spiritual comforts. Recently, I was called out to the sick and dying—to people who need the ministry of a priest in their final hours. I didn't become a priest to get involved in covert operations. That's for others to do. My duty is to the faithful.'

'I can hear it's been on your mind, Father Jos. I hope you don't want to pull out of the work I have planned?'

Jos hesitated. 'I know, Femke, you are committed to fighting the Nazis—'

'It's not fighting the Nazis,' she said, speaking over him. 'I'm not carrying any guns. There are no bullets in my bag. It's a merciful action, protecting people from the Nazis, vulnerable people who have no other means to escape death. It has the same quality of mercy as your priestly duties.'

Jos hesitated again. 'You put it well, Femke. But as a priest, I have exclusive duties. I must not pass them up for action others can do.'

'You have a special ability, Jos, an ability that will save lives. Few people can replace you. There was no one else to guide Bishop Eliott out of Holland and almost certain death if he were caught.'

'Nevertheless ...' Jos had no reply at that moment to Femke's powerful arguments.

Femke fell into silence while she walked around the attic space.

'You'll have to be very careful you do not attract the attention of the Nazis,' she said at length.

'We've taken precautions. Besides, we do not think the Nazis will be interested in a bunch of old people having a Bible meeting.'

'Perhaps,' she said, pondering. 'You must pray that it is so.'

Jos could see her mind was elsewhere. He waited.

'Let me suggest a compromise,' she said, turning her determined eyes on him. 'You continue your ministry with the utmost care, and I will only put operations to you that are vital and that no one else can do. Indeed, you are the only one at this point who has successfully smuggled someone out of Holland. As I said, you and your exploits have been noticed. Others will attempt it in due course. Time will tell whether they are successful.'

'You already have an operation planned, haven't you?'

'The Nazi invasion isolated two British officers in Holland. Actually, one is an Australian working for British intelligence—for the Secret Intelligence Service (SIS). They are both Catholic. We have held off moving them because of the special difficulties they present. I want you to take them as soon as possible to Zundert. The same arrangements. The difference this time is that you will guide two very fit men who speak a little Dutch. They have been prepared.'

'You're very convincing, Femke. I suspect if anyone is irreplaceable, it's you.'

'Well?' she said, ignoring his comment as usual.

'In such extreme circumstances, I cannot refuse. It belongs to my obligation to be merciful to those in need—as you have unerringly pointed out.'

'Thank you, Father Jos. The resistance is building. Catholic and Protestant groups are coming into action to help and protect the abandoned. Others, like the Communists, are preparing to meet the occupation with violence—sabotage and assassinations. It will bring a cruel reaction from the Nazis. It will make our task more difficult. So it's best to go now while the Nazis remain unprovoked.'

'All right, give me the details.'

Mevrouw de Vries was waiting for them at the bottom of the stairs.

'Oh, Femke, please don't send Father away. We need him.'

Jos saw irritation pass over Femke's face for the first time, as brief as it was.

'Mevrouw, you know the rules. Loose tongues are dangerous for everyone.' She softened. 'You and Meneer have been indispensably generous with your help. Please don't spoil things.'

'At least don't send him away during Christmas.'

'Please, Mevrouw, you don't know who could be listening,' said Femke, whose voice had dropped to a whisper.

Mevrouw, wringing her hands, glanced at the lounge room doorway. 'That's my only request, Femke. I won't mention it again.'

'I'm sorry to be so strict,' said Femke, stroking the old lady's arm. 'I will keep your wishes in mind.'

'Thank you, Femke.' The old lady returned to her guests.

'Don't look at me like that,' said Femke, turning to Jos. 'I have to be strict for reasons you know too well.'

'I'm not saying a word.'

'Don't. It's a full moon. You must take advantage of it.'

'I'll be ready tomorrow morning.'

THE SAME truck, a different driver, picked up Jos from Damstraat at 5 p.m. and deposited him at the same cluster of trees south of Amstelveen. They must change location, thought Jos as he righted himself after leaping from the moving truck. The two men appeared directly from behind the trees. He was relieved their disguise was convincing—unshaven, ragged cap, and dusty labourer's clothes.

They told us you would speak English, Jos,' said Captain Tony Hunt, after the greeting and Jos had briefly explained the next steps, 'but we did not expect so well.'

'You've been among English-speaking people—family?' said Captain Ross Crowe.

'I'm told you're fit,' said Jos, ignoring the question. 'I hope so because we will set off immediately and ride through the night.'

'Lead on, Jos,' said Tony. 'You're the commanding officer for this exercise.'

Possible doubts about the officers' suitability for the operation quickly faded. They kept up with him without difficulty. They did not speak unless spoken to and only stopped to eat and drink. Sleeping in rough conditions did not worry them. By the night of the fourth day, the bicycles were north of Breda. Jos decided not to call on farmer Vos. There was no need, and for the Vos's safety, he did not want to make contact unless necessary. He permitted the seminary a single glance as they glided by during the night. The moon was now on the wane, so the buildings looked less like a single-eye monster. By the morning of the sixth day, they came onto Bredaseweg. Jos halted in the same ditch, about a kilometre from the intersection giving entrance to Zundert. The officers took advantage of the stop and stretched out while Jos scanned the area. The farmers were already at work in the fields, and there was no more than the normal early-morning traffic.

'All right, we're here to take over,' came a voice from behind in Dutch about twenty minutes later.

'What's the password?' said Jos in Dutch, turning to face two men crawling through the crops. The two officers immediately sat up.

'Sorry,' said the leading man, "a nice evening for a walk."'

'It's important to follow the protocol,' said Jos in English. He calmed the officers with a wave.

'Yes, of course. A momentary slip,' said the man in Dutch. 'Anyhow, we can take over now.'

'A slip could mean death,' said Jos.

'All right, no need to make a thing of it,' said the man, still in Dutch.

'Jos is right,' said Captain Hunt. 'It's vital the protocols are adhered to. We have put our lives in your hands.'

The man gave Captain Hunt an inquiring glance. 'I apologise, Captain. It will not happen again. Come, we must go. Leave the bikes. They will be collected later.'

'Thank you, Jos,' said Tony, stretching out his hand. 'You're a real professional.'

'Yes,' said Ross, 'you've been a great commanding officer. It's like you've been in the services.'

Jos shook his head and smiled at Ross's curiosity. 'I wish you all the best.' He shook their hands. 'My prayers go with you.'

'We'll need them,' said Tony.

Jos watched until they had crawled away out of sight. He waited for half an hour before he emerged, mounted his bike, and headed back through the roundabout way he had come. He no longer dared to take the direct open route. When he came within sight of the Vos farm around midday, he stopped. Few people were around despite the village being about a kilometre away. No cars had passed him, not that he expected to see them. It was not a main route, and few villagers owned a car. Nevertheless, he would not show himself entering the Vos farm in the full glare of day. You never knew who could be watching. Catching someone spying on the farm on two occasions was a good lesson. Admittedly, it was in the evening. It did not matter. He moved into the fields on the opposite side of the road to the Vos farm and took up position behind some poplars where he had a direct view of the farm driveway. The evening would provide cover for him to approach the farmhouse.

He leaned back, relieved to have the opportunity to rest. Sleep overtook him, and he did not wake up until mid-afternoon. He sat up and unpacked his dry bread and cheese. He was chewing absentmindedly when a man came from behind the poplars, fifty metres from the entrance to the Vos farm. He was not wearing the clothes that farmers and labourers wore. They were more like clothes for recreation. The man fixed his eyes on the Vos farm. It was surprising that the dog did not bark. Perhaps he was too far away. Then, another similarly dressed man emerged from behind the poplars and joined his companion in surveying the Vos farmhouse. Hans de Jonge! What was he doing there?

Jos squinted to focus on the first man. No, he did not recognise him. The man gazed around the fields and waved his hand as if pointing out something. De Jonge raised binoculars and surveyed the area the man had indicated. He broadened his scanning. Seeing his position would come under his view, Jos ducked his head and lay flat. The men stood talking for around ten minutes, occasionally glancing and pointing at the Vos farm, and then walked towards the seminary. It was a long walk for a man of Hans de Jonge's fitness. But they did not go to the seminary.

Further up the road, they took bikes from behind the poplars and cycled towards Breda. Were they going to Breda or merely to the village? It was a long ride for De Jonge. He watched them cycle by. De Jonge seemed more at ease on the bike now. Why? Would ten months make such a difference to his fitness? Indeed, he had slimmed down. Jos focused on the unknown man. Now, he recognised him. It was Toon Achterkamp, one of the seminarians who had ridden out with them to visit the villages around Noord-Brabant. He was also slimmer. What were they up to? Whatever it was exactly, they were surveilling the Vos farm. If he were right, their surveillance likely had to do with the Vos couple's part in hiding him. Perhaps it was even connected to the major's intervention. In that case, the major and the Voses were in grave danger. When darkness fell, Jos crossed the road and made his way through the fields to come at the farmhouse from behind. The dog began barking but soon stopped.

'Is that you, young Father?' said farmer Vos at the back door, holding his dog's collar. 'We've been expecting you,' he added when Jos came into view. 'Come along inside.'

Mevrouw Vos went immediately into action, and within a short time, Jos was sitting at their table with a plate of food in front of him.

'Wait until you've eaten, Father, before you explain your presence. And you look tired, worse than last time.'

'Yes, lad, you need to stay a few days,' said farmer Vos. 'You'll do yourself a damage if you don't look after yourself.'

'Thank you, Meneer and Mevrouw, for your concern. I will rest tomorrow, but I must set off in the evening. I can't stay. There are, however, matters I must discuss.'

While he ate, Jos related how he had observed Hans de Jonge and his fellow seminarian surveilling the farmhouse. Did they know who he was talking about?

'Yes, we think De Jonge is some sort of helper to Fr. Muller, who seems to be Fr. van Rossem's deputy,' said Mevrouw Vos.

'The fellow is into everything,' said farmer Vos.

'That's not true, dear. He just takes care of the congregation, tells us what's going on and what needs to be done.'

'That's what I mean, wife. He's a snooty, interfering young man.'

'Can you think of a reason he is keeping an eye on your house?'

'No, we can't offhand,' said farmer Vos. 'Maybe it has something to do with you and the major.' Mevrouw Vos nodded her agreement.

'That's precisely my conclusion. If I'm right, you and the major are in danger. Have you seen the major since I was here?'

'No, but he left a list of vegetables and fruit in our mailbox,' said Mevrouw. 'We didn't see him. The list appeared there a few weeks after you had gone. He wrote a short message in German.'

Jos looked at the list that Meneer had fetched. It was in Dutch, but the message was in German. 'The apple pie was delicious,' it read, 'but too much for the soldiers' discipline.'

'Does it mean anything?' said farmer Vos.

'I think it does. You won't see him for a while, if ever, if I'm right. Something has happened to put him on guard.'

'You just didn't sneak around the seminary, did you? You had them coming out to investigate.'

'I'm embarrassed to admit it, Meneer Vos. It was clumsy of me.'

'Never mind, Father,' said Mevrouw. 'We understand what drove you. But you must be more careful.'

'You, too, Mevrouw and Meneer. You must not deviate from your regular farming activity. It seems clear that Van Rossem and Muller think you provided cover for me and that the major missed me during the raid—perhaps on purpose. The German command is at least aware of their suspicions. My clumsy action has raised the suspicion that I might be calling on you. Unfortunately, they were right.'

'But why would Fathers van Rossem and Muller want the Germans to capture you?' It does not make sense,' said Mevrouw.

'I'm not entirely sure,' said Jos, loath to reveal his suspicions about their ideological motivations. 'I would rather not involve you in their Byzantine world of intrigue.'

'Byzantine?' You've lost us, lad.'

'It's just as well, Meneer.'

Jos rested the following day and was ready to set off after a generous meal that Mevrouw insisted he ate to the last crumb.

'Make sure you have a good rest after you arrive where you're going. You're looking more than tired. Your body can only take so much, Father.'

'I'll be sure to rest. Thank you for everything. I can't express enough gratitude.'

'We're here to help you in your courageous action, lad,' said farmer Vos. 'It's the least we can do.'

Jos took his time on the return trip. He was aware of his exhaustion and was heedful of Mevrouw Vos's warning. He took the time to recheck his safe places. None showed any reluctance or fear of the danger. But they had not yet been tested. Mevrouw De Vries was overjoyed to see him when he arrived.

'Oh, Father, we're so relieved to see you,' she said after she had let him and his bike in. 'Come to the lounge. You look very tired. Jeroen, take Father's bike to the laundry. I'll prepare something to eat. You're probably starving.'

'Thank you, Mevrouw. I'll be saying Mass on schedule tomorrow morning.'

'I'll spread the news.'

Femke turned up four days later.

'That was a quick trip. Surely, you could've taken a little more time. The officers said you set a cracking pace they could barely keep up with.'

'They seemed to have had no difficulty,' he laughed, 'and they didn't say anything to me. How have you heard from them so soon, anyhow?'

'You look tired, Jos,' she said, ignoring the question. 'You must take a rest, otherwise you won't be good for anything.'

'Everyone is pestering me with the same advice. To stop the nagging, I will rest, I promise.'

'And don't get too involved in what you evidently see as a special apostolate. Say Mass and hear confessions and leave it at that. If anyone needs a visitation, let me know. You're not the only priest available.'

'You're a hard woman, Femke, but I will obey.'

'See that you do.' She gave him a warm smile and patted his arm.

Jos did not keep to his undertaking. Twice, he could not resist the call. He excused the broken promises by telling himself the two cases were urgent midnight appeals for which nobody else could be found in time. Someone would have to find Femke, and then she would have to organise a priest. No, it was a question of moral priority, and his Christian faith demanded it. They were wet and cold nights, with the rain drenching his clothes and the sleet lashing his face. The dying detained him at their bedside until late morning when their souls slipped peacefully from their suffering bodies. The families were fulsome in their gratitude. It was only doing his priestly duty, he said. By the time he returned home after the second visitation, he felt the beginnings of a fever. Christmas was only a few days away. He was loath to break his promise of conducting the solemn Christmas ceremonies, so he tried to postpone the full effects of the fever by doing what he had promised—staying in his room, keeping warm, and doing nothing.

'Are you all right, Father?' said Mevrouw de Vries when she brought him coffee on Christmas Eve. 'You don't have a fever, do you? Your face is flushed.'

'I'll be fine,' he said. 'But stay clear of me. I don't want you catching it if I have.'

'Should we put off the Christmas ceremonies?' she said, disappointed.

'It hasn't broken through yet. I will be okay for tomorrow's Mass at Dawn. I'll take a complete break afterwards.'

The attic was full of elderly people all rugged up against the chill when Fr. Jos approached the white cloth-covered table on which were the chalice, cruets, and missal. He counted the recipients for Holy Communion and began the Christmas Mass of Dawn. While reading the Last Gospel, he could feel the beads of perspiration and the heat on his brow. After his thanksgiving, he joined the festivity in the lounge room decorated with streamers and sprigs of pine and spruce. He patiently received his small flock's love and Christmas wishes and then excused himself. He did not wish to pass whatever illness was heating his body. But Mevrouw would not hear of it. He positively would not spend Christmas Day in his cold room at the back of the house. She cleared space for him in the corner of the heated lounge and draped a blanket around his shoulders.

'You're not going to make things worse, Father, by sitting in a freezing room. I forbid it.'

Femke arrived at noon carrying a parcel in Christmas wrapping. As she entered the now-empty lounge, she regarded him with a mixture of irony and reprimand.

'You are an incorrigible recalcitrant, Father Jos. You don't give up, do you, until forced?'

'There are things one must attend to,' he said wearily. He had expected a scolding from the determined Femke. 'I'll be all right after a day or two.'

'You hope. Here,' she said, handing him the parcel, 'Merry Christmas.'

'Thank you, Femke.' He unwrapped it to reveal a copy of Aristotle's *Politics*. He stared at it in surprise. 'This choice of book says something about you, Femke, but what, I'm not sure. Thank you. It's a good choice to distract me.'

'You struck me as an Aristotelian.'

'What are you, Femke, an academic at Amsterdam's university?'

'Is there a woman on the staff of Amsterdam University's philosophy department?' she said with a glint in her eye. 'You must tell me who she is.'

'I can't, as you know. But you're right. I am an Aristotelian, as interpreted by St Thomas. I'm sorry that I did not think to buy you a present. You deserve one. Merry Christmas.'

'I have the time and the occasion. You don't. Your present to me will be your health. Take more care of yourself. You're not invincible. There is important work to be done by a man in good health.'

'I promise I'll do better.'

'Until the circumstances demand otherwise, I imagine. Anyhow, I must go. Merry Christmas Jos, and Meneer and Mevrouw de Vries.'

'Oh, can't you stay for Christmas lunch, Femke?' said Mevrouw. 'We have enough food.'

'Thank you for the invitation, but I must be elsewhere.'

It occurred to Jos when she had gone that her visits were always short unless it was to discuss an operation. She never stayed for a social chat.

What did that mean? Of course, it meant she wanted to shield her identity. Was he right in thinking she had a husband and children and did not want the family connection known? But somehow, he could not envisage her as married. There was something about her that ruled that state of life out. What, he could not put his finger on.

The question did not preoccupy him for long. Very soon, the fever took over, and he was confined to the lounge room during the day and his bedroom at night while Mevrouw de Vries fussed over him. She subtly spread the news that Father was too sick for Mass, which provoked well-wishes and the arrival of food parcels. When Jos did not improve, Meneer de Vries called the doctor. The doctor came and said he could not do much. Jos must ride the fever out. It would help if the farm labourer looked after himself better—and stayed away from the drink. A child could see he was run down. It would take a few weeks to regain his health.

Chapter 11

More operations

THE FEVER WAS as stubborn as Jos. He took three weeks to shake its debilitating effects. He could not rouse himself to say Mass even after the two-week mark. All he could do was read for brief periods. He tackled Aristotle's *Politics* and mused that the intellectual discourse on political philosophy had hardly improved in two and a half thousand years. Indeed, some admired political philosophers like Edmund Burke reflected his influence. He could only manage a few chapters before the book dropped from his hands.

Femke came three times and stayed long enough to judge his health and encourage him to get better. Her usual determined expression softened as she looked at him. Concern and affection appeared in her eyes. She was not, after all, an automaton. He regretted at once the meanness of that thought. She was not worthy of it. She had her duty, as he had. He tried to make up for it by encouraging her to take the food gifts his congregation had sent.

'Take them, Femke. I'm sure you have people who need this food more than me. I've asked Mevrouw de Vries to discourage it.'

'That's generous of you, Jos. Thank you. Yes, I do have people who would appreciate extra provisions.'

That was another piece in the puzzle of Femke. She was involved with helping the needy. But it was a small piece and did not enlighten him much. He told himself again that it was none of his business who Femke was. It had nothing to do with his priestly life and nothing to do with the covert operations she was supervising. He should stop himself from wondering about such trivialities. Despite his undertaking, he could no more than push this competent young woman to the back of his mind. He remained on the lookout for more hints.

After three weeks, he felt fit enough to say Mass and provide pastoral care for his flock. Fortunately, despite the winter, the late-night calls were few, and his gravely ill or dying calls were during the day. When he did venture out in the cold night, he now had enough suitable clothing, provided by Femke, to keep warm and dry. To maintain his disguise, he managed to spend a few days at the market stall in Albert Cuypstraat. Surprisingly, Femke stayed away until mid-February. Her hair had been neatly clipped, and her dress was now that of a self-respecting domestic servant. The slovenliness had gone.

'Just what calling is your appearance meant to convey?' he could not help asking. 'Your dress has changed since the first time I met you. You would not be out of place working as domestic help in the bishop's residence.'

She hesitated, colouring. 'I'll just say, Jos, that your comment about the gap between my appearance and speech was helpful in my present work.'

'In your present work?'

'You can't help yourself, can you?'

'No, I can't. Sorry, but you are an intriguing woman, Femke.'

She coloured again. 'I'm a woman doing a job, Jos. Stop being intrigued. It's pointless.'

'All right. I'll try to control my curiosity.'

'Do more than try. Now, let's get off the trivial and talk about your covert activities. I need to give you a briefing.'

Femke had a lot to say. The resistance was well established and continuing to build. The Catholic and Reformed churches were cooperating, which was gratifying. Their help was entirely pastoral, caring for those targeted by the Nazis, especially the Jews. Over the winter, people in the east had helped escaped French prisoners of war make their way down south to Limburg and then onto France and Spain. It was like Jos's operations. Femke did not yet know the extent of the success. Groups had formed to carry out sabotage and assassinate the Dutch Nazis, some more daring than others. The most pressing problem, however, was the targeting of the Jews in the Jewish quarter of Amsterdam, the nearby area between Nieuwmarkt and Plantage. The Nazis had sealed off the quarter as a ghetto following clashes between the Jewish defence group and the Dutch Nazis. More violence was expected.

'I can't believe such persecution is happening in our country,' said Jos.

'It happened in Germany. It will happen here. I'm telling you so you can prepare yourself. Your apostolate to the elderly people around here is admirable. But we are on the eve of a descent into barbarity.'

'My elderly people are not less than anyone else in Holland.'

'Of course, they're not. You have to keep in mind the big picture. There's important work for you to do.'

'Does that mean you have another operation for me?'

'No. I want to wait to see how the persecution of Amsterdam's Jews plays out.'

Femke did not have to wait long. After further violent clashes between the Dutch Nazis, the so-called NSB-ers (*Nationaal Socialistische Beweging*), the Germans rounded up 425 Jewish men and held them hostage. The Communist Party of the Netherlands, itching for a substantial retaliation, called for a nationwide strike on 25 February. The Nazis acted in the way they knew best and applied a surplus of violence, culminating in nine unarmed Dutch citizens lying in a pool of their blood and 24 wounded being rushed to the hospital. The reaction was a warning to those Dutch people who rashly thought they could hinder the glorious advance of the Third Reich.

'Of course, the Nazis are too preoccupied with visions of Teutonic bravado,' said Femke when she came to brief Jos, 'to understand that the murder of unarmed Dutch citizens will only strengthen the resoluteness of the stubborn Dutch. The underground will grow with the help of ordinary people.'

'Teutonic bravado?' said Jos. 'Bishop Eliott said something about the influence of Germanic mythology on the Nazis.'

'Yes, he has looked into it. Many of the Nazi elite are deep into the occult. It's a driving force in their beliefs about blood and homeland. There are powerful hidden truths, they think, in the history and mythology of the ancient Germanic tribes. It reinforces the belief in the nobility and justness of their cause.'

'It's demonic possession; that's what it is,' murmured Jos absently. 'The Church has long regarded the Devil, the Evil One, as central to occult practices. St Augustine battled the occult as an element in Manicheanism. I can believe the occult is an influence in Nazism.'

'Whatever the influences,' said Femke to disturb Jos's musings, 'we must deal with the here and now. We must protect those who are priority victims of Nazi barbarism. It will get worse, Jos, much worse.'

'Was organising such a bold retaliation against the Nazis prudent?' Jos offered. 'Perhaps organising something more subtle but more effective in the long run would have been better than an industrial strike.'

'The communists are always up for the big act, the big radical measures,' said Femke. 'That won't change until the Nazis hunt them down. But Jos, what the radical groups do is not our concern. They will reap what they sow. Our task is to help and protect the vulnerable.'

'So you have an operation planned?'

'Not quite. We must still see how things develop. Other groups are planning to smuggle those needing protection out of Holland. With the victory of the British Air Force over the Luftwaffe, there will be bombing raids over Europe. We anticipate the need to guide the allied pilots shot down. We don't want to get in each other's way. Your first obligation, Jos, is to keep fit. Do you understand?' She wagged a finger at him.

'Yes, Femke, Sergeant Major, I understand.'

'Good,' she said with an encouraging smile, 'but I will supervise you more closely from now on.'

Femke was right. The brutal quashing of the February strike spurred the Dutch to resist the invader in whatever way they could. The organised resistance groups increased their sabotage and assassination actions, bringing ever more brutal reprisals. It seemed no horror was beyond the Nazi leadership, commented Femke, on one visit to ensure Jos behaved himself. Grabbing people off the street for execution ensured a loathing of the Germans likely to last a century. Jos could not help but agree. He tried to turn his mind from the horror and concentrate on the sacramental needs of his flock and preparing himself for Femke's operations. There weren't many during 1941.

A few weeks after the February strike, he guided a young Jewish man to the Belgian border, who had escaped the first pogroms. A family south of the Jewish quarter gave him temporary shelter. He was later transferred to an isolated farm, where Jos picked him up. What a miserable sight he presented—traumatised, fearful, and not knowing what awaited him. Jos could not blame him for regarding his surroundings with distrust. The advantage of his traumatised state was his careful attention to all Jos's instructions. They made good progress without the need to rest at the Vos farm. Jos delivered him in a better state of mind to an agreed point beyond Zundert. Jos had one other operation in late summer.

It was another British officer caught in Holland. Jos wondered why removing him from the country had taken so long. Femke, ever business-like, shook her head as the usual sign that she would not say. He, too, was fit and, like the two British officers before, cooperated in the operation, even anticipated his moves. Jos suspected he was some sort of spy and would not be the last. Though the operations to smuggle people out of Holland were few, Femke added a second use of Jos to her schemes. He would act as a courier of coded messages to the underground resistance. This task was more manageable. Jos had no one to guide, and his contacts were outside the towns. It usually took a week to complete the job because the contact points were rarely beyond the western side of Holland, where the big towns were. Femke could not help smirking with satisfaction after the third assignment.

'You are immoderately happy with yourself, I see,' said Jos.

'I am pleased the idea is working well. It's working well because of your ability to make your way around the country without being detected. You should know that before you tediously remark on my reactions. It's you who is being noticed.'

'By whom?'

'By people who matter. Now, Jos, no more questions because I won't answer. Just prepare yourself for the next assignment.'

'My tedious remarks are a natural reaction to your closed manner,' he teased. 'I'm working closely with a person who is shut up like a bank vault.'

'Goodbye, Jos,' she said, tilting her head. 'Don't forget. Your duty is to remain fit.'

JOS'S ROUTINE remained unchanged through 1941. He continued the pastoral care of his elderly flock for their sake and his. It distracted him from the horror of the war, which seemed to be going in the Nazi's favour. Femke came with her assignments, discussed them, and left. She returned for a debriefing after completion. Her manner became even more business-like. Jos thought her role in whatever group she belonged to weighed heavily on her. He refrained from teasing. She seemed to appreciate it. Her remarks now and then on the failure of some resistance operation resulting in executions confirmed his impressions. She was apprehensive about the infiltration of the groups guiding people out of Holland via Limburg in the southeast of Holland. The treachery resulted in the execution of those self-sacrificing people, often teenage girls, or being sent to the prisoner-of-war camps in Germany. Early in 1942, she asked him if he was still willing to carry out her assignments.

'Of course, Femke. Why would you doubt it? As long as you are risking your life, I will risk mine.'

Her bottom lip trembled in response to his warm, unexpected solidarity.

'Thank you, Jos,' she said, exerting herself to control her emotion, 'but the risks you run are far more acute than mine.'

'We're in it together to the end, Femke. So don't worry about me. My prayers and trust in Our Lord support me.'

'Spoken like a true priest,' she said, her eyes glistening.

'That's what I strive to be.'

In April, she came with a special assignment.

'No one else is willing to take this on because of the difficulty and danger. We think you're the only one who could pull it off.'

'All right, tell me about it,' he said, refraining from again inquiring who "we" was.

'Someone in Zeeland needs urgent extraction. He is in grave danger, and the people sheltering him likewise.'

'Where in Zeeland? The province is partly islands or former islands. That will make it difficult.'

'Walcheren.'

'The narrow peninsula shape of the land from Noord-Brabant to Walcheren means fewer avenues to evade the German patrols, but I know the area well. I have relations all through that part of Zeeland. It's twice the distance, too. It will need more preparation—and some good, detailed maps. How direct is your contact in Zeeland?'

'What do you need to know?'

'The pick-up point, of course. If there is some play in the arrangements, I suggest a secluded place near the village of Kapelle in Zuid-Beveland. Your contact can name a precise point. I will know where it is. My brother and I frequently bicycled through that area.'

'Thanks, Jos. I appreciate your willingness. This is a difficult assignment, fraught with danger.'

'Can you tell me who it is?'

'No—for good reasons. You will know when you rendezvous.'

Jos chose Kapelle, where an aunt and uncle lived, because he suspected Frans might be involved in the operation. He knew his forthright brother would not be sitting on his hands during the occupation. And he had a transmitter.

'How do you reach your contact in Zeeland?' he said a few days later. 'Transmitter?'

'No, Jos, you know not to ask questions like that. When will you give up?'

'I have a good reason this time to ask. I have—'

'No, don't tell me,' she said, interrupting him. 'I don't want to know. I don't have to know.'

He contemplated her urgent expression. 'Are you afraid the contact could be family?' he said, suddenly understanding.

'No, Jos, let's move on to other matters.'

'I suppose you only have a call code, anyhow.'

'I'm leaving if you insist on breaking the protocols.' She stood up, her face tense.

'Calm down, Femke,' he said, surprised at her uncharacteristic reaction. 'It's natural for me to wonder if my family is involved. I have a forceful younger brother—'

'I know you have a younger brother,' she said, interrupting him again. 'You told me about your family in our first debriefing.'

Jos now understood. She, too, suspected Frans might be involved in sheltering the unknown and found the possible loss of two brothers too painful to talk about. It was another glance into her closed character.

'The contacts have no idea who I am or where I'm coming from?'

'Of course not.'

'By the way, what's my code name? I assume I have one.'

'Pimpernel.'

'I assume of the scarlet type?'

'What do you think?'

'I'm impressed with the literary allusion—and flattered.'

'You have earned it.'

'Who are you, Femke? How many Dutch people would be aware of a novel about an Aristocratic English fop who had a secret life outsmarting the French revolutionaries?

'You, for one.' She raised an eyebrow.

'All right, I won't say anymore,' he said, smiling. 'If you can, please tell your contact to have enough food ready so the Pimpernel can have a substantial meal. He will be hungry by the time he reaches Kapelle.'

TWO WEEKS later, Jos was dropped off in the late afternoon at an isolated place south of Amsterdam. Femke had taken notice of his advice to vary the drop-off points. He had risked loading durable food like cheese and seeded bread into the saddle bags, which he intended to hide in places along the route. It was a long trip, more than twice as far, and he might be caught short, particularly after delivering his charge at the Belgian border. At Femke's sound urging, he kept at a steady pace on the outward trip to conserve his energy. It took ten days to reach the Vos farmhouse. Again, he surveilled the house for an hour before approaching it from behind. No one was on or near the empty road. Perhaps Van Rossem and Muller thought their suspicions were unfounded. Perhaps the self-indulged De Jonge had wearied of standing guard for no reason.

'Hello, lad,' said farmer Vos, who came at once to the back door on hearing the dog bark. 'We had a feeling you would turn up,' he continued after Jos had greeted Mevrouw and that kind lady had prepared supper for him. 'It's good timing. We have another list from the major, which looks like a message in a message.'

'Did you see the major?'

'No, the message was stuffed in our letter box overnight. I don't know how he did it without making a sound. We hear everything.'

'How do you know it was from the major?'

'See for yourself,' he said, handing Jos a dirty scrap of paper.

Under a list of vegetables was a message in Dutch.

'Mevrouw Vos, I have instructed my men not to order your delicious apple pie. It is not good for their discipline and causes resentment among others. They have worked out ways to get around my instructions. At least, they think they have. They don't realise they've been found out. You won't be bothered again.'

'It seems straightforward,' said Jos. 'Why do you think there's a message in a message?'

'They have had one pie from us,' said Mevrouw. 'There's been no request since. Why would he bother telling us what he does with his men?'

'Precisely, wife,' said the farmer.

Jos reread the note. They were right. There was no reason for the major to gratuitously tell the old farming couple about thwarting his men's sneakiness. If he were right, the obscured message was not for the couple but for someone else. That someone else must be him. It must be a coded message for him, just him. But what? What was the major trying to tell him?

'When did the message come?'

'About two weeks ago,' said farmer Vos, 'and we haven't seen hide nor hair of him and his men since they turned up while the bishop was here.'

'And you've got no idea what it could mean.'

'Absolutely none.'

'Leave it with me.'

After a three-day rest—Femke had made him solemnly promise to take a rest midway—Jos set off. He had refilled his saddlebags with durables, including Mevrouw Vos's special long-lasting seed bread. Although he knew the area well into which he was riding, there remained unknowns, like where the Germans usually patrolled. The German headquarters were in Breda, so Jos estimated that the farming country below Etten-Leur and Roosendaal, to the southwest of Breda, would have less attention than the northwest. He intended to take this route. Below Roosendaal, he would come close to the Belgian border. Jos had asked why he had to take his charge to Zundert. Why not here if he was to go into Belgium? But he received the usual shake of the head with the terse remark that the arrangement was a spot below Zundert near the village of Wernhout.

He estimated that Kapelle was around 70 kilometres from the Vos farm. If he added the extra distance of his roundabout route, it would be 75 to 80 kilometres. He planned one secure stop on the way. If Femke had succeeded, the parish priest at Hoogerheide near the Zeeland-Noord-Brabant border would be expecting him. For the rest, he would look for the forest areas near Roosendaal and bunk down under some trees. He prayed that it would not rain. The one problem was the narrow route from Hoogerheide to Kapelle. As it turned out, he found shelter among trees below Roosendaal, and the parish priest of Hoogerheide was welcoming. He had evaded the German patrols, only seeing one in the distance from the byway he was on. That gave him a day to rest. He set off late in the evening, intending to ride through to Kapelle without a break.

He arrived in Kapelle around 2 a.m. The arrangement was to shift a bale of hay on Vroonlandseweg on the village's south side and wait in the bush nearby. He prepared for a long wait in the cold. But he did not have to wait long. Within the hour, a man appeared from a side street, walked to the hay bale, and shifted it back to where it was. That was the sign. 'Bring your bike and follow me,' said the man in a thick Zeeland accent when Jos approached him. Jos followed the man to a house at the end of the side street, beyond which were fields. He took him to a back room heated by a wood fire.

'You can rest here for the day,' he said. 'There's bread, ham, and cheese on the table there if you're hungry. I expect you are. I'll bring coffee later. Have a good rest. I promise you will need it.' He pointed to a made-up bed and left.

The man's down-to-earth, Zeeland abruptness was reassuring. He was among his own. He did as he was told and enjoyed a generous helping of bread, cheese, and ham. Coffee and Boluses, Zeeland's pastry delicacy, were brought later. After gobbling the two boluses with the coffee, Jos lay on the bed and put a blanket over himself. The man returned at twelve with more food and left to return late in the afternoon when Jos was sitting staring at the fire. He carried a tray with more food and drink.

'Have enough to eat?' he said, placing the tray on the table.

'Plenty, thank you,' said Jos, suppressing his Zeeland accent.

'Now, here's the situation,' he continued, sitting down. 'Your man is not well but insists on going. He's had enough of waiting around, locked up, and in danger. I can't blame him. But he's very sick. You must decide if you want to risk your life.'

'What's wrong with him?'

'He has a fever, a very bad cold—could be influenza.'

'Can I talk to him?'

'Are you a doctor?'

'No, but the man's frame of mind is important.'

'I suppose you've had experience with this sort of thing.'

'Just let me talk to him, Meneer, if it's no trouble.'

'It's no trouble, but there's always a risk in moving him. I'll bring him tonight.'

Jos started when the man was brought into the room. He knew him. He was a friend or relation of Dr. de Weyl, a leading member of Middelburg's Jewish community. The doctor lived not far away from his family. He had regularly seen him visiting the De Weyl family. The man would have seen him, too, surely, but he gave no sign of recognition as he sat near the fire, coughing and hunching his shoulders. Of course, Jos looked entirely different now with his beard, long, scruffy hair, and labourer's clothes. He was also much older. Perhaps the man was too distracted with his coughing and fever to pay close attention to him.

'De Weyl,' he said, leaning back. His face was on fire, and beads of perspiration glistened on his brow.

'You are not well, Meneer de Weyl,' said Jos. 'Do you realise you have a demanding, dangerous journey ahead of you?'

'Yes, but it could not be more dangerous than here. Besides, I don't want to endanger the generous people who have protected me any longer.'

'What has happened to the rest of your community in Middelburg?'

'They were rounded up and shipped out somewhere on 24 March.'

'How did you avoid the Germans?'

'It was a miracle. I was with the rest of the community, all packed up. We were about to be marched to the station when there was a sudden jostle, and I found myself yanked aside by Frans van— Sorry, I'm not to mention names, am I? One of those crowding around us suddenly yanked me from the group, grabbed my bag, handed it to someone behind, and then he and others hemmed me in while the German soldiers were busy pushing everyone back. I was pushed back with the rest. It was a brave action.'

'Miraculous, indeed,' said Jos, unsurprised that his impetuous younger brother had risked his life. 'You may need another miracle to survive the journey before you. It is evident you are burning with a fever. Do you think you have the strength and determination to make a go of it?'

Meneer de Weyl focused a moment on Jos. A frown passed across his face before he answered.

'I will do my best, Meneer. You have my permission to save your life if I can't go on. I will not blame you.'

'Let's pray it does not come to that. Are you ready to leave in an hour? You have rested today, I hope. We will ride through the night and rest during the day.'

'He's been lying on his bed these last few days,' said the Kapelle contact. 'He could not be more rested.'

'I'm ready when you are,' said Meneer de Weyl.

They set off within the hour but had not been on the road for more than a half-hour when De Weyl stopped and leaned on the front handlebars, puffing, his head down. Jos expected it.

'Take your time, Meneer. We'll start again when you're ready. This first section will be thirty or forty kilometres. Try to suppress your coughing.'

It was painful going, both for De Weyl and Jos. At times, De Weyl had to lie in the grass beside the road until he gathered enough strength and spirit to continue. At one stage, they were surprised by a convoy of troop carriers emerging from the mist. Jos had just time to push De Weyl into the nearby ditch and follow him. He jammed his hand over the sick man's mouth to stop him coughing. The convoy passed hardly more than ten metres away.

'Sorry,' said Jos, releasing his hand while De Weyl went into a paroxysm of coughing and spluttering.

'It's all right,' said De Weyl, gasping for air.

When De Weyl had recovered enough, they continued and arrived at Hoogerheide's parish presbytery at 3 a.m. It took five hours with many stops to cover thirty-five kilometres. It should have taken around two hours now that Jos knew the way, even at a moderate pace. Fr. Keulemans was again welcoming. He did not object to being woken early and, glancing at the sick man, seemed to understand something important was afoot. He showed Jos and De Weyl to a room at the back of the presbytery. They were welcome to stay as long as they liked. Jos assured him they would be gone as soon as they could.

He expected it would take De Weyl two days to regain some strength. Fortunately, he looked no worse than when they had started. But he was concerned about his coughing. When Fr. Keulemans was free the next morning, he asked if he had a map of the area, including Belgium, whose border was no more than five kilometres away. The priest had a map of Belgium and Holland and was familiar with that northern part of Belgium. A brief look at the map confirmed his nascent plan. The Dutch-Belgium border was not regular. It zigzagged up and down below Hoogerheide and Zundert. A direct route to the rendezvous point south of Zundert would take him much of the way across Belgium.

'What's the land like if one travels east over the border in Belgium?' he asked Fr. Keulemans.

'It's not as flat as Holland and sparsely populated, much of it farming land.'

'I assume there are occasional forests of trees, similar to the country south of here.'

'Yes, they will give protection,' he said, understanding. 'You won't find many German patrols there.'

'Do you have some camping equipment you can spare?

'What I have, you can have—some sheets of canvas and props you can use to form into a rough shelter. It works. I used them when I was young. You'll stay dry.'

After studying the map, Jos fixed a route. The plan was to travel east along Huijbergseweg, pass below the village of Huijbergen, and cross the border on Hollandsweg. He would then pass below the Belgian villages of Wildert and Nieuwmoer, staying on Nieuwmoerseweg until he crossed again into Holland. He would pass around the village of Achtmaal and then take Achtmaalseweg to the rendezvous point below Zundert. It would be no more than twenty-five kilometres. He aimed to be at the rendezvous on the third day at the latest.

'You're not likely to run into Germans in Belgium, but it is a rough, isolated way until you reach the border again. Do you have enough food and water?'

Fr. Keulemans refilled the saddlebags and the water bottles. He listed the villages Jos was likely to come near and where he could camp. The two-day rest seemed to do De Weyl good. His condition still had not deteriorated. They set off at midnight two days later.

'I can only guess what you're doing,' said Fr. Keulemans when Jos thanked him for his indispensable assistance, 'but whatever it is, it takes a lot of courage and determination—perhaps a little madness. The least I could do is help. I wonder how far you will get with this sick man.'

De Weyl lasted a half-hour before he stopped and leaned over his handlebars, puffing and coughing.

'I wonder, too, how far you will get with me.'

'I don't give up, Meneer De Weyl. We'll get you there.'

'Where's there? I don't even know where I'm going. What do I call you? I don't even know that.'

'Call me Jos.'

'Jos?' He lifted his head and focused on his guide. 'There was Jos in Middelburg, a brother of— Sorry, I should not speak about such things, should I? But, no, that Jos is a priest and academic, not some sort of rugged, devil-may-care, undercover agent like you.' He leaned further forward and seemed on the point of toppling over.

'Keep up your spirits, Meneer De Weyl,' said Jos, grabbing his shoulder. He could not suppress a brief ironic smile. 'It will make a difference.'

'Call me Ben, Jos,' said Ben, lifting his head again. 'No need for all that meneer stuff in this horrible, degrading situation.'

'Keep positive, Ben. We need your cooperation to get you out of this degrading situation. I've done this before and am still alive and kicking.'

'I'll do my best. I don't want to be responsible for your first failure.'

'That's the spirit. Together, we'll complete this sector.'

Revived in spirit, Ben did his best. He suppressed his coughing as much as possible and only stopped when his strength would not take him any further. The stops were frequent. It took a half-hour for him to summon up the strength to go on. Nevertheless, when dawn came, they were well into Belgium, passing below Wildert. On the other side of Wildert, Jos stopped. He had planned to look for a place to camp here. Ben let his bike fall to the ground and tumbled into the grass beside the road.

'How do you feel, Ben?'

'I want to die, Jos,' he gasped, now with a terrible rattle in his throat. 'Give me the *coup de grace*, will you?'

'Don't give up. We've done well—come much further than I thought. We'll have something to eat and review our options.'

'Review our options!' Ben said drily. 'We're not having a business conference. Death is my only option—and perhaps yours, too, unless you leave me to die and save yourself.'

'You're not an actor in real life, are you, Ben?'

'No. Why do you ask?' he whispered, glancing up.

'You do melodrama well.'

'It's not funny, Jos,' said Ben, unable to suppress a laugh amid his coughing.

'I know, Ben. But it's better to laugh than despair.'

There were farms along the road out of Wildert, Jos had discovered to his surprise. The route was less isolated than Fr. Keulemans had made out. At that moment, a man approached from the nearest farm. Jos waited.

'Good morning,' said the man in a thick accent when he had reached them. 'Are you okay?' He looked at Ben, who was now asleep and breathing with a rattle.

'We're just having a rest,' said Jos, undecided about how to deal with this unexpected intervention.

'Your friend does not look well,' the farmer said, running an examining eye over Jos and Ben. 'You're a long way from home, too?'

'He has a little fever. We're on our way to Zundert.'

'Zundert? From where ...?' He continued to examine Jos and his sick friend. 'It doesn't matter,' he added, apparently understanding. 'Your friend has more than a little fever, Meneer. Come to the farmhouse. It will be more comfortable than lying in the grass beside the road. You'll have protection.'

'Are you sure ...? I don't want to make things difficult for you.'

'There's little risk here. You can rest as long as you need.'

'If you've got a hay shed, that will be sufficient. I don't want to endanger you and your family. If we can rest during the day, I'll be grateful. We'll leave at night.'

The farmer took Jos and Ben to his hay shed, where a barely conscious Ben collapsed onto the hay and continued his rattling. They were left to themselves most of the day, the farmer only coming to bring food and drink. When he returned in the evening, Ben was awake but barely had enough energy to speak.

'Thank you, Meneer,' he whispered to the farmer. 'I appreciate your generosity, but I fear it's wasted.'

'You can't give up now,' said the farmer. 'When do you plan to leave?' he said to Jos.

'Late evening. We'll ride through the night.'

'I can take you as far as the border.'

Jos protested that it was too dangerous. The farmer insisted there was little risk, perhaps over the border near Achtmaal, but not before.

'You would be unlucky to strike patrols on this side of the border.'

'It would be just my luck,' said Ben, as morose as he could sound.

Jos accepted the offer, and their bikes were loaded onto the truck around midnight. They were dropped off on the other side of Nieuwmoer, about five hundred metres from the border.

'Be careful when you approach Achtmaal,' said the farmer.

'Thank you, Meneer,' said Jos after the bikes were unloaded and they were ready to go. 'Your help has been priceless.'

'You're welcome. I understand what you're doing, but to do it so calmly would take almost insane bravado. It's the least I could do.'

'Come on, Ben,' said Jos after watching the truck disappear into the night. 'We've only got a little way to go, and you look in better condition.'

'Looks are deceptive,' said Ben, 'and there are limits no matter how positive one wants to be.'

Jos was careful in approaching the border. It was open country, but one could never be sure at such switch points. They walked on until he was certain there was no threat anywhere.

'Let's go,' he said, mounting his bike. 'We'll take it slowly to conserve energy.'

'There's little to conserve,' said Ben, laboriously mounting his bike and leaning over the handlebars.

On the outskirts of Achtmaal, they came across a man cycling towards the border.

'There's a German patrol on the other side of the village,' he said as he passed them.

Jos was ready for it. He had studied his map of the Zundert area while at the farm and saw byways around the village that would take him to the main road below Zundert. That's where he needed to be. The quarter moon gave enough light to negotiate the roads. At first, Ben kept up, but soon after branching off the main road, he had to stop.

'Rest awhile,' said Jos. 'We've got time. There are only a few kilometres to go.'

'I'm burning up, Jos,' Ben said, coughing and rattling, 'and my legs are like jelly.'

'Just two or three kilometres.'

But it was no use. After going and stopping for another kilometre, Ben was on the point of toppling off his bike. Jos grabbed hold of him and dismounted.

'Stay on your bike, Ben. Hold onto the handlebars. I'll steady you.'

So, wheeling his bike beside him, Jos pushed forward, holding Ben upright. He had to stop several times to rest, but after a kilometre and a half, he reached the main road near the village of Wernhout below Zundert. This was where he had to be. He guided Ben and his bike off the road, past a line of oak trees and helped him dismount. They both collapsed on the gr ass.

Chapter 12

Ben struggles

'AM I STILL alive?' said Ben, gasping and croaking.

'Stay where you are, and don't move,' said Jos, puffing.

'As if I'm going anywhere,' said Ben, moaning.

After five minutes, Jos got to his feet. 'Don't make a sound. I'll be back in a minute.'

'I'll resist banging on my drums.'

Jos calculated it was a little after 2 a.m. He walked to the edge of the road and looked up and down Wernhoutseweg. It was deserted, with a little mist above the fields. The village was in darkness. No lights shone from the nearby farms. The plan was to place a bike against one of the oaks as a sign they were present. But Jos could see a difficulty. The bike would be visible to everyone, and he and his charge had arrived several days later than planned for the rendezvous. What if a German patrol noticed the seemingly abandoned bike and stopped to investigate? It was not likely, Jos thought, but could happen.

As some security, he placed Ben's bike, with the saddlebags empty, at the far end of the long row of oaks and moved Ben, gasping and protesting, to the end nearest the village. If a patrol stopped to investigate, he and Ben had time to retreat into a ditch that ran across the fields to a nearby farmhouse before the soldiers fanned out to search the area. Jos settled down to take a rest. At around 5 o'clock, Ben roused him from his heavy sleep.

'Jos, Jos, a truck with soldiers has stopped,' he spluttered. 'Wake up!'

'What ...?' said Jos, taking a moment to assess where he was. 'Get ready to move, Ben. Take the canvas with you.' He crawled to a position where he could see the patrol. An officer and a soldier were on the roadside staring at the bike. The soldier took the bike and examined it. After some discussion, the officer signalled the soldiers to alight and search the area.

'Hurry, Ben. Crawl along the ditch—without showing yourself. Come on. Your life depends on it. Go as far as my bike. I'll join you if I have to.'

As another precaution, Jos had already hidden his bike with his provisions far along the ditch. Ben crawled away, dragging the canvas sheet behind him. Surprisingly, he did not moan or protest, even though the ditch was damp. He must be improving, thought Jos, relieved. He expected the soldiers to restrict their search to the nearby area. But he was wrong. For some annoying reason, the officer wanted the entire line of oaks systematically searched, a task that would take the soldiers at least a half-hour to complete. Jos joined Ben in the ditch about fifty metres across the field. The farmhouse was another fifty metres away.

'Come on, Ben. We'll move along a little further. It looks like the patrol is determined to find something. Are you okay?'

'I feel a little better—better than when we arrived.' He hesitated. 'Jos, if this is it, and they catch us, I want to say how much I value your unselfishness in this operation. I would not have gotten this far without your encouragement.'

'Thank you, Ben, but we're not finished yet. Glad to hear you're feeling better.'

For half an hour, Jos watched the soldiers searching around the oaks. They were now nearing the end of the row. He wondered if he should stay where he was or move closer to the farmhouse. But then, he risked endangering the farmer and his family. He decided to stay put.

'The days are cold,' a voice whispered in English.

'What's going on?' said Ben, turning in panic towards the voice.

'The nights are colder,' Jos returned in English.

Two men came out of the murky dawn light. 'Follow us,' said one, 'and keep down.'

'How did you know we're here?' said Jos.

'Someone saw the *Mof* looking at the bike. Hurry, we don't have time—

'My charge is quite ill,' whispered Jos. 'He will need help and a rest.'

'Leave him to us,' came the reply. 'You have finished your part.'

Jos and Ben followed the men through the ditch until they came to another cluster of trees away from the farmhouse. Further on was a road.

'Are you all right to go?' said one of them as the other helped Ben to the road. Ben turned and gave a wave before passing out of sight. 'Have you got enough food?'

'Yes,' said Jos, seeing that the men wanted to leave immediately.

'Good, I suggest you get the hell out of here. The Germans have become more active. Good luck.' He hurried after Ben and his companion.

Jos folded up the canvas and stowed it in his saddlebag. The soldiers had finished searching the oaks and stood around while the officer decided his next move. A soldier walked into the field and soon came across the ditch. He called the officer who ordered him to investigate. The soldier moved forward and stopped. He called to the officer, who ordered more soldiers to follow the ditch. Jos had no choice. To escape notice, he had to stay in the cover of the farmhouse and its buildings. That meant heading back the way he had come and taking a wide roundabout route to Achtmaalseweg. From there, he would have to cycle back towards Achtmaal before finding a route around Wernhout and Zundert. It was dangerous. Perhaps the German patrol was still hanging around Achtmaal.

It also meant a long, tedious alternative route where he must constantly check his map. He had no choice. He set off, cold and damp, feeling the heat in his face and ache in his limbs. Contracting Ben's fever was always going to be a risk. The Vos farmhouse was about twenty-five kilometres away. He had not planned to stop there, but realised he needed a day's rest after travelling for about an hour. It took another hour to arrive in the vicinity of the farm.

He wondered whether he should be careful about approaching the farm. Surely not. Surely, it was a fluke that De Jonge and Achterkamp were surveilling the farm just when he happened by. It was also early, about 8 o'clock, too early for amateur spies. But he had learned you could never be sure, and it was sound spycraft to make sure. He parked his bike behind a poplar and crawled across the same field to the same place where he had a clear view of the farmhouse and the poplars. Fortunately, the grass was dry. The open, dry air would allow his damp clothes to dry. He coughed as he settled down.

After an hour, he thought he had waited long enough and was about to crawl back to his bike when he heard the rumble of a car engine. It came from the direction of the seminary. He stopped and waited. A German staff car came into view, travelling at a leisurely pace. It halted about a hundred metres up the road from the Vos farm. For a while, it remained there with its engine idling. Then a door opened, and out stepped De Jonge, holding a small bag and dressed in tasteful casual clothing. He spoke at the back window for a minute before the staff car departed. Jos tried to see who was in the back seat, but the distance was too great, and the car's back seat was shaded. De Jonge took a fold-up chair from behind a poplar, pulled a book from his bag, and settled down.

De Jonge had a fine time for two hours, reading, snacking on cake, and drinking from a thermos. Occasionally, he stood and came forward to run an eye over the farmhouse and its surrounds. He didn't bother to look across the fields in Jos's direction. Shortly after ten o'clock, Achtercamp came into view, cycling leisurely, also dressed in tasteful casual clothing. De Jonge poured a cup for Achterkamp and offered him some cake. They stood chatting for about half an hour before retreating out of sight behind the poplars. Lazy, sloppy spies, thought Jos. But it was not their sloppy spying that occupied his thoughts. Why had De Jonge and Achterkamp turned up to do their surveilling precisely when he happened to be back there? Surely, it was too much to think it a second coincidence. No, it was as if he was expected. The senior seminarians had had enough by midday. De Jonge returned his book and thermos to his bag and mounted the bike behind Achterkamp, who doubled him back to the seminary.

'I caught De Jonge and Achterkamp surveilling the farmhouse again,' said Jos after farmer Vos had shown him into the lounge room. 'Didn't you hear anything during the morning?'

'Only a car,' said Mevrouw Vos. 'An occasional car drives by. We can't tell what sort of car it is.'

'We only know what it is if we see it,' said farmer Vos.

'The German staff car has a heavy engine. It makes a deep rumbling sound.'

'Oh, we hear that quite often, lad.'

'I urge you again, Meneer and Mevrouw, to be permanently on your guard.'

'Don't worry about us, Father,' said Mevrouw Vos. 'You should worry about yourself at this minute. You look tired and flushed. Take a seat, and I will get you something to eat and drink.'

Jos submitted to the care and fussing of Mevrouw Vos and endured the advice of farmer Vos while he ate a hearty meal. After eating, he retreated to his bed in the attic while the old couple attended to their work. He slept soundly until late evening but did not feel entirely refreshed. It was a bad sign. Bad sign or not, he had to leave. The old couple were in danger as long as he was around. De Jonge and his mate might make a more determined effort to find out if anyone had sought shelter in the farmhouse.

'I'm leaving,' he announced, appearing in the lounge room. 'It's too dangerous to stay, and it's better that I ride through the night.'

'No, you can't, *lieverd*,' said Mevrouw Vos, feeling his forehead as if he were her child. 'You have a fever. You'll make yourself sick.'

'Be sensible, lad. A day or two won't make a difference.'

'It could, and I can't risk it. No, I'm determined,' he said, embarrassed by his petulance.

The couple accepted his decision, and Jos set off after Mevrouw prepared a food package. It was gruelling going. After several days, Jos thought he might have been rash. Dying on the way would make a sad end to his activities. But he persisted. By the time he arrived at the Amstelveen parish nine days later, he was ready to expire. Indeed, he was sure it was only a few steps to his grave. The parish priest put him in the back shed, as he had done before. Two hours later, the same truck with its coal burner collected him and his bike and dumped them in Damstraat between the busy traffic. He did not have the energy to check if Nazi soldiers were patrolling nearby.

'*Goede hemel*,' exclaimed Mevrouw de Vries when she opened the door. 'You look dreadful, Father. Come in. Leave the bike. Jeroen will see to it.'

Jos had enough energy to wash and change into clean clothes before he collapsed on his bed at the back of the house. He awoke two days later to find the doctor standing over him. His face was burning, and his limbs were aching.

'I've warned you before, young man. Unless you take better care, you'll kill yourself. Eat properly and stay away from the drink. You labourers must learn the hard way. I've given Mevrouw a diet for you to follow. Of course, you're not fit for work and won't be for a week or two. I'll write a medical certificate for you.'

'Thank you, Doctor,' was all Jos could manage.

'You are such an obtuse priest,' scolded Femke when she arrived a week later and took a seat beside his bed on which he was lying fully dressed. 'It's like you have a death wish.'

'I notice you took your time visiting the sick,' he said, struggling to sit up.

'It's nothing to joke about, Jos.'

'If we're not joking, Femke,' he said wearily, 'it's difficult to understand the constantly changing circumstances an agent must deal with. Often, there's no choice.'

Sympathy and warmth appeared in Femke's eyes.

'Perhaps not, though I suspect it's not impossible for an agent to take the necessary precautions for one's own good.'

'You're a hard woman, Femke—just like a business boss.'

Jos noticed with surprise that the normally controlled Femke could not suppress an ironic smile. She quickly wiped it from her face.

'You're free to entertain whatever speculations come to mind. My job is to make sure you're fit to carry out our crucial operations. And don't irritate by asking again who "our" is.'

'Yes, Femke.'

'There'll be nothing until you are completely well. You are free to indulge your elderly flock,' she said, standing. 'Just don't overdo it and risk trouble with the German patrols. They've become very skittish.'

'Yes, certainly, Femke. But before you go, I've got some information for you. Actually, it's more of a puzzle. It could be important.'

Femke sat down again. 'I'm all ears.'

'I was given a cryptic message. It seems a warning that the Nazis have broken an Allied code. In other words, as I interpret it, the Nazis can decipher the messages coming to agents in Holland. I assume they mean coming from England.'

'Let me see the message.'

'No, it will compromise my informant. Just accept I've interpreted it correctly. It is now a simple task for the Secret Intelligence Service (SIS) to check if their agents in Holland have been compromised. It should be obvious if they have been. There is a special code that will tell the coders at SIS if the sender is genuine.'

'Indeed, there is. Leave it with me,' she said, again rising. 'You astound me, Fr. Jos. I chat with you, and when I am about to go, you pass on critical information as if it is just a passing thought.'

'No need to be astounded, Femke. I had not forgotten.'

Two weeks later, she returned.

'How shall I put this, Jos?' she said, a frown marking her hesitation. 'I passed on your message. There's been no direct reaction, but I'm led to believe SIS does not think it is important. Nothing explicit has been said.'

'I'm a little surprised. My source is absolutely trustworthy. He's not likely to get such information wrong. My worry is that I have not interpreted it correctly.'

'It would help if I could see the message.'

'No, it won't.'

'All right, if that's your decision. By the way, the Nazis rolled up the activities of one of the radical communist groups. The whole leadership was executed.'

'Talk about passing thoughts,' he said. 'I'm not surprised, though. I think more subtle means generally would be more effective. The communists must stage their grand action for the proletariat.'

'Indeed. I'll leave you now. There won't be anything for you for a couple of months. You must rest—and I mean rest.'

'Going so soon, Femke? Not willing to dally for a coffee and an everyday chat?'

'You are an annoying priest, Jos.'

'Just being friendly.'

'Rest. You still look dreadful.'

Chapter 13

The Occult

THE DOCTOR'S PROGNOSIS was a little out. Fr. Jos's fever lasted two weeks before it subsided, leaving him cooler but utterly drained. He had to abandon his Masses until further notice. His flock sent their love and best wishes, but no food presents. The Germans had imposed strict food rationing. One merciful outcome of the decrease in traffic to the De Vries's door was the decrease in risk for his congregation, who put attending to their faith above their safety. Indeed, the strong faith of these simple old people brought him to reflect on the last two years and what it meant for his priesthood and religious commitments. Cycling around the country, evading the Germans to help the war effort, was not exactly why he had committed himself to the priesthood—no matter how effective it had been.

His work and duty as a priest were above earthly matters. The same thoughts seized his mind. His central concern and duty were the supernatural destiny of the people under his pastoral care. His privilege as a priest was to provide the sacraments as indispensable aids to their journey's destiny. What was he doing now? His operations were works of charity, as Femke pointed out, but they were primarily covert military operations. One did not have to be a priest to carry them out—just a clever operative who took risks. He could not resist the feeling that he was failing in his priestly duty, however much Femke praised his success in taking stricken people to safety. And there was Femke herself. Was she a risk to his priesthood? He didn't think so, he had been telling himself.

Chance circumstances had thrown them together—two people the same age and of similar ways and temperament. That they had similar characters was not the danger. That he was a man, and she a woman—an intriguing one—was. Despite Femke's self-control in keeping their interaction businesslike, they could not help but become familiar with each other. He could not help teasing her in a perverse effort to break down her rigidity. She playfully accused him of flirting—improper for a priest, didn't he know?

Yes, flirting was improper behaviour for a priest, but he did not consider that he was flirting. It was merely an affectionate teasing he sometimes did with his sisters. There was nothing in it. It presented no danger. Indeed, he regarded Femke the way he regarded his sisters. The difference was that Femke was nothing like his sisters besides being a woman. He had an intellectual connection with her that was missing with his sisters. He admired her intellectuality and precise organisation. And there was something else that enhanced their familiarity.

He had arrived in Amsterdam as an unworldly twenty-eight-year-old, exhausted and suffering the shock of the first stages of the war. It was like nothing he had ever experienced. He could not comprehend the execution of Fr. Albers and his dear friend, the innocent, enthusiastic Bart Timmermans. Then, Femke came into his life to take charge of him for the next several years. Slovenly dressed, hair everywhere in an amateurish attempt at disguise, she was clearly as new to the enterprise of war as he was, despite her discipline, determination, and competence. It was two years ago that together they tackled the duties thrust upon them. Now thirty, they had grown together, just them, the two of them, isolated and enclosed. So much had happened, and so much had changed, that he felt it had been over two years.

Femke must have felt the same way. Their cooperation was more than two people working together. It was no wonder a close bond had developed. You would have to be made of rock, thought Jos, not to have felt an affinity with someone so close to you. Nevertheless, after these thoughts had occupied him for days while lying exhausted on his bed at the back of that Amsterdam house, he still thought his feelings for Femke were those of a brother for a sister. Temptation did not appear for him to resist. Said sister stayed away for nearly two months, which did not surprise him. In late August, she came to check on him.

'You're looking much better,' she said when he joined her and Meneer and Mevrouw De Vries in the lounge room. 'But you still need to improve. I'm pleased to hear from Mevrouw De Vries that you have not wandered often or far.'

'Just resumed Mass and confession for my little congregation—been out to the dying on several occasions.'

'Just restrict yourself to Mass and confession for the time being.'

'Yes, Femke, I'll try not to be a naughty boy.'

'It's all for—'

'Yes, I know. It's for my own good.'

'Good that you know because I rely on you.'

'Really? You have not given up on me?'

Femke shook her head as a sign that she would say no more in front of the elderly couple.

'How's the war going?' he said ironically to divert attention from him. 'I scarcely have time to think about it. If it's as bad as the Nazi savagery in Holland, then the Nazi propaganda here must be reliable. We must pray that the Nazi evil does not prevail.'

'The battles with the German U-boats in the Atlantic have until now been disastrous for the Allies,' said Femke in her usual businesslike manner. 'The loss of vital merchant shipping has been colossal. But there's hope there'll be a turnaround. We should not despair yet. That's as much as I know about the U-boat danger. On the Mediterranean front, a new British general has been appointed to face General Rommel's army in Africa. There is hope General Montgomery and the 8th Army will succeed where others have failed. Again, that's as much as I can tell you. Now I must go,' she ended, rising.

'You won't stay for a cosy chat?' said Jos.

'Yes, you don't have to hurry away,' said Mevrouw de Vries.

'Thank you, Mevrouw, but I have things to attend to. I can't sit around like those who wear themselves out and suffer the consequences. May I ask you to make sure Father continues to rest and not be a nuisance?'

'Of course, you can, Femke,' said Mevrouw. 'We'll keep an eye on Father and make sure he does nothing foolish. We rely on you, Father van Engelen.'

'That's a bit unfair, isn't it, Femke,' said Jos, 'calling on Meneer and Mevrouw to do your policing?'

'We are all concerned for your welfare,' said Femke with a triumphant smile. 'I'll see you at Christmas.'

Jos had to smile to himself. Femke now returned his gentle teasing with a bit of his own medicine. It was tactically better for her.

'How do you contact Femke, Meneer?' he said to Meneer de Vries while Mevrouw saw Femke to the door.

'We told you, Father, didn't we? We let it be known at the church that we want to see her. It doesn't take long for her to appear. We don't know any more. I think that's the way it's meant to be.'

'Of course, you're right. I'm sorry I asked you to break the rules.'

'I understand, Father. Femke is a rather intriguing young woman.'

'Do you have any idea what her normal situation or occupation is?' Jos could not help asking.

'None whatever. We can only tell she does not behave or speak like someone from Amsterdam.'

JOS'S HEALTH improved, enabling him to devote more time to his congregation than worry about the frightful actions the Nazis perpetrated in his country. He could not do anything about it, and his flock of frightened elderly people needed his pastoral attention. Every new horror—random reprisals, summary executions, and the continual threat of arrest—had them on edge. As he became fitter and more active, his pastoral reach extended beyond his area to marginal cases of sickness or dying and even to parents worried about their wayward children—some about daughters who flirted with German officers. He tried to impress on his people that his actions were unofficial and dangerous. That changed nothing for these abandoned, marginalised people. They had no one else to turn to and assured him they would be silent about his work.

An unusual case caught his attention at this time. One of his congregation urged him to counsel a mother worried about her daughter. Her daughter's fixation on ancient mythology seemed to conflict with her faith. The mother couldn't help because she could not understand what it was about. Her daughter waved the mother's worry aside by saying her interest in ancient mythology, particularly Germanic mythology, was merely an extension of her schoolwork. The mother pleaded to have someone from the church talk to her. But the parish authorities seemed to think it was nothing to worry about. There were more urgent matters for them to deal with.

Jos's first reaction was to agree with the parish authorities that other matters took priority over a harmless interest in ancient mythology, however deep that interest was. Then Bishop Eliott's words about the Nazis' obsession with the world of Teutonic knights came back to him. Was the daughter attracted to the occultist element in ancient myths? It would not hurt to talk to the mother—and the daughter if she was willing. A time was arranged, and Jos took himself off to an address in nearby Warmoesstraat. Mevrouw Borst warmly welcomed him.

'What exactly worries you, Mevrouw Borst?' said Jos after they were seated in the lounge room. 'An interest in ancient mythology in itself does not seem to conflict with the faith. After all, your daughter has said her interest carries on from her schoolwork.'

'I don't know exactly. That's why I asked you to talk to her ... Marlies's special interest in the religious ceremonies of ... actually, it's more than an interest. She celebrates and carries them out in her room. Her room has become a sort of shrine. She doesn't attend Mass anymore.'

'What does your husband say?'

'My husband was killed defending Holland against the *Mof* invasion.' Mevrouw Borst lowered her head and stifled a sob.

'I'm sorry, Mevrouw. That must make it difficult.'

'Yes, Father. That's why I've asked you to help.'

Marlies had taken her father's death hard, plunging her into a depression that lasted several months. Then, without warning, she came out of it and returned to her usual happy self. Perhaps her work as a waitress in an upper-class restaurant near Dam Square helped. Her interest in ancient mythologies later became known. Without her mother knowing, Marlies had got hold of several books on ancient rituals. She found others after rummaging among the books at the street markets in the neighborhood. Mevrouw Borst suspected this new interest was connected to the change—how exactly, she did not know.

'Would Marlies object if I spoke to her about it?'

'I'm not sure, but I will ask her. When not at work, she's in her room, where she spends most of her time with her shrine. She is home now.'

Mevrouw went to fetch Marlies and returned with a tall, very attractive girl of around twenty, dark-haired and poised. She raised her eyebrows when she saw Jos sitting comfortably in their lounge room. Jos got to his feet.

'Is this the labourer who you want me to talk to?' she said dismissively.

'My visit is confidential, Juffrouw,' said Jos. 'I'm not a labourer. Your mother is worried about your interests and asked me for reassurance.'

'Who are you, then?' said Marlies, sitting down. 'Why do you think you can give my mother reassurance, as you call it?'

'Juffrouw, my visit is confidential—and dangerous. I count on your discretion. Your mother wants to understand your interests in pagan ceremonies and has asked my assistance.' Jos decided there was no point in pussyfooting around.

'Pagan ceremonies?' she said evasively. Her poise slipped a little.

'If you celebrate such things as the winter and summer solstices, you celebrate pagan ceremonies. And if you seriously and wholeheartedly celebrate them, Juffrouw, you are playing with fire.'

'Playing with fire?' She raised her chin.

'There is nothing wrong with having an intellectual or historical interest in ancient peoples and their rituals. It's another to immerse oneself in ceremonies with a demonic element.'

'Demonic element?' she said, further raising her chin. 'That's the Church speaking, isn't it? But I'm not particularly interested in what the Church thinks—not after it did nothing to prevent the slaughter of my father. Besides, ancient ceremonies have much to offer in understanding oneself and the world. I'm not afraid of any demons—if they exist.'

'You don't know what you're getting yourself into, I assure you, Juffrouw,' said Jos. Blaming the Church was sure to be a pretext for her interest.

'I certainly do, and I don't need your advice—whoever you are—about what is my business and not yours.' She rose.

'One must consider the surrounding culture of those pagan ceremonies. There was a great deal of cruelty and violence—irrational violence—in ancient societies, particularly in their religious rituals. For example, wives in some German tribes were buried with their slain warrior husbands. The Church brought a culture of peace to those people. Christian culture civilised the rugged Germanic tribes.'

'Germany is hardly acting in a civilised way,' she sneered offhand but with some uncertainty.

'Germany has abandoned its Christian culture and replaced it with a callous irrational ideology. Reinvented Germanic mythology seems to be a part of it.' Jos surprised himself by articulating so fluently the little information from Bishop Eliott and Femke about the Nazis' obsession with Germanic myth.

Marlies coloured and looked more uncertain. 'As I say, Meneer, I don't need your advice.' With deliberate steps, she marched from the room.

'I'm sorry, Father,' said Mevrouw Borst. 'Marlies can be a very stubborn, self-centred girl. No doubt you've seen she's very attractive. Like many handsome girls, she has been spoilt. Unfortunately, she interprets the attention her beauty arouses as support for her opinions. She's easily flattered. I fear the attention she receives in the restaurant from upper-class men does not help.'

'You must not lose heart,' said Jos, sidestepping the issue of Marlies's beauty. 'I have challenged her. She looked uncertain at times. I hope I have seeded questions in her mind that she cannot ignore. I advise you to let things rest and avoid confronting her. If she is stubborn, challenging her will not be effective. I won't abandon you. I will give every help I can in a case that definitely shows worrying signs. It may take a while to get through to her. Contact me if there are any worrying developments. I will pray and reflect. You must offer your prayers, too.'

Jos left the Borst house shaken despite the confident face he had presented to the mother and daughter. He had never dealt with such a case. In Lae, he had had a congregation of natives who had received the grace of conversion. They had abandoned the spells and sorcery of their animistic beliefs and eased into the healing peace of Christianity. Marlies was the opposite. She presented an instance of an intelligent, well-educated young woman passing from the true faith to the animism of Northern Europe. What was behind it? Would investigating the ideas of occultism enlighten him? He sent a message via Mevrouw de Vries that he wanted to talk to Femke. Femke arrived a week later.

'This is a first,' she said lightly. 'What is so important that you have sent a summons?'

'I have a serious case to discuss with you. I am not sure how to deal with it. How much do you know about ancient myth—Germanic mythology, to be precise?'

'Not much—only what I came across in studying Roman and Greek history.'

'What about Germanic myth and the occult?'

'Good heavens, Jos. Who's involved with the occult?'

Jos related his meeting with Mevrouw Borst and her daughter.

'I understand your question. I know as much as I have already said. I agree with you; the girl's interest is worrying.'

'I don't want to get ahead of myself, but I might need your help dealing with this. I have little experience in dealing with a young woman like Marlies Borst. Do you have access to books about the occult and the Church's views about it?'

Femke returned a few days later with several books.

'That was quick,' said Jos. 'You must have access to a library. Thank you.'

'I thought the need was urgent. Look after them. I must return them in the same condition,' she said, raising her eyebrows. 'Now, Jos, a warning—don't overdo things. You need to stay healthy. Take your time in dealing with this matter. There is only so much that you, personally, can do.'

'Yes, Femke, Mother Superior,' said Jos.

She coloured and forced a smile. 'No jokes, Jos. Look after yourself.'

What the books offered was often confusing, but the more Jos read about occultism and the Church's views on demons and possession, the more worried he became. He cautioned himself not to run out ahead of the empirical evidence. A month later, however, he received an alarming note from Mevrouw Borst. Marlies had been seen chatting with SS officers outside the officers' club on Dam Square. He returned a message asking to talk to Marlies.

'Do you understand how imprudent it is for a Dutch girl to chat with SS officers, let alone ordinary German soldiers?' he said when she entered the lounge room.

'You again,' she said. 'What are you after? Who are you in your labourers' clothes?'

'Your mother is worried about you, Marlies. She has asked me to help. She would not have asked me if I weren't trustworthy. Others would be concerned about a Dutch girl chatting to an enemy officer. You must understand that.'

'Many people talk to me unasked, Meneer, not only German soldiers. I can't tell them to stop beforehand. Besides, I work in a restaurant where I necessarily attract attention.' She tilted her head and looked down her nose, fully conscious of her beauty—and its effect.

'It's who you chat to that's the problem. How do you think your fellow citizens would regard such socialising? You might invite retaliation for a perceived betrayal.'

Marlies's arrogant expression faded. 'I only talk to one, if you must know,' she said. 'I will avoid the others to please you and Mamma.'

'It's not a question of pleasing your mother—or anyone. You must be careful. We are in a war, and you are socialising with the enemy as if there is no danger. You attract attention, as you are clearly aware. Not everyone attracted has your welfare in mind.'

'But some do, Meneer.'

'If you think a *Schutzstaffel* officer will share your interpretation of Germanic mythology, you are mistaken. The Nazis are likely to interpret Germanic myth entirely differently.'

'That's just where you're wrong.' She rose. 'I have nothing more to say.'

'Don't be foolish, Marlies,' said Mevrouw Borst.

'I know what I am doing,' said Marlies, turning to walk from the room. 'You don't. And, Meneer, please don't bother to come again.' She disappeared into the hallway.

'I'm sorry, Father. Marlies was once a well-mannered child.'

'Manners are the least of our worries,' said Jos, more to himself than to Mevrouw. 'You were right to be alarmed, Mevrouw, about your daughter's developing interest.' He paused, considering. 'I will further investigate what we are dealing with here. In the meantime, convey your anxiety, but it's best to avoid confrontation. Let me know if there are further developments.'

Jos continued to read about the occult between his pastoral activities. To his relief, Femke had no work for him. She was serious about his need to regain his health. His reading did not bring a full grasp of the occult—it was such a wide subject—but there were fundamental aspects. The occult was essentially about inner knowledge, knowledge beyond our material existence. Bishop Eliott had said the occult was about the hidden matters of the mind and spirit. Furthermore, the occult was a category of esotericism encompassing a wider area of movements that rejected the knowledge gained from science, reason, and religion. Esoteric knowledge was intuitive. An important distinction was between transcendence and immanence, and that brought paganism into the picture.

In contrast to a transcendent religion, which sees God outside our material existence, immanence was about the deity permeating the material world. Knowledge of the immanent deity did not come through scientific investigation but through immersion in the natural world and how the people of old intuitively understood it. At this point, Jos thought it was best to hear what Marlies precisely saw in her pagan rituals. He planned to interview her after Christmas and the New Year, but an urgent request by mouth came from Mevrouw Borst.

'I was about to send a note,' said Mevrouw Borst when he arrived mid-afternoon, 'but I realised any written correspondence would be dangerous. Marlies is at work. She will be home shortly for a break.' She wrung her hands. 'Marlies has done what she promised. She no longer talks to German soldiers in the street. At least, no one has said anything. She said it was necessary to deliberately ignore them, which was not nice. Instead, she brings her SS officer home—here.'

'No,' said Jos, alarmed. 'That's hardly less imprudent.'

'He does not wear his uniform when he visits. It seems he doesn't want anyone to know. I must admit, Father, that he is a polite, respectful man, though a little stiff. He sometimes brings food, things that are not available to us.'

'The situation is far less dangerous, though still unsatisfactory. Is there something else?'

'Marlies and her SS friend go to Marlies's bedroom. They don't come out until he leaves. He sometimes spends a few hours here. At first, they didn't make a sound. But then they started to ...' She stopped, wrung her hands, and looked away. 'I'm sorry, Father, this is embarrassing. I don't know how to tell you.'

'Please continue,' said Jos. 'There is little a priest does not hear in confession.'

'You know, they made ... at first tried to suppress it, but they don't care now. Marlies is unashamed ... I can't understand it. How could she ...?'

Jos hardly knew what to say. All he could do was stare at Mevrouw Borst. 'She has never done anything like this before?' he said. 'Other boyfriends ...?'

'No, I'm sure there have been no other boyfriends—nothing like this. She has had a sheltered home life. Her father closely supervised her because she attracted attention from men of all ages. I don't understand how she could abandon all the moral teaching she—'

The front door opened and closed, and Marlies appeared at the lounge entrance.

'You again,' she sneered. 'I can imagine what my mother has said. Spare me your voyeuristic questions.'

'I have the same question as your mother, Marlies. Why have you turned your back on your upbringing?'

'I assume you mean about sex. The answer is simple. I don't believe in it anymore.'

Jos had an illumination—St Paul's Epistle to the Corinthians in which he deals with paganism.

'Has your abandonment of the Church's teaching anything to do with your interest in ancient Germanic ritual?'

She seemed surprised. 'My interest is in all ancient rituals and mythology. The same truth is in all of them. Look, Meneer, I don't have time to chat with you about the ancients' attitude to sex. I have things to do. However, I will say this. In ancient religions, the goddesses played a role just as important as the male gods. In fact, the goddess's power runs through all creation. I'm talking about Mother Earth and her life-giving fertility in which there is an inner truth—a divine truth. The female's fertility is the way to inner enlightenment.'

'You seemed to have studied it,' said Jos, testing a sudden suspicion, 'or even attended lessons, or discussions, or initiations.'

Again, she seemed surprised. 'Who are you, Meneer? As some sort of Church representative, how are you familiar with such things?'

'From the dawn of Christianity, the Church has struggled with different brands of Gnosticism.' Her reaction told him Gnosticism was unknown to her. 'The idea that there is some hidden special truth behind physical reality, that one must struggle to find it, has been present in many heretical movements.'

'Heresy has nothing to do with it. I reject the Church and all its evil baggage,' she said after several moments of thought.

'Do you belong to a group or association of like-minded people?'

Irritation passed over her face, and she shook her head. 'I have nothing more to say, Meneer. Please don't come again, even if my mother invites you. I will make it embarrassing for you if you ignore my polite request.'

'I warn you again, Marlies. You're playing with fire. Surely, you haven't forgotten the numerous cases of possession Our Lord dealt with. The Church has always had to confront demonic possession.'

She laughed. 'You're the one possessed—not me. Enlightenment is what I experience and what I offer.'

'You are mistaken if you think your *Schutzstaffel* officer is here for your truth.'

She shook her head, formed her lips into a snarl and continued down the hallway.

'I'm very sorry, Father ... I just don't know what to do.'

'Don't give up, Mevrouw Borst. We must pray that the right enlightenment comes. Marlies is yet to reach a crisis. When and how bad, I can't say. Call me if there is a change—some unusual development. I will pray and offer my Masses.'

JOS EXPECTED to see Femke before Christmas—she had been absent longer than usual—but it was not until Christmas Day that she appeared. He had turned to his congregation before the Mass of Dawn to count the number of communicants, and there she was, holding up her hand. Not only did she attend his Mass for the first time, but she stayed for the sparse Christmas breakfast Mevrouw de Vries and others had prepared. She waited patiently until he had spoken to everyone before she approached, holding a package wrapped in brown paper.

'Merry Christmas, Father Jos,' she said, leaning forward. 'May I give you a kiss? It's Dutch custom, after all.'

'Of course, Femke, Merry Christmas.' He bent forward to receive a light kiss on the cheek. 'I still receive kisses from my mother and sisters.'

'I'm honoured to be counted among your mother and sisters. Here, a small present for you.'

'You should not do this, Femke,' he said, taking the package. 'I can't return the favour.'

'Just accept it with humility. You deserve a little something.'

He unwrapped the package to find a secondhand book about exorcism.

'Again, Femke, I admire your powers of anticipation,' he commented, consulting the table of contents.

'I thought you may need a little background from the brief information you gave me. The girl sounds afflicted. I assume you've had little or no experience with the exorcism ritual.'

'You're right. My seminary professors had little to say. They seemed to think devil possession is a matter for modern psychology.'

'You know that it's not, don't you? Rome still has its exorcist.'

'How do you know?' he said, frowning at her.

'I made some inquiries. The information is readily available if you ask the right people before you start teasing me.'

'One of these days, Femke ...'

'Those days are well into the future. Now tell me briefly the latest with the girl.'

Jos was not brief. He gave a comprehensive account because he was sure he would need Femke's help in the end. Dealing with a beautiful young woman who had possibly become the hostage of the devil was fraught with danger for a young priest.

'I agree. You must be careful. Keep me abreast of what is happening.'

'You can count on it. Now it's your turn to update me on the war. I've hardly had time for the detail.'

Femke was brief. There were signs at last that the tide was turning against the Nazis. Allied victories were increasing. In particular, the surface raiders that caused havoc to Merchant shipping between the United States and Britain had been eliminated. The U-boats were still operating, but the British and Americans were now working on them. Montgomery and the 8th Army were making headway against Rommel's forces in Africa.

'I suppose that explains the increasing Nazi brutality in Holland,' said Jos.

'It will get worse. The Allies are dropping more agents behind the lines. Sabotage will increase.'

'That reminds me,' said Jos. 'Is there still no suspicion that codes in any operation have been compromised? As I said, my informant is trustworthy.'

'Nothing has been said. It's the German officer, isn't it?'

Jos shook his head. 'I suppose you'll have work for me soon.'

'Yes, but we must be careful,' she said with a knowing smile. 'The Nazis are hunting the people acting as guides along the escape routes. Many have been caught and executed. I don't want to sacrifice you for an uncertain benefit. It's more likely you'll be used as a courier for the time being.'

'As long as I'm not required to kill.'

JOS DID not hear from Mevrouw Borst until February. The lack of contact was surely a sign that things had improved. Perhaps he had prevailed on Marlies to reflect on what she was doing. Dabbling in ancient rituals was serious enough; imprudent and dangerous fraternizing with the Nazis was life-threatening.

'No, Father, things have got worse,' said Mevrouw Borst, now looking quite haggard. 'She seems even more determined in her role as—whatever it is. I began wondering after you asked if she belonged to a group of like-minded people. So I followed her one afternoon. She went to a gloomy, shuttered house in Warmoesstraat at the Zeedijk end. She knocked twice, and a young woman in a long cream dress opened the door and let her in. I stayed to observe. Her SS boyfriend and two other SS friends arrived shortly after. I huddled against a doorway to stay out of view. They knocked twice, and the same young woman opened the door.'

'Were they in uniform?'

'Yes, as bold as you like.'

'There was no indication what the house was for?'

'None. You don't think it's a brothel, do you, so close to the Zeedijk area?'

'Not likely, with no sign or indication of what it's for. It seems I was right. Marlies belongs to some sort of secret club, indulging in ancient rituals. There must be some connection, then, with the Teutonic fantasies of the Nazis. I can't imagine the SS officers were there because of the benefits of Mother Earth.'

'What miserable diabolical circumstances has my daughter gotten into, Father?'

'Whatever it is, our duty is to resist. We will resist with prayer. There is no practical way of stopping her. I'll think about a set of prayers fit for the occasion and—'

'I thought I told you not to come here again.'

Surprised, Jos swung around to see a furious young woman at the lounge entrance dressed in a long, flowing cream robe with her dark hair hanging wildly around her shoulders. Because Mevrouw Borst had not warned him, he had assumed Marlies was out.

'You have no right to ban anybody from this house, Marlies,' said Mevrouw, at last overcoming her timidity. 'I'll decide who comes here. Fath … Meneer is here at my request.'

'If you insist on being here, desecrating my religious space,' she said, approaching him, 'then you will be exposed to the seat of my power.' She loosened the top of her robe, wriggled free of it, and let it fall to the floor, revealing her voluptuous body.

'Marlies!' cried Mevrouw Borst, scrambling for the robe.

Fr. Jos had never seen a woman fully naked. This would not be the occasion to correct that omission. As her hands reached for the top of her robe, he had a flash of what she intended. He turned away, got to his feet, and hurried from the house with Marlies's loud mocking laughter following him. He turned only when Mevrouw Borst caught up with him.

'I apologise, Father. My daughter is out of control. I don't know what to do or say.'

'Your apologies are unnecessary, Mevrouw,' said Jos, stopping but not looking back. 'Like me, you did not expect such extreme behaviour. At least we know how far the devil has penetrated her soul. I will work on a program of suitable prayers to prevent deeper possession. I will be in contact, but call me if there is a change.'

'I agree,' said Femke, responding to his summons. 'The devil has her in his grasp. I can't judge to what extent, but it seems to be in the early stages.

'I would like a copy of the exorcism ritual. Have you access?'

Femke hesitated. 'Yes, I think I can get that for you. But, Jos, you need permission from the local bishop. There are requirements about the people present, particularly concerning a possessed female.'

'I know. That's why I want you if it comes to an exorcism. Can you ask permission from the bishop?'

She hesitated again. 'There's a limit to what I can do, you know, but I'll try.'

'Thank you,' said Jos, finding her hesitation odd. But he resisted asking the reason.

Two days later, she arrived with the ritual and the official requirements. 'It's a long service. It won't be easy to apply if the girl is not willing. As for the permission, you must provide more evidence that the girl is actually possessed.'

'Thank you, Femke. That was not difficult, was it?'

'What do you mean?'

'You seemed hesitant when I asked for the ritual and permission.'

'Did I?' she said, colouring in a way he was now familiar with. 'It's a serious matter, and I needed to reflect on it.' It was an evasive answer, and she seemed to know it.

'I wanted permission now so there's no delay if Marlies's condition worsens. It is anticipatory action. Are you happy to be present if I request it?'

'Of course.'

Jos returned to the Borst house at the end of March with Mevrouw and Meneer de Vries, who answered his request with holy enthusiasm. Without hesitation, they would take part in the prayers for demonic de-liverance. Jeroen de Vries was a big man and, though in his late seven-ties, would provide adequate physical protection if Marlies became vio-lent. Jos had prepared some Bible readings, the Litany of the Saints, and various well-known prayers, including Pope Leo's prayer to St Michael the Archangel, and the rosary. The improvised service would take a little more than half an hour. The little group knelt in the lounge room, facing Marlies's bedroom. They had barely reached the end of the Litany of the Saints when Marlies appeared at the doorway. Ignoring Marlies, they continued the prayers as Jos had instructed. Marlies stared, her lips silently moving. She came forward. A scream echoed through the house. The prayers continued. Filthy language in an unrecognisable voice filled the room. Jos, holding up the ritual close to his eyes to shield against unwanted sights, became aware of Marlies standing before him.

'Let me go!' the voice screamed, retreating from him. Gasps, hissing, and other noises of struggle followed. 'Let me go, you lecherous old man. Help, my flesh is crawling like maggots from your filthy hands.' Then, there was only the sound of the prayers. Marlies had fled from the lounge room.

'God, preserve us,' said Mevrouw Borst when the prayers finished. 'I can't believe ...'

'Most holy Mother, protect us,' whispered Mevrouw de Vries, barely managing her shock.

'Thank you, Meneer de Vries,' said Jos.

'You're welcome, Father. You were right, but I easily restrained her. There will be no threat to you during the service. I'll make sure of that.'

'Again, thank you, Meneer. We'll meet in a month to repeat our prayers. We now know what to expect. Prepare yourselves.'

They met again at the end of April. Marlies repeated her performance, screaming obscenities and struggling against Meneer de Vries, who prevented her from approaching Jos.

'Come and violate me, you vile, hypocritical priest,' the voice yelled while Marlies lurched to all sides in her struggle. 'That's what you're longing for, isn't it?' The voice described in lurid detail how Jos could make the best of its invitation to violate such a beautiful girl, a girl far beyond his youthful fantasies.

'Marlies!' repeatedly exclaimed Mevrouw Borst. 'My God, I'm sorry, Father.'

'Glory be ...' whispered Mevrouw De Vries.

'Don't listen to her,' whispered Jos. 'It's the devil talking.'

The May meeting produced the same performance and lurid invitation to Fr. Jos. But there were developments. Marlies now yelled in a foreign language. At least no one understood what she yelled. Then, ornaments flew from the table and shelves across the room. A picture fell from the wall. A frantic tapping sounded from the walls. Jos calmed the group; such happenings were common with possession. They had driven the devil to a hellish fury.

'How much worse could it be, Father,' said Mevrouw Borst after the prayers and Marlies had left the room.

'A lot worse, I fear,' said Jos. 'Marlies seems to be reaching a crisis point.'

Femke joined them at Jos's request for the June meeting. Pointing and stabbing the air, Marlies let out a howl when she saw her. She came towards her, her arm stretched out and her finger pointing menacingly. Femke backed away and reached out for Jos. Jos jumped to his feet before Meneer de Vries could act and shielded her. Marlies, keeping her clothes on, backed away. She skipped around the room in a wild manner, eventually stopping in front of Jos.

'Ha, ha, ha, ha, ha, ha,' she mocked breathlessly.

'Poor little Bart,
You lost your heart,
Who set you aflame,
You could not tame,
Gave you his trust,
Now lies in dust,
Ha, ha, ha, ha, ha, ha,
Poor little Bart lies in dust.
Poor little Bart...'

'You filthy abominable ...' Jos lunged forward. Femke grabbed his arm. 'No, Jos!' He recoiled. Mocking eyes stared at him from a dark abyss of an unearthly malevolence. 'Hail Mary, full of grace,' he gasped, resisting, 'the Lord is with thee ...'

Marlies let out a long, piercing, high-pitched squeal that penetrated the house. The abyss disappeared, the malevolence disappeared, her eyes glazed, and she slumped forward into Femke's arms. And Jos exhaled. 'Blessed art thou among Women, and blessed is the fruit of thy womb, J esus.'

With Meneer de Vries's help, Femke dragged Marlies to the settee, where she lay in a swoon. Jos continued the prayers to the end of the service. Marlies came to, rose, and left the room with an expression of utter detachment. A stunned silence gripped the group until Jos spoke.

'Unafraid, we must continue our prayers for Marlies's deliverance. She is surely at a crisis point. The devil is losing his grip.'

'Are you sure, Father,' said Mevrouw Borst. 'It looks the opposite. She is wilder than ever.'

'Does the SS officer still stay a long time?'

'Not as long anymore, no,' said Mevrouw Borst, her eyes widening.

'Does she go to her address in Warmoesstraat as often?'

'I don't think so. I can usually guess when. It's when she goes out between shifts in the same dress and makeup. No, it's not as often.'

'We'll meet again at the end of July.'

'Who is Bart?' said Femke while they returned to the De Vries house.

'I loved Bart like a brother.' He almost said, just like I love you as a sister. 'The evil, disgusting imputation was more than I could bear. Bart was one of the priests executed for operating the transmitter. That was a vicious lie, of course.'

'It was foul, I agree. But you must not pay attention. It's the devil speaking.' She took his hand for a moment and squeezed it.

They were halfway through the July service before Marlies entered, dressed in her long cream dress. But there was another change. Until then, Marlies had worn light makeup that accentuated her style of beauty, reminiscent of paintings of ancient folk. But now she wore bright red lipstick and dark eye shadow, matching her long, luxurious dark hair. It gave her fine, regular face the aura of the underworld—of the diabolical. The group stopped their prayers for a moment as they watched her stroll around the room, eyeing them maliciously with eyes that were not her own. They continued their prayers. She came to a stop in front of Femke. Femke anxiously looked up at her. Jos was about to rise.

'Don't worry, priest,' she sneered in the same diabolical voice. 'I won't hurt your girlfriend. She's in enough pain—deserves it, too, the hypocrite. You're all abominable hypocrites.' She continued her stroll around the room, and Jos resumed the prayers. He glanced at Femke. Her face was tense. Marlies stopped again in front of Femke and leaned towards her. 'Alone, alone,' the voice said in a hoarse whisper, 'abandoned.' Marlies continued her strolling. Femke's face tightened, and she stopped reciting the prayers momentarily. Marlies completed two more circuits before stopping again in front of Femke. The prayers ceased, and the eyes of the room fixed on her. 'No love, all alone,' the voice whispered. Femke bowed her head. 'Cold. Dead.'

To his dismay, Jos saw a tear trickle down Femke's cheek. She must not take the taunts seriously. She must take her own advice. He rose to shield her. More tears appeared on Femke's cheeks.

'Ha, ha, ha,' sang the voice while Marlies danced around the room and wagged her finger at Femke. 'The hypocrites don't care. All alone, all alone, all alone.'

Still, without sobbing, tears continued to flow down Femke's cheeks. Mevrouw Borst and the elderly couple rose and stood around her. Mevrouw de Vries helped her to her feet and took her in her arms. Jos held up his crucifix in front of the dancing, pointing girl.

'Go, out, get out,' he demanded, stepping towards her, 'you filthy ...'

Marlies screamed and fled from the room.

'Don't take any notice,' he said, caressing Femke's arm. 'It's the devil's malevolence speaking.'

'I'm all right,' said Femke, sniffling. 'She got me at a weak moment.'

'I understand.' He put his arm around her shoulder. She leaned her head against his chest.

'I'm all right, Father,' she said, quickly taking her head away. 'As I said, she got me at a weak moment.'

'You must take your own advice.'

'I will.'

By the time they arrived back at the De Vries house, Femke was her usual self.

'It's time to carry out the exorcism ritual,' she said.

'I was thinking the same.'

'I will consult ... I will arrange permission from the bishop.'

'Tell His Excellency I will attend confession a week before, as is the requirement for the exorcist.'

Back in his room, Jos wondered about Femke's reaction to the Marlies's taunts. She had left him with a look that said she had exposed herself more than she wanted. Indeed, she had. But what had she exposed? Marlies's taunt about loneliness seemed innocuous enough. Everyone feels lonely at times, sometimes for little reason. Indulgent self-pity often was a cause. Femke, however, was hardly one for self-pity and certainly not inclined to show it if it did unaccountably overtake her. No, until that moment, she had shown rigid self-control. So why did an innocuous taunt about loneliness affect her so deeply?

On the face of it, it seemed evident that she was not married, did not have a family, and lived independently of others, including a wider family. That said nothing specific about her. An alternative scenario was that she had a husband who, like Marlies's father, had been killed during the Nazi invasion three years before. As much as Jos thought about it, he could not form a clear picture. The most likely circumstances, he decided, were the loss of a beloved husband either through war or sickness. Such a loss could result in devastating loneliness. In any case, he did not have time to ponder the puzzle. He had to prepare for Marlies's exorcism.

Chapter 14

The exorcism

THE GROUP ASSEMBLED again in the Borst lounge room at the end of August. Jos wore a white surplice and a purple stole around his neck. Beside him, in the middle of the room, stood a table on which was the exorcism ritual, a crucifix, and a bowl of Holy Water. An upright armchair stood in front of the table.

'We're ready, Mevrouw Borst. Would you please fetch Marlies?'

Marlies frowned, staring at the group as she followed Mevrouw Borst into the room.

'Would you please sit in the armchair,' said Fr. Jos, pointing at the chair in front of him.

'What for?' objected Marlies, but sat as requested. The company gathered around her.

'We will pray to help you expel the evil that makes you unhappy.'

She threw her head back and laughed. 'I'm not unhappy, you stupid people. An angel has privileged me with the power I revel in. But if you want to indulge yourselves, I'm happy to please. Do you want me to please you, priest?' She leaned towards him with a seductive smile.

Fr. Jos made the sign of the cross over her and then sprinkled her with Holy Water. She yelped, barked and moved to lunge at the priest, but Meneer Vos held her with Femke's help. Her eyes glazed, and she fell into a swoon. A few moments later, her eyes cleared, revealing the demon's malice. Fr. Jos sprinkled Holy Water over the others and knelt. The others knelt with him. Meneer de Vries remained standing, holding Marlies, who struggled before giving up. Fr. Jos then began the Litany of the Saints, to which the company replied. After the litany, he read Psalm 53, a plea for help against the devil. All the time, Marlies screamed and barked obscenities. Several prayers followed, calling for help from God to confront the demon, after which Jos picked up the crucifix and held it in front of Marlies. Terrified, she tried to back away.

'I command you, unclean spirit, whoever you are, along with all your minions now attacking this servant of God, by the mysteries of the incarnation, passion, resurrection, and ascension of our Lord Jesus Christ, by the descent of the Holy Spirit, by the coming of our Lord for judgment, that you tell me by some sign your name, and the day and hour of your departure. I command you, moreover, to obey me to the letter, I who am a minister of God despite my unworthiness; nor shall you be emboldened to harm in any way this creature of God, or the bystanders, or any of their p ossessions.'

'Asmodeus, the Insatiate, you hypocrites,' screamed the voice while Marlies, still terrified by the crucifix, struggled against Meneer De Vries's unyielding grip. 'Joy flows from my embrace, you fools. Unending power and pleasure.'

Ignoring the demon's ravings, Fr. Jos continued, laying his hands on Marlies's head. He appealed to Jesus, Son of Mary, through the intercession of his apostles and saints to show favour and mercy. A selection of Bible passages followed, including those that showed Jesus casting out demons. He again asked God to grant him the power to confront the devil and cast him out. He paused before he pronounced the first of three exorcisms interspersed with signs of the cross.

'I cast you out, unclean spirit, along with every Satanic power of the enemy, every spectre from hell, and all your fell companions; in the name of our Lord Jesus + Christ. Begone and stay far from this creature of God. + For it is He who commands you, He who flung you headlong from the heights of heaven into the depths of hell. It is He who commands you, He who once stilled the sea and the wind and the storm. Hearken, therefore, and tremble in fear, Satan, you enemy of the faith, you foe of the human race, you begetter of death, you robber of life, you corrupter of justice, you root of all evil and vice; seducer of men, betrayer of the nations, instigator of envy, font of avarice, fomenter of discord, author of pain and sorrow. Why, then, do you stand and resist, knowing as you must that Christ the Lord brings your plans to nothing? Fear Him, who in Isaac was offered in sacrifice, in Joseph sold into bondage, slain as the paschal lamb, crucified as man, yet triumphed over the powers of hell.'

Fr. Jos traced three signs of the cross on Marlies's brow.

'Begone, then, in the name of the Father, + and of the Son, + and of the Holy + Spirit. Give place to the Holy Spirit by this sign of the holy + cross of our Lord Jesus Christ, who lives and reigns with the Father and the Holy Spirit, God, forever and ever.'

Prayers, supplications for divine assistance, and psalms and Scriptural readings, some of which reaffirmed the teachings of the Church, were repeated between the second and third formal exorcisms. The service lasted around an hour and ended with, 'Almighty God, we beg you to keep the evil spirit from further molesting this servant of yours, and to keep him far away, never to return. At your command, O Lord, may the goodness and peace of our Lord Jesus Christ, our Redeemer, take possession of this woman. May we no longer fear any evil since the Lord is with us; who lives and reigns with you, in the unity of the Holy Spirit, God, forever and ever. Amen.'

After Fr. Jos made the final sign of the cross, the demon's eyes faded, and Marlies returned to herself. She looked around, surprised. 'Is that it? Have you finished? Well, that wasn't much, was it?' she said, in denial of her screaming, shouting, and struggling.

'We prayed that you abandon the life you are living,' said her mother, putting her arm around her.

'You can pray as much as you like if it pleases you,' she said, disentangling herself. 'I must get ready. My *Schutzstaffel* adorer is expecting me at our temple of love.' She smiled indulgently at the surrounding company and strolled from the room.

'Do you think it does any good, Father?' said Mevrouw Borst. 'It doesn't seem to. I don't know how you put up with all the abuse and shocking language. It's frightening. I'll have nightmares from it.'

Mevrouw De Vries murmured her concurrence.

'I think we're doing good,' said Fr. Jos, aware that such responses often did not sound encouraging for the ordinary Catholic. 'I discern a faltering in Marlies, a sort of resistance to the demon's power. We must persevere and trust in the Lord.'

'I hope you're right,' she said, hanging her head. 'It's difficult,'

'We won't give up, Mevrouw Borst, until Our Lord has freed your daughter. We'll meet twice a month now. We'll take the battle right up to Satan.'

'I feel for Mevrouw Borst,' said Femke later. 'I, too, find it frightening—nightmarish. I've not experienced anything like the last several months. I knew possession was a reality, but—aren't you the least bit afraid? You don't seem to be.'

'It's not fear, Femke dear,' said Jos before he realised what he had said. 'It's more like wonder in the presence of primordial good and evil. Now, don't be alarmed. My familiarity is like that of a brother to a sister.'

'I hope so,' she said. 'It's not proper for a priest to address a single ... a woman like that.'

'Don't be scrupulous. This is your priest speaking. Scrupulosity is a fault.'

'It's not a joke,' she said with a reluctant smile. 'Are you sure the stress of the last three years has not changed you? I think it has. And you're not my priest.'

'Perhaps it has. But the stress is not responsible for my familiarity. It's more that we have grown and matured together in the most extraordinary circumstances. That has created a bond that does not affect my priesthood. Relax, Femke, my dear. You could not be safer.'

'At least, mind what you say in front of others,' she said, trying to suppress her smile.

Jos noticed she had almost said a 'single woman.' Single in what way? Was she unmarried, after all? There was no deceased husband. Or was there? Her status—what she was in normal life—was still inconclusive. He had to tell himself to stop obsessing about her.

The company assembled twice in September, and Jos performed the exorcisms unchanged. Marlies reacted in the same way, screaming, and yelling and taunting Jos and Femke— Jos about Bart and Femke about loneliness. Jos controlled his outrage, and Femke merely frowned. Jos could see it hurt her. The demon had struck something there. At the meeting midway through October, Jos discerned a change. Marlies's screaming and taunting were not as vigorous and spiteful. At different stages, she seemed to be struggling against her behaviour— against the demon's possession—however fruitless the struggle was. At the mid-November meeting, she submitted to the ritual, only struggling half-heartedly against herself. The screaming ceased, with only occasional animal groans and snarling coming from her. Meneer De Vries did not have to hold her in her chair. At the end of the ritual, she remained seated and looked up at Jos.

'I want to stop,' she said helplessly, 'but I'm torn.'

'Between what,' said Jos.

'Between staying here and going to the temple ... I want to stay away, but next thing I'm rushing to go there and do ... all that I must do.'

'Don't give up, Marlies. We will support you in your struggle with our prayers—'

A sharp knock at the front door interrupted Jos. Mevrouw Borst hastened to the window.

'Oh, it's your SS friend,' she said, coming from the window and wringing her hands.

Marlies looked around, paralysed in indecision.

'Go to your room, Marlies,' said Femke. 'We will call you. Mevrouw, clear the religious things away. Jos, throw the surplice and stole behind the settee. Quickly.' The SS officer knocked again, now more insistently. 'Answer the door, Mevrouw,' she said when order was restored and the guests sat comfortably.

They heard Mevrouw welcoming the SS officer in broken German and asking him to wait. The tall, imposing German wandered to the entrance of the lounge room while Mevrouw Borst fetched Marlies. He stopped and stared. His surprise changed to suspicion.

'Good morning, Officer,' Jos called in German.

'What are you doing?' he said, looking around the room. His eyes came to rest on Jos. 'Papers, please,' he demanded, holding out his hand.

Jos stood, pulled his identity papers from his pocket, and handed them to the German. He noticed an ancient symbol tattooed on his wrist, the same symbol he had already seen on Marlies's wrist. Marlies arrived, hurrying from her room while the German scrutinised Jos's papers.

'Oh, Anton, at last, so glad to see you. Rescue me from these stupid people and their prayer meeting.' She threw her arms around his neck. 'Come on, darling. Let's go.' She grabbed his hand.

Marlies's beautiful, inviting face peering up at him, and her voluptuous body pressed against his, were too much. He absently returned Jos's identity papers and, with a look of anticipation and scarcely a glance at the prayer meeting, let Marlies drag him from the house. There was a sigh of relief.

'Thank you, Femke,' said Jos. 'That was quick thinking.'

'Marlies helped.'

'But was it conscious, or had the devil drawn her back?' said Jos. 'She admitted her struggle.' He looked around the company. Femke did not offer an opinion. 'It doesn't matter at this point,' he went on. 'Our Lord has given us a breakthrough. Marlies is in a struggle against the demon holding her. She's fighting back. There should be no slackening on our part. Mevrouw Borst, could you persuade Marlies to undergo another exorcism in the next few days—as soon as she feels able?'

Three days later, Marlies appeared in the lounge room in a long white, unadorned dress and barefoot. She wore no makeup, and her dark hair hung loosely around her shoulders. She took her place on the chair without prompting while the company knelt around her. Marlies's head drooped as Fr. Jos read the exorcism prayers, Bible passages and psalms, but during the three formal exorcisms, she clasped the arms of the chair and moaned, her head moving from side to side, and her face contorted. Fr. Jos shook his head each time Meneer De Vries went to hold her steady. At the end of the service, Marlies, now lightly holding the chair's arms, bowed her head and did not move or utter a sound. Jos signalled the company to remain kneeling. A few minutes later, Marlies looked up.

'I want to stop,' she said, appealing to Fr. Jos. 'I want to be relieved of this terrible urge, but I don't know how. I don't know how to trust myself.'

Femke stood and put her arms around her. Marlies leaned into her embrace.

'We will continue the prayers,' said Fr. Jos. 'You must trust in Our Lord. We will not let up. He is already answering them.'

'How can I break away from the temple—from Anton and the others? I'm scared.'

This was something Jos had not thought about.

'Let me encourage you to submit to our prayers until you think you're ready to break completely,' said Femke, caressing her. 'I may have a solution to the problem of protection if you are willing to trust me. Do you trust me?'

Marlies turned to look at Femke. She hesitated and then nodded.

'We fully trust you,' said her mother, joining Femke's embrace of Marlies.

'Full of surprises as usual,' said Jos later when they were alone. 'What have you got up your sleeve?' Femke shook her head. 'Oh, so now we are back to headshaking when you don't want to answer.'

'You should know the rules by now.'

'All right, Mother Superior.'

'Don't be irritating, Fr. Jos,' she said, colouring. 'It's not a joke.'

She could not suppress the reaction Jos had observed on similar occasions to what he thought was mild teasing to lighten the atmosphere.

'No, it's definitely not a joke. Sorry.'

At the beginning of December, Femke arrived at the De Vries house accompanied by Marlies, who wore her waitress uniform. At a signal, the elderly couple left the house.

'Father,' said Femke without preamble, 'Marlies has decided to break from her present way of life. She will sever all connections with the people in Waarmoesstraat. I have guaranteed protection on the condition that she accepts there's no going back, that she must go into hiding until the end of the war, and that she will have no contact with friends or family. Her mother won't know where she is. Mevrouw Borst will only know she will not see her daughter until the end of the war.'

Fr. Jos, startled, looked from one to the other. He had no questions. He knew Femke well enough.

'Do you accept the conditions?' he said. 'Femke has set strict conditions, you must understand. Even I will not know where you are.'

'Yes,' said Marlies softly. 'I trust Femke.'

'You will now go about your daily business for the next several days,' Femke continued. 'Then send a message to your employer saying you are sick and can't come to work. If the German officer comes looking for you, tell your mother to say you are sick—too sick to do anything. I will send a message to meet me somewhere when all is arranged. You must come immediately as you are. No questions, and take nothing. Fr. Jos will tell your mother later that you have gone into protection until the end of the war. He will not tell her where because he will not know. Do you understand, Marlies?'

'Yes, Femke. I will follow your instructions.'

'There's no going back once we start on the road to protection. In fact, it will be dangerous to depart from that road.'

'I understand.'

Femke returned two weeks later. 'Marlies has gone,' she announced to Jos and the elderly couple. 'It's best we bury this episode until the war ends. The restaurant will be momentarily annoyed about losing an attractive waitress, but will soon look for a replacement. The SS officer, Anton, might prove more difficult. He might try to discover why she disappeared or, worse, where she is. The loss of an appealing girlfriend in which he has invested some feeling might motivate him, or he could act from suspicion that something subversive was happening.'

'You mean I aroused his suspicion,' said Jos, 'and he might try to find me?'

'Something like that. We must prepare for a follow-up. Our story is short. We were at the Borst house for a prayer meeting, as Marlies said. If Anton persists and finds you, Fr. Jos, your papers will cover you. I suggest you appear regularly at the Albert Cuypstraat market for the next few weeks. Finally, we must make sure we support Mevrouw Borst.'

Jos visited Mevrouw Borst to assure her Marlies was safe and would remain safe until the Germans were defeated. She must contact him if she had any worries. Above all, she must join him in thanksgiving prayers for the release of her daughter from the demon who possessed her. It was not a small favour from Our Lord and Saviour. Mevrouw Borst agreed. As for the street market, he later thought Femke might be too scrupulous in advising regular attendance. She had a tendency to overmanage. Two weeks later, there was Anton alone in civilian dress, calmly wandering along the stalls.

'Papers,' he said when he came to Jos's stall.

'What have you done with her?' he said out of the side of his mouth as he pretended to scrutinise them.

'Who do you mean, Officer?' said Jos, thinking it was wiser to speak plain German and not pretend otherwise.

'You know who I mean, labourer,' he said, fixing angry eyes on him, 'if you are a labourer.'

'My papers say I am a labourer. Would you like me to demonstrate my knowledge of the produce?' Jos cheerfully launched into a description of the fruit and vegetables before him.

'Shut up,' said Anton, 'and don't play games with me. How come you speak German, labourer?'

'You must not think country people are ignorant, Officer,' said Jos, feigning indignation. 'I'm an admirer of German literature. Many Dutch people are.'

'What have you done with her?' he repeated. There was now desperation in his eyes rather than anger.

'Done with who?'

Anton regarded Jos closely as if unsure how to proceed.

'I'm going to keep an eye on you. The others in that prayer meeting, including her mother, may not be involved, but I think you have something to do with Marlies's sudden disappearance.'

'What is Marlies to you?' Jos dared to risk the question, relieved that Anton saw nothing suspicious in Femke. 'An impressive SS officer like you would have his pick.'

'That's my business,' Anton said after some hesitation.

'If, as you say, I have something to do with Marlies's disappearance,' said Jos, deciding to broaden his risks, 'then it is in your interests to ensure nothing happens to me.'

'You should be careful you don't get into business you can't handle, labourer.'

'I'm merely responding to your questions about Marlies.'

'You're not what you say you are,' said Anton, after more hesitation. 'A labourer does not speak German like you. You must get it in your head that I intend to find out what happened to my ... to Marlies.' With that, he left Jos and wandered off along the stalls.

'You took a huge risk,' said Femke later, 'but your intuitions were right. It's uncanny. Marlies is to him more than the physical ...'

'He might even be in love with her,' said Jos with his ironic smile.

'Whatever the case, you must be careful. For the moment, you will be free from courier and guidance work, at least until Anton gets tired of tracking you. It comes at a good time. You're looking tired again. You cannot afford to make mistakes. The Nazis know what we're doing and are looking in the right places, and to be frank, you've become too complacent about the dangerous work you do.'

'Yes, Femke, I will act with due care. You know, with all your marshalling of me, I'm getting an idea of what it means to have a wife.' It was another of his attempts at humour, but the reaction was not as before with his teasing. Femke turned pale, and her face tightened as a prelude to tears. 'I'm sorry, Femke. My jokes are a little thoughtless at times. I don't mean to upset y ou.'

'No, it's all right, Jos,' she said, recovering her self-control. 'I know you mean to be humorous as a relief to the horror around us. I'm a little too sensitive sometimes. But the warning is still there. This year, we had an example of the disaster that can follow from carelessness and complacency, didn't we?'

Jos knew what she was referring to, but his thoughts remained with her unexpected reaction. What was she so sensitive about?

Chapter 15

The hunger winter

FR. JOS HAD been so preoccupied with his courier work, pastoral care, and Marlies's exorcism that he had paid little attention to the war outside Holland. Femke had to keep him informed. By the end of 1943, she said, the battle had swung against the Nazis. Montgomery had defeated General Rommel and the Axis forces in Africa. Montgomery and US General Patton had entered Italy and forced the surrender of the Italian forces. The Russians had retaken Stalingrad. The Nazis were on the defensive, and the Allies were preparing for an invasion across the Channel. However, there was one British disaster in Holland—the one Femke had alluded to while berating Jos for his complacency. She had barred Jos from smuggling operations during 1943, but an urgent case arose. At the beginning of August, while they were preoccupied with Marlies, a British pilot was shot down near Amsterdam. He was on a dangerous low-level reconnaissance flight over Belgium and Holland. He had vital information, and getting him back to England was urgent.

'I didn't want to do this, Jos,' said Femke, 'but the case can't wait. Central command wants the Pimpernel to do the job.'

'Are you serious?'

'Of course I am. You have acquired some fame, or should I say your recklessness has acquired fame.'

'I'm not reckless,' said Jos. 'The risks are calculated.'

'It's not often I can turn your teasing back on you,' she said mischievously. 'I know you calculate the risks. I'm just concerned you don't go too far. I want you to survive the war.'

'All right. I'll go, but I'll have to pay close attention to you from now on.'

The operation went off smoothly despite the extra attention the Nazis were paying to the escape lines. The British pilot was fit and eager. They rode through the night and part of the day and reached Zundert on the third day. He made his usual call at the Vos farmhouse on the way back. This time, De Jonge and Achterkamp were nowhere to be seen. He had not expected to see them because Van Rossem and Muller could have no indication he was in the district. Mevrouw and farmer Vos were delighted to see him and fussed over him like he was their son. Did the major have a message?

'Indeed, he did, lad,' said farmer Vos, taking a scrap of paper from the sideboard and handing it to Jos.

'*My men will never learn. They get caught each time making the same mistake,*' Jos read. '*How many warnings do they need?*'

'It cannot be more explicit,' said Jos after relating the message to Femke. 'My contact clearly means that Allied communication with Holland has been compromised, and agents are being caught.'

'And probably killed, if correct,' said Femke

'You should ask your superiors to check again.'

'They are still ignoring the message,' said Femke two weeks later.

'Who is "they"?'

'I just pass the message on,' said Femke. 'I'm a small cog in all this.'

'You may be a small cog,' said Jos, 'but a vital one. Ignoring a message from inside the Nazi army would be foolish.'

'It's your major, isn't it?'

In December, Femke unexpectedly arrived at the De Vries house during the preparations to remove Marlies.

'Your major was right,' said Femke, appalled. 'It's been an unmitigated disaster. The British created a separate secret service to place agents behind the lines to give the Nazis a taste of their own barbarism. Killing, sabotaging and relaying information back to London was their task. So, it's not the SIS involved. It is a new section called the Special Operations Executive (SOE). Sometime during the last year, the Germans ambushed a Dutch agent while he was transmitting and forced him to cooperate. With the Nazi-instructed messages, the Dutch agent sent an arranged code signaling he was messaging under duress, but SOE in London continually ignored the warning. Around fifty agents were captured and killed or imprisoned. Two escaped from prison in November and made it to Switzerland. The information the Nazis were waiting for them was relayed to SOE in London. They suspended the operation.'

'How could they be so stupid?'

'It stresses the need to follow protocols.'

It signalled a serious warning, and Jos felt uncomfortable about the risk he took with Anton. As far as he could tell, it was paying off. Anton was more interested in finding where Marlies was than unmasking Jos's cover—at least for now. The next few weeks would show where he would go. Jos had to wait until February before he appeared at the street market, again in civilian clothes. He was ready for him.

'I thought I would see you before this,' he said cheerfully. 'Our produce here is better than our competitors. You haven't been going elsewhere?'

'I've had you checked out,' said Anton, glancing either side of him and ignoring Jos's nonsense. It was a cold winter's day, and snow lay around. Few people were at the stalls. 'It seems the people I met at Marlies's house were, in fact, a prayer group, and you're their leader.'

'I'm happy your informants vouched for my innocence.'

'Stop your nonsense and listen. Mocking me won't help you. You are still at my mercy. Don't forget it. I could have you arrested and shot before you knew it.'

'No doubt you could, Anton. But I perceive a trace of decency in you that keeps me safe.'

'Don't be too sure of yourself,' said Anton, frowning. 'You're not who you say you are, despite your role as some sort of religious leader. But I'm not interested in you. I want to know where Marlies is and why she disappeared without telling me. I will keep on your back until I find out.'

'I don't know where she is,' said Jos, understanding that he was safe as long as Anton did not know. Was Anton so fixated on discovering where Marlies was that he did not see his disadvantage?

'My patience has limits, I warn you.'

'I'm speaking the truth. I don't know where she is. You can torture me as long as you like, but you won't get what you want.'

Anton contemplated Jos closely. 'But you know how to get in contact with her?' He paused, still scrutinising Jos. 'All right, I know enough at this point ... what is your name? It's not the false name on your identity papers. What do I call you?'

'You can call me Jos.'

'Now, Jos, give me a selection of vegetables and their price,' he said, waving at the boxes in front of him and glancing around. Jos selected a range of vegetables, named their price, and handed them over. 'Think carefully about what I have said,' said Anton, placing a handful of coins in Jos's hand. 'I'll be back.'

'The war's over for you,' said Femke after Jos related the meeting. 'Your cover has been blown. You can now devote yourself entirely to your pastoral work, which is what you want, anyhow. You've taken a frightening risk. It could backfire on you. You're on your own, you know.'

'I know, but I don't think it will go that way. Anton is desperately in love with Marlies. His love is dominating his thinking.'

'We'll see,' said Femke. 'I hope you're right, but given this house is under surveillance, I will stay away for the moment. I will send a message if I need to talk to you.'

Surprisingly, Anton did not turn up at the street market until April. But now he was in full SS uniform, walking casually along the stalls until he came to Jos.

'Give me your papers,' he demanded. Jos handed his papers over. 'I can't meet you here,' he continued, pretending to scrutinise the papers. 'I will come to your residence in a few days, late in the afternoon.' He handed back the papers and continued his walk along the stalls.

Jos now felt more secure. Anton had compromised himself further by arranging a furtive meeting with a covert agent. He arrived as promised a few days later. Mevrouw De Vries, in trepidation, led him into the lounge room.

'Here is some coffee,' he said, handing a paper bag to Jos. 'Ask your landlady to make us a cup. She can keep the remainder.'

'Thank you, Anton. That's a generous gift. Mevrouw De Vries will be grateful. None of us has tasted coffee for more than a year.'

'Now let's get down to business,' said Anton, acknowledging Jos's gratitude with a nod. 'And let's remove the pretence. My sole interest is Marlies. I don't care about the rest. I'm desperate to contact her. I accept you don't know where she is. That knowledge is outside your role as an agent. That's standard practice. But I'm sure you know who to contact to send a message to her.' Jos raised his eyebrows but did not commit himself. 'I offer you a bargain.'

'Which is?' said Jos, startled by the extent of Anton's willingness to compromise himself. Compromise in any form meant an instant bullet in an SS officer's head.

'I have a letter.' He took the letter from inside his breast pocket and held it out to Jos. 'I would like you to translate it into Dutch and send it to Marlies. I would like her to know exactly how I feel.'

'And in return?' said Jos, taking the letter.

'I will answer a limited number of questions about military placements as soon as I have confirmation that Marlies has received my letter.'

'You must care about Marlies to run such a risk,' said Jos. A quick perusal of the letter showed it pulsated with passion.

'I do.'

'All right, Anton, I will try. You have exposed yourself unashamedly to enormous risk. It's the least I could do.'

'I think I can trust you, Jos.'

'Don't expect a speedy answer. I'll contact you when I have a reply. Tell me about your relationship with Marlies before you go. It might help.'

While they sat back and drank the coffee Mevrouw De Vries had prepared, Anton related that he had met Marlies in the restaurant where she worked. Naturally, a beautiful girl like Marlies attracted everyone's attention. To his surprise, it was only his attention that she returned. He surreptitiously arranged to meet her away from the restaurant. The relationship speedily developed from there. Indeed, Marlies's unrestrained passion stunned him. Then she revealed she was a member of what she called the Temple of Enlightened Love. The adherents believed in totally unrestrained sexual freedom, but it was all inextricably tied to a strange religious context of ancient Germanic symbols and myth, which opened a pathway to enlightenment. Anton did not fully grasp the religious element, but threw himself into the highly theatrical, intoxicating orgies. But then something unexpected happened. He fell in love with Marlies, the prime escort along the pathway to enlightenment.

'Why was it strange to you?' said Jos. 'Isn't there an obsession with the religious aspect of Germanic myth within the German army? Isn't there the same idea of enlightenment? Have you heard of Gnosticism?'

'No, never heard of it, whatever it is. The religious aspect is Himmler's obsession. Many pretend to take it seriously. The appeal of Germanic myth is its tribal loyalty, the undying submission to authority, and the courage of the Germanic warrior. That motivated me to join the *Schutzstaffel*.'

'But Marlies shook you out of it.'

'Yes, I became obsessed with Marlies instead of the myth and the pathway to enlightenment. Marlies became my enlightenment, and I didn't want to share her with anyone.'

'You told her?'

'Of course. I didn't want the grubby hands of others ...'

'What was her reaction?'

'She tried to explain her religious vision. I said I was in love with her. True love was exclusive. I could not have it any other way. I felt she was in love with me despite her ... I wanted her to leave the Temple ...' He stopped, examined his hands, and looked away.

'What happened then?' said Jos to bring him back to his story.

'I tried to convince her ... She seemed to be responding to my appeals ... My love seemed to be convincing her when she suddenly disappeared.' He opened his hands in an appeal. 'What happened at those meetings? She said you prayed for her release. But I can't believe that a bunch of old people sitting around in a circle could make a difference, and I can't believe she was abducted.'

'No, Anton, she was not abducted. She came to see the demon driving her behaviour.'

'Demon? You're not serious ...?'

'She overcame the demon and removed herself of her own free will. I had nothing to do with the arrangement.'

'I know. But your talk about demons demonstrates you have been a crucial influence. That's why I have given you the letter.'

'I will do my best to convince those responsible of your sincerity. How do I contact you?'

'I'm at the Grote Club on Dam Square on Friday afternoons. Position yourself near the Palace at around four o'clock if you have news.'

'I'm speechless,' said Femke after hearing Jos's report and reading the letter that Jos had already translated. Just when I think I've got control of you, you go off on another adventure.'

'I'm just as surprised as you. I didn't expect it. Besides, I don't choose my adventures, as you put it. They choose me. It's Anton's burning love that's determining it.'

'Don't be modest. He saw he could trust you. That was critical in his decision to risk certain death if found out. Leave it with me. I will return when I have news. In the meantime, concern yourself with your pastoral activities—if you can.'

Jos received a message a week later.

'Marlies wants proof that it's Anton—something only he and she know.'

The following Friday, Jos stationed himself near the Royal Palace. Soon, Anton came strolling across the square from the Officer's Club. He summoned Jos with a nod. Jos followed him into Damrak, where he stopped at a shop window. He came up beside him as Anton pretended to gaze at the window's display.

'Marlies wants proof you're the letter's author. She needs something only you and she know.'

'What? Surely she would know ... of course, it's not Marlies who wants the proof. Let me see ... she has an illustration of the goddess Freya on her dressing table. She bowed to it before we—'

A week later, they stood again in front of the display window in Damrak.

'A letter from Marlies,' he said, slipping it into Anton's hand. 'Here's the deal. You provide useful information, and we will pass on your letters to Marlies. Do you have a collection point?'

'There are benches near the entrance to Vondelpark. I will place the information in the bushes behind the second bench. To alert me, stand in front of the Royal Palace at the same time. I will replace Marlies's letter with my information. Here's the first.' He pushed an envelope into Jos's hand. 'A week after I have received Marlies's letter, I will place my reply there without fail.'

'That was very useful information from the point of view of the coming invasion,' said Femke less than a week later. 'Of course, the Nazis know an invasion is coming. We want to speed things up a bit. Arrange a time for me to discuss things with Anton.'

At 4 p.m. the following Friday, Jos stood outside the Royal Palace. He had to hang around for an hour before Anton appeared and walked across Dam Square to Damrak. Jos followed him to the same display window.

'What's up?' said Anton. 'Is there a problem?'

'My handler wants to meet you. When can you come—same house?'

'This Monday at 8 p.m.'

'Thank you for coming, Anton,' said Femke without ceremony when they were seated in the De Vries lounge room with coffee made from Anton's gift. 'Call me Femke. I have a few questions. Is it only your love for Marlies that motivates you?'

'Well, you surprise me, Femke. Your disguise is utterly convincing. I had no idea that the rather dowdy woman sitting among those old people could be Jos's handler. And you speak German as well as Jos. I see now you are younger than I thought. Are you a married team?'

Femke shifted a little and shook her head. 'Let's keep to the script, Anton.'

'Keep to the script?' he said with a brief smile. 'What other motivation could there be?'

'The war is not going well for you.'

Anton hesitated. 'Indeed, there's no denying it.'

'What do you think about it? Where do you stand?'

'I see where you're going. I'll be brief. I came into our campaign with the enthusiasm and loyalty of a Germanic warrior. I was in my early twenties. I particularly wanted to join the *Schutzstaffel*. They seem to embody my ideals of the loyal soldier—'

'But you have been disappointed,' said Femke.

Anton hesitated again. 'Yes. As the war progressed, I began questioning the goals—and myself. If our leaders were so concerned about Germanic racial purity, why were we in a death struggle against our racial brothers in England, Holland, and Denmark? We in the *Schutzstaffel* swore loyalty, but there are limits. General Rommel is my ideal.'

'Are there others who feel the same way?'

'Yes, there is growing dissatisfaction. There are rumours. One has to be careful.'

'What sort of rumours? Speak plainly.'

'Removing Hitler.'

'If General Rommel led those planning to assassinate Hitler, would you join him?'

'Without hesitation.'

'Even before your love for Marlies?'

'There is duty above individual commitments.'

'Good. If you provide information to help the coming invasion, I will ensure your correspondence with Marlies flows smoothly. You will not see

Marlies until after the war. Like Jos, I don't know where she is, but I assure you she's safe and isolated—and resigned to her situation until the war finishes. That's all I have to say. Jos will keep me informed.' She stood up.

'Is that all? said Anton.

'Yes, that's all. I don't need to know any more. I wish you a good evening. Wait a few minutes before you leave. Good night, Jos.'

'That's an intriguing woman,' said Anton after Femke had left. 'Is she always so coolly business-like?'

'She is focused and to the point—and as committed as you. And before you go asking a whole lot of questions, she is my handler. I know nothing else.'

'I think she likes you.'

'I like her, too. We work well together.'

Anton raised his eyebrows with obvious irony and made ready to leave. Jos missed the heavy irony.

ANTON'S INFORMATION and the Allies' invasion of Europe dictated Jos's activities. Femke took the information away and returned with questions for Anton and messages for Jos to deliver to resistance points, mostly around the middle of the country. As before, the work was not as demanding as his smuggling operations. He did not have to think about the messages. His job was to pass them on and escape detection. That was a relief because his mind was increasingly focused on his congregation and their spiritual needs. That was his prior concern. Military matters were for those with military responsibility. The Allies invaded in early June and worked their way north from Normandy. In July, Anton reported a failed assassination attempt on Hitler. He feared Field Marshall Rommel, who had been badly injured in a bombing, was in the assassination group. Executions were expected. It was depressing news, said Anton. As the Allies slowly made gains, the Nazi command in Holland became ever more brutal. Summary executions of civilians were more frequent. In August, Anton asked to see Femke.

'You're taking a big risk,' said Femke after they met late at night at the De Vries house. 'We would rather you didn't take such risks. Your information has been valuable. We don't want to disturb the arrangements.'

'I want a guarantee from you.'

'What sort of a guarantee?'

'I did not join the army to brutalise and slaughter defenceless citizens, especially those we regard as family. Until now, I have not been involved in the worst of it. I'll do my best not to be.' He paused meaningfully. 'Germany will lose this war. We will win some battles, but it will make no difference. The Allies will gradually move north and force a surrender. Reprisals will follow. I want you to promise that my cooperation is officially recognised. Here are all my personal details.' He handed over a neatly folded sheet of paper that Femke took and perused. 'I want your guarantee on official stationery.'

'It's an added risk,' said Femke after reflecting on the request. 'If any suspicion comes on you for leaks, you'll be searched. We don't want your needless death—for your sake and ours.'

'I won't keep it with me. I will sight it and give it to Jos for safekeeping—if Jos is agreeable.'

'There's still a risk, but this time, you risk Jos in addition to yourself.'

'It's less a risk. Jos is too clever to be caught. And I trust him.'

'How do you feel about it, Jos?' said Femke.

'I'm happy to safeguard Anton's papers. We must remember that Anton not only provides valuable intelligence. He and Marlies have undergone a process of redemption. They help each other in this process of redemption.'

'Thank you, Jos,' he said, regarding Jos as if sorting his thoughts. 'There has always been something about you. I haven't been able to decide what until now. I suppose my Protestant background is partly a barrier. 'You're a priest, aren't you? Your faith and clerical state dominate what you do.'

'Yes,' said Jos. 'It's how any priest would behave. But now we're talking about it, Anton, my pastoral care is for the old people who gather here. I hope you will help preserve them if their well-being comes within your reach at any stage.'

'You have my promise, Jos.'

'Good,' said Femke, rising. 'Our mutual guarantees have been given. It's time for me and Anton to depart. I will let you go first, Anton.'

'Indeed, you're always the priest, Jos,' said Femke after Anton had gone. 'It is good that I'm reminded now and again.'

'We have worked so closely. It's understandable ... it's now four years.' He paused. 'I hope I don't embarrass you if I say I've come to love you like a sister.'

'You don't embarrass me,' she said, her lips quivering slightly. 'I count myself honoured.'

'We have experienced very special circumstances, but it will come to an end one way or another.'

'Have you read any of Anton's letters to Marlies?' said Femke after some silence that did not discomfort either.

'No, I have regarded them as private.'

'In my case, I have to read them. Just between us, Anton is so sweet and romantic it's hard to believe such feelings come from a tall, imposing SS officer, often stiff in his manner and trained to distribute brutality randomly.'

'Anton reminded me of a possible threat,' said Jos, paying scarce attention to Femke's thoughts about his romantic expressions. 'You know that starvation has been used as a weapon in the past, don't you?'

'It was a weapon in Holland during the Spanish occupation. You don't think the Nazis would resort to it here, do you?'

Their savagery and desperation are increasing. It's a possibility. I think we should be prudent. Winter is approaching, too. I will ask Mevrouw De Vries to stock up as much as rationing will allow. I advise you to do the same.'

'That would be too terrible,' said Femke, 'but I will suggest it to those responsible.'

IT ROUGHLY happened as Anton forecast. The Allies were not entirely successful in their attempt to take the bridges around Arnhem in September, but continued to move north towards Fortress Holland, where the greatest concentration of the population was around Rotterdam, Den Haag and Amsterdam. In late September, the Dutch responded to the exiled Dutch government's appeal to stage a railway strike to support the

Allied campaign. Reichskommissar in Holland, Arthur Seyess-Inquart, warned he would unmercifully crush any attempts at sabotage. The railway strike went ahead, and the Nazis blocked all transport of foodstuffs and heating supplies to the west. It was a typical case of the Nazis going well beyond adequate measures. In November, Anton reported that the fear of causing chaos and disease forced the command to suspend the starvation tactic. However, the delivery of supplies did not restart because the disruption to the transport did not end. During November and December, the food stock and coal in the west began to run out. In January, the unusually harsh winter froze the rivers and canals, stopping the supply by boat. People were dying of cold and starvation.

The extra stock Mevrouw De Vries bought in was shared with Jos's congregation, but it had also run down by the end of January, even after tight rationing. Femke's contacts were in the same situation. Jos had the impression they had not been prudent. She lost weight and looked sickly. Anton provided as much food as he could manage without risking detection. Femke insisted he continue supplying intelligence. He was desperate to hear that Marlies was safe. Marlies was safe, said Femke. He need not worry. His beloved was outside the starvation area, but he must resign himself to a break in communication. By the end of January, Anton had ceased to make contact. Femke had expected it.

The German command allowed people from the cities to spread out into the countryside to fetch food from the farms that were little affected by famine. Jos was among them. One from his congregation commandeered a bike trailer. His time was now taken up in journeying into the country west of Amsterdam. Soon, the competition for food became too great and too expensive. The farmers had a captured market. He was forced to turn towards the southwest. Breda had been liberated in October, and in late January, he had made the Vos couple his destination for food. The elderly couple, overjoyed to see him, fed him up and gave him as much food as could fit in his trailer. In February, he returned from an excursion to find Femke lying on his bed, looking pale and ill.

'She collapsed yesterday,' said Meneer De Vries, 'while here.'

'What have you been doing to yourself?' said Jos, sitting by her bed and taking her hand.

'Most probably what you've been doing to yourself,' she struggled to whisper. 'You don't look a picture of health either.'

'Mevrouw De Vries will make you a meal from what I have brought back. You must regain your health.'

'You must share whatever food you have,' she said, closing her eyes.

The following day, Femke looked much better. Colour had returned to her cheeks.

'That's much better,' said Jos. 'You must eat enough to sustain yourself and not work so hard.'

'I give you the same advice,' she said with a warm but weary smile. 'You forget you're not invincible.'

'I have a contact outside Breda. They feed me. I'm just about to leave.'

'Jos, look after yourself,' Femke said, coming to him. 'The war is ending, but there are still dangers to negotiate. The Allied bombing is increasing.'

'I will take care, Femke. I've learned to dance between the bombs and orange clouds.' He took her hand. 'You must take care, too.'

'May I give you a hug?' she said. 'Would that be proper?'

'Is it improper for a brother to hug his sister?'

Jos had a feeling as he cycled away that Femke's warm hug was her goodbye. It must just be a feeling, he said to himself. Surely, she had more work to do, but when he returned ten days later, Meneer De Vries said they had not seen her. He waited four days, but she did not appear. Ten days later, when he returned, she still had not appeared. No message had come, and the elderly couple could not contact her other than by leaving a message at the parish church nearby.

Jos resigned himself to her disappearance with feelings of deep grief, despite realising that there must be a good reason for her sudden disappearance. He concentrated on ministering to his congregation and making trips to secure food. In March, the Swedish flour that had arrived at the docks in January was at last distributed to bakers. Loaves were rationed to the people. Though the famine had been broken, people were still dying at an alarming rate because of the deprivation they had suffered. There was no lessening in the need to provide the sacraments and holy consolation. He made his last call to Meneer and Mevrouw Vos at the end of March. As usual, they received him joyfully. Mevrouw Vos immediately went to the kitchen to prepare a meal.

'The horror is ending,' he said when seated at the table. 'Meneer and Mevrouw, you have amply carried out your Christian duty. Our Lord will reward you, but I want to thank you sincerely for the indispensable aid you have given me.'

'No thanks necessary, lad,' said Meneer Vos. 'It's you who has given the example.' He reached across the table, laying a gnarled and weathered hand on his arm.

'Thank you, Father,' said Mevrouw. 'It's been Our Lord's privilege to help you in your important work.'

'You gave your trust,' said Jos, 'when you had little idea of what I was doing and especially when I acted with deplorable imprudence.'

'What will happen now?' said Mevrouw. 'What will you do?'

'When the war finishes, I will return to the seminary where I belong.'

'Return to those vipers?' said farmer Vos. 'You can't be serious, lad.'

'It's where I belong, for better or for worse.'

'Then you must take the major's advice—watch your back. You can't trust anyone there.'

'Has there been any sign of the major?' said Jos, remembering the extra-ordinary risks the major took.

'Nothing since the last correspondence,' said Mevrouw. 'We pray that he has survived the war.'

Jos stayed overnight. With his trailer again packed, he said his last good-byes.

'Thank you again, Meneer and Mevrouw. The next time I see you, I hope I'm shaven, hair cut, washed, and in my habit. May I give you a blessing before I depart?'

The elderly couple knelt before him and bowed their heads.

Fr. Jos made the sign of the cross over the old couple: *'Benedictio Dei omnipotentis Patris, et Filii, et Spiritus Sancti descendat super vos et maneat semper, Amen.'* [May the blessing of Almighty God, Father, Son, and Holy Ghost, descend upon you and remain with you forever. Amen.]

FATHER JOS van Engelen's time was now spent visiting the sick and providing the sacraments, often the last rites, and spiritual consolation in the last hours. So numerous were the calls for his priestly services that he hardly had time for anything else. He frequently thought of Femke, wondering where she was and how she was doing. They had been together for five years. It was sometimes difficult to accept she was no longer there to support him with her decisive manner and wise advice. He missed her. He prayed for her health and security, confident he would hear from her when the world returned to peace.

His visits took him to all parts of Amsterdam, which meant he sometimes did not return to the De Vries house until early morning, exhausted. But he could not afford to indulge himself with a refreshing break. He would snatch a rest where his priestly duties took him and sleep later when his work was done. Mevrouw De Vries urged him in vain to slow down. It was not only exhaustion and lack of sleep that preyed upon him in April. It began slowly and almost unobtrusively and then quickened.

Odd sounds and something like distant screaming and shrieking accompanied his late-night visits. Sometimes, he felt a dark shape brush by him in the backstreets. He tried to tell himself that he was imagining things. It was his exhaustion playing tricks on him. He hesitated when taking a shortcut through dark streets whose walls were flowing with the grime and slime of the centuries. The sounds increased in the vicinity of Warmoesstraat. Then, odd things happened in the De Vries house. Pictures fell from the wall, and furniture moved, seemingly of itself, mostly when he was alone. Mevrouw De Vries witnessed a picture unaccountably falling from the wall. She appealed, frightened, to Fr. Jos. He tried to reassure her, but she could not be reassured when it happened again, with Meneer De Vries present. Then, strange and evil visions plagued him on visits to the sick.

'We must again pray for protection from the demons,' he said. 'Just as we had prayed over Marlies. Our Lord will protect us.'

He blocked out the demonic torment and wandered through the ancient city's narrow streets and along darkened canals to his assignments in what he felt was a dream that often turned into a nightmare of devilish assaults. Through it all, he felt the absence of Femke, and prayed that she was safe.

Chapter 16

Truus van den Donker

GENERAL FOULKES, commander of the Canadian army, sat opposite General Johannes Blaskowitz, the commander of the German 25th Army Corp, whose men had occupied The Netherlands for five long years of horror and brutality. It was Saturday, 5 May 1945. They sat at a miserable wooden table in De Wereld, a crumbling hotel in Wageningen, a small bombed and blackened provincial town along the route from Arnhem to Amsterdam. Without ceremony, the Canadian commander read out the unconditional terms of surrender to the stony-faced Blaskowitz, whose final terse 'Jawohl, Herr Oberbefelhshaber' acknowledged his new masters.

News of the formal surrender sent a shudder of joy through the Dutch population. For despite the spontaneous unfurling of flags hidden for five years, despite the handshaking, hugging, and dancing on the streets, the Dutch mind and spirit were pierced through by the suffering and murder of so many innocent people, pierced with memories of the ruthless, unrelenting Nazi jackboot, the forced labor, the summary executions, and the unforgiving group reprisals for resistance to the occupation. Nor could anyone ignore the fate of those fellow Dutch citizens who had been rounded up and transported to Germany and Poland. And now, in the spring of 1945, many of the population still suffered from the recent *hongerwinter*, the cause of widespread starvation. Still, it was time for celebration. It was time to celebrate their restored freedom. The following day, Sunday, people giving thanks filled the churches. The celebrations continued throughout the day, spilling onto Monday.

It was a fine sunny day that Monday in Amsterdam, 7 May 1945, a day to lift the spirits. While glinting and whirring Allied planes dropped desperately needed supplies outside the city, people gathered in the city center to welcome the Canadian army. Streams of people filled Het Rokin, Kalverstraat, and Damrak, the chief roads to the Dam, Amsterdam's central square. Sometime after two o'clock, an emaciated, unkempt, unshaven man dressed in rags and with a rucksack on his back emerged from Vondelpark, the grand public park just beyond the outermost canal on the southern side of the city. Fr. Jos brushed bits of grass and other plant matter from his ragged clothes and set off along Stadhouderskade, the road running along the canal. He stopped and gazed towards busy Leidseplein on the other side of the canal. A patrol of German soldiers moved among the people on the square. He stood there for a minute, expressionless. Then, he crossed the road and walked along the canal in the direction he had come.

With the Rijksmuseum on his right, he crossed the bridge over the outer of the canal rings that formed the defences of the ancient city on the Amstel. He continued along Spiegelgracht towards the city centre, taking no notice of the peaceful glimmering waters around him. He crossed over the following two canal rings and came to Herengracht, the first of the canals marking in the early 1600s the expansion of the medieval city limits to make room for Amsterdam's fabulously wealthy merchants and businessmen. Here, he paused. The vacant look faded from his face. He was in the centre of the most affluent residential area of Calvinist Holland's heyday. The sumptuous examples of Dutch Renaissance, classicist and Louis architectural styles were all around. Residences, less grand but in similar styles, stretched back along the way he had come. The southern area of Amsterdam, formed by the canals Singelgracht, Prinsengracht, Keizersgracht, and Herengracht would forever testify to the city's most glorious period of business, trade, finance, artistic achievement, and learning. Worn and unkempt, Jos contemplated the surroundings for some minutes. At length, with an inaudible sigh, he turned left and headed along Herengracht towards Leidsestraat.

Shortly after, he mingled with the stream of people surging along Kalverstraat towards the Dam. He took little notice of the people around him, and they noted yet another of their countrymen who had lived the life of a beggar during the German occupation. The only sign that the beggar was aware of his surroundings came with a few glances at a watch hidden under the sleeves of a ragged coat several sizes too big for his emaciated body. Halfway along Kalverstraat, he stopped outside the Saints Peter and Paul Church, known locally as the *Papegaai*, the code word used to indicate the clandestine Catholic church behind Kalverstraat when the Calvinist elite would not tolerate papist superstition. It was open.

Glancing up at the stone parrot sheltering in a niche in the narrow neo-Gothic facade of the church, the beggar took off his soiled black beret and went inside. The cool, shaded atmosphere seemed for a moment to overwhelm him. He gazed at the carved wooden Gothic-style altars until his eyes became accustomed to the dimly lit interior. He sank into a back pew. His head nodded forward a few times before he jerked it upright. He knelt beside the crucifix that hung on the left-hand side. At the sound of a clock in the distance striking three, he put his left hand on the feet of the crucified Christ and struck his breast three times. A minute later, he was on his way again in the same vacant manner. Within sight of Dam Square, he came to a stop.

Ever cautious despite the effectiveness of his disguise and vacant expression, Fr. Jos fixed his eyes on the people milling around the Grote Club, the German officers' club, at the end of Kalverstraat. The building overlooking Dam Square was barricaded, and his countrymen did little to hide their scorn. German officers came to the first-floor window on the Kalverstraat side and looked down. The priest sidled to an alleyway on his right and arrived shortly after on the square by way of Het Rokin. The officers' club was now on his left in the next block. Several SS officers appeared on the front balcony and then disappeared.

Bumped and pushed, he made his way between the people. Over near the entrance to Damrak, the street leading to Centraal Station, the barrel organ *Het Snotneusje* was lustily grinding out its tunes. The familiar sound of the organ music seemed suspended in the air, unwilling to grasp the people. The priest could not help dropping his guard as he surveyed the packed square and the officers' club. A flock of pigeons fluttered up over the crowd and flew away over the Royal Palace. He walked on. A shot rang out. He swung round. A German soldier on the roof of the Grote Club rushed forward, his rifle at his shoulder, firing. Then, sputtering machine-gun fire sounded above the single shots. The crowd stampeded towards the streets leading from the Dam.

A wave of humanity dragged him into Damrak. Tumbling forward, he pushed himself into a shallow recess of the nearest building as the wave of people streamed by. There was no screaming or crying, just the heavy sighing and breathing of the people trying to keep from being trodden underfoot. A terrified young woman carrying a baby was jostled towards him. He reached out as she began to topple and squeezed her beside him. Grasping bodies fell and piled up while others crawled over and between them. Then it was over. Dam Square was empty. The streets were empty, and the shooting had stopped. All that remained were the fallen bodies, the mangled bikes and small tradesmen's carts, shoes, prams, and the un-recognisable debris, once objects carried or worn by people. Those who had saved themselves by crouching behind the bullet-riddled *Snotneusje* had taken their chance and fled towards Damstraat.

The priest took the woman by the shoulders and hurried her to the nearest shop entrance. Still clutching her baby, she sank to the floor among the battered and traumatised people who had sought shelter there. She breathed in gasps and leaned against the display window. A man beside her was clutching his arm, trying to stem the flow of blood. Further into the shop, another man lay groaning on the floor. Jos gave the woman a reassuring pat on the shoulder and looked at the baby in her arms. It was still asleep. He left them and knelt beside the man.

'I am a Catholic priest, Meneer,' he whispered.

The man rolled his head from side to side and, in a faint voice, said, 'Reformed.' The priest rested his hand against the man's cheek and, still bending over him, bowed his head. The man took him feebly by his sleeve. Jos brought his ear close to the man's mouth.

'From Leimuiden ...' The man stopped to get his breath. 'My bike ... somewhere ...' He stopped again.

'May I say a prayer with you?'

The man nodded and, with eyes rolling, tried to focus on the priest. His effort to speak was in vain. He closed his eyes.

'Jesus, Lord and merciful Saviour,' the priest whispered in the man's ear, 'look with mercy on your servant who in this hour humbly confesses all his weaknesses. Forgive him his sins and accept him into the bosom of your love.' He stopped, keeping his head bowed and his eyes closed. There was another feeble tug on his coat. The priest glanced at the man's face. His eyes were closed, and the expression of pain was fading. He again put his mouth to the man's ear.

'Remember what Simeon said to Jesus's mother in the temple: Lord, take me now because my eyes have seen Thy salvation.'

The man no longer moved. Jos remained in prayer for a minute. When he lifted his head, a look of peace had replaced the contorted expression. '*Deo Gratias.*' He realised his knee was in the way of a trickle of blood. He looked around. Shock gripped the people. He returned to the young woman sitting on the floor, staring at the ceiling. He knelt and took her hand.

'You're safe now. It's finished, I think.'

'Yes, Meneer,' she said, shaking a little. 'You saved my baby and me. Thank you. Thank you.' She glanced at the man lying in his blood. 'Poor man, to be killed on this day. But my husband, Meneer, we were together just before the shooting. Then he went towards Damstraat to find a friend. He said he would be back soon. Where could he be?'

The fresh, innocent face—she could not be more than twenty—the absence of any make-up, her hair drawn back around her head, and the loose-fitting, modest, dark-coloured clothing said much to him. The accent was that of Zeeland. Still holding her hand, he said, 'Let's say a prayer that he has not come to harm.' The young woman composed herself, leaving her hand in the priest's and closing her eyes. When she opened them again, she said, 'Thank you, Meneer. I should have done that at once.'

'I think it's best that you wait here. Your husband will be looking for you. He'll likely begin where he left you. He must think the people pushed you in this direction.' He let go of her hand and stood up.

The young woman stroked her baby's head a few times. 'Yes, Meneer, I think you're right. Thank you again.'

'I'll stay with you until he finds you.'

She nodded and then looked at the priest as if she had just noticed his appearance. Questioning eyes passed over the sunken cheeks, long hair, unshaven face under the soiled beret, and ragged clothes covering a deprived figure. She appeared on the point of saying something, but looked away. A few moments later: 'Look, Meneer, my baby has hardly noticed a thing. She has slept through it all.'

'What's her name?'

'Gerda.'

The young woman stiffened as bursts of gunfire from the Dam rent the air outside the shop. There was a nervous shuffle among the people, some crouching. Then, the gunfire ceased, to be replaced by the swelling roar of an approaching vehicle.

'They're heading for the station,' said Jos as the roar faded in that direction. 'They won't bother us anymore. It is the last of it. I'm sure.'

She relaxed, as did the others. Some moments later, a young man came rushing into the shop. He stopped dead in front of the young woman. 'You're safe.' He knelt and put his hand on the baby's head. The baby stirred. Jos gave him a comforting pat on the back. The young man started and stared up at the priest.

'This man saved us,' said his wife. 'We owe him our lives.'

The young man stood up and looked Jos up and down. He looked down at his wife and then back at the priest.

'She was being pushed along with the crowd. I prevented her from falling.'

The young man continued to stare at the priest.

'Cees, he saved our lives. We would've been trampled to death.'

Still, the young man did not speak. Instead, he looked at his wife and then again at the priest.

'I'm not what my appearance would lead you to believe,' said Jos.

'I believe you, Meneer. Who are you?'

'I have been working with the resistance, with the underground—'

'What doing?'

'What does it matter? Cees, please help me up and take me out of here.'

Cees gave the priest one more glance and then, as if shaking himself out of his mood, helped his wife to her feet. He took the baby from her arms and turned to head out of the shop, but stopped. 'Thank you, Meneer.'

Jos nodded, thinking the thanks had been grudging.

'Yes,' said his wife, 'we are indebted to you. Please tell us who you are.'

'It's not important. Do you have somewhere to go?'

'Oh, Meneer,' she said, coming to him, 'we have nothing. All our family have been killed. Our village has been destroyed. We are from Walcheren in Zeeland. There's nothing there.'

It was as he suspected. They were from one of the villages that the German bombing had destroyed. They were on their own. He took a grubby piece of paper and a pencil stub out of his trouser pocket and scribbled a few words.

'Much of Walcheren is underwater because of the bombing of the dykes, but you won't starve if you can return there.' He handed the piece of paper to the young woman. 'If you can make your way there, you will get help.

In the meantime, go to that address in Amsterdam. You will get temporary aid and assistance to return south. God be with you.'

'Thank you again, Meneer,' she said, glancing at the paper. 'We owe you ... But who are you?'

'It's not important. Take yourselves to safety.'

With a nod of gratitude, she returned to her waiting husband. By this time, a glowering man of the same age and appearance had joined him. A small, undecipherable tattoo on their right wrist caught the priest's attention. The young mother followed them out of the shop. Jos stood, staring at the vacant entrance, and then turned to the dead man on the ground. The pool of blood had grown. He looked around. Indistinct and haphazard conversation hung eerily in the air. Then, people from the Red Cross, accompanied by the Dutch scouts, entered the shop and busied themselves with providing aid. The priest left to continue his journey. Without bothering to maintain his disguise, he crossed Damrak and turned into a narrow street that led to Warmoesstraat. He could hear occasional gunfire coming from Centraal Station. A few minutes later, he was knocking on a familiar door, his fatigue and worn spirits now weighing on him.

'Father, thank the Lord, you're safe!' said an elderly man, whose eyes appeared in the narrow opening of the door. Two women looked anxiously over his shoulder. 'We heard gunfire. Some men have joined a detachment and are on their way to the station.' He noticed the blood on the priest's trouser leg.

'It's nothing,' Meneer De Vries. 'I'm safe, but I'm afraid some poor people have met their death on the very day of rejoicing.' With much attention, they led him inside. There was more gunfire. 'There'll be no more shooting after this. The Nazis have performed their last barbarous act in Amsterdam. And now, I need to rid myself of this appearance. Come on. Now is the time for the *Te Deum!*'

Half an hour later, in the secure attic of that house, Fr. Jos, washed and vested for Mass, stood in front of a makeshift altar decorated with flowers. Gleaming candles lit the dull, windowless space that his flock of old people had used to attend to their faith during the Nazi occupation. Fr. Jos van Engelen made the sign of the cross and spoke the psalm that Catholics worldwide heard at the beginning of every Mass. While Fr. Jos and his small, aged congregation attended to their thanksgiving Mass, the last deadly skirmish played out between the Third Reich soldiers and the local forces guarding Amsterdam's *Het Centraal Station*.

The priest was kneeling in prayer after Mass when someone tapped him on the shoulder and slipped a note into his hand. He looked around at the disappearing message bearer. After a glance at the note, he summoned the last of his energy and prepared to depart. 'I am needed,' he said to the inquiring looks from the raised heads around him. The air was still and unbroken by gunfire as he made his way along the canal. He put out his hand to steady himself on the bollards and the occasional railing. Just one more task, and he could rest. Then he stood at the door of the unknown address marked on the note. Glimmering in the canal waters, the bright sunlight behind him shed no light on his wandering mind as he waited.

A door opened. A young, smiling, unrecognisable face welcomed him. He thought it strange that the unblemished, youthful face with full red lips had escaped the ravages of the war. She showed him to a comfortable armchair in what looked like a waiting room, a richly furnished and decorated room. She brought him a cup of tea. Again, he thought it strange as he sipped the welcome sweet drink. He struggled to draw the note from his pocket to ensure he understood. But a greyness enveloped him, followed by incantations, and intermittent darkness and light as time seemed to stand still. Feelings of pleasure and revulsion passed over him as he struggled to keep his arms crossed over his chest. And the lovely, innocent face of the young woman with her heartfelt appeal intruded as an unfathomable recrimination.

Chapter 17

Fr. Jos is found

AFTER THE ALLIES landed in Normandy on 6 June 1944, they fought north to secure Walcheren and Antwerp harbour's strategic points. Stubborn resistance slowed progress. On 4 September, they wrestled Antwerp from the Germans. Fierce fighting followed through Zeeuws-Vlaanderen to the river Schelde. Across the Schelde was the heavily fortified coast of Walcheren, with Vlissingen guarding its mouth. The Allies had no choice but to bomb the dykes and the fortifications. Water flooded the island, forcing many to flee to higher ground. Middelburg grew to an unheard of 40,000 people. Emergency dykes were hastily built to hold the water back from the city centre.

At Westkapelle, higher up the coast, the bombing killed 152 people. The invading allies attacked the Germans on all sides until they were cornered and forced to lay down their arms. The first army duck arrived in Middelburg from Vlissingen on 6 November. After parking in front of the ancient *Militair Hospitaal* in Zandstraat, Captain Jones jumped down. With the duck 'Spider' following, he made his way with a column of Middelburgers up Lange Viele, across Marktplein, and down Lange Delft to Damplein, where Commandment General Daser at 6-8 Damplein faced surrender.

Simon and Frans van Engelen were among those waiting for the humiliation of the German commandant. Daser made himself ridiculous by refusing to surrender to an officer under the rank of colonel. It had to take the ruse of Major Hugh, who arrived later, posing as a colonel, for Daser to give up. They watched as Johnston and his men took Daser into custody to be transported to Vlissingen, shipped to the other side of the Schelde, and on to processing. They watched as the weary German troops assembled on Damplein, eager to get out of the place and return to their homes in Germany.

'It had to come to this,' said Simon.

'Look at these sad creatures who made life so oppressive for us. They just want to get back to their families.'

Frans had said a prayer of thanksgiving as he joined Captain Jones in the procession to Damplein, not only for the end of the war on Walcheren but for his deliverance. He had gone to ground to conduct his covert activities. Through unfaltering caution, he had escaped the roving detection units and the desperate German soldiers who ultimately faced annihilation. Now that it was all behind him, his thoughts turned to his brother Jos. Where was he? Had he survived? By the end of the week, they learned the 1st Polish Armoured Division had liberated Breda on 29 October, a week before Walcheren's liberation. As the communication lines were down, Frans wrote to the superior general. A reply came back after four weeks with the brief information that Fr. Jos had disappeared from the seminary in the first weeks of the war and regrettably had not been seen since.

'What does that mean?' said Simon.

'I have no idea other than that Jos is missing—not confirmed as dead. I will write again.'

The reply from Fr. van Rossem scarcely provided more information. He repeated that Fr. Jos had left the seminary without informing anyone and had not contacted them since. They did not know whether he was alive or dead. They could not search for him or make inquiries because of the tight restrictions the Germans had placed on them.

'I must go there,' said Frans. 'This Van Rossem knows more than he is saying.'

It was necessary, however, to postpone any plan to travel to the seminary. It was winter, the war was still on in the north, and Walcheren's rebuilding took priority. So, Frans had to wait until the German forces' formal surrender in May before he could take the train to Breda. He met Fr. van Rossem and Fr. Muller, who, though friendly and sympathetic, could not tell him much more, but that little more was significant. Fr. Jos had disappeared on the evening the Nazis raided the seminary and found Fr. Albers and Fr. Timmermans, a former classmate of Fr. Jos's, operating a transmitter. The Nazis executed them the next day.

'Was there any warning that the Nazis were watching them?' said Frans. 'I assume they had information beforehand if they raided.'

'None,' said Fr. Muller. 'Fathers Albers and Timmermans gave no signs of what they were up to.'

'And Jos?'

'We don't even know that Fr. van Engelen was working with them,' said Fr. Muller. 'He just disappeared without warning. Nobody remembers seeing him that evening. We are sorry, Meneer van Engelen. We can tell you nothing more about your brother. I suggest you wait to see what may turn up. It's early days.'

'What may turn up?'

'He may be somewhere in the north. For whatever reason, he may have gone to Amsterdam. It's possible he somehow got wind of the execution and feared returning to the seminary.'

'That suggests he was working with Fr. Albers,' said Frans, testing them.

'We really don't know,' said Van Rossem. 'We can only speculate. We will inform you at once if we have news of him.'

Frans had heard enough. He thanked the two priests and left. The evidence suggested, indeed, that Jos had taken flight because of the raid and the executions. For some unaccountable reason, he was absent when the Nazis raided in response to suspicions of covert activity or information they had received, possibly from within the seminary.

'There are signs someone betrayed them,' said Simon, after Frans had reported his findings, 'from within.'

'Yes, it's possible. The missing piece in the puzzle is why Jos was not at the seminary when the Germans raided. It seems significant Muller thought he might have gone to Amsterdam. They both know more than they're saying.'

'Don't be overly suspicious.'

A day later, a young woman approached Frans at the market on Marktplein.

'Oh, hello, Meneer—,' she began, putting out a hand, but stopped. 'Oh, I beg your pardon. I have mistaken you for someone else.'

'No apologies necessary, Juffrouw,' said Frans with a reassuring gesture.

The pretty young woman kept staring.

'Juffrouw?'

'You look like someone I met in Amsterdam recently. Do you have a brother?'

'Yes,' said Frans, now all attention.

'Do you look alike?'

'People say they can see we're brothers. I'm a little stouter, not as tall. Tell me more, Juffrouw, where—?'

'It's Mevrouw, Meneer, Mevrouw van den Donker. In Amsterdam. He was dressed like a beggar—said he worked for the resistance. He didn't appear at all well. That's why I was surprised.'

'The resistance?'

'He saved my baby and me from being trampled.'

'Where in Amsterdam?'

'In Damrak—' She stopped and looked past Frans. 'I must go, Meneer.'

A frowning young man stood at the end of the row of stalls with his eyes fixed on her.

'But Mevrouw, where—?'

'He crossed the road as if he were going to that neighborhood behind Damrak, you know, that dirty area. I can't stay. Goodbye, Meneer.' She hurried away with her head down.

Frans watched her walk to the frowning young man, who mouthed a few words at her before turning and walking off towards Vlasmarkt, the road that took them out of the town centre to go to the north of the island. The young woman followed, her head still down and her shoulders hunched. Frans was determined to know more. At first, his inquiries led nowhere. No one he spoke to knew of her or the young man.

'They must be farm people,' said Simon.

'And I would say Strict Reformed by the look of the young woman.'

'If they are as young as you say, they'd only be known to their family and closed church community at this stage. The water has driven them into town. Perhaps you should try to find out where the man works.'

'And then? He was such a disagreeable-looking fellow, and she seemed afraid of him.'

It was their only hope, Frans decided. Much building and restoration work was going on in the town centre. He would search there. The next day, he toured the building sites, careful to avoid the impression he was searching. He did not trust the man's reaction. Eventually, he found him in a work party near the Abbey complex at the Damplein end. It was just after midday, so he would not finish work for a few hours. Frans returned at 5 o'clock to find the work party had moved inside to Abbey Square. He guessed the man would come along Lange Delft and across Markplein on his way home. He guessed correctly.

With a perpetual frown and pursed lips, the young man emerged from Lange Delft shortly after half-past five, crossed the square, and entered Vlasmarkt. Frans followed at a distance and was in time to see him turn right into Kromme Weele. At Seissingel, the road along Middelburg's outer canal, the frowning man, without greeting, boarded a rowboat, one of the vessels taking people and provisions to the island's dry areas. At 10 o'clock the following day, Frans waited for the same boat.

'Goeiemorgen, Meneer van Engelen,' said the man at the rudder when the boat returned, 'off to visit the properties in the north, I imagine.'

'Goeiemorgen, Meneer.' Frans was happy to have a pretext without inventing one. 'Yes, many property matters await resolution because of the bombing and flooding.'

He boarded the boat, and they set off after a short wait for other passengers. The boatman was keen to talk about the damage, who had lost what, and how long it would take to rebuild.

'It's sad to see the loss of life and property. People, as well as their farms, have perished. I don't know how one will sort all that out. I suppose you will help.'

'Yes, Meneer. Tragically, people will need my services.'

'You know, I've seen a particularly sad case near Vrouwekerke,' the boatman continued without encouragement. 'A young couple has returned with their baby from Amsterdam to find both their parents deceased and their houses a pile of bricks. What a tragedy. The man doesn't have a friendly word to say, but his wife—you couldn't see a lovelier young woman. They are Strict Reformed, which accounts for his sullen looks.'

It must be his couple, thought Frans, relieved that the chatty boatman saved him from asking questions that might have seemed purposeful. The boat reached dry land after covering a short distance over the water towards Grijpskerke. The area over which Frans now walked had mostly escaped the bombing. It was tragic for Meneer and Mevrouw van den Donker that stray bombs meant for the dykes and other coastal targets had struck their parents' properties. On the outskirts of Vrouwekerke, on a side road, was a half-destroyed house with its barn reduced to rubble. Although work had begun to repair the house, there was no sign of life. Frans walked on to the untouched village. The villagers were going about their daily routine, many of whom greeted him. He stopped to talk, patiently listening to their stories while looking around. There she was, sitting in the middle of the grassy square, looking at her daughter on a blanket.

'Goedemorgen, Mevrouw,' said Frans, pretending he had happened across her. 'Stay calm,' he encouraged, seeing her grab her child into her arms. 'People expect me to be looking around at the property damage. I want to know more about—'

'I can't tell you any more, Meneer,' she interrupted. 'I would rather not—'

'Mevrouw, please, just a few questions. You say he looked sick.'

'Yes, quite ill. I can't add any more except that he was very kind to me. I will always remember what he did and the way he did it. He looked so ill, but it made no difference to the kindness he showed me and others in shock over what had happened.'

'What?'

'There was a stampede when the Germans fired at everyone on Dam Square. I told you. Your brother saved my baby and me from being trampled to death.'

'What were you doing there? What was he doing there?'

'I was waiting for my husband.' She rose. 'There's nothing else to say. Please thank your brother ...' She stopped. 'I imagine he needs help. Think of him rather than question me.'

'That's exactly why I want to know more, Mevrouw.'

'Please thank him for the kindness he showed me if you find him in time. He said a prayer with me. I will say one for him.' She hurried away, leaving Frans staring after her.

He strolled around the village centre for another half-hour before turning towards the embarkment point for the trip back to Middelburg. Mevrouw van den Donker was in the front yard of the half-blasted house in the side street he had passed on his way in. Her daughter was on a blanket before her, playing with a toy. She did not look at him. The boatman was right. Mevrouw van den Donker, the wife of that frowning, disgruntled man, was all loveliness, even in her anxiety.

'I'm going to Amsterdam,' he told his parents after returning. 'I can't delay. Jos is on the edge of death if Mevrouw van den Donker is telling the truth. We can't take the chance she is exaggerating.'

'You be careful, Frans,' said his mother. 'Don't trust the Germans even if they say they've given up.'

'Make sure you take enough money,' said his father. 'You don't know what circumstances you'll be landing in.'

Frans left the following day, not knowing how easy the transport would be to Amsterdam. Despite the work and rebuilding everywhere, he arrived in the afternoon at Centraal Station with surprisingly few delays. He walked the short distance to the seedy area behind Damrak, long known for its brothels. He wondered what Jos was doing there as he ambled around the streets and along the canals, the sly looks and the eyes at split curtains making it unmistakable where he was. Few people of everyday appearance passed him. He saw nobody of whom he felt confident enough to ask questions. As darkness fell and the houses along the streets and canals were stirring with blinking lights and the opening and shutting of doors and windows, he left to seek accommodation elsewhere. He strolled down the Oudezijds Voorburgwal, stopping at the Oude Kerk. With a cursory look at the premises, which now surrounded the ancient church, he continued his way. The further he walked away from Centraal Station, the less seedy the area became until he found a cosy hotel with a friendly, welcoming manager. As he was leaving the following morning, he put the purpose of his search to him.

'He was quite sick. I assume he was going to someone he knew.'

'If you're looking for someone last seen in the Warmoestraat area and who you claim was unlikely to be a patron of the businesses, I suggest you ask people on the other side of Oudezijds Achterburgwal, in the streets nearer to Nieuwmarkt. There are some very old residents there. If they can't give you some news, nobody can—or he's not here.'

After arriving at Nieuwmarkt Square, Frans wandered along all the streets between the square and Oudezijds Achterburgwal, asking people he judged to be long-time residents if they had seen a man who looked like him but was ill. The old people were friendly, suggesting who he could turn to, but they had seen no one of that description, sick or otherwise. Late in the afternoon, he was ready to give up, thinking he should find the government office handling missing person inquiries. While walking down Monnikenstraat on the way to Dam Square, he met an old couple. He posed the same question but added that he was looking for a Catholic priest, something he had neglected to do before.

'We have not seen the person you're looking for,' said the woman, 'but we know someone Catholic hereabouts. If a sick Catholic priest has been wandering around here, they would know.'

'Where can I find them?' Frans clutched the woman's arm.

'We will take you there if you don't mind walking slowly.'

'Go as slow as you like.'

The couple took him to Oudezijds Achterburgwal, then to a narrow street two blocks away. They knocked at a weather-worn door.

'It'll take time for them to answer,' reassured the woman.

At last, there was a stirring within, and after a tense delay, the door opened a little. A pair of inquiring eyes appeared at the crack. After they explained the intrusion, the door swung open a little more, with the eyes focusing on Frans. The eyes widened, and the door opened, revealing a woman as the owner of the wary eyes. An old man was at her shoulder.

'Yes, come in, Meneer. We think we can help you.'

Frans thanked the eager couple and entered the house, the old woman acknowledging the couple with a nod and then shutting the door.

'We feel we can't be too careful, even now, Meneer van Engelen,' said the old man, who walked with a stoop. 'There are scores to be settled.'

'I understand.'

They took him to a room at the back of the house with a window overlooking a small back garden. The afternoon light revealed a neat, clean room with an emaciated man lying in a bed and breathing in weak gasps. His eyes appeared half-opened. Frans fell to his knees and took his brother's hand.

'Jos! My God!'

'We found him two days ago after looking for more than a week,' said the woman. 'He received a message after Mass and left without saying where he was going.'

'We knew something was wrong when he did not return that evening,' said the man. 'He was already starved and exhausted. We knew he could not have gone far.'

'Where was he?'

The couple hesitated, the woman glancing at her husband.

'He was in a filthy room in a filthy house on Zeedijk, near death. They didn't know how he got there, they said. More likely, they wouldn't say. But the sooner he was gone, the better. We did not have to ask for their help. A car appeared at the front of the house. They bundled him in and brought him here. They even gave us money to care for him, which we gratefully accepted. We're looking after him as best we can.'

'Have you called a doctor?'

'No. We're very careful, Meneer van Engelen. The people who did this are still around. We think they wanted to disgrace him and then cause him a miserable death.'

'Who? Why?'

'His cooperation with the underground caused the Nazis and their collaborators a lot of trouble. But others were after him.'

'Who?'

'We're not sure. During the last month, we had the feeling—so did Fr. Jos—that fiendish forces were stalking him. They took their opportunity on that day of surrender when Father dropped his guard.'

'Well, I'm here. Those demonic forces will get at him over my dead body. We must call a doctor. Now.'

The old couple, Meneer and Mevrouw de Vries, appeared reassured by Frans's presence and called a doctor. The same doctor arrived within the half-hour and, after a close examination, said Fr. Jos was suffering from extreme exhaustion and malnutrition. Disease was not an issue. He needed rest and a strict diet to return him to health if it was not too late. His recovery would take time. The doctor wrote out a diet and made a list of requirements to nurse the patient. He would return in a few days to observe the progress—if any. Frans made arrangements for an extended stay.

He sent a letter to his parents while the old couple bought provisions and nursing necessities. They set up a bed in the same room so Jos had his total care and attention. The first step was to get him to eat and drink, which was difficult because he was in a delirium, barely conscious of his surroundings. Then, by little steps of encouragement, Frans got Jos to sit up, supported by cushions, to take fluids, after which he lay back in exhaustion until the next effort. The doctor returned as promised four days later and praised Frans for his care. He was now hopeful that starvation and exhaustion had not dealt too severe a blow to his brother's heart. After a week, the glaze disappeared from Jos's eyes, and he seemed to recognise Frans. Frans squeezed his arm and told him not to say anything.

'Just lie back and rest. I'm here, and we're looking after you. No need to worry. All you need to do is eat and rest.'

'Frans?' said Jos a week later.

'Yes, Jos. I'm here.' Frans leaned close to him. 'You're safe.'

'Where am I?'

'You're with Meneer and Mevrouw de Vries. You're in good hands.'

'Those dear friends. Thank them for me, Frans.'

'I will. Mevrouw de Vries has been preparing your meals.'

'That dear, generous lady.' He lay back and closed his eyes.

Frans stayed with him, never venturing from the room unless necessary. He did not press Jos to talk, leaving him to say what he wanted, which was not much, just regular expressions of his gratitude for the care he was receiving and asking after his parents, hoping they were not too anxious about him. Meneer and Mevrouw de Vries supported Frans, taking on tasks that did not need his attention—fetching food, buying clothes, and taking Frans's letters to the post office, among others. The rags Jos had worn for so long ended up in the rubbish bin.

'What has Fr. Jos been doing all this time?' Frans asked one day, leaving his brother to sleep after one of their brief conversations.

'We don't know very much,' said Meneer de Vries, 'but he was working with the resistance in some way—with a young woman. He and Femke didn't want to talk about it unless necessary. It was too dangerous, they said. He just wanted us to give him a place to sleep. He would leave and sometimes stay away for long periods. He would come back often starved, ready to collapse.'

'He said Mass for us and others,' added Mevrouw de Vries. 'Provided the sacraments. He was our priest during the war.'

'You have a very brave brother, Meneer van Engelen,' said Meneer de Vries.

'Self-sacrificing, brave brother,' added Mevouw de Vries.

'Do you know who this Femke was?'

'No, only that she worked with the resistance,' said Meneer de Vries. 'We weren't allowed to know more.'

After three weeks, when Jos could sit up for extended periods, Frans read to him from Saint Augustine's *Confessions*, which Meneer de Vries had on his bookshelf. In the fourth week of his convalescence, Jos was strong enough to wear his new clothes and sit outside in the narrow garden to enjoy the summer weather. Those old people who had given Jos cover and for whom he had exercised his priestly ministry now had permission to visit. The uninhibited affection these simple people showed brought Frans to tears.

'I suppose you're wondering what happened to me,' Jos said one day while they sat outside.

'Yes, but you don't have to say anything until you're ready. First, you need to regain your health.'

'Thank you, Frans. Thinking exhausts me.'

They sat in silence for some time.

'The last I remember was sleeping in Vondel Park. It was terribly cold.'

Frans waited for him to go on.

'How did I get here?' he said a few minutes later.

'I think it's best to leave that until another time.'

'It's that bad, is it?' said Jos, glancing at his brother.

'It needs context.'

'Well put, brother.'

Another period of silence followed.

'Have you contacted the seminary?' said Jos at length.

'No, not yet—at least not about finding you.'

'So, you have contacted them?'

'Yes, of course.'

'You spoke to Fr. van Rossem, no doubt.'

'Yes.'

'And he said he had no idea where I was.'

'That's about it.'

'And you haven't contacted him now because you weren't entirely satisfied with his answers.'

'Right again, but I spoke with Muller as well as Van Rossem.'

Jos looked at the ground in front of him. When weariness and tension appeared on his face, Frans decided they had said enough.

'I will contact the seminary after we return to Middelburg. Now, when do you think you can travel?'

Jos looked up. 'Whenever you want. I can sit in a train carriage, I imagine, as well as here. I want to return home to Middelburg, Frans, as soon as possible. Maybe I'll get my thoughts together then. Thank you for all you've done.'

'No thanks necessary. It's what a brother would do.' He hesitated. 'Who is Femke?'

Jos looked wearily at Frans. 'Yes, Femke ...,' he said, looking away.

'Meneer and Mevrouw said you worked with her in the resistance.'

'I ... I can't talk about it now. Perhaps another time.' A tear trickled down his cheek.

'Don't worry, Jos,' said Frans, putting his hand on his brother's arm. 'No hurry. We can talk about it when you're ready.'

Later, when alone with Mevrouw and Meneer De Vries, Frans asked again who Femke was.

'We don't know, Meneer van Engelen. We just know that she and Fr. Jos worked with the resistance. We were strictly told to ignore what they were doing. It was for our safety as much as theirs. We stuck to the rules.'

'Where is she now?'

'We don't know. She suddenly disappeared. To be frank, we don't know whether she's alive or dead.'

'Where did she come from?'

'We don't know. It is pointless to ask us about Femke, Meneer. We know nothing. She just turned up one day and spoke privately with Fr. Jos. If Fr. Jos wanted her, which was not often, we had to go to the parish and leave a message. The strange thing is that nobody knew who we were talking about. But Femke would always arrive a few days later.'

Frans could not resist inquiring further. He went to the parish office and spoke to various people, including the parish priest, and all said they didn't know who he was talking about. Nevertheless, he left the message that Fr. van Engelen was very sick and perhaps Femke would like to know. A letter arrived a few days later, addressed to Fr. Jos.

'You couldn't resist, could you, brother,' said Jos, after perusing it.

'You know what I'm like. Anyhow, it might help if I knew who this Femke is. Well, what does it say?'

'It's not directly from Femke. It says that Femke has returned to her life before the war and wants to put her war experiences behind her. She is sad to hear I have been sick and wishes me a speedy recovery. She may be in contact sometime in the future. Here, read it yourself.' Jos held out the letter to Frans. 'I feel the same way, Frans. I want to consign my war experiences to the past. But to satisfy your curiosity about our activities, we were engaged in covert operations for the resistance. I don't want to say any more.'

'All right, Jos, I won't persist, though it will be difficult to keep my mouth shut.'

'Offer it up as penance for your sins,' said Jos, forcing a smile.

Frans let it rest for the moment. He prepared Jos for travel and organised a farewell lunch for Meneer and Mevrouw de Vries and those who had helped him and been under his care. During the lunch, a woman accompanied by a beautiful dark-haired woman of around twenty arrived. Frans, taken by the young woman's arresting beauty, assumed they were mother and daughter.

'Oh, Father van Engelen,' said the young woman, hurrying to the priest in his armchair. She knelt before him and took his hand. 'I'm so grateful for all you and Femke have done. I can't thank you enough for delivering me from that evil.'

'We are happy to have been instruments in God's work,' said Jos, raising her. 'It was an answer to our fervent prayers.'

'Oh, yes, I've said many prayers in thanksgiving.'

Mevrouw Borst also added her thanks and explained that two of the sisters of the convent where Marlies stayed brought her to Amsterdam and safely delivered her.

'She only arrived yesterday,' said Mevrouw Borst. 'I'm so happy she's in good health in mind and body.'

'There's only one thing on my mind now, Father,' said Marlies.

'Anton, I imagine.'

Oh, yes, Anton said you have a document testifying to his work for the resistance. Femke wrote that she has informed the authorities, but I would like to have the document he left with you.'

'Yes, of course, Marlies. It's hidden in the attic. I will have to fetch it.'

'No need, Father,' said Meneer de Vries. 'I removed it for safekeeping after the surrender. I fetched it while you were talking. Here it is.' He handed a folded sheet to the priest.

'Do you know where he is?' said Jos, handing it to Marlies.

'No. His last message said he would contact me as soon as possible. He thought he and his unit would come under scrutiny, but I was not to worry.

Just be patient. He would come for me no matter what or how long it took.'

'I'm sure he will, Marlies. He took a life-threatening risk in helping the resistance and maintaining contact with you. We must continue to say our prayers that he will be with you soon. Please let me know if there are any difficulties. My brother, Frans, will give you the contact details.'

Seeing his brother's energy and spirit straining under the attention, Frans tactfully brought the lunch to a close. All departed with heartfelt wishes for his future, with special thanks from Marlies and her mother.

'Who is Anton?' said Frans later, 'apart from that stunning girl's lover.'

'Not now, Frans, please. It's a long story. I will tell you when I have the energy.'

'My curiosity is torturing me.'

'He was an SS officer who helped us in the resistance. He had fallen in love with Marlies. No more, Frans. I will tell you the rest later.'

'*Allemachtig*, Jos. What were you mixed up in?'

A taxi took them to Centraal Station two days later, where Jos brightened.

'Just the thought of being back in Middelburg cheers me, Frans,' he said when they were comfortably seated in their carriage.

'That's the spirit.'

Chapter 18

Fr. Jos recuperates

JOS'S PARENTS could not hide their shock on seeing their son.

'Oh dear, Jos,' said his mother, taking him into her arms.

'Don't worry, Mamma. I have survived. Others, more worthy than me, didn't.' He brushed a tear from his left cheek.

'But you're our son,' said his father. 'You're going to stay with us until you completely recover, no matter what your superiors say. You're not going anywhere for a long while.'

Simon van Engelen did not have to worry about a strict, uncaring attitude from Jos's religious authorities. When informed of his survival, Fr. van Rossem was all joy and insisted that Jos not return to his priestly duties, including his religious dress, until fully recovered. If any help was needed, all they had to do was give him a sign.

'That's being kind and cooperative,' said Mevrouw van Engelen.

'Yes, I appreciate it,' said Jos, with a glance at Frans.

The doctor visited, carried out an examination, and heard Frans's account of how and when they found Jos. Then, with a wagging finger, he stressed Jos would need at least six months to regain some semblance of health.

'I fear starvation and exhaustion have permanently damaged your son's health,' he said to Simon when he was about to leave. 'He needs complete rest, exercise, and a healthy diet. I hate to say it, but he may no longer be capable of fulfilling his priestly duties. You should take that up with his superiors. Dispensation of vows is possible in certain circumstances.'

Arrangements had long been made for Fr. Jos's accommodation. Ada, the oldest sister, had married during the war and had left the family home. The other three sisters were happy to go to relations in Zuid-Beveland, where they were close to their fiancés. That left Jos and Frans in the parental house, where Jos settled in with his mother's help. As the weeks passed in the mild summer weather, he regained some of his health.

Sitting in the spacious back garden, chatting with his parents and Frans, and drinking coffee or tea with a stroopwafel or a bolus helped restore his mental and physical health. He was often on his own, which gave him time to reflect on what he had been through. Femke often came to his thoughts, but he resigned himself to a complete break with her. It could not be otherwise. Although he could not yet bring himself to talk about it, not even with Frans, those last few days before he went missing became clearer in the sequence of events, from his sleeping in Vondel Park to the tap on the shoulder after Mass.

An unknown person slipped a message into his hand, saying someone was sick and wanted a priest. How had he entered the room? Nobody knew. Although he felt on the point of collapse, he had gone to the address scribbled on the ragged piece of paper, an address he could no longer remember. A young woman welcomed him and took him to what looked like a waiting room. There she brought him a cup of tea, sweetened more than he liked. After that, his memory was cloudy. What happened then, he strained to think? But he had to stop. The effort to recall brought him to tears of exhaustion. He must let it go until he could cope.

Gradually, his strength increased, and he accompanied Frans on short walks beyond the town limits into the country, where it was dry. The calm rural landscape in its natural cycle soothed his exhausted spirits. It also relieved him of meeting people who had all sorts of questions he could not answer. In time, he felt strong enough to walk into Middelburg town centre to see the damage wrought by the German bombing. One day, in late summer, he wandered with Frans around Marktplein, viewing the restoration work. He walked with a slight limp and rested his hand now and then on his brother's shoulder.

'Let's stop for a moment,' he said, grasping his brother's arm. 'I'm sorry, Frans.'

'Nothing to be sorry about, Jos. Take your time.'

They had stopped in front of the ruins of what, until the war, was one of Europe's finest Gothic town halls. It was a priceless victim of the senseless destruction and cultural vandalism when the German air force sent its planes to bomb the people of Walcheren into submission. The brothers regarded the blackened shell in silence. The stone figures representing the Counts and Countesses of the once Catholic province stood intact, protected high up in their decorative niches.

'What would they say if they could talk?' said Frans. 'I don't think we would want to hear.' He paused. 'This beautiful building, so much connection with our past, all destroyed in a moment. Will we ever rise above it, and will proper punishment ever come to those who did this?'

'We've got to have hope,' murmured the priest after a while. He looked with affection at his younger brother, whose care had been untiring. 'The war has finished,' he continued. 'Surely, people have learned what it means to turn away from God. Peace is ahead of us. No resentment now. Forgiveness and solidarity must motivate us.' He found himself saying this as much to himself as to his brother, perhaps more so. 'Our fellow Zeelanders will see the wisdom in rebuilding everything, in bringing it back to what it was—to its former glory.' He broke off. The mechanical sound of his voice was unendurable. He roused himself. 'Come on, let's go and see Our Blessed Lady's Abbey—remind ourselves of Middelburg's Catholic past.'

Frans took him by the arm, and they walked towards Nieuwe Burg, a new street on the left-hand corner of the square constructed from the ruins of that old quarter. As they turned into Nieuwe Burg, they glanced to their right along Lange Delft, Middelburg's main shopping street. Although the authorities had cleared the rubble away, it was still a scene of devastation, with its glorious medieval and Dutch Renaissance buildings in dust and piles of bricks. They said nothing as they walked up the incline to Groenmarkt, one of the oldest streets in Middelburg, going back a thousand years to when it was a mere dirt pathway. They stopped in front of the blasted shell of the Nieuwe Kerk and what remained of the great Abbey tower, t he *Lange Jan*, both covered in scaffolding. Then, they made their way to Balanspoort, one of the ancient passageways to Abdijplein.

As they emerged on the square, the cruel sight of the ravaged abbey buildings, occupied by the provincial government since the Reformation, confronted them. On the opposite side of the enclosed square were the ruins of the complex's oldest buildings: the Abbot's living quarters, his private chapel, and the cloisters. They walked across the square and stopped. To their right was a work party stacking and arranging building materials. In quiet conversation, the brothers lingered there. They continued past the workers, giving them a greeting as they passed. A young man pushing a wheelbarrow arrived at the group. He put his wheelbarrow down and looked up as the brothers strolled by. He was about to acknowledge their wave but halted, frowning. Jos, his attention caught by his reaction, also s topped.

'I know this fellow. Wait. I want to say hello.' He limped to the man. 'Goedemorgen, Meneer, I'm glad to see you made it to Middelburg safely. Things seem to have worked out for you. How are your wife and child?'

'They're all right,' said the young man, refusing the priest's offered hand, 'but I can't say things have worked out, as you put it.'

'No need to be so bleak. You have work, and I assume accommodation for your family.'

'I do have a job, and my wife and child are safe ...' He hesitated. 'It was written all over you. Why didn't you confess you were a papist priest? What were you up to?'

'Steady on!' cried Frans, stepping forward with his hand held up.

'It's none of your business ... Oh, a colluding brother.'

'Wait, Frans,' said Fr. van Engelen, putting a hand on his brother's arm. 'Meneer ... what is your name ...?'

'Van den Donker.'

'Meneer van den Donker, I was concerned about your wife and child's safety. I had a reason not to reveal who I was. While the Nazis were still around, my identity had to remain hidden for security reasons. I also guessed your wife belonged to the Strict Reformed community.'

'Very Strict Reformed,' corrected the young man. 'I was relieved my wife and daughter were safe, but I wish their rescuer had not been an agent of that oppressive papist organisation.'

'Have you taken leave of your senses?' exclaimed Frans. 'Do you know what my brother has ...?'

'Frans, please ...'

'I recognise evil, no matter how it's dressed.'

'You ignorant fool. Do you know where you are?'

'As well as you do.'

'This complex is called the "Abbey." That should give you a clue about these buildings if you've ever bothered in your Calvinist arrogance to think about it.'

'Frans—,' Fr. Jos appealed again while the young man raised his chin.

'No, Jos, these things need to be said to a person like Meneer here,' said Frans, jabbing a finger into the man's chest. 'This was once truly an abbey, established by Norbertine monks in the 12th century. A thriving Catholic community grew around it. Was that evil? It all came to an end when the Prince of Orange's troops laid siege to Middelburg in 1574.'

'They were traitors, collaborators, just like the NSB-ers. They were the tool of the Spanish oppressors. Get your finger off me.'

'Oppressors! Who was the oppressor? The prince's supporters drove the monks from Our Blessed Lady's Abbey with only the clothes they stood in. Theft by violence—that's evil. Whether it's the Nazis doing it or the prince's troops, the act has the same name!'

'Frans, please, it's not necessary—,' Jos appealed yet again.

'They were kicked out just like the Nazis,' said the man, speaking over the priest. 'Nazis or papists, out with the oppressors!'

'You compare a group of dedicated monks administering a thriving community over three centuries with the Nazis? You're in the pits of the darkest confusion!' The closest labourers looked up.

Jos took his brother by the arm and drew him away. 'Frans, you will not get anywhere with this sort of talk. That young man and his wife have been through terrible hardship. They've likely lost everything, family and property. Hardly a wonder if his resentments were raw. In any case, you don't deal with prejudice this way.'

Frans huffed and then nodded. 'Okay. But he got under my skin. There's something really weird about him, let me tell you.'

'Frans, I appreciate your concern, but please wait near the Balanspoort. I'll be with you in a minute.'

'Okay, but be careful. I don't trust that fellow. He's got a strange smell about him.' He shuffled off towards the Balanspoort.

As Jos hobbled back, he recalled the young man's strange reaction when he discovered he had helped his wife and daughter survive the stampede.

'Meneer van den Donker, please forgive my brother. He's very protective of me.' The young man began emptying his wheelbarrow. 'The war is over. Now is the time to build on the peace and forget our differences.'

'We can never ignore the differences between you papists and us.'

'I meant the differences between us as people and citizens. Let's get rid of the animosities that have dogged us since the political events of the 16th century. Forget the actions of fallible men and women. Goodwill motivates most people. That is the basis for fraternal cooperation. We can do this without denying our real differences. I would want you to change your beliefs only when convinced otherwise.'

'The tiger will never lose its stripes. In any case, you're the one who should change.'

The priest hesitated, shifting his weight on his weakened legs. 'Do you believe in the Holy Trinity, three persons in one God?' The young man glanced at the priest. 'Do you believe that the Second Person of the Holy Trinity became incarnate of the Virgin Mary?' Still, there was no more than a glance from the young man. Jos continued to count off the essential beliefs of the Christian faith. The young man kept on working but eventually stopped and stood up straight.

'I live according to the true meaning of the Scriptures—all the Scriptures—especially those your Church has subverted or ignored.' He looked the priest up and down. 'What about your priests in their queer uniform? What about all those black chiefs who parade as clergy, live in palaces, and enjoy a lifestyle that the poor ordinary Christian can only dream of? Have a look at these buildings. They were once the home of your clergy, your brother said. Not a place for the Zeeland peasant. And what about *Kasteel Zaligheid* up there on the coast? I've looked at that castle all my life. No peasant would have seen the interior of that castle, the summer residence of those same papist priests when they had us under their heel.'

Jos's heart sank. There was no way he could respond to these objections on the spot. And the other labourers were looking at them, some making comments.

'Look, Meneer. I just wanted to say we share the same essentials of Christian belief. Let's start from that positive point—that point of agreement—and discuss our differences honestly, openly, and with goodwill. Perhaps the Holy Spirit will enlighten us.'

The young man let out an ironic laugh and then, glancing to the side past the priest, bent down to his work. 'The foreman's coming. Leave me alone if you want me to keep my job.'

Jos turned to see a big man in dusty work clothes approaching them. 'I'm sorry to hold up your worker, Meneer foreman,' he called. 'No fault of his. Just inquiring about his family. I'll be off.'

The foreman stopped, grunted, and turned back in the direction he had come.

'I wish you and your wife and baby all health and blessings. God bless you,' Jos said and turned to walk away.

'How do I know you weren't in with Nazis?'

It seemed more than a question—more like defiance supported by something unknown to Jos. But it hurt. It was not that this angry young man brought to nothing his work; he did that without thought of reward. No, it was that someone could think he would abandon all notion of right and betray his country and fellow man. He stopped and turned around.

'How could you think such a thing?'

The man stood erect, smiled, and then returned to his work. With a heavy heart, Jos limped to his brother standing inside the Balanspoort.

'Can't see you made much of an impression.'

'Yes, you're right, Frans. In fact, I probably confirmed his worst opinions.' The priest held out his open hands as he contemplated the cobblestones under their feet.

'Jos, don't let it upset you. The man's a bigot. He was that way before the war. I've seen him swaggering around the town with his arrogant mates. I doubt whether his hardships have made it worse. The German army would have trouble penetrating that mentality.'

'No, we mustn't give up. We must trust that Meneer van den Donker wants to do the right thing. You might see him as a bigot, full of impenetrable prejudice, but he's convinced he's right about the Church and its clergy.'

'Hitler was convinced he was right. Not much hope in that quarter.'

'No, Frans, I'm not talking about manifestly evil views. We're all capable of recognising such evil. But in Meneer van den Donker's case, we must admit he has grounds for his opinion. The behaviour of some Church prelates, right up to the pope in the Middle Ages was hardly edifying. The trouble is that Cees van den Donker and those like him take the small part for the whole. When the clergy fail, it is a failure of momentous proportions. Perhaps the Abbot's expulsion, together with his confreres, on that day in 1574, was God's punishment for the clergy's sins. We, priests, bear a grave responsibility.'

'Perhaps so. Our friend Van den Donker is, I fear, an exception.'

The priest took his brother's arm, and they walked under the brick archway.

'Nevertheless, we cannot—we must not give up trying to explain to people like him what the Church is really like. We must try to separate the human failure from the purity of the faith, and the Church committed to guarding it.'

Despite the optimistic spirit Fr. Jos tried to project, he could not help pondering the savage war that had just ended. God seemed to have withheld his mercy. But was there a God to withhold mercy? That was the question many were asking. How could a merciful God allow the murder of so many innocent people? Before knocking on that door in Amsterdam, he had not seriously asked that question. The Church of the crucified Saviour had an answer. He had an answer. That richly furnished room with the unblemished face and the red lips threatened to sap the answers of meaning.

'Are you all right, Jos?'

'Yes, Frans, just a little tired.'

'Come on. Sit here for a while,' said Frans, stopping at an iron bench in front of the Town Hall.

'I'll be right in a while.'

He could not remember how he had ended up in that dirty, dark room after the slaughter on Dam Square and the rescue of that young woman, no matter how much he thought about it. Indistinct shades in swirling darkness intruded on his consciousness; all he could recall was cramping pleasure followed by feelings of uselessness and despair. Was it the Nazis who had sought final retribution for the nuisance he had caused them? No, it was more than the evil of Nazism. There was something else, something of intangible evil, something demonic he could not face—at least not alone. Who had led him to that place? Then there was Van den Donker's strange reaction to him when he found him with his wife. He could not make sense of those lost days of darkness and despair. And how was that innocent young woman and her baby faring with that man?

'Frans, I'm ready to talk about what happened.'

'Wait till we're at home and you're rested.'

Later that day, Mevrouw van Engelen brought them coffee and a plate of buttered boluses while they sat in the back garden.

'That will help the conversation, *lieverds*.'

Fr. Jos appreciated the coffee and boluses, as well as his mother's care, but he did not need those refreshments to recall what had happened on that day in Amsterdam. It had now come back in stark relief. He recounted the intervention to save Mevrouw van den Donker and her baby, her husband's reaction, and the message that brought him to that address where the healthy young woman brought him a cup of sickly sweet tea. After that, it was as if he were caught in a nightmarish world where he had snatches of consciousness.

'Do you know where it was, that house?'

'No, I can't recall exactly, but it wasn't among the brothels.'

'You were found in a filthy room in a house on Zeedijk.'

'Was I?'

'Did that young woman with the red lips look like a prostitute?'

'Well, I didn't think so. She was like an attendant in a clinic of some sort. Wait—'

Jos's mind fixed on the hand that handed him the cup of tea, like a camera focusing. There it was, a mark, a symbol, like the one he had seen on Van den Donker's wrist—similar to the one he had seen on Marlies's and Anton's wrist.

'What?'

'That woman had a mark on her wrist like the one Van den Donker has.'

'Has he? I didn't notice. What sort of mark?'

'I don't know—some sort of strange occultist mark.'

'Occultist? Does that ignorant fellow have enough brains to get involved in such weird stuff?'

'Don't underestimate him, Frans. There's depth to that anger.'

'To think that lovely young woman is paired with that misfit.'

'You saw it, too, then?'

'You mean Mevrouw van den Donker? Yes, what a fine example of a Zeeland maiden. You know, you have her to thank for finding you.'

Jos sat up. 'No, really?'

'Yes, she saw me on market day and thought I was you. When I told her I was your brother, she asked me to thank you for your kindness if I found you alive. She didn't have much hope, I might add. You said a prayer with her?'

'She was worried about her husband. She didn't know where he was.'

'Well, she said a prayer for you. It seems it was answered.'

Jos fell silent. Frans, with a glance, did not speak.

'Why haven't you told me before?' said Jos.

'I didn't want to overload you. I've let you decide what to talk about.'

'You've done right,' said Jos after some thought. 'Thank you, Frans. Your support has been unfailing.' He patted him on the arm.

'You'll recover, Jos. Give it time.'

Their mother came to collect the plates and cups. 'You look tired, *lieverd*. You should go and rest.'

'Perhaps, I will. Excuse me, Frans.'

Jos sat in the chair beside his bed, looking out over a vista of partially flooded farmland. For a while, that fresh, innocent face with its heartfelt pleading filled his mind. What if she had not mistaken Frans for him? Would he have survived? It was like a direct intervention of Providence. Now, gratitude added to the sympathy he had for her. The turmoil in his mind subsided, leaving some questions.

On the next market day, he wrapped himself warmly for the cooling autumn weather, donned a beret and sunglasses, and walked into the town center—without Frans. He waited at the corner of Nieuwe Burg and Lange Delft, prepared for a long wait. There was no certainty she would come to town. The water around her village would be a disincentive. After an hour, he could no longer stand. He looked around and was on the point of going to a nearby cafe table when she appeared at the other end of the row of stalls, wheeling a stroller. He steadied himself against the shop wall.

'Hello, Mevrouw,' he said when she arrived at his end of the stalls.

'Oh, Meneer,' she said with one hand to her mouth. 'I didn't know ...' Her eyes filled. She looked around, fidgeting.

'I want to thank you for telling my brother you had seen me. It saved my life.'

'It's me who should thank you,' she said, looking around again. She wiped a tear from her eye. 'You've been unwell.'

'Yes, I'm recovering with the help of my family. Mevrouw, I would like to ask you—'

'What are you up to?' came a voice behind him.

'I'm not up to anything,' said Jos, catching the pleading in the young woman's eyes before he turned. 'I'm merely asking after your wife and family.' It was a half-lie, excusable in the circumstances.

'We're not interested in your papist inquiries.'

Mevrouw van den Donker's expression of surprise told Jos her husband had said nothing about their meeting at the Abbey.

'It's merely a person's concern for ....' He saw an almost imperceptible shake of the young woman's head. 'It's just normal concern.'

'There's nothing normal about you papists. Come on, you,' he said out of the side of his mouth. He turned and walked away.

'I'm sorry,' she mouthed. 'Thank you.' Turning the stroller around, she followed her husband with her head down.

Jos watched until they had mingled with the crowd near the Town Hall. How could that man treat his wife like that? Surely, she was a wife to be treasured and proud of. He returned to his parents' house, frustrated that he could not receive an answer to his questions.

'You can't pin his obnoxiousness entirely on his cramped Calvinist background,' said Frans when Jos told of his meeting. 'I hear he gives his church community heartburn. I can't see that enduring for very long.'

The clash did not deter Jos. He must speak to her; the only way was to seek her out on market day. Her village was not an option. Suspecting she would come to the market at the same time, he arranged to meet Frans late in the morning at one of the cafes on the square. He was right. Mevrouw van den Donker appeared in the same row around the same time. She did not look in his direction as she moved along the stalls, now without her baby and stroller, but she glanced at him at the end of the row and shook her head.

'It looks like she doesn't want to talk to you.'

'Or is not allowed to.'

A short time after she had disappeared into the next row of stalls, Van den Donker, dressed in his work clothes, hastened by, looking around. He did not notice the two brothers.

'He obviously keeps an eye on his wife. That's taking a risk if he has left his work.'

Jos did not reply, again frustrated. The following market day, it was the same. A little shake of the head, and she walked on, but Van den Donker did not appear this time. Jos was without Frans the following week. Frans said it was not likely she would ever be free of that ruffian's supervision. Besides, his workload was increasing. He was wrong. She gave him a nod as she turned into the next row of stalls. Jos followed.

'Meneer, I mean, Father, please walk behind me as if you are viewing the wares,' she said as he came up to her. 'I have five minutes.'

'It's not necessary to call me Father, Mevrouw. Whatever you're comfortable with. Thank you for seeing me. I wanted to ask you about that day.' She nodded. 'Did you see me after you and your husband and his friend left me?'

'Yes, when we reached the Dam, Cees and his friend stared up Damrak as if they were looking for something. Then I saw you cross Damrak and walk towards Warmoestraat, at least in that direction.'

'Were they looking for me?'

'I don't know. I couldn't see what interested them.'

'What did they do, then?'

'Cees's friend whispered something. Then Cees took my baby and me to a nearby cafe and told me to wait until they returned. He returned about forty minutes later without his friend.'

'Where did they go?'

'I don't know. I didn't pay attention. Cees was always going off with his new friends and leaving me alone. Meneer, I can't talk anymore.'

'New friends?'

'Yes, people he had met in Amsterdam.'

'What's that mark on Cees's wrist?'

'I have no idea—something to do with those friends. He told me to forget about it. Meneer, I must go. Please.' She turned, facing him. 'I hope you get well soon. I'll say a prayer.'

He looked down at the innocent, pleading face—the face of an angel. 'Thank you, Mevrouw. God bless you.'

Knowing she feared her husband catching her in the act, he turned and walked in the opposite direction. He sat at a cafe table and ordered a cup of coffee. Sitting outside made him visible, something he tried to avoid. He was a priest on leave, after all. But it could not be helped. As he sat there sipping his coffee, he owned up to a growing interest that he should be careful of, an interest Femke had never excited. But she was suffering—unfairly, unjustly. A priest's duty was to succour the afflicted. Van den Donker emerged from the milling people and, seeing him, stopped. He stared for a moment and then approached.

'What are you doing here, you papist snake? As if I didn't know.'

'Your manner has now exceeded the bounds of acceptability, Meneer.'

'To hell with your bourgeois manners. You keep away from my wife.'

'What's that mark on your wrist?'

Surprised, Van den Donker looked at his wrist and pulled his sleeve over the mark.

'Just keep away from my wife.' He came closer and wagged a finger in Jos's face.

The threat and the action made Jos uneasy. He was losing control of the situation. His concern for that vulnerable young woman and the conflict with her belligerent husband were a dangerous development. But he just wanted to clarify what happened in Amsterdam. That was all, he told himself. Twenty minutes later, as he left the cafe, Van den Donker again confronted him.

'I won't tell you again. Keep away from my wife, or I'll do something about it.'

'I've not done anything wrong, Meneer. Neither has your wife. You shouldn't threaten people.'

'You and your class. Yes, your father and brother will protect you, won't they?'

'Now you're contradicting yourself. My father and brother have responsible positions in this town, but they are also Catholic.'

'Just keep away from my wife. You are warned.'

With a snarl on his lips, Van den Donker marched off, his head erect. Shaken, Jos watched until he merged with the people entering Noordstraat on the right of the Town Hall. As he left to return home, his legs locked and buckled, forcing him to steady himself against the chairs outside the restaurant. He feared he could not manage the distance to his parents' house. By stopping frequently, however, he made it without collapsing, though it was a near thing. His mother helped him to his room and made him lie down.

'You're doing too much, *lieverd*. You must rest. If you're not careful, you'll make yourself sick.'

The warning came too late. Jos caught a cold that worsened over the week. The doctor came and, making many points with a poking finger, subjected him to a long lecture. It was obviously not getting through to him that his deprivation during the war had severely weakened him. Time was needed to regain his health. Moreover, the winter was almost on them, which could mean his death if he did not stay warm. Resignation to his incapacity was tough, but there was no getting around it. He must rest. Besides, he must not now seek out that young woman. It was not because of any wrong he did or any threat that the brute made, but because of the possible scandal. There was something else, too, something he was reluctant to face, something that had never happened to him.

The months keeping him inside were not too tedious. Frans was an eager partner in conversation, keeping him up to date with the town's restoration and rebuilding. He had much to read from his father's library. His sisters came to visit, bringing their fiancés with them. Cheery folks, they were, full of farm talk while their future wives looked on, beaming. Aunts and uncles turned up and delighted him with their gossip. Willeke, his second oldest sister, married just before Christmas. His mother made an exception by wrapping a blanket around his heavy winter clothes and having him driven to the church, there to sit like an enormous stuffed animal.

He had set up an upstairs room to say Mass each day. Then, there were the feasts of Saint Nicholas and Christmas, the verses composed for Saint Nicholas, causing laughter and merriment. He even received Christmas greetings from Fr. van Rossem, with a postscript asking him to send a doctor's report about his health. He waited until the new year to carry out that instruction, offering the busy Christmas period as an excuse for his tardiness. A reply came asking him to be more specific about a date for returning to his priestly duties. Arrangements had to be made, Fr. Jos should understand. The doctor said he would write to the superior general. It was silly to go through a third party.

'Before I write, I think you should consider laicization. I don't think you're fit to continue as a priest. The work will be too demanding. I will provide medical evidence that will pass the highest tribunal in Rome.'

'You think I'm so damaged?'

'I don't think, Fr. van Engelen. I know. I am a doctor.'

'No, not for one moment will I consider it.'

'Don't be foolish, Father. I've known your family for a long time. I have an idea of your vulnerabilities.'

'No, doctor. Please don't express that opinion in your letter to Fr. van Rossem. That's my request. I will return to health, won't I?'

'Yes, reasonable health. That's not the issue. It's whether you'll have sufficient stamina to do the work.'

'I'm a priest forever after the order of Melchizedek. There will be something I can do, even if it's sweeping the refectory floor.'

'As you wish, Father, but I don't think they'll have you sweeping the refectory floor somehow.'

Two weeks later, a letter arrived asking him to report to the seminary at the end of May when the weather was warming. There would be discussions about his next assignment—with his state of health in mind. On the first sunny day in spring, Jos ventured outside after receiving permission from his mother, who had strictly overseen his progress in consultation with the doctor. She set him up with Frans in the back garden.

'Now you're to come inside if the sun disappears behind the clouds.'

'Yes, Mamma. Thank you.'

She brought them coffee and stroopwafels while they talked.

'I feel a lot better now, much better than before Christmas. It won't be long before I return to my duties.'

'You appear a lot better, I have to admit. So what's going to happen to you?'

'I don't know. Nothing has come from the motherhouse.'

'What do you hope?'

'To return to the missions in Papua and New Guinea.'

'What are the chances?'

'I have no idea. The reason I was recalled to Holland, I assume, is buried with Fr. Albers.'

'Were his suspicions correct?'

'I can't be entirely sure. There were indications of changes in attitudes, but I can't be definite about what and who the agents were. It was clearer in Bart's mind. He agreed with Fr. Albers.'

'That there was subversion?'

'Yes, along Marxist lines.'

'Poor unfortunate Bart.'

'Yes, I feel responsible for dragging him into it. I'm sure he had little idea what he was getting into.'

'No, Jos. Bart was a solid, straightforward fellow. No delusions. He took on the same risks as you and me. On your account of things, you were all betrayed.'

'That's what Bart would say.'

'Again, from what you've told me, Van Rossem and Muller were likely the culprits for whatever reasons they had. I never liked Muller—such a slimy character.'

'Please, Frans.'

'No, Jos, don't let your worthy feelings of charity blind you to the truth.'

Jos frowned. They fell into silence for a few minutes.

'Bart was missing an element in the change of attitudes. It was not wholly Marxist, you know, all that talk about capitalism and class. It had a Hegelian colour about it, a sort of dialectical changing of spirit, not particularly linked to the material.'

'Now you're losing me, Jos.'

'It was reflected in the conversation of one of the advanced seminarians, a smart fellow named Hans de Jonge.'

'The question remains: what will you do?'

'I don't know. Anyhow, it's likely I won't be able to do anything much. Fr. van Rossem has hinted that my responsibilities will be light. The missions will have to wait if I get there at all.'

'Poor Jos and you're just going to swallow it from those two suspicious characters.'

'Don't be silly, Frans. You know the commitment. And, please, a little more respect for my superiors.'

'Yes, older brother.'

The conversation moved away from Jos's position and prospects and meandered through the family's concerns and Walcheren's clean-up. In his work as a notary, Frans had much to do. His business was thriving. Sadly, much of his work came from restoring and reorganising Middelburg and the surrounding localities.

'Have you seen Van den Donker and his wife?'

'I've caught a glimpse of Truus van den Donker on market days. Otherwise, she's seldom seen. Her obnoxious husband is another matter. I pass him in the streets. If he weren't so busy going somewhere or other, I'm sure he would stop to abuse me. As it is, he just gives me a sneering look. They tell me he's very busy sorting out his family's property. He's already rebuilt the farmhouse outside Vrouwekerke, using cast-off material, which he has got from next to nothing. He has initiative if one has nothing else to say about him.'

'And their religious activity?'

'Sorry, Jos, I've no interest in those wacky Calvinist groups.'

'Remember, Frans, that young woman who so impressed you is a member of one.'

'Yes, well, I'm sorry for her. She deserves more.'

Jos was silent for a while.

'Would you find out how she is going? I would like to know before I leave.'

'Just out of pastoral interest?' Frans glanced at him.

'I would just like to know how she is. I owe her a debt.'

'Yes, brother. It so happens I will be out that way in the coming week. But let's leave that. There's something I want to show you.' He looked at his watch.

'What?'

'In a few minutes. Be patient.' He again glanced at his watch.

Jos waited, observing a cheeky smile on Frans's face. A few minutes more, and they heard the front doorbell. 'Frans!' their mother called. Frans rose and hurried inside to return with an attractive young woman a minute later.

'Fr. Jos, let me introduce Marijke Martens. We've been seeing each other for a few months.'

'Well, this is a surprise. Please to meet you, Juffrouw.' Fr. Jos rose and held out his hand.

'It's Marijke, Father. It's a pleasure. Frans has said much about you.'

'I didn't want to say anything until things progressed,' said Frans, unusually sheepish.

'And they have.' Marijke took Frans's hand and drew him to her.

Frans had seen Marijke in December when he visited the family home to discuss business with her father. He had had a slight acquaintance with her as a member of the Catholic community. She was six years younger and had been in England since before the war.

'I noticed she had changed,' he said, laughing.

'Yes, Father, I was in London, furthering my education when the Germans invaded.'

'She seems a delightful young woman,' said Jos after Marijke had left to drive home.

'We hit it off immediately. I mean, when I saw her at home last December.'

'Are you engaged?'

'No, just seeing each other for the moment. Testing things. But I have hopes. And I hope you'll be around to fulfil those hopes. Do we have your blessing?'

'I've only seen her this once, but she seems a most charming, cultivated young woman. Of course, you do.'

Frans's developing relationship and the meeting with Marijke seemed to conclude Jos's convalescence in Middelburg, as did Frans's news about Truus van den Donker. He had been out to Grijpskerke and stopped at Vrouwekerke on the way back. The water had receded in that area because of the work to repair the dykes. He cautiously checked to see if anyone was at home as he cycled past her street. Truus was in the front yard, attending to the gardens. Her daughter, now mobile, was close by. He stopped, allowing her to wave him away. She did not.

'How are you, Mevrouw?'

'I'm all right, thank you, Meneer van Engelen,' she said, leaning lightly on the spade she had used to turn the soil.

'I'm happy to see much improvement in your house.'

'How is your brother?'

'He is a lot better.'

'I am relieved to hear that.' She looked down at the fresh soil she had turned. 'God has preserved him.' She looked up. 'I imagine he will soon depart.'

'Yes, not long now.'

'Please pass on my best wishes—and my prayers.'

'Certainly, Mevrouw van den Donker.'

He did not stay any longer. She made it clear she did not want to extend the conversation, though showing no anxiety. He wished her the best and continued his way.

'I think she only allowed me to approach to hear about you.'

'She's grateful for my action during the stampede.'

'Is that all?'

'There's nothing else. We are grateful for each other's kindness. There cannot be any more.'

Frans could see his brother did not want to pursue the subject. He, too, understood Jos wished to return to the motherhouse and his life as a priest. The suspicion that there could be another reason did not escape him.

JOS WROTE to Fr. van Rossem, assuring him he was fit and ready to return—the sooner, the better. It was earlier than planned, but he was ready to go. He informed the extended family of his plans and thanked them for their support and warmth. In response, they came to gossip, drink coffee, eat boluses, and hug him tightly. A reply came a week later from Fr. van Rossem with instructions. He had a special dinner with his parents, Frans, and his sisters, expressing his gratitude for their support. A few days before he left, he asked Frans to walk with him around Middelburg centre, the same route they had taken when he had had trouble walking. It was market day, a day he had chosen deliberately, a day on which Middelburg was most vibrant. It would be his last taste of the town of his birth, which had instilled his love of the countryside. After finishing their tour, they sat again at an outside table and ordered lunch.

'It's a fitting end to your stay,' said Frans, looking around. 'It's a beautiful day, and the market is humming. If it weren't for the rebuilding, you wouldn't know the war had happened.'

'Yes, indeed.'

Their chat wandered around the family, avoiding the subject of Jos's return to his priestly duties. Frans spoke about Marijke, expressing his pleasure that his brother had found her so charming and cultivated.

'You know, she has had the best education, considering the times, achieving a bachelor's degree—fluent in English. I think proficiency in English will be very important in the coming years. The countries with stable economies are all English-speaking.'

Jos did not have a chance to remark on this observation. Truus van den Donker, wheeling a stroller, came out of the row of stalls in front of them and, on seeing the brothers, came over.

'Goedemorgen, Father and Meneer van Engelen. Please stay where you are,' she said as they began to rise. 'I won't stay. I understand you'll be leaving Middelburg shortly.'

'Yes, Mevrouw, I'll be gone in a few days.'

'You're enjoying your gallows meal,' she said with a brief smile, using an expression popular in the area when someone was setting out on a long voyage.

'You could say that,' said Jos, returning the smile.

'I thank you again for your kindness, and the Lord be with you.'

'Same to you, Mevrouw, and no thanks necessary.'

'Yes, there is. Goedemorgen, Meneer van Engelen.' She turned the stroller around and went on her way.

The brothers watched her go.

'You could cry when you see such a sweet young woman so unhappy.'

Jos nodded and looked away.

Chapter 19

Return to the seminary

SIX YEARS EARLIER, he had made the same trip, Jos mused as he looked out of the train window at the dew-soaked fields rushing by. Was it portentous that the weather was clear and sunny in contrast with the cold, the wind, and the sleet the train had travelled through in March 1940? A lay brother was at the station to pick him up. He welcomed him but was not talkative, providing brief answers to Fr. Jos's inquiries about the community. On arrival, the brother led him to the reception room and, taking his bags, told him to wait for Fr. van Rossem, who would be along shortly. That 'shortly' extended to forty-five minutes. No worry. Jos was content to wait, taking in his surroundings after an absence of six years, some of which took him to the depths of the netherworld.

The windows of the reception room looked out over the avenue and the fields beyond. It was the same scene as six years before. The image of the silhouetted figure on the poorly moonlit night flashed through his mind, but he resisted searching for its meaning. He still could not return to a sustained appraisal of what that image meant. But now, he had to prepare himself. Fr. van Rossem was sure to bring up the gap in his memory. Or perhaps not. Fr. van Rossem strolled into the reception room to save further soul-searching.

'Welcome, Fr. van Engelen,' he said, holding out a hand. 'You look well enough, I am happy to say. You seem to have recovered from your ordeal.'

Dr. van Rossem had changed little in six years, except for the scowl. It had gone as well as the disgruntled waspish tone.

'Thank you, Father. I feel quite well.'

'Very good. Now, we will speak later about your experiences, if you wish to talk about them, that is. I understand you might feel reluctant to dwell on unpleasantness and would rather make a clean start. The sooner we put the war behind us, the better, wouldn't you think? It might be wise to concentrate on your next assignment. In any case, we'll discuss those matters with Fr. Muller, my right-hand man and deputy superior general. It's nearly noon and time for chapel. At lunch, you will sit with me so I can introduce you to the community, and they can welcome you. There are new faces, as you would expect.'

Van Rossem made much of Jos's return at lunch, and the community responded with welcoming smiles. Muller, stationed on the other side of Van Rossem, made an effort to greet him in the same friendly way but could not banish the irony from his eyes.

'Well, Fr. Jos, you're back with us again, are you? I suppose you could write a book about your experiences.'

'Yes, Father, I have been through much. Some of it I would rather forget.'

'I can imagine.'

'Let's leave that for later,' said Van Rossem. 'There is time enough for those matters. We want a relaxing lunch.'

After lunch, Van Rossem took him to the community room to meet the old and new staff. The reception was warm and friendly, but with a superficial allusion to the war and Jos's experiences. It was as if someone had instructed them not to burden him with painful, unwanted questions. When he had exchanged words with everyone, Van Rossem beckoned.

'You can talk at leisure with your colleagues later,' he said, leading Jos from the community room.

'I did not see Hans de Jonge. I assume he was ordained.'

'Oh, yes, Hans de Jonge, is now Fr. de Jonge. We've sent him to the Oceania Province. He is in Sydney. We have high hopes for Fr. Hans.' He glanced at Jos. 'Hans has a keen interest in the liturgy.'

It was unclear what the connection was between high hopes, Sydney, and the liturgy, but Jos let it pass. No doubt, an explanation would follow. Muller joined them in Van Rossem's office, the very office where Fr. Albers had plotted resistance to the Nazis. Jos struggled to rid his mind of those memories as Muller opened the conversation.

'Now, about your sudden disappearance. It seems to us, considering what happened, that you were involved with Fr. Bart and Fr. Albers. Is that right?'

'You don't have to go into a lot of detail,' said Van Rossem, frowning at Muller, 'just confirmation of what we've concluded.'

'Yes, I was, and I am devastated Fr. Bart lost his life.'

'So are we,' said Muller. 'He wasn't in it at first, was he?'

'No. It was just Fr. Albers and me.' Jos was on his guard at the tone of Muller's questions.

'How did it happen?' said Van Rossem before Muller could continue.

'I don't know about Fr. Albers, but the British approached me when I arrived in London.'

'That's where the transmitter came from?' said Muller.

'That's right.'

'Pretty amateurish stuff, don't you think? Two people dead because of it.'

Jos frowned and stared at Muller. 'How did the Nazis know? I hear it was a sudden raid.'

'Because you were stupid.'

'How did they know Fr. Albers and Fr. Bart were the ones with the transmitter?'

Jos fixed his eyes on Muller. Muller blinked, the irony disappearing for an instant.

'You made mistakes, young Jos. Albers was stupid enough to be operating the transmitter from this room when the Germans raided.'

So that was it. A plant. There's no way he had made mistakes in transmitting, and there was no way Fr. Albers would have been so careless for the simple reason that he did not know how to operate the transmitter or knew the necessary codes. Moreover, transmission had to be brief and from an isolated place. Muller was giving himself away. He didn't know what he was talking about. But who had planted the transmitter in the room? And how come Fr. Albers and Bart were allegedly operating it just when the Nazis raided? If, indeed, it all had happened that way, and his superiors were not concocting a story. Jos's staring silence caused Muller to shift.

'If that's what you think. It hardly matters now.'

Van Rossem and Muller exchanged glances.

'How did you escape the raid?' continued Muller.

'Fr. Albers sent me on an urgent errand.'

'For what and where to?'

Fr. Jos hesitated again. No, he would not cooperate.

'I would rather not say.'

'What does it matter if you tell us?'

'Indeed, it doesn't matter. There's no point anymore.'

'You're required to answer your superior's questions.'

'Where did you go?' said Van Rossem, with an admonishing glance at Muller.

'It's a long story. Let me just say I ended up in Amsterdam cooperating with the resistance. And I had the care of a small group of elderly people.'

'I can see you're tired,' said Van Rossem after a short pause and another glance at Muller. 'We'll leave it for another time. We were going to talk about a possible assignment, but we might postpone that, too. Just one question. Is there anything in particular you would like to do?'

'I would like to return to New Guinea, where I was before the war.'

Van Rossem and Muller seemed pleased.

'Well, we'll talk about it tomorrow,' said Van Rossem. 'This afternoon, you can relax—take a walk around the grounds in this mild weather. The flowers are blooming, and there's a lovely scent in the air. Join us for afternoon tea.'

'Where are the graves of Fr. Bart and Fr. Albers?'

For the first time, Van Rossem appeared uncomfortable.

'I will ask Br de Beer to show you. Don't be disappointed. We need time to erect a suitable monument for them. You understand the Germans would not allow any elaborate ceremony.'

The young lay brother showed him to his room on the ground floor, not far from the reception and away from the priests' rooms. It was more like a guest room. He found all that he had left behind packed in boxes. The boxes would probably stay unpacked. His stay at the motherhouse, he suspected, would be short. Br de Beer left him to settle in. Twenty minutes later, he returned to lead him to the graves. His manner was rather stiff, with polite responses to Jos's questions about the community. Jos wondered if he had instructions not to be free about the community. He hoped his fears were groundless and he was not letting his imagination get away from him. Since the execution of Bart and Fr. Albers, circumstances had made him question everything about the seminary. He should check that inclination. Br de Beer was, however, more responsive when he remarked on the state of the grounds.

'The gardens are bursting with colour and life,' Jos said as he followed him towards the bottom of the property. 'You wouldn't think a war had gone on.'

'The Germans didn't bother us too much. Life went on as usual for most of the time. We attended to the gardens, perhaps more because of the restrictions.'

'Restrictions?'

'The Germans permitted only the seminary's religious routine. We couldn't go anywhere. Otherwise, they left us alone.'

'I would've thought the Nazi jackboot was everywhere here.'

Br de Beer glanced at Jos. 'No, the commandant came now and then, sometimes with officers, one an SS officer, spoke with Dr van Rossem and left. I attended them. They were very military, but treated me okay. The commandment seemed to get on with Dr van Rossem. I suppose that was fortunate for us. Fr. Muller said everything would be all right if we didn't cause any trouble. And we didn't.'

'That was fortunate, indeed. The Nazis elsewhere acted like barbarians.'

That seemed the signal to Br de Beer that he had said enough. By this time, they were near the boundary. Jos looked around for the graves. They had already passed the cemetery. Where could they be? When they reached the fence, Br de Beer, with Jos following, left the path and walked to a tall oak tree whose branches fanned out over a wide space. He pointed to two small, rough wooden crosses stuck in the ground amid thick grass and weeds. Bart's and Albers's names were scratched in the wood.

'There.'

Jos collapsed to his knees, his hands covering his face. He bent over until his forehead pressed against the wet grass and weeds. The moist earth filled his nostrils.

'No, no.'

'The Germans made us bury them here,' Br de Beer hastened to say, alarm in his voice. 'We weren't allowed near them after that. It was a strict order, Fr. Muller warned us.'

The strength sapped from Jos's limbs, and he rolled over onto the grass and weeds. Br de Beer gaped at the prostrate priest.

'Let me help you up, Father,' he said, grabbing his arm. He lifted Jos to his feet and steadied him. He waited while Jos composed himself.

'Thank you, Brother. I'll be all right. Thank you.'

But he wasn't all right. Br de Beer had to assist him back to his room, where he collapsed on his bed.

'It's clear you have a way to go before you are fit enough for normal duties,' said Van Rossem when they had summoned Jos to another interview.

'A long way from it,' said Muller, shaking his head.

'Your doctor warned us. I see what he meant.'

'I was just shocked at the state of the graves. Fr. Bart was a close friend.'

'We weren't happy with it, either,' said Muller, 'but we didn't see the need to roll in the dirt ...'

Van Rossem raised his hand at Muller. 'The detail doesn't matter. What is important is your condition. So, taking Fr. Muller's advice, I have decided. We are assigning you to a rural parish in South Limburg, assisting the parish priest. It will not be hard on you. It's a small parish, and Fr. Vroom is known for his easy-going ways. We'll see how you go before we decide anything else.'

Jos bowed his head. He was too tired, his head too much of a muddle to discuss his future.

'I have just one request,' he said, looking up. 'May I have your permission to visit Meneer and Mevrouw Vos? They became close friends. I owe them a debt.'

Van Rossem and Muller looked at each other.

'One moment,' said Muller, going to the door. 'I will be back in a moment.'

He returned with Br de Beer, who stood at the door while Muller resumed his seat.

'It is with great sorrow and regret that I have to tell you that those faithful people were killed during the liberation of Breda,' said Van Rossem.

'Oh, no. Not them, too.' Jos felt a steadying hand on his shoulder. 'How?'

'Shot. They were found dead after the Germans surrendered.'

'Where?'

'What does it matter?' said Muller. 'They were tragic casualties of the war.'

'Where? I want to know.'

Van Rossem glanced at Muller. 'Their son found them dead at their farm.'

'Why would anyone want to kill that old couple? What use was that?'

'Who knows?' said Muller. 'There was chaos in the final fighting.' He paused. 'What was the debt?'

Jos hesitated. How much should he reveal? He would test them.

'They gave me shelter when I learned of the Nazi raid.'

In the uneasy silence that followed, Van Rossem and Muller stared at him without glancing at each other, as they had been doing.

'You probably got them killed,' said Muller.

'Five years later? And what was the point? How would the Germans know there was a third spy?'

Despite his effort to remain composed, Van Rossem gave Muller an angry look.

'Where did you go after that?' said Muller, ignoring Van Rossem.

'What does it matter?' said Jos, his head in his hands.

'Indeed, it does not matter at this stage,' said Van Rossem, again checking Muller with a raised hand. 'The important task for you now is to regain your health. We have made arrangements for your immediate passage to Limburg. Br de Beer, would you please help Fr. Jos to his room? Fr. Jos, will you join us in the common room later, if you are up to it? You can say your farewells to your priestly brothers. You may not have another chance.'

'Yes, of course, Father,' said Jos while Br de Beer helped him to his feet. At the door, he glanced back at his interrogators. They had their eyes fixed on him, Van Rossem straining to appear composed, Muller making no effort to check his customary sneer. Back in his room, it suddenly occurred to Jos that he had visited Mevrouw and farmer Vos after Breda had been liberated. It was another concocted story with the necessary implications—and warnings.

FR. VAN ROSSEM was right about Fr. Vroom. He was a jovial, overfed parish priest who preached an uncomplicated faith to an uncomplicated congregation whose minds were open to the parables of the Good Samaritan and Prodigal Son and Jesus's mercy to the woman caught in adultery. Charity was the cement of the community in that little rural parish. It reminded Jos of his congregation in Lae. There was the same simple faith that made sense of their lives. He settled into his duties with full support and encouragement from Fr. Vroom.

It was a pleasant routine of saying Mass, hearing confessions, marrying, baptising, giving the last rites, and hearing all the petty troubles that beset his good-hearted country folk. Fr. Vroom only intervened to gossip, make a joke, or invite him to share his dinner wine. The tension of the last six years flowed out of him. It was like a valve had been opened. Soon, he was so at peace with the world that he began questioning his long-held suspicions. Could he really be right about the monstrous deeds he suspected of his superiors? No, it was too terrible to conceive. They could not do such things and remain priests. The conflict would be too great. They would surely snap under the guilt. No, he should let it go.

To aid him in rationalising some very dark deeds, Fr. van Rossem wrote solicitous, encouraging letters. Jos should not hesitate to contact him if he had any worries. He promised to look kindly on his wish to return to his parish in Lae. The friendliness extended to permitting Jos to attend the weddings of the two remaining sisters. To top off this generous support and encouragement, he allowed him to officiate at Frans's wedding as long as Fr. Vroom was agreeable. A hearty laugh was Fr. Vroom's reply to the request. 'Of course, lad, go and enjoy yourself, don't drink too much, and give my blessings to the couple.' Jos heard nothing from Fr. Muller, not that he expected it. It was just that Muller had his nose in everything.

Jos was so pleasantly engaged in his duties that he hardly noticed three years had eased by before Fr. van Rossem wrote to inquire whether he still felt the call to return to New Guinea. Being confronted so abruptly by the question broke him out of his dream. Could he now leave his parish and the dear people he cared for? It was a troubling decision, but he shook himself out of his dream and wrote to Van Rossem, saying he was ready to go whenever he allowed. Things moved quickly after that as if someone feared he would reverse his decision. Papers were prepared, passage booked, and instructions sent.

So, three years later, in May 1949, Fr. Jos van Engelen sat with his family at a table outside a cafe on Marktplein in Middelburg. Before setting off for his next assignment, he was enjoying a coffee with his family. It was a sunny Thursday, market day. Rows of stalls and a multitude of people walking between them crammed the square. Many women and men still wearing their district's traditional costume added colour to the crowd, milling about and pushing each other as they made their way from stall to stall.

'This is one of the great sights of Middelburg, isn't it? It's like the war never took place,' said Jos, scanning the scene.

'Take a good look, Jos,' said his father. 'You may not see it for some time.'

'You are right, Pappa. But as much as I love my old town, it's time to return to my old job. I hope you won't forget to write.'

'Of course, we won't,' said Marijke, who held her baby daughter Anneke. 'We'll ensure you regularly get a little Dutch cheer through the mail.'

'I appreciate that, Marijke. Truly.'

They chatted and drank their coffee while watching the people bustle from row to row. Jos's eyes came to rest on a young woman with a child of about five years struggling alongside her. 'Excuse me,' he said, getting up, 'I won't be a minute.' Leaving his family staring after him, he hastened to the woman on the point of entering one of the rows.

'Mevrouw van den Donker.'

She swung around, putting her hand to her mouth. 'Oh, Meneer, I mean, Father, it's really you.' She stepped to the side, pulling the little girl with her.

'Yes, it's really me,' he said with a smile.

'I ... I hoped I would come across you someday.' She shifted and blushed. 'The last time I saw you was more than three years ago ... here, with your brother.' She glanced at the family, looking at them. 'You were sent elsewhere?'

'Yes.'

There was a nervous pause.

'You look better, though still thin.'

'Thank you, Mevrouw,' he smiled again and then turning to the little girl: 'Hello Gerda, are you enjoying the market?' The little girl scarcely glanced at him. 'Yes, I have been in Limburg. I am back here for a few days to spend with my family. Tomorrow, I set off for New Guinea. That's where I was until shortly before the war's outbreak, when I came home for a visit. The war kept me in Holland.'

'That was my good fortune.'

'Providence works in strange ways.'

She nodded and rubbed her daughter's head, leaning timidly against her.

'Yes, Providence does act in strange ways. Not only did you pluck my baby and me from death that day, but you gave us hope, at least me. We were desperate. I am sure you guessed that. Little did I realise a man dressed as a beggar would come to our aid. Do you want to know how things are ... what happened after I saw you in Amsterdam? Do you have time? You asked before when I couldn't talk. I was sorry about that. I can now.'

'Of course, Mevrouw,' said Jos, pleased but surprised at the change.

'Well, after much urging from me, Cees decided we had no choice but to return to Walcheren. He refused to go to the address in Amsterdam. So, we made our way by ourselves to Middelburg. The trip was difficult, and we were exhausted when we arrived. Pastor Hendrikse provided us with food and accommodation. Cees soon had work. You know, they had to repair the bombed dykes. He worked on the dykes until he could get labouring work at the Abbey. It was not as backbreaking, he said. When we were settled, he set about rebuilding the family house and finding out what happened to the family property. You may guess what resulted from Cees's single-mindedness. The shocking tragedy of having the whole family wiped out meant that all their property came to us from both sides of the family. We actually inherited quite a lot of property and money. We are quite well off now. Terrible, isn't it?'

'It is sad, but I'm glad to hear you're comfortable.'

'Yes, we are materially comfortable. But, in other ways, it's just like we remained in the war.' Her eyes filled. 'You must excuse my husband, Meneer, I mean Father.' She brushed an encroaching tear from the corner of one eye.

'Please, you don't have to call me Father. Whatever suits you.'

'No, no, I'll call you Father. Cees was already an intense, sombre person before the war. The war just made it worse. He became very bitter about the destitute circumstances we ended up in. Perhaps we should have stayed in Zeeland. We have heard there was enough food here to prevent people from starving. But Cees thought the Germans would force him to work in their factories. Anyhow, there we were in Amsterdam, struggling to survive.'

'Actually, we weren't even married when we fled the Germans. Of course, we had always intended to get married, but at the time, our parents thought we were too young. We got married as soon as we could because ... you know. Then I fell pregnant. Instead of making Cees happy, it made him even more bitter about the world. Why did we have to bring a child into all that misery? he exclaimed. Nothing I could do or say would appease him. That day on Dam Square, he had arranged to meet someone about work. The poor man was trampled to death. Cees already knew that when he found me. It only increased his bitterness. I'm so sorry about the way he acted towards you.' She put her hand on his arm, but quickly withdrew it.

'His mood became even darker after that. His anger ... I thought he would burst. Then he left me that morning, not long after you—and I don't know why. He went with that friend you saw. I sat alone in that cafe with my daughter, but he was better later. Well, you know all that ... the last time we spoke.' She shrugged. 'I always wanted to thank you more fully than I have. Now, I have the chance to do so. Thank you for saving our lives. I will never forget it.'

'I was doing what every human being should do in the circumstances.' He gazed at her fresh, young face with the smooth, rounded cheeks, limpid eyes, and lustrous hair tied back. 'Is Cees really not at all improved in spirits?' Surely this compassionate, lovely young woman, dressed modestly and conscious of her duties, was all a man could wish for in a wife?

'I'm afraid not,' she said, looking down at her daughter and brushing her hair. 'In some ways, it's worse. It has become very political. He associates all the ills of his life with people of authority, and he associates all authority with the Nazis or people like them. I just don't understand it. We're well off. Cees is a hard worker, and it wasn't long before the farms made good profits. With those profits, he could buy into other businesses. They're all doing well. And still, he's as bitter and obsessive as he was when the war ended. I had hoped for a change ...' She shrugged again.

'Doesn't your faith make it easier for him?'

'No, he has so twisted it that it supports his views. I don't understand it. It's like there's something else there ... and I can't do anything about it. He gets ...' She hopelessly shook her head. 'Anyhow, I suppose I must move on now. You're with your family. And we're standing in the way here, you know.' A nervous smile brightened her face. 'Thank you, Fr. van Engelen. You see, I'm comfortable with your name now,' and then, as if another thought came into her head, 'I won't forget we prayed together. It's so strange when you are a Romish priest.'

'I'll keep you in my prayers,' he said as she moved off, leading the little girl by the hand. 'Goodbye, Gerda,' he called, but the little girl ignored him. He watched them disappear into the bustling crowd and then walked absently back to his family, who looked at him without saying anything. He sat down and ran a hand over the leg that was still weak.

'I don't have to tell you who that was, do I?'

'No,' said Frans. 'Truus van den Donker is as lovely as ever.'

'Yes, she is a fine-looking woman,' said Marijke. 'It's such a pity she is trapped with that unpleasant husband.'

Jos was on the point of inquiring further, but Frans spoke before him.

'That abusive fellow, you wouldn't believe it, has fallen on his feet, gone from a labourer to a well-to-do farmer and business proprietor. He rebuilt and extended the farmhouse at Vrouwekerke. If I'm not mistaken, he'll end up a big boy in this part of the world.'

'She told me they had inherited a lot of property from family killed during the war.'

'Well, he's putting it to good use. And I'll probably have business with him in the end. I don't look forward to it.'

'Oh, that's so sad,' said his mother. 'They won't forget how that money came to them.'

'We will all feel the effects of the war,' his father observed. 'I hope that young man learns how to deal with it for the sake of his family.'

'I do, too, Pappa,' said the priest, but he did not like their chances.

That evening, during the family farewell, he could not help thinking about Cees van den Donker and his wife. On the train the next day on the way to Rotterdam harbour, he still had them on his mind, especially the sad, appealing expression on the fresh, youthful face of Mevrouw van den Donker. He felt a nagging despondency about her. No, he told himself, he must shake it off. He must keep hope as he encouraged others to do. But dark, indistinct visions came back to him and mingled with the effort to stay optimistic. It was not until he was back in New Guinea in the coastal town of Lae and bearing the full load of his work that his mind was released from obsessing about the war, Femke, the motherhouse, Cees van den Donker, his pining wife, and passive little daughter who did not share her mother's good looks. Those stories had ended, he tried to convince himself.

IF HIS workload did not give much mind space to wonder what was happening to Truus van den Donker, Marijke made sure that whatever there was, filled that space. She wrote every few months, and in each letter, she included some snippets, trivial things, but enough to ensure her story continued. Not even when his superior in Lae, the parish priest, was recalled to Sydney, leaving him with a crushing workload, did the little items cease to focus his mind. Truus was seen at the market, her husband's business interests were growing, and he had branched into property acquisitions and the like. As Frans had foreseen, he had occasional dealings with Van den Donker. To his relief, wrote Marijke, the irascible country boy understood the things at stake and restricted himself under his heavy eyebrows to the bare details of the transaction. Such was the news about the family over the next few years.

The only change was the deepening sadness of Mevrouw van den Donker's expression and Gerda's development into a rather plain, slovenly girl that her pushy and impudent manner accentuated. Marijke, voicing Frans's opinion, could not help remarking on the mother and daughter's unfortunate difference. Other news took attention away from the mismatched couple. In 1950, Frans and Marijke's second child, Joop, was born, and two years later, Pieter came. Another three years and Lodewijk came to the great joy of the family. Marijke had nothing much to report about Cees and Truus other than that Cees was still a brute and his pretty wife still put upon. Then things began to happen.

Cees van den Donker's growing conflict with members of his religious community consumed the gossip mill. He made life uncomfortable for the community leaders by airing his strange religious views and expecting everyone to listen. The conflict grew to an acrimonious break with people everywhere, not just the gossipmongers, deploring the savagery of Cees's unrestrained abuse. It was clear, too, that Mevrouw van den Donker disagreed with her husband's mad ideas and was too frightened to say so. Speculation filled the town about where it would lead.

The troubles seemed not to affect Gerda, who displayed more affection for her brutish father than her revoltingly pretty mother. If that scandal was not enough, wrote Marijke, there was something else, not unexpected if she thought about it. One of Cees's business rivals, a member of his former religious community, began paying attention to Truus. It looked all very innocent, but not innocent enough to escape the ever-suspicious and cantankerous Cees van den Donker. Something was bound to happen.

'Father Jos, I have never seen or heard anything like it in Middelburg,' Marijke wrote, devoting a letter to the affair. 'Geert Cornelissen, I learned, began approaching Mevrouw van den Donker on market day. The few who noticed thought nothing of it because they are both Strict Reformed. Why wouldn't they stop to chat? On all accounts, Meneer Cornelissen is a charming man. What began as brief conversations became longer as they lingered to talk among the people pressing around the stalls. Someone said it was not just the growing length of the conversations. Truus perked up. She lost that sad look for a while. She seemed to like Meneer Cornelissen and enjoyed their talks. I don't know how true this is. I mean about her liking Meneer Cornelissen. It came to a head when he invited Truus to have a coffee out of the way of the market crowds. They chose a table in full view of everyone. This is when people noticed Truus liked the attention. So, they said.

'Anyhow, Meneer van den Donker appeared from nowhere and abused Cornelissen. It was the usual thing, they said. He wanted to know what he was doing with his wife. Cornelissen said he was doing nothing with his wife, and he thanked him not to be insulting if he could manage it. Cornelissen's smooth manner riled van den Donker all the more, and he threatened to punch him. Cornelissen jumped to his feet and said he should expect one in return if he dared. The more the exchange went on, the more uncouth Cees van den Donker appeared. Truus remained seated, full of apprehension, while this was going on. Van den Donker tried to grab Cornelissen by his coat, but Cornelissen brushed his hands aside and warned Cees to back off. There was never any backing off for Van den Donker, and he threw a wild punch that Cornelissen easily evaded. Cornelissen, also a hardened country boy, again warned Van den Donker. Van den Donker came at him. Cornelissen grabbed him, and they went into a clinch, pushing this way and that, knocking over chairs and tables. Truus hastened out of the way.'

'The two men fell over, crashing into more tables and chairs. Those around them now intervened. Women came to comfort Truus. When Van den Donker and Cornelissen were standing apart, held by those who had separated them, Van den Donker warned Cornelissen to stay away from his wife or suffer the consequences. This is where it became fascinating.

Cornelissen held up his fist and said he would not restrain it next time. If Van den Donker really cared about his wife, he would treat her a lot better. She was wasted on a crude brute like him. Van den Donker laughed and said, "But she *is* my wife." He nodded to Truus to follow him, and they left the market.

'As you can imagine, Fr. Jos, Cornelissen's words set tongues wagging. Was this a love triangle, the gossipers said? For many, the answer was yes. That's what it looked like. That's what it was. But it wasn't. The following market day, Mevrouw took me aside. She was lucky I was there. I don't go every Thursday. Anyhow, she told me there was nothing between Geert Cornelissen and her. I must believe her, she said. He had always been friendly to her inside and outside their community. He was a nice man. There was no reason she shouldn't talk to him. She hadn't seen him for a while because of Cees's split with the community, and because she was interested in the friends she no longer saw, she agreed to have a coffee with him. That's all.

'Besides, Geert, she said, was married, and she would never become involved in a relationship with a married man. Nor would Geert with a married woman, she believed. She asked if Frans would talk to Geert Cornelissen and say she was sorry she could no longer talk to him. It made things difficult for her. She hoped he would understand. She had nothing against him. Frans spoke to Cornelissen, and Cornelissen did understand. Having spoken with him, Frans said he was not so sure there was nothing on his side. Things died down after that. Most accepted that Cees van den Donker's nasty character caused the whole thing. As usual, a little group of gossipers isn't convinced and stays alert for signs of a relationship.'

Jos read and reread the letter. He kept it with him, taking it out when he paused to eat or have a break, which was not often. His parish priest had not returned. His workload—overseeing the sacraments, the liturgy, counselling, and the school—was for two priests. He had to put the letter away. He should put the letter away. However much he sympathised and deplored the exposure of Truus to the questionable attentions of other men, he could do nothing. He wrote to the Sydney house to ask when his parish priest would return. A letter arrived saying he could not return for the moment and that Fr. Jos should carry on. When Jos wrote that the parish required two priests, the reply was that he should manage. He resigned himself to the task.

Marijke's letters and the occasional one from Frans were the best dis-
tractions from the constant weighing up of what duties took priority. The
trivial family matters that Marijke related so well were a real relief. The
two older children, Joop and Anneke, were doing well at school. Anneke
was the boldest little girl around, and many said the prettiest. Marijke
feared Anneke would need restraint on her exuberance. Frans's accounts
of business and developments on Walcheren were engrossing. He always
looked out for news about the Van den Donker family. There usually was
some, but more of the same.

The gossip was that Cees van den Donker was extending his business
activities, now travelling away from Walcheren. Whatever it was, Cees
had all the appearance of flourishing. Gerda was just as unattractive and
slovenly, but she was a good student, very bright, apparently. That was
compensation for her unfortunate appearance, said Marijke. Mevrouw
van den Donker continued to attend Thursday's market day but kept to
herself. She had always worn smart, modest clothing, but now her dress
was dour as if in mourning. The Geert Cornelissen affair seemed of the
past. He no longer came near her on market day.

Jos embraced his workload with the feeling that he was muddling
through. He was grateful for having two supportive native parishioners
who did their best. But it was not enough to cover work that exceeded the
powers of one person. He feared his weakened constitution would break
in the end, as his doctor in Middelburg had warned. His fears were not
baseless. He fell ill with the flu. The parish doctor came and warned that
he needed a rest. He offered to write to his superiors in Sydney, but Jos
declined. The doctor spoke with leading parishioners who rallied around
to give him time to get over his flu. Reluctantly, he agreed to take a week
off. He did it as much to please his dear parishioners, who were anxious
about him.

As he sat in the front room of the presbytery, feeling guilty and wondering whether it was wrong to ignore the possibility that the war had
rendered him unfit for mission work, a small group of European tourists
came into view on the road outside. They carried a booklet in one hand
and looked around while consulting it. Jos started. He stood up and came
closer to the window, taking care to stay out of sight. There, among the
group, were Cees van Donker and the friend with the tattoo on his wrist.
Cees's eyes came to rest on the presbytery and then the church next to

it. He nudged his friend and nodded towards the church. They had time for a grimace and a brief exchange before the five people moved on. What on earth was Cees van den Donker doing in Lae? It took a few days and discreet inquiries to learn that the group had anthropological interests and was on a tour of native New Guinea. What the exact purpose was, he could not discover. One thing was sure. Meneer van den Donker and his occultist friend were not just tourists.

Chapter 20

Fr. de Jonge

ELEVEN YEARS after Jos had seen Truus van den Donker and her silent little daughter disappear into Middelburg's market crowd—it was 1960—he was on his way back to Holland. He had been ailing for some time with a strain of flu he could not shake. He did his best to overcome his lack of energy, pushing himself, thinking he would be all right for the rest of the day once he got started. One morning, his limbs were like lead, and his body ached. Dizziness took over when he tried to raise himself, forcing him onto his back.

He lapsed into a semi-conscious haze in which he saw people coming and going amid hushed and anxious conversation. He sank deeper and deeper where the shades of the war reappeared, then further into the dark, miserable hollow where he was conscious of moving candlelight and robed people around him. Intermittent waves of despair flowed over him, accompanied by the bright red lips of the unblemished young face whispering spells and incantations. He penetrated still further to depths hitherto unknown. A rush of joy and pleasure forced back the spells and sirens as he became aware of a holy presence. Truus van den Donker's lovely, innocent face rose before him.

The doctor was beside his bed. He felt the prick of a needle. It was evening, and his housekeeper put a tray in front of him with a cup of tea and two slices of bread. She helped him to sit up and eat. He drifted off again, this time into an undisturbed sleep. A few days later, the doctor was back at his bedside. By this time, he was clear in mind, although still crushed by exhaustion.

'You silly priest, I've been telling you, you'll kill yourself unless you change your ways. I will be writing to your superiors today.' He outlined what he was to do and the strict diet he was to follow. 'You've been starving yourself, haven't you? Well, that's finished. And you can forget any work for the moment. You are simply incapable of it. But don't worry. I will be discussing that, too, with your superiors.'

The doctor was quick to carry out his threat, writing a long letter to his superiors in Sydney. Fr. van Engelen was good for nothing, and if they wanted their priest to survive, they should pay attention to him. He could not go on the way he was. It was probable that his hardships during the war had severely weakened his constitution, making him now unsuited for work in the missions. He must go somewhere where he could enjoy absolute rest. The Provincial of the Oceania Province decided to send him back to Holland for convalescence. A replacement would be sent. Besides the rest, Father would have the chance to catch up on developments within the order and the extended Church. The new pope, Pope John XXIII, against all expectations, looked like shaking up their ancient establishment, the provincial informed Jos in the letter containing his instructions. Jos submitted without complaint but gave the anticipated shake-up scant attention until he arrived at the order's monastery in Sydney a week later.

The first hint of the importance of his catching up on the developments in the Church came when the provincial told him there were high expectations for the Second Vatican Council. Due to open in two years, the council was expected to make long-overdue changes in the Church. His role as a missionary priest would be vital in preparing the formal discussions on the liturgy. When Jos returned this information with a blank expression, the provincial told him not to worry. He should rest in Holland and get back on his feet. He was sure to hear exciting developments while there. They could talk about those developments when he stopped off in Sydney on his way back to New Guinea.

The following two weeks were a welcome break. Friends and relatives of members of the order, many of whom were recently settled Dutch migrants, invited him to dinner, organised social club celebrations, and took him on sightseeing trips around Sydney. One occasion he enjoyed was the trip to the junior seminary, the Apostolic School of the Blessed Virgin Mary, at Ringbark Park, about sixty miles out of Sydney. During the afternoon, the seminarians peppered him with questions about the missions, the missionary priest's role, and the people who had not received the message of redemption. Fr. Hans de Jonge appeared at the back of the room at the end of the conference. He displayed the same fastidiousness but now radiated an air of imperturbable confidence.

'Goedemiddag, Father,' said De Jonge, offering his hand. 'I'm pleased to see you after so many years. I'm sorry you're not in better health. You will be in my charge from now on.'

'Pleased to see you, too—and to speak my native language. You might even have news from Holland.'

'Yes, there's much to tell you. The car's waiting for us. We'll get on our way at once.'

They left the seminary with a lay brother at the wheel and Jos and De Jonge in the back. Jos contemplated the landscape with its green hills made lush by the winter rain.

'Not much like home, is it? You know, the landscape,' De Jonge explained, seeing Jos did not understand, 'It's different from the flat country in Holland.'

'Oh, yes, of course. I wasn't sure what you were referring to.'

They drove on in silence, with Jos aware of glances coming his way.

'That was a gratifying talk with those eager young seminarians,' said Jos to discourage the furtive glances. 'You know what is said: if the Church's priests are sound, so is the Church.'

'We haven't had the chance yet to talk about the situation in the Church,' said De Jonge, seizing on the subject. 'You've been so preoccupied.'

'Yes, I know. But it's been restful. I appreciate the provincial's efforts, indeed, everybody's efforts, to make me comfortable. It's also a nice change to speak Dutch.' He glanced at the driver. 'Perhaps we should speak in English now.'

'No, no, Br Johnson is fine. Besides, what I want to say is confidential.'

'Confidential?' said Jos, intrigued by De Jonge's enthusiasm.

'Are you aware of my specialty?'

'Your specialty?'

'Yes, what my training is for. You know, you were sent to the missions. Well, I have been attending conferences in Holland, Belgium, and Germany on liturgical development. My brief is to develop the ideas discussed in liturgical circles. Some of the finest and most progressive minds on the liturgy and other doctrinal questions are at the University of Oost-Nederland. We are at the forefront of developments.'

'At the forefront of developments?' said Jos, sitting up and facing the eager liturgist.

'Yes, it's accepted that the liturgy needs a thorough overhaul. We must consider the age we live in and the people we must reach. The modern world is breathing on us.'

'Thorough overhaul?' Jos said, conscious of how he must sound. He tried to stay composed, but the idea of thoroughly overhauling the centuries-old Latin Rite alarmed him. He was aware of the desire of some to change the sacred liturgy. Such talk had been bubbling for years. That movement was restricted to small, restless groups in northern Europe. At least, that's what he thought. Their views had never attracted much attention. Any genuine feeling for changing the beautiful, solemn, sacred ceremonies and rituals developed over the centuries had never cropped up among his congregation. Those ceremonies represented an unassailable defence of the essential truths of the faith. It was unimaginable that anyone could contemplate touching ceremonies and rituals that had the sanction of time, which surely meant the sanction of the Holy Spirit.

'Father, you have been too long in the missions. You're missing out on these important developments. Change is necessary so the Church can move forward in the modern world. That's a widespread opinion. The Church needs to be updated to spread the message of the Gospel more effectively.' He looked across at the older priest. 'We know you were an outstanding philosophy student in your seminary days. You could have gone to Rome. Dr. Albers brought you back from New Guinea to pursue your doctorate. Your lectures were engaging, at least for the short time you gave them.'

'I do have an abiding interest in philosophy, but spreading the Gospel to the non-believer seemed to be a priest's duty.' Jos was surprised at the open reference to Fr. Albers's plans for him. If De Jonge was not guilty of disingenuousness, he was not in on the collusion he suspected. That, too, surprised him if true.

'Your gift in philosophical understanding,' continued De Jonge, oblivious to Jos's frown, 'demands you acquaint yourself with the current thinking about all the critical issues of the contemporary Church. The Church must reflect on its governance, the papal office, the curia, the priesthood's exclusive nature, the clergy's role, and its triumphalist face. Well-trained, philosophically attuned minds are needed to articulate the issues and bring about change. You could conduct a different form of missionary work. Tutoring those young seminarians in the latest thinking would better aid them. You would equip them to deal with the social problems they confront as new priests in this modern world. We don't want to send them into the world with an obsolete, even harmful message.'

Jos looked askance at his younger confrere. Could he be serious? But he was. Just one glance at the animated face said enough.

'Is it true? Is there so much support, as you say, for change?'

De Jonge spent the rest of the journey expounding his views with frequent references to well-known theologians' academic research in universities in Germany, Holland, and Belgium. The frequently named connection between the Dutch and the Germans in these theological and ecclesial matters brought to mind the only connection with which Jos had any experience. Just fifteen years ago, his countrymen were liberated from their German neighbours' cruel, oppressive ideology. Fifteen years ago, he thought he heard the echo of Schopenhauer, Hegel, Nietzsche, and other German philosophers in the Nazis' rhetoric. It was fifteen years ago that he could not fathom how a Christian country could soak up the ideas of a mad, self-indulgent, psychologically stunted misfit like Nietzsche, whose admirers fanned the dimmest spark of his lunacy.

When, at last, they pulled up outside the monastery's main entrance, De Jonge ended his furious discourse by saying that he would give Father some literature to read. He would be happy to discuss things in greater detail before he left for Holland. Jos thanked him and said he looked forward to reading the material, which was the truth. Over the next week, they had no further opportunity to talk. Jos was grateful to be left alone.

He picked a place of solitude under an enormous Morton Bay Fig growing on the monastery's Sydney side. To the north, he had a view of the city buildings. To the south, although the spot was out of the direct route of the monastery traffic, he had a good view of the comings and goings of his religious brothers. Visitors' arrival and people passing from the main administrative building to the chapel, the study, and the living quarters came under his observation. Early on, what struck him was that De Jonge was often in the company of the same three or four priests. That included the provincial. Then there was something else, too. None of the other priests he spoke with ever brought up the Church and its need to change. De Jonge joined him under the tree the day before he was due to leave for Holland.

'Well, your time with us is almost up,' he said cheerfully. 'You must have had time to read the literature I gave you. What do you think? Are you now convinced of the need for change?'

'You gave me an agenda for significant change, even radical change. I have been out of circulation, as you say. Much of this is new to me.'

'I understand. It is a broad agenda. Most are not as acquainted with it as I am. But about the liturgy, surely you, as a missionary priest, can see the need for adjusting the Church's services to the people's culture in the different mission territories. What affinity would the natives of Papua and New Guinea have with the profoundly medieval origins of the present liturgy, a liturgy in a dead language?'

'Well, firstly, the origins of the Latin Rite are not only medieval, but to answer you directly, much affinity.'

'What ... what do you mean?' said De Jonge, recoiling, as if he had been struck across the face.

'Well, there are wide anthropological, philosophical, and cultural issues here, but let me keep it brief and simple. Most ancient societies had harvest festivals as part of their religious ritual. Some societies still do. A harvest festival in one culture, I suggest, is recognisable by another culture with a different form of festival. If I can use Thomistic categories, the substance is the same, only the accidents or secondary features are different.'

'But hardly a comparable example in discussions about the Mass.'

'Isn't it? Take a ritual that's closer, then. Take the Aztecs ...'

'The Aztecs with their human sacrifices? That's taking it to extremes.'

'No, consider. The Aztecs sacrificed prisoners of war by the thousands in lengthy ceremonies; they beheaded young girls to encourage successful crops. The preferred victim, though, to appease the gods was the young, stainless male. In an elaborate ceremony, the male victim was led to the top of the temple, where the priests seized him and held him over a stone altar while they cut his heart out and burnt it in a nearby bowl. The priestly class conducted themselves with great dignity. I suggest that people of traditional societies would have no trouble recognising that the Aztecs developed a comprehensible form of religious ritual. What revolts us is that they killed humans to appease their deity.'

'You seem to destroy your own argument.'

'No, no, consider again. The Aztec priest would surely recognise and understand the elements of our Mass as it is, right down to the vestments. If the Aztec priest were to receive the grace of faith, he would have no impediment in fervently attending in mind and body. All the more so, considering that it is a re-presenting of Christ's sacrifice on the cross to atone for the sins of mankind. He would understand it as the human sacrifice to end all human sacrifices, a self-giving sacrifice on behalf of others. It would be an enlightened move away from the darkness of killing one's fellow man in a deluded attempt to appease an erroneous idea of God. The natives of my mission have no difficulty with the Mass as it is. It incorporates all their ideas of what a traditional religious ceremony should be, but with the difference that it highlights the central mystery of our faith: Christ's death on the cross for the redemption of mankind.' He paused and waited. De Jonge stared past him.

'Many people would disagree with you.'

Jos waited for him to elaborate, but he remained silent, his face reddening.

'The course Fr. Albers asked me to teach,' continued Jos, 'some of which you attended, was meant to show how the Enlightenment philosophers deviated from the realist philosophy of Christian Aristotelianism and ended up in atheistic materialism.' He stopped and gestured with his open hands. 'I must tell you I have detected the spirit of those philosophers in the literature you gave me—particularly the Hegelian dialectic.'

He rested his hands on his lap and took hold of the breviary lying there. But De Jonge still said nothing. Curling and pursing his lips most oddly, he gazed at the ground before him with darkened looks. Finally, he stood up and took hold of the chair he had brought with him. 'I am sorry you are not more receptive to these ideas.' He fidgeted with the back of the chair. 'This is a great disappointment. I must even say it's tragic that you cannot discern the signs of the time. The signs are with us, and the blind will be left behind. The demand for equality between people, for basic rights, the demand for freedom from an authority based on a persecuting principle, the irresistible move to a more just democratic form of social organisation, all these things will happen. These are prophetic times. You must see this.'

'Authority based on a persecuting principle?'

'The history of a persecuting authority is there for everyone to see.'

Jos stared open-mouthed. 'Are you talking about the actions of a duly constituted temporal authority or corrupt secular authority? Or are you referring to the actions of a divinely appointed authority in contrast to the actions of a corrupt prelate?'

'How do you distinguish between them?'

There was a heavy silence while Jos tried to grasp what he was hearing. De Jonge took up his chair, preparing to depart.

'I am sorry we have not been able to understand each other,' he said, looking at his watch. 'The world has changed—is changing. We must adjust to our modern life. The liturgy must reflect that adjustment. I could say more, but I fear it would be pointless.' He looked down at Jos. 'Well, eh ... look, I have a meeting to attend. An important meeting. With the provincial. We can perhaps discuss these matters later when you consider the issues a little more—with a spirit of discernment.' With that, he was off, carrying the chair awkwardly in one hand.

Jos watched the retreating De Jonge in astonishment until he entered through the main building's side door, bashing the chair up against the doorway as he went. He sat for some minutes, pondering what he had heard. 'A persecuting principle,' he said out loud. 'No, he could not mean it.' That evening, De Jonge was nowhere to be seen, and nobody knew where he was. Jos did a discreet search because he wanted to confirm the arrangement for the next day. Giving up the fruitless search, he sought the provincial before he retired. The provincial brushed off his concern and told him not to worry. He would get to the airport on time. He then excused himself.

After breakfast the next morning, Jos was informed that a taxi would take him to the airport. Many of his brother priests came and said goodbye while he waited for the taxi. The provincial sent a lay brother to say he had been detained and could not see him before Father left. He wished him well. The lay brother gave him an envelope containing his instructions. He should not bother reading it until he was on board the plane. His instructions, however, did not occupy his mind. De Jonge's long tirade on the Church's future forced him to return to the pre-war years. He saw a development of the mind he had observed during the philosophy classes and the bike rides, justifying his uneasiness at the time. When he sat in the plane, the letter remained unopened. His meeting with Cees and Truus van den Donker after the stampede on the Dam replayed in his mind. It was odd that his recent collapse had shed more light on what had happened in those dark hours. Something other than the Germans had been stalking him. Some sort of evil had ambushed him—the same demon he had exorcised from Marlies. Was it a coincidence that De Jonge's zeal had revived those memories?

Chapter 21

Return to Holland

AS THE QANTAS 707 banked southeast of Schiphol Airport to make its final approach, Jos gazed at the Dutch landscape below. A lump came to his throat while he surveyed the broad, flat fields hemmed in by water-filled ditches, canals, dykes, poplars, narrow roadways, fences, and here and there, great waterways. Then, there were the clusters of houses forming villages dotted around the countryside. He saw the steeples of the churches and the marketplace in the centre of the villages. It brought back so many sights, sounds, and smells for him.

'*Goeie hemel*, Jos!' Frans exclaimed when the priest finally appeared from customs. 'What have you been doing to yourself? You haven't improved much, have you?'

'What do you mean?' the priest said, smiling at his brother's frank, open manner. He looked at the two children standing beside his brother. 'And who have we here?' continued Jos to evade inconvenient questions.

'I'm Anneke, Father,' said the pretty blond 11-year-old, 'and this is my younger brother, Joop. Pieter and Lodewijk stayed at home.'

'Jos, what have you been doing?' Frans repeated when they were heading out of the car park. 'You look terrible, not as bad as in Amsterdam, but terrible. No wonder they sent you home.'

'A severe case of the flu. It sapped my energy.'

'Sapped your energy—and the rest.'

'Frans, I'm always grateful for my younger brother's concern. But the younger brother can be too nosy sometimes.'

'Why aren't you wearing your habit?' Frans persisted, looking at his brother dressed in everyday trousers, shirt, jumper, and coat. 'The last time I saw you like that was not auspicious.'

'They have instructed me not to wear my habit while I'm resting,' said Jos, realising he could not avoid the question. 'I am to have a thorough rest and not attend to or invite any religious activity for several months. My religious habit would make that difficult, I was told.'

'Do you think that?'

'It's not for me to question. You know that.'

Frans frowned and glanced at his brother, who turned to his niece and nephew sitting in the back. Jos ensured the conversation for the three-hour trip back to Middelburg was about family and anything except his appearance. When the restored Lange Jan of the Nieuwe Kerk appeared in the distance, signalling they were not far from Middelburg, he turned again to his brother.

'Frans, I want to mention a couple of household items.' Frans inclined his head. 'Although my superiors have relieved me of my pastoral duties, I am still a priest. So, I would like it known I would rather behave like someone on retreat during the week. I don't want to be inflexible about this. If someone needs to speak to me or happens to be in the area visiting Mamma and Pappa, I won't ignore them, of course. The thing is, I would like to reserve the weekends for social occasions. Apart from Mamma and Pappa, the exception is you. I want to discuss important matters with you when I settle in. Will you let people know—discreetly?'

'You're asking me to be discreet? But, of course, I will, seriously.'

'Thank you.' There was a pause and a hesitant glance. 'Do you know anything about the ecumenical council the pope has announced?'

'Not much. Why?'

'I'll explain later. That's one thing I want to talk about.'

Instead of taking the road around the old medieval boundaries, Frans turned onto the bridge over the *Kanaal door Walcheren* and drove through the heart of the town. Jos marvelled at the restored buildings, especially the Abbey and the Town Hall. Over the last bridge, they came to the Singel, the road running beside the outer canal. A short time later, they pulled up outside a neat, two-story house in typical Dutch style. Jos was not surprised to see the many smiling family faces crowded at the front window.

'Oh, Jos, what have you done to yourself!' exclaimed his mother, hurrying from the house to greet him. The priest's father and Marijke followed her. They exchanged kisses and hearty handshakes while Frans and the two children took charge of his luggage. Inside, Pieter, Lodewijk, his sisters, and their families, plus cousins, nieces, nephews, aunts, and uncles from all parts of the province, greeted him.

JOS DID not take long to settle in. His mother and father did all they could to make him comfortable. He arranged with Fr. Matthijs, prior of the Augustinus chapel, to say daily Mass. With that settled, he followed an agreeable routine of religious duties and strolls into the surrounding farmland. Occasionally, he walked into the town centre wearing sunglasses and a beret to avoid recognition, always conscious of someone he might meet. More often, he would set off on a walk into the countryside, making for Domburg on the northern coast.

He avoided the road into Vrouwekerke. Though Truus van den Donker was on his mind, he must not make any move to meet her. In time, she would learn he was back in Middelburg. What then? He did not know. His conversations with De Jonge about the affairs of the Church returned time and again to his thoughts. That priest's views on updating the liturgy and his allegations about a persecuting principle gnawed at him. Sometimes, Frans accompanied him on his walks. On one such walk, he asked Frans what he thought of the Church.

'What do you mean? That's such a vague question.'

'Well, say what comes to mind.'

'I don't know what to say,' said Frans, shrugging. 'You know, the Church has always been there for us. We accept it, and we try to live according to its teachings. It's our whole life, all organised in a typically Dutch way, and yet most of us don't think about it too much. In a way, we only think of it when we're aware we're doing wrong, not living up to the way the Church expects us to live, or when we are in trouble. Otherwise, the Church as an organisation, the pope, the Vatican, and the clergy are just there.'

'I think you're right. I mean, you're right that most people these days regard the Church in that manner.'

Frans collected his brother a week later and drove to Domburg to walk along the dunes to Oostkapelle and back again. The fresh sea air would spark him up, he said. Frans was right. The fresh breeze blowing in from the

North Sea gave him life. At around two kilometres along from Domburg, they came into sight of *Kasteel Zaligheid*.

'Oh,' said Jos, stopping, 'that castle had passed out of my mind. It's a beautiful, dignified building, isn't it? Unostentatious, sober, a symbol of when the clergy administered the province's affairs.' What Cees van den Donker had said all those years ago came back to him. The castle meant something entirely different to him. He said as much to Frans.

'The man is an ignorant bigot. He has little idea of the province's history. What does he say about the many clandestine churches Catholics were forced to establish after the Calvinist takeover? And just look at him now with all his wealth and property. I don't think many of the farmers on Walcheren share his vast holdings. What a hypocrite.'

'Who owns the castle now?' said Jos, wanting to divert the conversation.

'It was bequeathed to a charitable organisation, but they don't seem to do much with it. Witness the disrepair into which it is falling. You can count on it coming up for sale soon.'

They gazed at the castle in silence.

'That reminds me, Jos. I've been thinking about your question, you know, about how people regard the Church today. As I said, I'm afraid the ordinary Catholic doesn't think too much about it. Take the members of our family, for example. From their behaviour, you would think they gave little thought to it. At least, they never mention it outside their family circle except for Mamma and Pappa. But why the question? What was on your mind?'

Jos hesitated. Having broached the subject, he felt a perverse reluctance to pursue it outside his religious order's confines.

'You remember I asked you about the ecumenical council organised for 1962. The object of that council, I am told, is to bring the Church into line with modern times, with the aspirations of modern man.'

'Adapt it to modern times? God forbid. What? Do they plan to bring Elvis Presley and his Dutch imitators into the liturgy?' said Frans, evidently reaching for the most absurd idea.

'Now, Frans, let's be serious. No, I don't know much about it, but it seems the intention is pastoral. We should wait and see how the plans of Pope John and his curial assistants develop.' He stopped to choose his words. 'Adapting the Church to our modern times should not make us uneasy. Leo XIII boasted the Church does not favour any particular political system or culture as long as the one true God and His one true Church are recognised.'

'Then what's making you uneasy?'

'Do I appear uneasy?'

'You do.'

'Well, I've heard an opinion that the Church needs thorough-going reform, especially the liturgy.'

'Change the Mass?'

'Yes.'

'Unthinkable!'

'Have you ever heard anyone claim the Church needs reforming, that the liturgy needs a thorough overhaul?'

'Thorough overhaul? No, never.'

'Have you any idea how the Mass could be improved or better adapted to particular circumstances?'

'No, I have never thought about it. But I don't doubt that others have. You know, we Dutch aren't reluctant to meddle in things that don't concern us, as if the world will perish without our interference.'

'Yes, we are a busy interfering folk,' said Jos, smiling. 'For a little country, we have much to say for ourselves.'

They turned away from *Kasteel Zaligheid* and set off towards Domburg. After walking in silence for a while, Jos resumed the conversation.

'Frans, tell me. When I say to you that certain authorities work on a persecuting principle, what do you think of?

'Lord, Jos, what sort of question is that?'

'What do you think of? Come on.'

'Okay, the Nazis, the Russian communists, any tyranny, I suppose.'

'And the Catholic Church?'

'The Catholic Church! *Allemachtig*, Jos, who have you been speaking to?'

'Well, come on, does the Church operate on a persecuting principle?'

'No, it doesn't. If it did, then all authority does.'

'Perhaps that's it,' murmured Jos, after reflecting on the notion.

'What? Stop being mysterious.'

'Never mind. Let's leave it for the moment and enjoy our walk.'

The brothers let the conversation drift on to other matters. Jos was glad of it. The whole subject made him anxious and uncomfortable. Developing social attitudes was just as worrying. He had been away from Holland for eleven years. So, any changes came out in sharp relief as he mixed again in Dutch society. In contrast with the immediate post-war years, when people were thankful they had overcome evil people with evil ideas, he now saw a growing preoccupation with material wealth and sensual pleasure.

It was as if the moral scheme of things ceased to exist after the defeat of Nazism. He heard troubling political ideas. The young were besotted with the new cinema, popular music, and the latest fashions. The films, television, songs, and the behaviour of some stars idolised by the young were not always edifying. There was an unwillingness to face the implications of some popular trends that even he could see around him in his reclusive routine. Worse still, in some quarters, a voice of justification sounded for such trends.

He was curious to see what was happening in the religious life of the ordinary Catholic. On two successive Sundays, he attended Masses in the district. The lack of fervour among many of the congregation was no surprise. Immersing oneself in the spiritual realm, solemn acknowledgment of the Almighty, and reflecting on one's behaviour were incompatible with the desire for the material in the here and now. Some people were present only in body. Their minds were elsewhere. How could this be, he thought, with the terrible war years just fifteen years behind them? If what he saw was a growing tendency among Catholics, it seemed reasonable for the Church to take stock of the situation. Perhaps this is what 'good Pope John' had in mind—rejuvenating the faithful. But that was not what seemed to be motivating De Jonge.

He dealt with these anxieties by continuing to discuss his thoughts and observations with Frans, still aware of a certain perversity on his part. He could not help it. The growing feeling that the world was on the brink of some outbreak overtook him. There were signs he could not ignore. The movement for reform in the Church and the preoccupation with popular culture were just some signs.

He had the impression that the same stirring was happening in the other Christian denominations. Attitudes and behaviours that did not harmonise with the Dutch way of life were growing. Holland looked like it was on the point of a social explosion. Frans consoled him to some extent. He could see the basis for his worry and agreed with his observations. He admitted he was surprised and embarrassed that he had not seen it for himself. The changes were insidious, he said. He found himself going along with questionable trends. The Dutch spirit of tolerance seemed a convenient cover for these worrying trends.

WHEN JOS was up to it, Frans took him on bike rides around Walcheren. Marijke and the two older children joined them on the weekends, while Pieter and Lodewijk stayed with their grandparents. Riding, chatting, stopping for coffee or lunch, and seeking places and buildings important in Walcheren's history were the routine. On one of these outings, the family group ended up mid-afternoon on Marktplein. Frans stopped outside The Townhall and suggested they enjoy a beef croquette.

Jos and Marijke sat on an iron bench before Middelburg's restored Gothic splendour while Frans and the children headed for the nearest croquette and chips stand. Still wishing to avoid recognition, Jos kept his beret and sunglasses on. Soon, Marijke, Frans, and the priest were tucking into the warm croquettes with the children propped against the bikes behind them. The square was busy with people coming and going, some shopping. A few tourists, the last of the summer holidaymakers, wandered a round.

'Do you see those girls over there, Jos?' Frans said, nodding towards two girls in their mid-teens who had stopped on their bikes to greet each other.

'Yes. What about them?' said Jos, focusing.

'Can you see who one of those girls is?'

The priest looked closely at the two girls. 'No, I recognise neither. A second or third cousin I have not yet seen?'

'Wrong.'

'One of them is Gerda van den Donker,' said Anneke.

'Hey, you spoiled my fun!'

One girl was slim and attractive. That was not Gerda van den Donker. Although they seemed to be chatting as friends, Cees van den Donker's daughter's demeanour was like his: assertive and frowning. In contrast to her friend, who was smartly dressed, Gerda wore loose-fitting and poorly matching slacks, a blouse, and a jumper over which she had hung a jacket that looked like something the farmers throw on to work in the muddy fields. She had none of the feminine prettiness of her mother's face; it was all Cees van den Donker's strong jawline and challenging expression.

'Yes, I can see the likeness with her father. I wonder now and then how that family is going.'

'Well, as we told you, the man has a real nose for business opportunities, especially in the property market. He converted several rural holdings into cash and bought into businesses and assets that have realised enormous gains. His farms on Walcheren and in Zuid-Beveland are under management, and he and his family live at a smart address in Middelburg.'

'And Gerda is such a bore and a nuisance,' Anneke broke in.

'Why do you say that?' said Jos.

'She was one of our leaders in the Girl Guides, bossy, always wanting her own way. She never stopped nagging about everything. Her and her stupid stories about earth goddesses—'

'Earth goddesses?' said Jos.

'She was difficult to manage and sometimes rude to the adults,' said Marijke, lifting a warning finger at her daughter. 'In the end, the movement expelled her. There's a story there that's best left untold.' She gave Anneke an admonishing look.

A woman, approaching on her bike from Vlasmarkt, drew Jos's curiosity from the warning and admonishing look. She stopped at the two girls. In turning to face her, Gerda noticed they were under scrutiny. She frowned, said something, and nodded in their direction. The woman gave the group a hurried glance and turned back to the girls. She was about to say something, but stopped. She looked back. With a few words to the girls, she came over.

'Goeiemiddag,' she said, as a general greeting, and then addressing Jos, 'Yes, it is you. I would know you anywhere. I will never forget the image of your face under that black beret. I heard you had returned. You haven't been well, I see.'

Jos and his brother stood up and returned the greeting.

'Excuse me, Meneer and Mevrouw van Engelen,' Truus continued. 'Do you mind if I say a few words in private to Father?'

'Of course not,' said Marijke.

The priest removed his sunglasses, preparing to go aside with her.

'Just a moment while I speak to my daughter,' she said as Jos walked with her. He stopped when they were a few yards away from the girls and put on his sunglasses. He had the faint impression that Mevrouw van den Donker preferred not to introduce him. There was a brief exchange between mother and daughter while the daughter glanced at the priest. Gerda and her friend then mounted their bikes and headed towards Lange Delft.

'I am sorry,' said Truus, rejoining the priest. 'I thought it best not to complicate things by introducing you to Gerda. She still doesn't know what happened that day. My husband has strictly forbidden me to talk about it.' She looked at his clothes. 'You are still a priest?'

'Yes, I am on leave for a couple of months. I have not been well, as you have observed.' He removed his sunglasses.

'Of course. I can see from your manner that there have been no changes.'

By this time, they had walked to the right-hand side of the square. Truus stopped at the entrance to Vlasmarkt and leaned her bike against the wall. 'I won't keep you long. I can see you're on an outing with your brother's family.' She glanced at Frans and his family, who were looking at them. 'They're such a happy-looking family. Beautiful children. I've only had one child. My husband's insistence, you know. He didn't want any more children after Gerda, but that did not stop him from ...' She stopped herself. 'Somehow, I'm not embarrassed to admit something so private to you. I know now you have heard such things many times before.'

Jos nodded. She spoke in a sad and haphazard way as if unsure of what she would say. Her face still had the smooth, rounded, pretty cheeks of fifteen years earlier. Her figure had not filled out much. Her hair, tied back in the same unpretentious, modest manner, had not lost its colour and sheen. But her expression, especially in her eyes, was marked by a sadness to which she was resigned. It was the sad face of his visions.

'Do you remember our conversation the last time we met? It was over there.' She pointed to the cafe on the opposite side of the square.

'Yes, I remember it well. I have kept you in my prayers.'

'They don't seem to have done any good, the prayers, I mean.' She looked away, and tears came to her eyes. 'But thank you.'

'The Lord answers our prayers in unexpected ways.'

'I know.' She took a flimsy handkerchief from under her sleeve and dabbed her eyes while she looked away. 'Cees has not improved. He has gotten even worse. He has been very successful in business. We're now wealthy, exceedingly wealthy for this town. But the more prosperous and the more successful he becomes, the more intense and bitter he is about his political ideas.' She waved her hand in a short, helpless manner.

'It's still about established authority and how it oppresses the ordinary person. I don't understand the reasons for it. I don't understand what he means by "ordinary people." He's certainly not an ordinary person. I don't know what he is talking about half the time. I'm afraid we have drifted apart. The truth is he has drifted away from me. I don't think I have changed.' She looked up at him, but he said nothing. 'He's not the same person I wanted to be with when I was sixteen.' She continued to look at him. 'He still thinks the same way about the Catholic Church. He thinks the Catholic Church is a criminal organisation. As I said, he has forbidden me to talk about the incident in Amsterdam. It's almost as if he wished Gerda and I had been killed instead of a Catholic priest saving us.'

'Mevrouw ...'

'Please call me Truus. I feel that I know you well, very well, even though I have only spoken to you a handful of times.'

'Thank you, Truus. I understand your feelings. I understand your disappointment. Is there nobody in your family to talk to about it? As terrible as you feel, speaking about it to a family member will offer consolation.'

'You have forgotten that most of my immediate family were killed in the war.'

'Oh, I'm sorry,' he said, taking her hand. 'It slipped my mind. Please forgive me.' He looked at her slim feminine hand in his. He released it.

'Don't worry. I don't expect you to remember everything about me.'

'I should have remembered that. I'm sorry.'

She regarded him in a way that made him feel self-conscious.

'You know, and I find this hard to understand, I have had few expressions of sympathy and understanding in the last fifteen years. My husband has isolated me from people I would normally mix with. The most sympathy and understanding have come from a Catholic priest. Regarding Catholic priests with sympathy was not part of my upbringing.'

'I'm sorry you have been alone in your sadness and grief.'

Her eyes passed around the square. They settled on Frans and his family. They were busy talking together and not paying heed to them.

'I took the time to learn more about the Catholic Church. I wanted to know what a priest like you does. Because of what happened that day. I had to be very careful. Cees would have been infuriated if he had known what

I was doing. When we were in Amsterdam a few years ago, I stole into a Catholic church in Kalverstraat one morning while Cees was busy to see what it was like. A priest was saying Mass for a small group of elderly people.' She stopped and looked at the handkerchief she was unconsciously wrapping around the index finger of her left hand.

'What did you think?'

'It was not what I expected.'

'What did you expect?'

'I don't know, really. Some sort of hocus pocus, as they always told me. Oh, there were the candles and statues and the priest's colourful clothes, all those things we make fun of, but it did not appear to be a magical show or a celebration of superstition. The priest said the prayers—or whatever you do—quietly and solemnly. The people were very reverent, reading prayer books. I didn't stay long. I was so worried Cees would be wondering where I was. It was enough, anyhow. My picture of the Catholic Church did not correspond with what I saw.'

'A lot of misunderstandings have survived the political conflicts of the past. I'm pleased my actions as a priest caused you to look behind those misunderstandings.'

'It was your kindness, not the ...' She looked away again. Jos waited. 'Are you happy being a priest?'

'Well, yes, but that's not the question I ask myself as a priest. The question is whether I am doing God's will and my duty as a priest.' He paused. 'There are difficult times, times when I think I can't carry the burden, but in the end, I am happy, perhaps not in the way the ordinary person would think about it.'

'Don't you miss a wife, children, a family—all those things? You are a priest, but you're also a man.' She blushed.

'No, I don't really miss those things.' She did not know how often he had heard that question. 'It was a conscious decision to give up that part of life to devote myself to the religious life. The commitment to Our Lord is willing and total. Perhaps it's not so clear from the lay point of view, but I don't miss them because they are not there. My family becomes those under my pastoral care. Of course, I miss my parents, my brother, and his family when I am away. But anybody working away from the family would feel that way.'

'Still, it seems a big sacrifice, a very big sacrifice ...' She hesitated. 'What would you say to me if I were a Catholic? I mean about my marriage.'

'What would I say as a priest?'

'Yes.'

'I would start with what we both believe in—Christ, the perfect, spotless victim, died on the cross to redeem mankind. The act of redemption was the willing correspondence of the Lord's will with the Father's will. He's our model and example to accept God's will in our lives, even though sometimes it means suffering. But suffering in following God's will does not mean we will be unhappy—' He stopped. On the other side of the square near Nieuwe Burg, he saw Gerda van den Donker holding her bike and staring at them. Truus turned to look. Fear passed over her face.

'Oh, I told my daughter I would meet her in a few minutes. I must go. I have kept you long enough, anyhow.' She took her bike and mounted it. 'Please say a prayer for me. I'm happy I have seen you again.' She went a little way and then stopped. 'I wish I were under your pastoral care.' Then, without looking to see his reaction, she rode off.

Jos watched her go. He watched her until she reached her daughter. He watched while the daughter mouthed a few words at her mother and then rode up Nieuwe Burg. He watched while Truus rode after her daughter and then disappeared. How could such a tender-hearted, honest woman end up with such an insensitive, dominating man and a daughter who seemed to inherit all the father's qualities? It was a mystery. Head bowed, he walked back to Frans, Marijke, and the two children.

A FEW DAYS later, a letter arrived containing brief instructions. If Father was well enough, he should prepare to return to the missions. He must organise his affairs and proceed to the motherhouse, where he would spend a day or two and receive further instructions. Jos was surprised. He thought the issue of his health would prevent a return. The unexpected decision pleased him for more than one reason. Truus van den Donker and her circumstances were none of his business, and he had no business thinking about her. The next day was market day. He resisted the urge to engineer a meeting.

The letter caused a flurry of social activity. Aunts, uncles, cousins, nephews, and nieces—all wanted to say their goodbyes. It left little time to make his preparations, let alone attend to his religious duties. He had time for just one walk into the countryside with Frans, for which he was thankful. They arranged regular contact about the affairs of the Church and what was happening in the Netherlands. He thanked Fr. Matthijs for his hospitality and the use of his chapel. He set aside special times to talk with his mother and father, for he realised it might be the last time he saw them. Through all this busy period, the one thing that kept appearing before his mind, despite his efforts, was the sad, apprehensive face of Truus van den Donker before she turned to go and join her daughter. As it turned out, he spent one night at the motherhouse. There was a perfunctory meeting with Fr. van Rossem, who, after inquiring about his health, told him he would assist the parish priest who had returned to Lae. He was not well enough for more.

'You know,' said Fr. van Rossem, tapping his desk, 'it's not too late to review your health regarding your priesthood.'

'What do you mean?' said Jos. Questions by his superiors about his priesthood had never arisen until now.

'I am aware of your fervour for the missions, but your health has been precarious. Your doctor gave us a serious assessment of it after the war, and your latest collapse has demonstrated little improvement.'

'Your meaning is not clear, Father.'

'My meaning is this, Father van Engelen,' said Van Rossem, tapping the desk again, 'your health may bar you from carrying out a priest's duties. The condition of your health would provide a smooth path to laicization.'

'Laicization?' said Fr. Jos, straightening himself.

'Yes. You can still go to the missions as a layperson. Dutch lay organisations are in Papua New Guinea. We could help you there. You would not have a parish's heavy workload.'

'I am a priest forever after the order of Melchizedek.'

'Yes, Father van Engelen, no need to be pompous about it. But I must warn you. This is your last chance. Burdening our priests with duties they find too onerous or placing a similar burden on your co-workers is not responsible.'

'I will be all right.'

'Make sure you are.'

Apart from a few organisational matters, the interview finished there. There was no mention of the ecumenical council, which surprised Jos. He asked whether the order was taking much of a role in the preparations. A very significant role, said the superior general, tapping the desk again. He was proud to reveal that the order's best theologians and liturgists were active throughout the whole of Holland in laying the groundwork for discussions. They were working closely with their German and Belgian colleagues. When he asked if he was permitted to receive information about the preparations, Van Rossem said he would keep everyone abreast of developments.

Jos did not pursue the subject as the superior general showed no interest in discussing it. He spent the rest of his time in silence, either in the chapel or walking around the grounds. He was grateful for the seclusion; he needed to prepare himself spiritually. He visited Bart's and Fr. Albers's graves, where he knelt beside Bart's tombstone and bent over, letting his tears fall on the hard, dry stone. It was regretful that he did not have the chance to meet and talk with his brother priests, some of whom he had been in the seminary with. He also wondered why his superiors did not avail themselves of a missionary priest's presence. In his experience, a conference with a priest from the missions always encouraged the seminarians.

The following afternoon, Jos had his nose again pressed up against the window of the Qantas 707 as it took off from Schiphol, banked to the left, flew out over the coast, and then around again to head in a southeast direction. He looked down at the green fields, the patchwork of canals, the lines of poplars, the clusters of houses around the church spire, and again, Truus van den Donker's apprehensive face appeared before his mind. A lump came to his throat.

Chapter 22

Return to Lae

WHEN FR. JOS returned to Lae late in 1960, he found himself under an Australian priest's direction. Why nobody in Sydney had said anything about the replacement was a mystery. But he was pleased to see Fr. Tom Connolly, a relaxed, uncomplicated man, about fifteen years younger, who behaved as if he had been in Papua New Guinea all his life instead of one year. His favourite expression of 'no worries' to end discussions baffled Jos until he realised it was just a way of agreeing about what they should do. Beneath Tom Connolly's relaxed, laconic manner was a dedicated priest whose overriding concern was for his congregation's souls and those outside it. Fr. Tom's uncomplicated faith matched that of his native parishioners, making it easier for him to convey the faith he had received from the cradle. Jos thought they would get on.

'You enjoy it here, don't you, Father?' he said not long after he had settled in.

'Like a pig in mud. And, eh, when we're in private, it's Tom. Okay, Jos? There's nobody around to check on us.'

'Like a pig in mud?'

'Yeah, like a pig in mud,' repeated Tom, not catching Jos's irony. 'I became a priest to go forth and teach all nations and the rest—you know the verses—and that's what I'm doing.'

'I think you even like the climate.'

'I'm from Brisbane in Queensland. Gets bloody hot there, too, though not as humid as here.'

'A little different from Holland. I took some time during my first stint here to get used to the humidity.'

'Yes, I heard. Now, look, Jos. Now we're talking about it, I've been told not to overwork you.'

'Overwork me? They told you that, did they?'

'Yes, I know all about the war and how it left you. Our superiors don't want you collapsing and being shipped off to Holland again. It's very inconvenient, apparently, and costs a heap of money.'

'Very solicitous,' Jos could not help remarking, but regretted it as soon as the words came out. This was a change, though. Fr. van Rossem's last words were about getting him out of the order. He resisted the thought that his superiors in Holland had adopted another tactic to get him out of the way.

'So,' continued Tom, 'I am to restrict you to pastoral activities within the local congregation—you know, Mass, confessions, baptisms, and all that. No wandering around the countryside in search of souls. That's my job. Okay? I'll take care of the school, too—all that heavy administrative stuff. Oh, and you can keep the nuns happy, too.'

'Yes, of course.'

'If I see you flagging, I'm to send you to the nearest pub to relax with a beer. Well, not quite, but you get the message.'

'But I don't drink beer.'

'Don't drink beer? Well, we must change that, mustn't we? I can't drink alone.'

For all Tom's light-heartedness, he could not hide his total commitment to his priestly duties. And when he did relax with a beer, it was never more than a few glasses to accompany his regular chats. He even prevailed on Jos to have a glass during the hot, humid weather. Tom's congeniality, as Jos foresaw, enabled them to settle into a comfortable routine where the parish's tasks were agreeably divided. Jos would behave himself and not go outside the boundaries Tom had set. This light routine allowed him to return to the academic reading that circumstances had forced him to neglect for most of the last fifteen years. Now, it was not just for pleasure. De Jonge's strong ecclesial views and preoccupation with liturgical change made him realise he was behind in the academic discourse in Holland.

'What do you think about this council that His Holiness has called?' he said one Sunday afternoon when they were relaxing.

'I don't think about it. That sort of thing is not only outside my intellectual interests but outside my intellectual abilities.'

'You see it as an intellectual activity, do you?'

'From the information so far, that's what it looks like.'

'What information?'

'All that stuff from gifted theologians in the bulletins. They are always gifted, these theologians and so-called liturgists.'

'You mean information from within the order?'

'Yes. In the bulletin. Haven't you seen it?'

'No,' said Jos, surprised. The superior general had been cagey in response to his request for information.

'Really? Well, I'll give you what I haven't thrown out. It's all the same stuff. They don't send me much anymore because they know I'm not interested. I don't say that, of course. I just say I've too much work saving souls to read the bulletins. I suspect I'm to toe the line, anyway, whatever I think about such elevated matters.'

The bulletins were not so much information about the council as praise for the idea of the council. It was the same rhetoric De Jonge had poured out in his enthusiasm about the same theologians and liturgical experts. Jos suspected De Jonge authored the bulletins, which amounted to attempts to bring members of the order on board with his 'positive' attitude to the council. He asked Tom if he would not mind requesting Sydney to send whatever they had on the council.

'Of course, mate. I'll tell them I've got an intellectual here that'll lap 'em up.'

'Oh, I wouldn't say that.'

'Just kiddin', mate. I'll get onto it.'

The Sydney office did not delay. The information came in a steady stream. Conferences were happening all over the place in northern Europe about a new era breaking upon the Church. The Church must modernise and update to cater to our new modern society with new needs, new aspirations and so on, and so on. In a word, the Church must progress. It must engage with modernity. Tom was right about the continual appeal to expert theologians and specialists on liturgical development, especially in Holland. Indeed, the order should be proud that one of its very own is at the centre of the discourse, namely, 'our gifted Fr. Hans de Jonge.' Jos wondered in this fervid intellectual atmosphere of the expert that it did not occur to De Jonge that he was running a fallacy that a first-year philosophy student should detect. The constant reference to experts was an appeal to

authority. There was no substantial argument for the claims of necessary chan
ge.

'What do you think of this proposal to change the liturgy?' said Jos, late one afternoon when Tom summoned him away from his reading for a quiet beer.

'Liturgy is the new word, it seems,' said Tom. 'I assume they're talking about the Mass.'

'Well, mostly about the Mass, but all the ritual of the Latin rite is in question.'

'I'm glad, Jos, you understand what they're talking about. But just between us, I think the idea is daft. Apart from these experts, have you ever heard the ordinary faithful mention the need to change the Mass?'

'No, never.'

'What's wrong with our centuries-old Mass, the Mass of the saints? It's beautiful. The native converts love it—love its mystery, love the meaning in the mystery. They get it. They see the mystery of the sacrifice, of the act of redemption.'

'That's been my experience.'

'Do you know what I think, Jos?' said Tom, after a contemplative sip of beer and leaning towards him.

'Tell me.'

'I think they're bored.'

'Bored?'

'Yeah, don't laugh. I'm serious. They've got to do something with all those years of study.'

'But the Church needs competent philosophers and theologians to explain and protect the faith.'

'From whom?' said Tom, leaning a little closer.

'From those seeking to undermine it.'

'From a small band of other intellectuals.'

'Well, yes. It's important, though.'

'Look, Jos. I just scraped through philosophy. I wouldn't have a clue now what substance and prime matter, act and potency mean. I've never had to use them in my work in the missions. The natives would be just as baffled as me about it all. But they're not baffled about the Mass. It's boredom driving it all. Take it from me.'

'You put your case well.'

'It's common sense.' Tom righted himself and raised his glass. 'Come on, Jos, relax. Drink up. Surely you can manage the one glass. I'm giving you the benefit of the philosophy of the beer. Cheers.'

In a way, Tom, who had been in the building trade, had a point about the distance between the Church's intellectuals and the ordinary man in the pew. Needless indulgent disquisition was pointless, it was true. But responding to intellectual streams undermining the Church, some of which were intended to undermine the Church, was not. His thoughts returned to Fr. Albers's bringing him back to the motherhouse to counter what he thought were Marxist ideas creeping into the order's priestly training.

The capitalist order was not the first issue, as he had begun to suspect, but Marx's materialist dialectic. Indeed, he had to go further back to Hegel's dialectic, from which Marx had borrowed. It was significant that Fr. Muller wanted him to spend half of the new course on Hegel, whose logic was a striking departure from the reasoning that established an objective order in the world. Hegelian reasoning unhitched the world from an objective order as understood in Catholic philosophy. It was time to return to his books on the German Georg Hegel. In the meantime, he asked Frans to give him an idea of the chatter in Holland about the council. Frans had nothing significant to report. It was just over a year before the Second Vatican Ecumenical Council was due to open. It was not general news, but he would remain on the alert. Then, two weeks before Christmas, Jos received a letter from Marijke that occupied his mind for weeks.

'Dear Brother-in-law,' she wrote, 'Frans, Anneke, Joop, Ludwig, Pieter, and I send you hearty greetings and Christmas blessings. We hope you have a restful break in the heat and humidity while we cosily crowd around the fire. There's nothing dramatic to report in the family. Frans is very busy with his work (fortunately), and Anneke and her brothers are doing well at school. Anneke is as bold and pretty as ever. She gets away with too much, that little girl with her innocent airs. And her father just encourages her. No more babies to report from Frans's sisters since the last letter. None from us either. Your mother and father are frail but doing well. Such sweet people. We had the families over for Sinterklaas this year. There were the usual frivolities, with Frans and Anneke excelling (as usual) with their witty poems. If there's nothing much happening in our family, there have been developments elsewhere—with you know who.

'As I think you are aware, Cees bought a house on the Singel not far from us, on the other side of Seis Bridge. One of the best houses overlooking the canal. You wouldn't think there was anything in that, would you? Can't get away from us (ha, ha). Well, now poor Truus has returned to the farmhouse. It's common knowledge that she and her cranky husband are more or less separated. She now has a dog to keep her company. But all that, I'm told, doesn't stop him from interfering in her business. Sweet lady, she just takes it. Anyhow, the attention has not stopped—I mean, from interested men in the reformed community. Despite Mevrouw doing her best to look dowdy, the attention is still there.

'What do people expect? Dowdy clothing won't hide her beauty or her sweet temper. She's in her late thirties but still looks young and attractive—and delightfully feminine. In most men's eyes, she's a prize. The attention is not about taking advantage of her. No, the men are interested in a wife. Though something of a scandal, divorce is not forbidden in the Reformed groups, strict or otherwise. These men think that if Cees van den Donker doesn't want her, then he should release her to others who do—and would treat her as she deserves. Cees is regularly away on business these days, so the men court her during his absence. It was never going to escape his notice. No violence this time, just abuse, telling the men to keep away. Truus is still his wife. What a dog in the manger! And a hypocrite. The men—there are two of them—have ignored him. What's Truus's attitude to all this?

'She tries to put them off. She's polite but makes it clear she is not interested. She is married. She doesn't believe in divorce, and she doesn't believe in marrying a divorced man. One of the men is divorced, and the other is a widower. Both are successful, outstanding men of the community. And they won't take no for an answer. I don't mean they're intrusive. They don't pressure her. They just make it clear what their intentions are whenever they meet. There are no long conversations or meetings for a drink. How do I know all this? Well, Truus approached me again on market day a week ago and asked if we could have a chat. We went to the most public cafe on Marktplein and sat at an outside table. We had a long chat over coffee, during which she told me what I have just related.

'The men did not offend her, and their interest flatters her. But it also embarrasses her. They must realise it was pointless. They must understand she would not divorce her husband. For financial reasons, she did not expect Cees to divorce her. But if she ended up alone for some reason, she already had an interest that ruled out marrying anyone else. I was staggered. I was lost for words. When I got my wits together, I asked who. She didn't answer. She just shook her head. I asked her why she was telling me all this. She said she wanted us, Frans and me, to be her witnesses. We were kind to her. She said you had been kind to her. She trusted us. The community trusted us. She hoped our witness would dissuade the men and anyone else. A response to the men's advances would not happen.

'I said I would pass on the message if the subject came up, but I did not think the men would take notice. She shrugged and said they were sensible men. In the end, they would give up. Fr. Jos, I felt so sorry for her. She seemed so resigned to the hopelessness of her circumstances. There's no sackcloth-and-ashes look. She is ready with a small smile and a content expression, but you can see it in her eyes. I might sound like I'm exaggerating, but she has the eyes of a martyr—a white martyr—at least what I imagine a martyr's eyes to be. I agree with Frans and those suitors. What a waste. How terrible for such a woman to be subject to the obvious contempt of her husband and daughter.

'About Gerda, I hear she's doing brilliantly at school. She certainly rewards her father's interest in her. Her association with The Companions of Creation takes up much of her time. She's built quite a following of young people interested in the environment. Frans says it has become very political, very radical. He expects they'll carry out some sort of political action sometime. Nothing has happened yet. And it may not happen. She will finish school in a couple of years. Anneke tells me she will be off to Amsterdam to study linguistics or something like that. What that has to do with the environment is anybody's guess. Nobody expects The Companions of Creation to survive her absence. Fortunately, our naughty daughter, Anneke, has obeyed our instructions to keep clear of her since their last clash. There have been no repeat incidents. Anneke says Gerda keeps clear of her, too. Whenever Gerda or her father sees her, she says they just stare at her. She looks away, she said, so as not to invite trouble. As I say, for once, our single-minded daughter is doing what she is told.

Well, Fr. Jos, that's the end of my news. I've brought you up to date on the excitement in Middelburg. I expect that tongues will start wagging once people hear Truus has an 'interest' in Middelburg. Who could it be? I thought she meant it was someone in Middelburg, but later realised she did not mention Middelburg or Walcheren. It could be someone outside of Walcheren, though nobody would have a clue who. She had been to Amsterdam several times with Cees, but that was years ago. It is a mystery.

'Dear Father Jos, have a happy and holy Christmas, and we look forward to hearing from you. Much love from us in Middelburg.'

Jos read and re-read the letter. He carried it around with him, pulling the bundle of pages out to read in his spare moments.

'You're going to read the words off the paper,' said Tom one evening after dinner in late January.

'Eh? I beg your pardon,' said Jos, looking up.

'That letter. You've read it so often. I hate to be nosy, but is there bad news or something?'

'No, not really,' said Jos, folding the letter. 'It's local gossip—in my hometown, I mean. So it won't mean much to you.'

'It must be more than mere local gossip. It's had your attention these last six weeks. It draws a frown from your normally serene face. Do you want to talk about it?'

'Not really,' said Jos, surprised that Tom had noticed. He did not think he was so observant. 'Yes, I suppose it's more than mere gossip. It's a long story, something that happened after the war. I would rather not discuss it. It's personal.'

'Perhaps that's all the more reason to discuss it. I'm your parish priest, don't forget.'

It was the first time Tom had pulled rank. His laconic Australian manner could be misleading.

'If it affects your priestly life,' Tom continued, 'then you need to tell me about it—for your sake and mine.'

'It's a letter from my sister-in-law. She writes about circumstances I was involved in at the end of the war. As I say, it's a long story, and that story is finished. I don't want to talk about it. It's pointless. I will tell you if I think it's affecting my life as a priest. I promise.'

Tom nodded and was silent for a while.

'I know more about you than you suspect.'

Jos was on guard. Whatever Tom knew about him could only have come from within the order and, indeed, from one or two sources.

'You don't seem surprised,' said Tom before Jos could answer.

'No, I'm not,' said Jos, his mind now concentrating. 'I assume my superiors told you about my collapse and return to Holland.'

'That and more.'

'I suppose they mentioned I was quite sick at the end of the war, that I had a weakened constitution.'

'That and more.'

'Well, you had better tell me what you've been told before we begin to sound like a radio quiz show.'

Tom laughed. 'I know you were mixed up in some sort of maverick espionage that went horribly wrong. You got two of your priestly brothers killed, after which you disappeared for the rest of the war. What you did during that time is not known.'

'It's perhaps not known to those who have given you this information.'

'Who was it known to, then?'

'What you have said are claims—one-sided claims.'

'Well, correct them.'

Jos hesitated. How far should he go? How far could he trust this Australian priest he knew so little about? To this point, he had no reason to distrust him. But now, he thought he could hear Muller's voice in the Australian's words. He would be careful.

'It is true I was engaged in espionage work. It was on behalf of British intelligence. They had put me through intensive training. Did they tell you that?'

Tom whistled and shook his head.

'No, they didn't tell you that because they didn't know. The only person I told was the superior general whom I had to tell. He didn't become directly involved because he seemed to have something else going on—some plan against the Nazi occupation. I don't know what it was, and I never found out. Tragically, I allowed my good friend Fr. Bart Timmermans to join me, something I bitterly regret now. Early one evening, after the Nazi command had settled in, Fr. Albers sent me to an outlying parish to say Sunday Mass. Later that same evening, the Nazis raided the motherhouse and found Bart and Fr. Albers working a transmitter. Allegedly. They were in the superior general's office. What they were allegedly doing was absolutely against our established routine. Absolutely against our agreed protocol. Besides, Bart and the superior general didn't know the codes. The Nazis executed them the next day. Someone betrayed us.'

Tom's wide eyes and open mouth reassured Jos. He had just repeated what he had heard.

'Who betrayed you?'

'I have my suspicions, but I am not at all sure. I will never say unless I'm convinced I'm right.'

'Good heavens, mate. What did you do then?'

'I couldn't go back to the motherhouse. So I made my way to Amsterdam, where I worked with the Dutch resistance while ministering mainly to old people too frightened of the Nazis to leave their houses.'

'That's when you became sick?'

'Yes, but it resulted from the many hardships caused by the war. I wasn't the only one to suffer. You probably haven't heard, but there was the "hunger winter" in the war's last year. In retaliation for the nationwide strike, the Germans blocked food supplies to Holland's heavily populated west. A nasty winter made it all the worse. The big cities like Amsterdam and Rotterdam suffered terribly. Many people died of starvation. People resorted to eating tulip bulbs, sugar beets, and things like that. There were soup kitchens. People died before my eyes. I would have died if those poor, suffering people had not made me eat. Their priest needed to survive.'

'No, I never heard about it. My goodness, Jos, I'm sorry, I had no idea.'

'Nothing to be sorry about.'

'Yes, there is. I've been fed a story.'

Jos hesitated before he spoke. 'But now you have the story from the horse's mouth, so to speak.'

'Yes,' Tom murmured, 'from the horse's mouth.'

Jos and Tom had passed over a hump in their work relationship. Having adjusted his assessment of Jos, Tom showed more understanding in allocating their work. Not that Jos had less work. Tom arranged it so there was less physical work and more organisational input. Jos said he did not have to change anything. Of course, Tom replied, he could manage how things were, but he just wanted to take advantage of a superior mind, which made Jos laugh. Their chats over a beer or two became more relaxed and more enjoyable. Jos's thoughts returned to what had preoccupied him before the hump.

That letter. What should he do? Do nothing was the advice his mind whispered. It was none of his business. But he could not leave it. His sympathy overruled his intellect. But was it sympathy? He did not want to answer that recurring question. Who was that special 'interest' Truus spoke about? He continued to complete his duties with those same questions never far from his mind. He kept the letter with him but was careful to bring it out in his private moments. In the end, he gave in to his sympathies. He wrote to Marijke, asking her to hand the enclosed letter to Mevrouw van den Donker. Discreetly, please.

'Dear Truus,' he wrote, 'it's been around a year since our conversation on Marktplein. You had asked my advice as a Catholic priest about your circumstances. I began talking about those fundamental beliefs that we—you as Strict Reformed and me as Catholic—both share. We share in Christ's act of redemption and his death on the cross. If we suffer, so did Christ so much more. Suffering is a burden, but there is also a joy and consolation in suffering for what is right.

'Knowing we are acting right gives us strength and hope. At that stage, our conversation was unfortunately interrupted. As you left me, you said you wished you were part of my pastoral family. I wish you were, too. But it cannot be. What I can do—which is just as effective as direct pastoral care—is offer my prayers for you. I will always have you in my special prayers.

'May you receive the abundant blessings of Jesus and his Blessed Mother. Fr. Jos van Engelen.'

'What do you make of this?' said Marijke, handing the letter to Frans. 'Jos has asked me to give it to Mevrouw van den Donker. Discreetly.'

'It's a fine, sensitive letter,' said Frans, handing it back after perusing it, 'just like Jos.'

'Yes, it's a beautiful letter, but is that all?'

'What do you mean?'

'Well, he has not kept it from us for a start. Don't you think that strange?'

'Not really. He probably wants to avoid any suspicion of an improper connection with Mevrouw van den Donker.'

'Yes, but why?'

'Oh, I can't guess. Is your female intuition sniffing out something?'

'He seems to make a point of being open about it to us.'

'You're too subtle for me.'

'Do you think ... could it be that Truus's particular interest is your brother?'

'What? No, no, Jos is a priest. He has sympathy for her and feels for her, but he's behaving like a priest. No, there's nothing to support such a suspicion. I know. Besides, Mevrouw has been too vague about her interest. You assume it's a person. It could be a something.'

'What?'

'I have no idea.'

'All right. But it's intriguing, isn't it?'

'Not really.'

Marijke found Truus van den Donker the following market day at the cheese stall.

'Have you got time, Mevrouw van den Donker? I have something for you, but we must be discreet.'

'Yes, of course, Mevrouw van Engelen. Where do you want to go?'

'On second thoughts, it's better we don't do anything unusual. Let's have a coffee, but a little out of the way.'

Truus followed Marijke to a cafe on the square and sat at an inside table. After they were served and indulging in small talk, Marijke pushed the letter into Truus's hands under the table.

'Don't look at it now. Put it in your bag for later. It's a letter from Fr. Jos.' She looked around and missed the flush in Truus's cheeks. 'I know what's in it. It was in a letter he sent us. I put it in an envelope for you.'

'Thank you. You know what's in it, do you?'

'Yes, it's a beautiful letter.'

'A beautiful letter?'

'Very sensitive, as Frans said.'

'Meneer van Engelen read it, too?'

'Yes, he thought it was just like Jos.'

'Oh.' She looked blankly at Marijke. 'Did Fr. van Engelen want you to be discreet?'

'Yes.'

'Oh.'

That evening, Frans asked whether Marijke had handed over the letter as she intended.

'Yes, of course. I found her at the market, and we had a coffee.'

'I hope you had a lookout for our dear friend Cees.'

'She said he was away on business.'

'He's often away these days. I wonder what he's up to. Anyhow, what did Mevrouw say?'

'She didn't say much. She looked bemused the whole time. She wasn't expecting it, of course.'

'No hint about her interest, then?'

'Don't be annoying, Frans van Engelen.'

TRUUS PLACED the unopened envelope on the dining room table and stared at it. She went to her sideboard and took a letter opener from a drawer. She stared at the letter. She put the letter opener beside the envelope and went to her back patio. A light breeze from the fields caressed her cheeks and ruffled the wisps of hair that had come loose from her hairband. The fields were wet and silent in the serenity of their winter slumber. The chill got the better of her, and she returned inside. One more glance before the letter opener did its work. The single page fluttered a moment in her hands. Her eyes ran quickly over the contents, then again. The letter lay on the table, a sigh and her hand instinctively over her heart. The following market day, she caught up with Marijke on her way to Frans's office.

'I won't keep you, Mevrouw. Would you please include this in your next letter to Fr. van Engelen?' She pushed the envelope between the purchases in Marijke's bag.

'You're not keeping me, Mevrouw,' said Marijke, wishing to detain her.

'I can't stop. Please be assured, I appreciate your concern. I can't tell you what a comfort it is.'

'You're welcome. It's no trouble. It's normal.'

'But my circumstances are not normal.'

'I understand. If there is anything …'

'Thank you, but I don't expect an answer.' She hesitated. 'He's still in New Guinea, is he?'

'Yes.'

'Goedemorgen, Mevrouw.'

Marijke watched her disappear among the bustling people. After reflecting on her sad circumstances, she turned to continue her way. In front of her, walking towards her, was Cees van den Donker. He blocked her way.

'I keep wondering what my wife's doing with the Catholics of Middel-burg?' he said, his lips forming into a sneer.

'Please move out of the way, Meneer van den Donker.'

He stepped to the side. 'I wasn't aware I was in your way, Mevrouw. It's a public way here, don't you see?'

She walked on without looking at him.

'What's my wife doing consorting with Middelburg's Catholics?' he called.

'He's going to the limits of offence,' said Frans when Marijke related what had happened. 'He won't go further. He's not that stupid. You needn't be afraid.'

'Oh, I'm not afraid. I just abhor the feeling of dirtiness his manner causes. That poor woman—she doesn't deserve it. I wonder whether he would harm her.'

'I don't think so. His business reputation is too important. He wouldn't hold back from assaulting a man. But not a woman. No. That could cost money.'

'IT'S ANOTHER letter from your sister-in-law,' said Tom, placing it on his desk.

'I can't keep anything from you, can I?'

'No, and keep that in mind.' He gave Jos a friendly pat. 'What's her name, by the way? I don't want to keep referring to her as your sister-in-law.'

'Marijke. The words in Dutch for sister- and brother-in-law are short, unhyphenated—"schoonzus" and "zwager." Marijke has been in the habit of affectionately calling me "zwager," that is, brother-in-law.'

When Tom left to visit the nearby primary school run by an associate order of nuns, Jos sliced open the envelope. He was not surprised to see a folded envelope inside.

'I caught up with Mevrouw van den Donker at the market,' wrote Marijke. 'She seemed rather bemused about receiving a letter from you, but did not say anything other than inquiring whether you were still in New Guinea. We chatted over coffee and exchanged small talk about our families. She spoke about us as if we were her model family, praising Anneke and Joop as fine young people. I wanted to tell her that the pretty little miss she so admires is not always as angelic as she seems, but I glowed shamelessly.'

'She told me what I already knew—that she lives alone at the farm. Gerda does not stay with her when Cees is away on business, which seems to be often. Gerda can look after herself. She said Gerda has already chosen the university she will attend when she finishes school. It's De Witt University in Amsterdam. I would have thought a more prestigious university would be the choice—certainly the choice of her rough country father, who, I am told, wants the best for his clever daughter. After I left Mevrouw and was walking to Frans's office, Meneer came and stood in my way. What a rude man he is. He stood aside when I requested and acted as if I were standing in his way. It's funny. He seems to turn up at the oddest times.'

Jos put the letter aside and picked up Truus's letter that he had laid on the desk in front of him. He stared at it and put it down again. Leaving the presbytery, he set off towards the harbour. It was a fair walk, but the sight of water was always invigorating. One thing he missed, just second to his family, was the water, the canals, the waterways, and especially the view of the North Sea and the entrance of the Schelde River at Vlissingen. It was mid-morning. There was time for the walk that Tom had prescribed for him, each day if possible. He took his rosary with him. An hour and a half saw his return. It was still half an hour before lunch, and Tom was not back yet. He picked up the letter, hesitated, and then tore it open by sliding his finger through the gap at the top.

'Dear Fr. van Engelen,' Truus wrote, 'Thank you for your kind letter. You have always been kind. I understand your position. I can't be part of your pastoral family as much as I wish I could. But it's enough to be in your special prayers. I know from my reading that prayer intentions during your Mass are important. I hope I am in those intentions. You will always be in my prayers. God bless you, Truus van den Donker.'

Jos laid the letter on the desk and looked through the window at the road, busy with people and commercial activity. He placed it in a small box with other letters. That was it. It was finished. It must be finished. He resolved to end a pointless preoccupation. His dedication to his pastoral duties would help him forget. The months passed by, and Truus was forced into the background by the news about the council in De Jonge's swollen rhetoric, although it was still only about the Church's high hopes for a thorough revival of Catholic life. It was the same with Frans. He, too, had nothing special to report. Jos suspected Frans had not yet had access to the information driving De Jonge. He hoped the council would bear fruit, but the hollow-sounding rhetoric, more like propaganda, filled him with unease. He kept it to himself. One Saturday afternoon, while chatting on the verandah with a glass of Tom's favourite Australian beer, a tall, solid man dressed smartly wandered into view, looking around. He stopped in front of the presbytery and scrutinised the two priests.

'What have we here?' whispered Tom as the man approached. 'He's not from here but seems interested in us.'

'Good afternoon, Fathers,' the man called cheerfully from the road.

'German,' said Tom, and then to the man, 'Good afternoon, my friend. Can we help?'

There was something familiar about the grey-haired man with an air of success, but Jos could not place him. The man came to the front gate.

'Fr. van Engelen?'

'Yes,' said Jos, rising. 'With whom do I have the pleasure?'

'You don't know my name,' the man said in a slight German accent, 'but we've met before.'

'*Goede hemel*,' cried Jos after looking more closely.

'Yes, it's me. May I come in? I would like to talk to you if there's no inconvenience.'

'By all means,' called Tom, glancing at Jos, who seemed unable to reply, 'please join us. Can I offer you something?'

'Gerhard Bann,' the man said when he had joined them, 'I'm in Lae on business. I learned that Fr. van Engelen was here.'

'Well, come inside, Mr Bann, and let me get you something to drink before we talk.'

'I met Fr. van Engelen during the war,' Gerhard Bann began in fluent English when they were settled in the lounge room. 'I came across Father and a colleague helping people caught in the bombing. A few other connections followed.' Tom glanced again at Jos, who said nothing. 'After the war, to keep a long story short, I returned to my work as an engineer and helped rebuild Germany. I ended up establishing my own firm, which grew to be very successful. I never forgot my meeting with Father, and I made inquiries during a business visit to Holland a few years ago. I wondered if you had survived.'

'Mr Bann was in a position to kill me,' Jos remarked to Tom. 'I always wondered why he didn't.'

'It was not difficult to track you down to Middelburg,' the German said. 'I discovered you were in New Guinea. I was pleased to hear you had survived.'

'That must have been before 1960.'

'Yes, that's correct,' said the major. 'You have nothing to ask?' he continued when Jos did not respond.

Jos glanced at Tom, and Herr Bann seemed to understand.

'If you have anything to say in private,' said Tom, 'I'm happy to leave you.'

'No,' said Jos, after some hesitation and raising his hand, 'I should not be so rude.'

'I understand your hesitation, Fr. Jos. You can trust me.'

'Yes, of course. I am sorry, Fr. Tom. This has been such a surprise—almost a shock. Okay, then, Major, why didn't you shoot me when you found me at the farmhouse? That's what you were there for, wasn't it?'

'Not quite. We were out looking for you. Indeed, I had tracked you down to the farmhouse. At least, that's where the evidence pointed. I didn't shoot you because I had orders to bring you in if I found you. Several units were out looking for you. The Gestapo wanted to interrogate you. That would have been the end of you—after a bout of torture.'

'The Gestapo?' interposed Tom.

'Not every German soldier was a Nazi, and not all of us were bereft of a sense of justice. You had saved a big group of people, some old and some very young. You didn't deserve to be handed over to the Gestapo. That's why I let you go.'

'I thank you, Major. I am grateful because you obviously compromised yourself.'

There were moments of silence while Tom looked from Jos to the German and back again.

'You have nothing more to ask?' prompted the German.

'I caught someone near the barn a few days before your visit. Whoever it was, fled on a bicycle towards Breda. Do you have any information about that?'

'No, I'm sure it was not us. I was close to the organisation of the search.'

'Why did you come a second time, then, just after the unknown visitor who was clearly spying?'

'I had a hint from my superior officer that I should recheck my suspicions. We were all cautious about the SS.'

'The hint had some ground, then?'

'Yes, indeed, I had not considered that. If it was us, it was out of my area of intelligence. A major has a wide responsibility.'

'Who tipped you off about the transmitter? And how did you know to raid precisely at the time it was in use?'

'I had no information about the SS raid beforehand. From what I could gather—it was a risk to pose questions when the SS were involved—the information came from within the seminary. But I cannot be sure. Who else would have known, besides?'

'Yes, you are right. Nobody else knew, I was sure.'

Anything else?

Jos thought for a moment.

'The couple who lived at that farmhouse was shot dead allegedly during the liberation of Breda. Do you know anything about that?'

'No. My unit was hemmed in. I surrendered as soon as the opportunity arose. I didn't want any more of my boys killed. I knew nothing about the couple.'

'How did you know I was at the farmhouse in the first place?'

'The information about your activities came from within the seminary. From whom, I don't know. We narrowed your possible whereabouts to a few places.'

'What happened when I was not found?'

'Nothing. There was always the possibility you had fled. That was the conclusion.'

'Did no one know I was sent to an outlying parish north of the seminary that evening?'

'It appears not. Where did you go afterwards?'

'To Amsterdam.'

'You surprise me. How did you escape detection? Indeed, how did you survive after the work you did smuggling people out of Holland?

'I was careful.'

'You were very clever and very lucky.'

'I'm a Catholic priest, Herr Bann. I trust in the efficacy of prayer. Besides, I had training in covert operations in London.'

'Yes, I'm Catholic, too. I attribute my survival to my poor, ragged prayers.'

'You speak excellent English, Mr Bann,' said Tom when the exchange appeared to come to an end.

'I had a lot to do with American companies, still do, but less now. It seemed learning English would be essential for business in the coming years.'

'Do you have a family, Herr Bann?'

'Yes, four children, three girls and a boy.'

'I bless them.'

'Thank you, Father.'

In contrast to the stern, reticent major of the war, Gerhard Bann turned out to be an agreeable conversationalist. The two priests and the German businessman chatted until late afternoon. Bann was in Papua New Guinea to survey the possibilities of infrastructure work in which his company specialised. He had not come to Lae especially to visit Fr. van Engelen, he smiled. It was a happy coincidence. Shortly before five o'clock, he rose.

'Thank you for your hospitality, but I must return to my hotel to make a few calls. Besides, I understand you have religious commitments.'

'You are understanding, Herr Bann,' said Jos in German. 'I am so pleased you took the time to see me. Your information has been helpful.'

'I understand,' said Herr Bann in German and then in English to Tom. 'Please excuse our little exchange in German, Fr. Connolly. Fr. van Engelen speaks perfect German.'

'No worries, Mr Bann, nice to meet you. Call again,' said Tom, leaving Jos to accompany the German businessman to the front gate.

'You were betrayed, weren't you? I did not want to say it in front of your brother priest.'

'Yes, I was betrayed. It could not be otherwise. I trust Fr. Connolly. He's a down-to-earth, sensible person. But I can't help being on my guard.'

'I would feel the same way. Is there anything you want to ask now we're alone?'

'The two things that concern me are the raid at precisely the time the superior general and my colleague were operating the transmitter and the murder of that old couple who gave me cover. Herr Bann, I had intensive covert training and spycraft in London before arriving in Holland in March 1940. We did not fail to adhere to the protocols I established for my colleague and me. The superior general had nothing to do with the transmitter. That was agreed. Nor did he know the crucial codes. I can never believe Fr. Timmermans and Fr. Albers deliberately broke the rules. I must conclude that the reasons given for the raid were a sham. There was collusion between someone at the seminary and the German command in Breda. Someone was aware of my activities despite the care I took. But who?'

'I've told you all I know about the raid. I only came into the picture when the command concluded a third spy was on the loose, namely you. They gave me the details of your frequent contact with farms in the seminary's neighborhood and businesses in Breda. I concluded the farms were the most likely places to offer you cover. I was right about the farm I picked. They did not tell me why they thought you were the third spy. I assumed the information came from the same source. I did not know until our confrontation in the attic that the third spy was the priest I had met chasing down the Breda evacuation.'

'Think, Herr Bann,' said Jos after reflecting, 'was there any sign afterwards of who the person or persons could have been?'

The German pondered the question.

'My duties did not bring me into the sphere of the relations with the seminary, but I do remember the commandant was an occasional visitor there. If I remember correctly, he found the seminary leadership agreeable and cooperative. I assumed that was a facetious way of saying the raid had frightened them into compliance. I see it could have been otherwise now. You must understand, I had little to do with that side of the command. I was a soldier first. Espionage and trickery were not my thing. Excuse me for saying so.'

'No apology necessary, Herr Bann. I thought the same way before I understood the precariousness of our country. What about the murder of the old couple? Anything to add?'

'No, nothing, except perhaps I did not search the surroundings. I guessed you had enough sense not to stay in the house, and you probably hid somewhere in the fields. I thought you would surface eventually. Afterwards, when it was obvious you were gone, I assumed the old couple had cleared away any signs of an encampment. As far as I'm aware, there was no harassment of the couple in the weeks following.'

'Well, I thank you for your information, Herr Bann. In a way, it doesn't matter now. It is simply for me to know what happened.'

'If you were betrayed then, those same people could betray you now.'

'I've thought about that, too, but there seems no point or opportunity now.'

'I'll tell you what I'll do,' said Herr Bann after some thought. 'When I'm back in Germany, I'll make inquiries. I'm still in contact with fellow officers.'

'I would appreciate that. Write to me here.'

Jos stood at the front gate and watched the German businessman walk briskly and upright towards the harbour, where he assumed he was staying in one of the international hotels.

'Well, there's no end to your talents, Jos,' said Tom. 'You speak German, too.'

'That's no great thing, I assure you. Germany is next door to Holland, and the two languages are related. Moreover, some of the books I studied were in German.'

'Well, did you learn anything more?'

'Not really. Just confirmation of what I suspected.'

'You were caught up in something big, Jos. Me, in my little carefree world in Brisbane, I had no idea. It sounds like someone in the seminary betrayed you. It's shocking to contemplate.'

'Yes, it is shocking, but it hardly matters now, as I said to Gerhard Bann. More than twenty years have passed.'

'I'm not so sure,' said Tom, frowning.

Chapter 23

The Council Opens

DURING THE following weeks, the conversation with Herr Bann continually churned in Jos's mind. He hardly got any further than suspecting all or one of Muller, Van Rossem, Koeman, and even De Jonge. Indeed, it could have been someone he had never imagined, one of the lay brothers, for example. But, no, that was too mad. The big problem with Van Rossem and Muller was their suspected Marxist or Hegelian agenda. If the influence was Marxist, which Fr. Albers assumed, and not so much Hegelian, which he increasingly suspected, why would Marxists collude with the Nazis? It did not make sense unless the diabolical intention was to manipulate the Nazis for their purposes, as Bart dared not openly suggest.

A letter arrived from Frans to distract him from his pointless scrutiny of the same details. Frans still had nothing more than the usual to report about the council, but he did have a suggestion from Fr. Matthijs at the St. Augustinus chapel. Fr. Matthijs recommended Fr. Jos get hold of Pope Pius XII's encyclical *Humani Generis* 'concerning some false opinions threatening to undermine the foundations of Catholic Doctrine,' published in 1950. He should also find Fr. Garrigou-Lagrange's paper 'Where is the New Theology Leading Us?' It was released in 1946. Fr. Matthijs suspected this 'New Theology' would be a key motivation among some bishops attending the council.

The release dates were curious, thought Jos. In 1946, he was almost too ill to read a newspaper, let alone attend to an obscure piece of theology by one of the great Thomists of the modern era. In 1950, he arrived in New Guinea to find all the Lae parish's responsibilities on his shoulders, a burden that resulted in his collapse. He heard nothing about *Humani Generis* among his fellow priests. A crucial papal encyclical about modernist thought, a little more than ten years old, would have interested him. It occurred to him why he might have missed the publication of both works, even if he had been in a fit state to attend to them.

'Have you read Pius XII's encyclical *Humani Generis*?'

'Who mani what?'

'*Humani Generis*,' said Jos, thinking he had the answer. 'It's Latin for "Of the human race."'

'No,' said Tom, reluctantly taking his eyes from his newspaper. 'Should I have? You know, papal encyclicals are not high on my reading list here.'

Jos did not inquire further but asked Tom to request copies of both publications when he reported to the Sydney house. Jos had to remind Tom a couple of times. With much apologising for his 'slackness,' Tom eventually sent off the request. Several bulletins arrived, but not the requested publications. A letter from Fr. de Jonge came four weeks later, saying Pius XII's encyclical was misleading in many respects.

The obsolete, superseded Thomistic ideas of the notorious Fr. Garrigou-Lagrange had infected the pope's thinking. Indeed, rumour has it that Garrigou-Lagrange had ghostwritten it. There was sound evidence for it. The theological dialogue, certainly among the Dutch theologians, had moved on. Frs. van Engelen and Connolly would do better to get involved with enthusiasm in the order's preparations for the great ecumenical council that was about to open, instead of persisting with literature that many found mistaken, besides stale and dated. To help, Fr. de Jonge enclosed a summary of Fr. Enrico de Leon's key theological ideas. Fr. de Leon was a leading theologian of the *Nouvelle Theologie* and would play a leading role in the council as a *peritus*, a theological expert to one of the bishops.

'Now look what you've done,' said Tom, handing the letter to Jos. 'You've got an innocent man into trouble.'

'You'll survive,' said Jos as he perused the letter. 'But somehow, I think it's me De Jonge has as his target.'

'I'll have to discipline you,' said Tom, returning to his newspaper.

Jos took the three-page summary to his room to study. It was more of the same tedious stuff, but in more detail. The Church had to be open to the modern world. The liturgy—De Jonge's preoccupation—must be adapted as a vital pastoral step, especially in the missionary lands. What would the natives of Papua New Guinea make of a liturgy in a foreign language and steeped in centuries of medieval history? Quite a lot, thought

Jos. There was, however, something new, at least philosophically. The most respected theologians of the present time, wrote De Jonge, agreed that Thomistic realism was too restrictive and limited by its medieval origins.

De Leon's claim that life was ever-changing and evolving——new situations, and new ideas——demanded the Church's theologians break out of a stationary notion of truth. Truth was ever forming, and the Church, in its teaching, must consider that. It was all very vague, but Jos caught a whiff of Hegel's dialectic in those vague passages. If so, De Leon was swapping stationary for unstable. The issue was essentially philosophical, not theological, more about fundamental ideas of reality and knowledge acquisition. He was determined to get hold of *Humani Generis* and Garrigou-Lagrange's paper. He wrote to Frans but did not expect an answer before the Second Vatican Ecumenical Council's opening, which was only weeks away.

ON THE eve of the council, Jos was at the natives' fruit and vegetable market. He came to buy provisions and enjoy the bustling crowd's tropical and indigenous atmosphere, though he was not too keen on the drums in which the natives spat out their chewed betel nut. For the rest, it reminded him of the Middelburg market despite the enormous difference in people and stock. From the corner of his eye, he noticed a group of Europeans coming along the vendor displays towards him. He took no further notice. European tourists were a common sight at the native markets. He made his choice of tropical fruit and vegetables and paid the vendor. Turning to move on, he came face to face with Cees van den Donker and an attractive woman hanging on his arm.

'Meneer van den Donker. What a surprise to see you here?'

'I can't say the same, Meneer Pastoor.' He smirked at his attractive companion, who showed no interest. 'I know you're here and what your purpose is.'

'And what would that be, Meneer?'

'To indoctrinate the natives with that pernicious religion of yours.'

'Would I be right in thinking you are here to stop me?'

The smirk disappeared from Cees's mouth, and he looked unsure. He quickly regained his composure.

'You flatter yourself, Meneer.'

'Do I?' said Jos, noticing the others watching. 'Are you here on a tour?' he said in English. 'We see many groups of Europeans coming through on visits.'

'We're not a tourist group,' said a woman who appeared to be the leader, 'at least not in the usual sense.'

'I didn't mean just tourists. Many businessmen, government, and non-government organisations visit. Papua New Guinea is a developing country. Others have a cultural interest.'

'We have a cultural interest,' said the woman.

Jos noticed Van den Donker shake his head at the woman.

'So do we.'

'Not the same as ours,' said the woman, nodding at her companions and preparing to move on. 'We don't think religious indoctrination is a positive influence.'

'We have religious motivations—spreading the Christian faith, the message of charity to all. But we are also concerned about the health, work, and vocational education of the native population. We want to see the deadly tribal conflict end, as well as such things as cannibalism. You might be surprised, madam, to hear there are still reports of cannibalism in the hills.'

'We see these things differently. Good morning, sir.'

'You're all about blind cultural destruction,' sneered Cees in Dutch as the group walked on. 'And you can't have her, see. She's still married—to me.'

'I suppose this woman is your cousin?' said Jos, immediately wishing he hadn't.

A few filthy words in English slipped out the side of the woman's mouth, and with Cees smug and smirking, they caught up with the group. Jos watched them amble along the displays, stopping now and then. They gathered around a native with carved wooden artifacts, picking them up and passing them around with keen interest.

As Jos made his way back to the presbytery, he wondered, not about the group's purpose—that had something to do with Cees's strange interests—but the comment that he could not have his wife. Did Cees have any solid reason to think he was after his wife? Or was he just making something out of nothing to carry on his hatred of the Church? Surely, his sympathy for Truus would not convince the average rational person that he was scheming to run off with her. It was ludicrous. Besides the lack of evidence, he was thousands of kilometres away in a developing country, which was difficult to travel to.

The question returned to why Cees was in Lae. There were thousands of places in Papua New Guinea to satisfy the group's anthropological or occultist interests. Why should they choose Lae? And how did Cees know he was in Lae? Besides asking his family not to reveal his precise where-abouts, he had heard that Cees avoided all contact with them. A week later, these questions ceased to occupy him. He collapsed with food poisoning. Alarmed, Tom sent for the doctor, who, on examination, rushed him to the hospital. Jos vaguely found himself attached to intravenous tubes amid very busy people in white. When his vision became clearer, he saw Tom at his bedside.

'Where am I?'

'Where do you think, mate? You're in the hospital. They've just shifted you from the intensive care ward. The doctor said if I had left it, you might now be in serious trouble.'

'You don't call this serious? When can I get out?' he said, squinting at Tom.

'No, you're staying put. You're too drugged to go anywhere.'

'What happened?'

'Your food poisoning was developing into septicemia.'

He dozed off again.

'How come you didn't get it?' he asked on Tom's next visit.

'Strong constitution, mate.'

'Don't give me that,' Jos said, now less drowsy. 'If we eat the same bad food, you should get it, too.'

'What are you suggesting? I poisoned you?'

'Don't be silly. I just find it strange.'

At that moment, the parish doctor swaggered into the room.

'Floored again,' he said. 'I told you, your war experience has weakened you. This is going to happen again, you know. I can still write that recom-mendation.'

'You can put your pen and paper away,' said Jos, sighing with fatigue. 'I'm not going anywhere.'

'Okay, I can only give you advice. Now, you'll be here for a week or two until you're completely fit to resume your duties.'

'A week or two?'

'Yes, they've got to get the poison out of you. Besides, I know you wouldn't rest if we let you out.'

'Let me out?'

'Fr. Tom will give you some pleasure reading to distract you, a nice novel, or something. You must have mental and physical rest. You're not to concern yourself with Church matters for a few weeks.'

'I told him about your preoccupation with the council. I'll keep the reports for you.'

'Bring some decent fiction, if I'm to read a novel—a Dickens or a Greene or a Waugh, something like that. It's not likely you'll find some nice Dutch novel here.'

'I'll come each day. Let me know if there's anything you want.'

'Don't worry about the bananas and grapes. You understand.'

'You're almost a different person under sedation. It's amusing.'

'Is that what it is? Who's going to pay for all this?'

When Jos opened his eyes, the nurse was at his bed, feeling his pulse and taking his blood pressure. The light indicated it was late afternoon. The hospital doctor stood behind the nurse, waiting for her to finish.

'Your doctor told you that you landed in hospital because of septicemia caused by food poisoning,' the doctor said in a low voice, taking the chair beside the bed when the nurse had departed. 'We're not so sure about that.'

'What do you mean?' said Jos, much clearer than in the morning.

'You might have been poisoned—a natural poison, the sort the natives make out in the hills. How trustworthy are your staff, you know, the natives who work for you?'

'I've never had any reason whatsoever to distrust any of them. Those who help us are fine, dedicated people.'

'Fr. van Engelen, I don't know how much you know about the natives of New Guinea or their traditional religious beliefs, but sorcerers have played a big role in their brand of animism.'

'Yes, I know. What are you getting at?'

'It's possible that a sorcerer has targeted you as the cause of the harm suffered by someone or a group.'

'No, no, I can't believe that. That's too easy. Our native parishioners gave those animist beliefs away a long time ago. Besides, how certain are you about the poison?

'Less than a hundred per cent sure. We don't have the facilities. It is significant that Fr. Connolly was unaffected when you both ate the same food. You should be aware that some natives mix their Christian beliefs with the old animist beliefs. Sorcerers are still active with their magical arts.'

After Jos had exacted an undertaking not to make public his suspicions, the doctor left him to ponder his warning. One should not underestimate the social and political harm such public knowledge could cause, apart from upsetting Jos's congregation. Over the next week, the stubborn stomach pain and discomfort forced Jos to consider that the hospital doctor might be right. Something was wrong with his stomach, something he had not felt before. Three weeks later, he returned to the presbytery with the solemn promise he would do as he was told. He stuck to his promise. The state of his stomach was an incentive. It would also be foolish to ignore the hospital doctor's warnings.

He stuck to a bland diet of food he prepared himself. Tom took discreet notice of the food and its preparation. The cook and her casual assistants, all natives, did not question the new procedures. They were more concerned about Fr. Jos and his illness. Two weeks later, Jos was fit enough to take his turn in the confessional. One Saturday afternoon, there were no penitents near the end of the two-hour session, and the church fell silent. Jos took out his rosary beads. He was threading his way through the beads when the door of the confessional opened and shut softly. He waited a moment before sliding aside the door of the grille. Silence followed his introductory prayers.

'Do you need help?' he said, peering into the darkened cubicle. He made out the silhouette of the top of a head. Whoever it was, man or woman, that person was not kneeling in the usual way. 'Do you have difficulty in confessing your sins?' he prompted. Now, he could hear laboured breathing. 'You have nothing to fear. Your confession is between you and Our Lord.'

'I poisoned you,' said a voice in a barely audible whisper. 'I'm sorry.'

'Why?' said Jos, not recognising the voice.

'I don't have to tell you,' the voice said after a lengthy silence.

'Did you mean to poison me?'

'Yes.'

'Was it entirely your decision? I must know your intention, your free will to commit a grave act, a mortal sin.'

Laboured breathing was the only answer.

'Did you feel compelled by something or someone?'

There was no answer.

'Are you afraid?'

Still no answer. The breathing ceased. Jos looked into the cubicle that now had a little light, showing it was empty. He leapt to his feet and swung open his cubicle's door. The penitent's door was ajar, and the church was empty. He shut both doors and resumed his seat. Ten minutes remained before the end of the session. What was he to do? He would never break the seal of confession, but was it a confession in the sacramental sense? Whoever it was—he still did not know whether it was a man or a woman—that person did not follow the usual procedure. He simply informed him of the act rather than confess it. There was a distinction. But did that distinction make a difference for the seal of confession? There was no problem with identity—he did not know who it was, only that it was a native. Was he free to reveal something said in an irregular and incomplete confession? As he sat chatting with Tom that evening, he decided he could not. He had heard a partial confession that might have become a full confession if he had not posed those questions.

On the pretext of going for some fresh air, Jos made his way a few days later to one of Lae's tour operators, where he made inquiries about inland excursions. The tour operator, a parishioner, was expansive about his products and the wonderful sights to be had. When Jos casually asked about cultural tours, the operator exclaimed in surprise.

'All our tours target a cultural aspect of the hinterland and its people, Father van Engelen. That's the focus.'

'Yes, of course. I should have realised.'

'Are you making inquiries for someone?'

'Not really. I came across a group of tourists here specifically to study native culture. I wondered what the possibilities were for such a group.'

'I can guess who you mean. A rather pushy woman asked if I conducted tours into the wilds where natives still practised sorcery and witchcraft, unaffected by foreign belief systems—evidently meaning Christianity. I had to pass her through to the young blokes down the road who are silly enough to take people there. I heard they were out there a week and paid a big bonus to the young fellows with their guns and four-wheel drives. Those people have been here before, you know.'

Yes, Jos knew they had been in Lae before, but he did not say so. He thanked the parishioner and returned to the presbytery to ponder this fresh information. The drift of his thinking led him to unacceptable conclusions. He could not believe Cees van den Donker's hatred was so consuming that he came to New Guinea to arrange to kill him by inciting some sorcerer's magic arts. It could not be. It was as unimaginable as thinking van Rossem and Muller were the ones who betrayed him. No, it could not be. It was insane. Such madness, such wickedness, could not possess rational beings. But why did that native admit to trying to poison him? What was behind the attempt if Cees had nothing to do with it? Who had he upset? He could think of nobody. Then again, there was nothing rational about sorcery if it had taken possession of a person. It belonged to the diabolical—to the demonic. Demons seemed to have followed him across the oceans. Other matters, however, pushed the poison and sorcery into the background.

PATTING HIM on the shoulder for being a good boy, Tom released the bulletins from Sydney on the Second Vatican Council's first session, which had started on 11 October.

'They'll keep you busy for a while,' he said. 'Better you than me.'

'What's your impression?' said Jos, leafing through the bundle. 'Are you inspired?'

'You're usually not so facetious, mate.'

'You're right. My apologies. I should be more respectful. It was just that I didn't see much point.'

'No, no,' said Tom, wagging his finger. 'None of that respect stuff. You've got to become more Australian. We descendants of convicts are born with disrespect for authority, especially unproven authority. It must be earned. Say what you think.'

'I wonder whether our respected provincial realises he has a potential rebel among us.'

'My name's not Connolly for nothing.'

'I beg your pardon.'

'Connolly, Irish, rebels. Come on, Jos, don't tell me you don't know what a bunch of rebels the Irish are. Anyhow, truth is,' he continued, dropping his voice, 'don't tell anyone, but I find all that intellectual stuff boring. It's hard to concentrate on it. You read and summarise it for me. I'm too busy saving my congregation's souls—and my own, of course.'

'Well, theological and philosophical perspectives may be behind it all, but the public conversation has been about renewing and updating the Church, throwing the windows open to the modern world, and letting in fresh air. With such a grandiose purpose, the results may be far-reaching, reaching all the way to us in Lae.'

'What could they do that'll affect us?'

'It's hard to say. With the wild talk in some quarters, anything is possible.'

'Come on, Jos, that doesn't sound very positive.'

'No, it doesn't, does it?'

The rhetoric about updating and renewal filled the first lot of bulletins, but then came the concrete information. The tone was triumphant. Despite fears that the all-powerful curia cardinals would prevail, the opposite happened. Those fearful and distrustful of change had to bow before the Holy Spirit's movement among the world's bishops. The order of the Wounded Heart of Jesus was proud that the Dutch contingent, with its gifted theologians, had taken a leading role in showing the need for change.

They had set up their information centre before the council opened and were turning out reams of discussion papers on all the contentious issues. In Holland, bishops and theologians, under the leadership of gifted Dutch theologian Fr. Eenwoud Schilferbek, subjected the discussion papers prepared by the curia conservatives to devastating analysis. The whole preparatory work, accused of 'lacking a charitable, missionary, and ecumenical approach,' was thrown out. The harshest critics accused the curia authors of 'triumphalism, clericalism, and legalism.'

Jos put the bulletins on his desk and stared through the window before taking them up again. Hans de Jonge could not suppress his joy in reporting the turn of events. After the close of the first session on 8 December

1962, his bulletin crowed breathlessly that one of the most outspoken expert advisers, Fr. Hilarius de Koning, could hardly believe the success in thwarting the traditionalists' domination of the council. Those for change, the progressives, were a minority, but they had prevailed. No one, the curia least of all, could stop the new spirit that had permeated the gathering of bishops. 'The spectacular outcome of the first session,' he said, 'was the demonstration that the bishops, and not merely the Roman Curia, make up the Church.' The apparent success of the progressives was dispiriting enough, but the proposed changes to the liturgy caused Jos the most pain. Hans de Jonge's radical vision was more than vindicated. Jos dreaded further developments.

'You don't look pleased,' said Tom a few days later, after evening dinner. 'Those bulletins are giving you indigestion.'

'It's worrying, I must admit.'

'Okay, give me a brief roundup, no taxing detail.'

'Let's see,' said Jos, picking up the bundle of bulletins he had at his side and shuffling through them. 'Pope John says the council is to be pastoral, meaning no changes to doctrine. The Church's teaching remains untouched. Despite that declaration, a group of bishops from Northern Europe—mostly from Germany, Holland, France, and Austria—have set the pace for big changes. They support theological ... actually, I would call them philosophical ideas at variance with the philosophical presuppositions underlying Church teaching. Thomism has been—'

'You're losing me, Jos.'

'Right, well, as brief as I can, then: on one side, you have those who want to defend the Church as it is; on the other, those who want radical change—traditionalists versus liberals or progressives. De Jonge seems to be using these words interchangeably. The liberals are steamrolling the traditionalists and appear unstoppable.'

'Sounds like a political barney.'

'A political barney?'

'A fight, a brawl, you know. I need to give you lessons in Australian English.'

'The worst of it is that radical changes to the liturgy, the Mass, seem certain. Use of the vernacular, cultural adjustment, even having the priest facing the congregation.'

'You're kidding.'

'Read it for yourself. And prepare yourself. Liturgical change is De Jonge's special advocacy and is inextricably connected with the need to modernise. The political and the liturgical are the same for him.'

'De Jonge should pull his finger out ... I'm sorry, I shouldn't say things like that, old habits from mixing with plumbers and bricklayers. He's in his own little intellectual fantasy world. I'm uneasy with someone who's so neat and precise in everything. If I had my way, I'd make him spend time on a building site.'

'I wouldn't use your colourful Australian expressions, but I agree, at least about his fixation with the liturgy.'

Tom was not the only one to descend into colloquialisms about the council. Frans added a few lines in Marijke's Christmas letter. 'Who in the hell is this Schilferbek?' he wrote. 'Does the rest of the world know what a great big fat finger busybody Holland has in the Rome proceedings? It's embarrassing. You remember the joke I made about Elvis Presley in the Mass when you told me about the agitation for far-reaching change in the liturgy? Well, I wasn't far wrong, was I? All that talk about simplification, spontaneity, introducing everyday speech, blah, blah, blah—where will it end? Once these radical fellas get the bit between their teeth, there'll be no stopping them. Fr. Matthijs and his fellow monks are very worried. I feel sorry for you, Jos.' Marijke was more moderate in her language but also wondered about the point of it all. Nobody she knew was aware that the Church needed radical change. Her parents were just as bemused. She did add news about the Van den Donkers, something Jos could not help looking for.

'I saw Truus last market day. We stopped for a brief chat. Although the sadness was still in her eyes, she was more relaxed than I've seen her in a while. Cees must have been out of town. She never stops otherwise. He's frequently gone these days. She said he had recently been on an overseas trip for about a month. She had no idea where he went. He just told her he would be away for a while, and she did not have to concern herself with Gerda, meaning she should stay at the farm in Vrouwekerke. He doesn't want her interfering in his business, she said.

'She has become quite open with me. She said she had my confidence. I reassured her, of course. The attention of the two suitors has died away. The message got through, apparently. Thank heavens she has stopped wearing those dowdy clothes. It was a shame to see her deliberately spoil her feminine looks. She wished us a merry Christmas. She included you, too, you know. Isn't it odd that a person with a strict reformed background has chosen us for her confidences?'

Jos read and pondered those passages many times. It was a relief that he did not write home about his poisoning. He returned to studying the ideas on which Pius XII's encyclical *Humani Generis* focused. In the meantime, he had received copies of the encyclical and Garrigou-Lagrange's commentary. That gave him a taste of the *Nouvelle Theologie*, the New Theology, and the fervour of its promoters. All the time, he had a sense of the overwhelming influence of a Hegelian spirit, the idea of continual change, conflictual change, as the fundamental reality of human existence. The more he read, the more pessimistic he became about where the council would go in the second session. He was thankful Tom allowed him some leeway in his study. Better he studied the business than he, repeated Tom. The unexpected appearance of Gerhard Bann, who turned up one Saturday afternoon in January, broke his preoccupation with the council.

'Come on in, Mr. Bann,' said Tom. 'You're very welcome and, no, you're not disturbing our routine. Would you like a cup of tea?'

'Thank you, Fr. Connolly. No, I will not stay long. I have a meeting later in the afternoon. I am only here overnight—for business. Our company has possibilities in Lae. Would you mind if I chat in private with Fr. van Engelen? It's easier for me to speak in German.'

'Of course not. Please feel free. I've got things to do.'

'Can I suggest Father and I go for a walk? I do not want to impose. That would not be fair.'

'You're not imposing, but please yourself.'

'I wasn't entirely truthful about speaking to you in private,' said Herr Bann when they were outside walking towards the harbour. 'I wasn't sure how much you wanted your colleague to hear. I hope I did not offend him.'

'No, not at all. Fr. Tom is very relaxed. He understands. So, you have some news, I take it.'

'Yes, I succeeded in contacting a few of the officers from that time, June 1940. Only one had something of interest—something that might be critical, at least to you. He thinks the information about the clandestine transmitter came from one of the *Schutzstaffel* officers. He didn't know who. Who told him, he can no longer remember. It was a passing comment, and we knew it was best not to chat about the SS.'

'SS? How?'

'Yes, and here's the interesting part. The SS officer was homosexual, which had something to do with the contact in the seminary. The commandant's occasional visits to the seminary were always in the company of the SS officer. Nobody thought that unusual. I would not have thought it unusual if I had known. The *Schutzstaffel*, especially the officers, did what they wanted. But there's more than the homosexual connection.'

'What?' Jos's thoughts returned to Fr. Albers's remarks about Marxist infiltration and the plant of a homosexual priest.

'Did you know there were rumours about the SS and the occult?'

'Yes, I am aware ...,' said Jos, not wanting to disturb Herr Bann's account with what he knew.

'Fr. van Engelen, it might be interesting for you as a Catholic priest to research how connected Nazism, homosexuality, the esoteric tradition, and neo-paganism are.'

'What prompted your interest in all this?'

'I come from Bavaria, which, as you may be aware, is Catholic. Talk of connections in the German army with the occult, homosexuality, and paganism would always arouse my interest. After the war, I followed up with some research. We weren't all bloodthirsty *Krauts*. Many of us wanted to discover how ordinary people, some of our neighbours, descended into barbarism.'

'You have given me something to think about, Herr Bann,' said Jos, unwilling to go into his experiences with the SS and the occult. 'I appreciate your taking the time to inform me.'

'There's something else. We did some research on Papua New Guinea when the business opportunity arose—cultural research. Although many natives have converted to Christianity, especially in places like Lae, the old animism with its sorcerers and witchcraft still exists in the backwoods.'

'I'm aware of that. Do you have a point?'

'The revival of esotericism and the occult in the West, particularly in Germany, has a natural link with unspoiled indigenous animism. Catholic priests are the spiritual enemy of sorcerers. I hope you and your fellow priest are careful.'

'We try to be prudent with all indigenous matters, but as concerns our native parishioners, we have full confidence in them. In any case, thank you for your advice. It's more than valued.'

'You're welcome. I'm glad to be of service in something clearly of deep importance to you.'

'Again, Herr Bann, I'm grateful for your help in understanding what happened all those years ago. Please drop in any time.'

'Thank you, Father. While I am with you, would you please hear my confession?'

AT THE end of January, Fr. Tom handed Jos a message from Sister Ambrose, the principal of the local convent run by the Sisters of the Assumption. It was an invitation to meet Mother Augustinus, the mother superior of an associated Dutch institute of sisters, on a research visit connected with the council.

'Did Sister Ambrose say what it was about?' said Jos, looking at the note. 'I don't know any Mother Augustinus. What would she want with me in her research?'

'No. You'll have to go and find out for yourself,' said Tom, showing he had finished with the subject. 'Even less do I know any Dutch nuns. That's your business. Wish Sister Ambrose a good day for me.'

Jos racked his brains on his way to the school. He could not think what a mother superior of a Dutch order had to say to him. He was not familiar with the female religious orders in Holland. If she were on a research visit, wouldn't speaking to Tom be more courteous? When he arrived, Jos wished Sister Ambrose a good morning and passed on Fr. Tom's greeting before being shown into the convent parlour where two sisters sat, one with the dignified bearing of a mother superior. Jos stopped, stared, and gaped as the two sisters rose.

'Femke!' He staggered and reached for the nearby chair.

Sister Ambrose and Mother Augustinus's companion looked askance at him.

'I'm sorry, Fr. van Engelen,' said Mother Augustinus, coming to him. 'I did not mean it to be such a surprise. Please take a seat.' She took his arm lightly and indicated the nearby lounge chair.

'It's more a shock than a surprise, Fem ... Mother Augustinus,' said Jos, taking his breath as he sat. 'You were the last person I expected to see in Lae after ...what is it ... seventeen years?'

'First, let me introduce Sister Paulus,' said Mother Augustinus, typically taking charge. 'She has accompanied me on my rather long informational trip.'

Introductions were completed with the usual pleasantries before Sister Ambrose excused herself.

'I will leave you to your business,' she said. 'Sister Paulus, let me show you around the school.'

'Well, Femke,' said Jos when they were alone, 'if you did not mean to shock me to the bone, you failed. I'm still reeling.'

'I'm sorry, Jos. It's best we keep our history confidential. Sister Paulus only knows that I met you during the war years. I anticipated you would want the same.'

'Yes, of course, it's better that way.' He looked at her and shook his head. 'The questions are teeming in my brain. What happened? Why did you suddenly disappear?'

'Your questions are understandable, and I have long wanted to answer them. I could have done so on other occasions—before you left for Papua New Guinea in 1949. And I could have contacted you in 1960 when you were so sick. But the time was not right.'

'Why ever not?'

'Didn't you ever consider,' she said, sidestepping the question, 'that I could have been like you—a religious person, given an unexpected role in the war? There were enough signs, I thought.'

'No, never. It never entered my head. The clues pointed to several organizational roles, but never a religious one. Were you really a religious sister all through those years?'

'Yes, Jos, the whole time. My mother superior sent me to help the bishop with his administrative work. Plans were being made for the Church to aid the resistance. One day, however, I was dispatched to talk to an unknown priest who had turned up from nowhere at a parishioner's house, dirty, ragged, and exhausted. Nobody else was available, and it did not seem important. A lowly sister was good enough for the job. It all started from there. I saw almost immediately the use of your experiences and ability. Already, there was talk of smuggling people out of Holland.'

'So you accidentally became a covert agent handler—originally in a terrible, unconvincing disguise.'

'Yes, in a word,' she said with a warm smile. 'But I learned quickly with your help. The bishop thought I should continue and keep the work exclusively ours because we both belonged to religious orders. The resistance knew generally what the bishop's office was doing, but none of the details. Nobody knows who the Pimpernel was except me.'

'Good heavens,' said Jos. 'I would not have been so teasing and familiar if I had known.'

'That was one reason I hid my background—at the cost of embarrassment and discomfort. You would have acted differently and inhibited our work. You needed free rein.'

Jos contemplated the familiar face and expression, though now more mature, framed by a white wimple and veil. 'I'm not surprised you eventually rose to the position of Mother Superior. Your management ability was already evident.'

'Thank you, Jos, but I never aimed for the position. It has its burdens, believe me, especially with the council and the changes it has unleashed. That is the other reason I wanted to talk to you. I will rely on your frank, open manner.'

'You will get it in all its rawness, I warn you, but you have not answered my question. Why did you disappear, and why have you left it till now to contact me when there were opportunities? Didn't you realise I would have been worried?'

Femke hesitated. She rose and walked to the parlour window overlooking the busy road. The cries and chatter of schoolchildren drifted into the room from the playground. She turned, deep in thought.

'As you say, Fr. Jos, it is seventeen years since I abruptly disappeared from your life—and you from mine. I have matured. The responsibilities as the order's superior have matured me. The feelings I have now are not the same as then.' She hesitated again.

'Yes, I understand,' said Jos to encourage her. 'I'm not the same person, either. Things have happened—'

'Oh, Jos, you haven't changed at all,' said Femke, returning to her seat. 'I saw that immediately. But let me say what I find difficult to explain. There were two reasons I disappeared. First, I was not well. The intensity of the work, the worry about your safety, and starvation were the main causes.'

'Yes, I could see it. I remember your collapse. I was very worried.'

'Mother Superior decided it was time to stop. She sent me to the motherhouse outside Den Bosch. I spent the rest of the war recuperating and reviving my religious vocation.'

'Reviving your religious vocation? Was it that bad?'

'Yes. Definitely yes.'

'And the second reason?' said Jos.

'It also has to do with reviving my vocation.'

'Well? Jos said, seeing her colour as of old and hesitate.

'You said you loved me like a sister—'

'That was true. I have no trouble admitting that after—'

'But I could not love you like a brother.'

'But ...'

'Mother Superior recognised my struggle without saying anything at the time. Later, much later, we spoke about it. I thanked her for her intervention because I wanted to pursue my religious vocation like you. Over seventeen years, I have resolved that struggle. There, now you know the reasons I disappeared.'

'I had no idea,' said Jos. 'I assured you ...' Jos could not stop his thoughts from returning to Truus and her growing place in his feelings.

'I know. You were oblivious to my feelings. Just as well, I realised later. It was of supreme importance that you continued your work. But let's put it all aside, Fr. Jos. It belongs to the past and is no longer an issue. My affection has taken a different form. We are the brother and sister you thought we were. I've told you because I owe you an explanation for running away like I did.'

'Thank you, Femke. I understand your—'

'Now, let's talk briefly about the Second Vatican Council,' she said with a dismissive wave. 'It would be discourteous to remain in private conversation. Sister Paulus and Sister Ambrose may become suspicious that there is more involved than resuming acquaintance with a priest I met during the war.'

'Well, Femke—'

'It must now be Mother Augustinus, Fr. Jos.'

'Of course ... Mother,' he began, struggling to shift his attention from Femke's startling admission. 'I haven't had access to the documents. My views have been formed by the Sydney house's one-sided information and the colourful, equally one-sided accounts in the newspapers and magazines. The latter have reduced the council to a conflict between liberals and conservatives. It's more than that sort of conflict. At this stage, I must admit that I am worried about the direction the sessions have taken.'

He went on to outline the same concerns he had expressed to Tom. Most worrying were the proposed changes to the liturgy and the discussions within a philosophical framework that was incompatible with Church teaching and the perennial philosophy of St. Thomas. Mother Augustinus listened closely without commenting. Jos had to ask for her views.

'I'm not sure what to think,' she said. 'My philosophical knowledge is nowhere near yours, but I heard a dissonance in some of the discussions and the backgrounding discussion papers.'

'It's more than a dissonance,' said Jos.

'That would have to be explained to me and my sisters,' she said. 'I fear much of it will go above our heads unless someone competent can explain it all. It will be the same in other female orders. We risk being pushed in a direction we will only understand after the changes are fixed.' She paused, reflecting. 'On the other hand, the pope has the authority to modernise the Church, and modernisation does not in itself suggest a departure from the Church of the ages. I suppose my attitude is to wait and see what happens. We will be studying the documents.'

'Do you have access to the documents?'

'Yes, of course,' she said. 'I see to it that we have all the necessary information. I'm surprised your superior has not sent them to you—to someone with your academic background.'

'I must be tactful. My superior in Sydney does not share my views on the liturgy and philosophy.'

'I will be tactful, too, and not comment. You should have access to them, though. Would you like me to send the important ones? I will seek your advice as an academic—as a *peritus*.'

'My vow of obedience?'

'You have to resolve that, Jos ... I mean Fr. Jos.'

Jos laughed. 'Come on, Femke, I can't call you "Mother" in private conversation. It will be "Mother" only in public. By the way, what is your Christian name?'

'I'm reluctant to tell you.'

'Don't be silly.'

'It's Femke.'

'Ah, a lovely feminine Brabants name. I promise I won't tell anyone.'

'Seventeen years ago, I would have accused you of flirting as a defence.'

'Seventeen years ago, I would have said I don't know what flirting is—still don't.'

'All right, Jos,' she said, not hiding her amusement, 'to return to my offer, if your vow of obedience stands in the way, let me ask if you will reply to questions about the documents. That's legitimate, isn't it? They can't stop you from speaking your mind.'

'No, indeed, they can't. I will speak up, no matter what. Send me your questions.'

As Jos returned to the presbytery, he reflected that there had been no change in their relationship despite Femke's unexpected admission. They were just the same, like brother and sister. That would not change. At least, he hoped it wouldn't.

'Well, how did it go, mate?' said Tom. 'Who was it?'

'It was a sister I met during the war. I hadn't seen her since. Just stirring old memories. It was good to see her.'

'Had a good old chin-wag in Dutch, no doubt?'

'Yes, we did. Very enjoyable—being able to speak my own language.'

Just as well. It's all double Dutch to me,' said Tom, amused with himself.

Chapter 24

The New Mass

THE COUNCIL reconvened for the second session in September 1963. Pope John XXIII had died in the meantime. The papal conclave had placed Cardinal Giovanni Battista Montini on the papal throne as Paul VI. It was difficult for Jos to judge what precisely was going on in the council meetings. De Jonge's sympathies coloured the papers he sent, deploring the spoiling tactics of those fearful and resistant to change that continually disrupted the council's discussions. Nevertheless, those determined to drag the Church out of its paralysis, out of its fortress mentality, and take its rightful place in the modern world were prevailing.

As Fr. de Koning said, there was a spirit there that no one could stop—not even the powerful curia conservatives. Fr. de Jonge was fully confident it would do its work in the years following the council. From Frans, relaying the views of Fr. Matthijs, Jos received a similar message, but from the other side. He said it was like a tug-of-war going on in the council. It was pulling the council Fathers this way and that. Just when the council seemed to be heading into heresy, the pope intervened to drag it back from the edge.

When the Second Vatican Ecumenical Council ended in a glorious ceremony two years later, on 8 December 1965, Fr. Jos had the feeling the Church was close to toppling over the edge. In Holland, liturgical chaos reigned, wrote Frans. Jos agreed with De Jonge, whose star was scaling the heavens, about the success of the liberals. The 'spirit' had been let loose on a long leash—if there was any leash there at all.

Already before the council closed and changes were introduced throughout the Oceania Province, De Jonge announced alterations to the Masses in the order's parishes and establishments. The council had agreed on urgent liturgical changes, wrote the enthusiastic liturgist in a special missive, and they were proclaimed in the official document, *Sacrosanctum Concilium*, on 4 December 1963. It remained now for the changes to be implemented. To set an example and to take a brave lead, the priestly fraternity of the Wounded Heart of Jesus would introduce the vernacular (English) in all parts of the Mass except the Canon. It had started, thought Jos. It was May 1964.

'What are you going to do?' he said after reading the letter Tom had handed to him. It was again Saturday afternoon, and they were having a cup of tea and chatting about parish matters.

'What do you mean, Jos? Ours is to obey. We'll start the implementation immediately, of course.'

'We'll need time to prepare, won't we?'

'Yes, there'll be some preparation, but that's not too difficult, is it? I have the English translation. We read it until we memorise it. Okay? It'll be like before but with some parts of the Mass in English.'

'You're very trusting.'

'And you, Jos, have a great deal of distrust and scepticism.' Tom patted him on the shoulder. 'Relax, mate. It'll work.'

'I wouldn't bother memorising the English text,' said Jos after some thought.

'Why not?' said Tom blankly.

'You've read all that talk about "accretions" in the liturgy, haven't you? Mark my words. The first simplification will remove the beautiful penitential Psalm 42 at the beginning and the last Gospel of St John at the end. Other so-called accretions, what they call unnecessary additions, will go, too, as if they're bits of chewing gum stuck to the priest's shoes.'

'Come on, Jos. You're far too pessimistic—and negative.'

'Am I?'

'I'll tell you what,' said Tom after considering. 'You leave it to me to introduce the changes in my Mass. You go on as before. We'll do you when everything is running smoothly, as I expect. Deal?'

'Okay, deal. You're very considerate, Tom.'

Two months later, in July, the same changes were introduced into parishes throughout Australia. Jos still said his Masses unchanged, and there was no pressure from Tom. January 1965 saw the first universal change. The Vatican announced that parishes worldwide were to drop the introductory psalm and St John's last Gospel verses.

'It seems you were right,' said Tom, handing Jos the formal announcement from the Sydney house. 'De Jonge says we can drop Pope Leo's prayer, too. He can scarcely contain his jubilation.'

'It won't stop there.'

'I'm afraid to ask what you're thinking.'

'Mass facing the congregation—the turn from *ad orientem* to *versus populum*—from facing the east to facing the people. The talk will be about celebration, a communal meal, rather than sacrifice, as it has been for nearly two thousand years. Such talk has been there from the beginning, I have discovered.'

Tom was silent for a while.

'Look, Jos, I'm just a small fish in this enormous pond,' he said. 'I knowingly took the vow of obedience. What I was giving up was clear. I must trust the Church authorities. I must trust they're making changes for the good of the Church—that they're carrying out Our Lord's mission. You took the vow of obedience, too. What are you going to do?'

Jos was ready for this moment.

'I have learned from newspaper reports that they are making allowances for older priests and parishioners. So let's say I'm an older priest saying the unchanged Mass for older parishioners here. I am, after all, fifty-three.'

'You're getting me off the hook. I appreciate it. But how long can we run this excuse? De Jonge will eventually find out. He's not ready to tolerate deviations, in my view.'

'We'll face it then. Tom, again, I appreciate your generous understanding.'

Jos not only appreciated Tom's understanding. He had started to worry about him. Under that easy-going matey manner was a conscientious, sympathetic priest. How great a burden would his trust take?

LATER THAT same month, Tom handed an envelope to Jos while he sat in the lounge room, rereading some of De Jonge's council missives.

'Here's a letter from your Dutch war friend,' he said, showing no interest. 'I hope it's more interesting than what you're reading.'

'How do you know it's not from family?' said Jos playfully, meaning to shake Tom out of his mood.

'Easy, mate. Official stationery and different handwriting.'

'Can't fool you, can I?'

'I'm just about past caring.'

'Cheer up, Tom,' said Jos. 'We must not lose hope. That's what our faith is about.'

'Lose hope?' said Tom, unmoved. 'An important reason that the role of priest appealed to me was the rock-solid Church and the certainty of its teaching. Now, the council has thrown everything into the air to be the plaything of the likes of De Jonge.'

'We must persevere.'

'Yes, persevere,' Tom said, shaking his head. 'Well, I've got things to attend to, mate. I'll leave you to plough through your friend's pages.'

Jos watched Tom walk from the room, his shoulders a little hunched. He feared Tom was approaching a crisis. He sliced open the envelope and took out Femke's pages.

'Dear Father Jos,' she wrote, 'I have often been on the point of writing since we spoke about the council. The surprising developments, the obvious conflict in the council, and its aftermath have delayed me. Much information has come to us about the council's proceedings besides what is available in Holland. Of course, we also have the developments in our country steered by the so-called progressives. The papers are full of references to Fr. Schilferbek and his theological views. One could easily get confused, as I'm sure many of the faithful are. As for Fr. Schilferbek, I have the impression that few people in the Anglo-Saxon world know about this powerhouse progressive figure and the influence he wields. He exercises far more influence here in our country than high-profile *periti* like Frs. de Koning, Rathuis, and Cullen. Knowing you, I imagine you're in constant dismay over the Mass.

'The reaction to the changes in the liturgy differs among our sisters. A minority is enthusiastic, a middle group doesn't know what to think, and a third group cannot understand the reasons for dismantling our ancient rituals. The minority favouring the liturgical changes, I might add, are among the best-educated and most competent of our sisters. I'm in the third group, though I understand the intent of the innovators. Jos, would you please give us your perspective? We need sound orientation from someone who understands what's going on, doesn't have some agenda to follow, and is firm in his judgment. All this business about the council is in your area of expertise. I am a manager and organiser—that's where my competence lies—not an academic, though you suspected me of being one

.

'The council's changes to the Mass have understandably preoccupied the Catholic faithful because they are concrete and immediate. The debate will rage for some time, though I suspect the innovators will have their way and continue to innovate. There is, however, another dramatic change afoot that has not captured the attention of the Catholic masses. It is the so-called modernisation of religious life. To the extent the council texts have gained attention—it is very little—it is about the life of the male religious. The proposed modernisation for religious men threatens to be disruptive enough, but I fear it will be a destructive revolution for female religious.

'It seems the council's final decree on religious life is to be proclaimed in December at the end of the fourth session. Once again, the council's discussions and the background papers make plain the goals of the progressives. Belgian Cardinal Schuermans—ironically a man—has long been the standard bearer for radical changes in the structure of female religious life. I have included a selection of discussion papers and some of the council's reported discussions to give you an idea. However, I can summarise Cardinal Schuermans' principal ideas.

'Fundamentally, the governing structure of the convents should be radically altered to take the "concentration of power" away from a "single Mother Superior" and distributed evenly among the order's members. The ordinary nun or sister should not be reduced to a "passive, infantile, obedience." (The cardinal clearly does not understand female psychology.) A preferable equitable system of government would allow the selection of leaders through the input of its members, representing the entire congregation. In other words, Jos, the cardinal wants to restructure convents along the democratic lines so familiar in Enlightenment thinking. (My history studies have informed me of that much about the Enlightenment thinkers.) The lowly postulant entering the convent would have the same selection value as the mature, long-experienced senior sister who has risen to the position of authority and been appointed by her peers.

'But the restructuring is not only to satisfy the higher principles of democratic government, as envisaged by Cardinal Schuermans and his agitating supporters. More importantly, a democratic structure would allow the individual sister to engage freely in apostolic work, independently of the supervision of an all-powerful authority who will disappear, anyhow. Finally, consistent with the cardinal's democratic ideals, he wants the removal of the "ridiculous garb of many communities" and practices based on "outdated notions of the inferiority of women." The cardinal seems more concerned with lay political arrangements than with the ascetic nature of religious, particularly that of the female religious.

'Fr. Jos, if the progressives have their way, chaos will follow, leading eventually to the collapse of some female institutes. That's what I foresee. Let me know what you think. Am I too pessimistic? Am I fearful for nothing? Will the female orders and congregations reject the radicals' plans and introduce the modest changes proposed by those wanting to preserve the traditional ascetic life of the female religious, from which customs and governmental systems flow?

'I repeat my offer to send you the council's documents. I believe some issues are so critical to the Church and faith that they fall outside the notion of obedience. Yours in Christ Our Lord, Mother Augustinus.'

Jos read and reread Femke's letter. He went for a walk to clear his mind and think. It was a critical matter, and he had to be sure he understood Femke's position before he responded. In the end, he had to agree with her about the progressive influence in the council and the effects of restructuring religious orders according to Enlightenment thinking. It would be explosive for male and female religious orders, not just female orders. He could see Femke's argument for it being so much more destructive in female orders. It was just like Femke, free of any ideological commitment, to have coolly examined the implications of democratic government for religious orders. She had a practical mind rather than an abstract mind that can lead to fanciful theories. But he must see the full council texts before he wrote back. His attention returned to the liturgy, for it was, as Femke said, the more immediate and concrete issue. Again, it was the unseen document that was critical.

The early proclamation of *Sacrosanctum Concilium* showed the liturgy's prior importance in the minds of the council's bishops, particularly of the progressive faction. At Jos's request, Tom asked De Jonge for a copy. In response, much information about the council flowed to the Lae mission, all to push forward the great changes wrought by the 'spirit' of the council. But the document on the liturgy was missing—so, for that matter, were the other proclaimed council documents. Jos asked Tom to renew the request. Tom was reluctant to interrupt De Jonge's burning enthusiasm but did so

.

De Jonge sent back a curt lecture about the order's heavy responsibility to interpret and introduce the prescriptions of the council's documents. The priestly members of the order had a duty to respect and obey the directives. He insisted on their cooperation. Jos understood the mounting pressure Tom was under. He did not ask again, figuring the documents would eventually turn up. But by mid-1965, with no slackening in the speed of the liturgical changes, he could not wait any longer and resorted to Femke.

He apologised for the delay in commenting on the council's texts about modernising religious life. He still had not received the documents from the Sydney motherhouse. He would be grateful if she could send the relevant texts as well as the document on the liturgy. A month passed before versions in Dutch arrived with a brief note from Femke saying there was no hurry. She would wait until he had studied the texts and had time to write. He decided not to speak to Tom until he read the texts. The pressure Tom was under had only increased. His decision turned out to be justified.

Tom no longer took notice of the mail coming from Holland and only gave the thick envelope a cursory glance. That relieved Jos of explaining the disobedience of going outside his supervision and De Jonge's expressed commands. Though he thought Tom too preoccupied to pay attention even to the 30-odd pages, he decided to wait until he set off on his weekly visit to the nuns at the primary school. They loved Tom and always kept him much longer than he planned. Sure that Tom was on his way, Jos settled in the lounge room with a cup of tea and a biscuit while he read at leisure. He took the bundle of loose pages from the envelope, which he had thus far only glanced at. There was a letter from Femke together with the decrees on the liturgy and religious life. He would tackle the decree on the liturgy first.

He threw four pages on the coffee table before standing up and glancing around as if caught in some diabolical act. He shuffled the pages and sat down again. Five minutes later, he was on his feet again, throwing more pages on the coffee table. He walked around the room, running his hand over his forehead. He stepped onto the verandah to let the light breeze vaporise the perspiration on his face. He returned to the lounge room, took up the pages, and resumed reading. He read to the end while pacing up and down. 'My God,' he said, flinging page after page onto the dining room table, causing them to scatter, some falling to the floor. 'This is an atomic bomb.' Tom's voice sounded from the street, hailing someone or other. Jos gathered the pages and assembled them neatly before resuming his seat in the lounge chair.

'Is there something wrong?' said Tom, sitting down with a faraway look on his face.

'No, why do you ask?'

'Well, you don't look your usual serene self, mate.'

'No, no, I was just reading this about the council.' He held up the pages.

'Yeah, well, I wouldn't look serene if I had been reading about that bloody gathering.'

'Do you mind, Tom, if I go for a walk to scoop up some fresh air, as we say in Dutch?'

'Go and scoop up as much fresh air as you like. You need to get out and have some exercise. You spend too much time with your books.'

'Oh, I hope I'm not neglecting my duties.'

'Of course not, mate. Don't take me so seriously. You'd think you'd have understood me by now. Go on. Go and relax. Get your mind out of gear. Take a long walk. You're not needed until this afternoon.'

The last thing Jos could do was get his mind out of gear. He set off towards the harbour, where the soft breeze over the blue waters of the Pacific Ocean would calm the turmoil of his feelings. He had hoped De Jonge's whole approach to the liturgy was exaggerated, representing the progressive faction, and that the final council document would limit the urge to innovate. But he was wrong. Terribly wrong. The document had put into unmistakable words precisely what De Jonge had been broadcasting. The council's aim, the initiators had said, was to update the Church and adapt it to the modern world. This applied most assuredly to the liturgy. But a mere 'updating' was not the core purpose of *Sacrosanctum Concilium*.

The document began talking about 'restoration' and 'reform' as if these two words meant the same thing. Restore to what? The present Latin Mass—the Tridentine Rite—had grown organically over fifteen hundred years, with little change in five hundred. Stripping the Mass of its so-called accretions, simplifying it so it was 'short, clear,' and 'within the people's powers of comprehension' was more than reform. Insisting on the laity's 'full active participation' with 'actions, gestures, and bodily attitudes,' together with unbridled 'acclamations, responses, psalmody, antiphons, and songs' would leave nothing of the unity, dignity, and mystery of the Tridentine Rite. And then add the 'allowable' mother tongue and traditions of the world's many cultures, even those emerging from violent animism, would be to complete the ruin of this liturgical atomic bomb. A completely new liturgy would arise from the ashes. Discontinuity was written all over it.

These thoughts churned over and over in Jos's mind as he walked on, scarcely paying attention to his surroundings and the people who greeted him. Whatever the soundness of his judgment, he could not ignore his feeling of self-centred disobedience—even of betrayal. How could he entertain such thoughts about the august assembly of the world's bishops—of an ecumenical council guaranteed inerrancy by the Holy Spirit? Was he the one guilty of exaggeration, of wilful blindness to the legitimate authority and intentions of the council? Did he lack a true understanding of the document?

Whichever way he looked at it, however much he tried to fit *Sacrosanctum Concilium* into legitimate change to the Church's liturgy, he could not resist the thoughts he knew would plague him from then on. Frans had spoken of liturgical chaos in Holland. He understood exactly what he meant. Indeed, the council's document was a recipe for liturgical anarchy. Strangely, at that moment, the rumbling noise of aircraft and bombing by the Allies and the return fire of the Nazis as he weaved his way through the Dutch countryside took possession of him. He tried to push off the intrusion he had blocked for twenty years, but it followed him like the demonic sounds he heard in the dark streets of Amsterdam. The roar of war and orange flashes of explosions seized his mind. Only as he approached the presbytery could he escape it. He caught sight of Tom on the verandah, staring into a glass of beer. No, he would not speak his thoughts to Tom.

'Hope you have cleared your mind,' said Tom, when at last roused from his thoughts as Jos mounted the steps. He showed no uneasiness about the glass in his hand.

'It was a pleasant walk,' said Jos, evading an honest answer.

'If you've cleared your mind, mine is becoming more confused by the day.'

'Perhaps you need a walk to the harbour.'

'No, what I need is a beer. Jos, you must join me. I order it. Go and get yourself a beer. I need to talk to you.'

This was one occasion when Jos was grateful to sit with Tom and quietly drink a glass of beer. He needed relief from the storm of his feelings, visions of the war and the conflict brought on by his judgement of the liturgical document and feelings of betrayal. He listened to Tom prattling wistfully about his work as a builder before joining the priesthood, which relieved him of having to reply. The next day, he found time to read Femke's letter and the document on religious life. There was no joy in either.

AS TOM had predicted, De Jonge eventually learned Jos had not followed his instructions. He did not say how he knew. Tom received a sharp reprimand.

'It was probably one of the parishioners,' said Jos. 'There's a little group among our congregation who can't get enough of the changes and can't wait for the next ones. I will write to De Jonge, requesting some allowance if it's all right with you.'

'That's okay, but I must answer the reprimand.'

Jos put his case to De Jonge—on his behalf and the people who preferred the old Mass. A terse reply came back, saying the provincial was willing to grant him more time to adjust, but Fr. van Engelen must eventually join his fellow priests in following the great council's spirit. He must fall in with the democratic, egalitarian spirit of the council. Tom also received a short reply.

'It's another reprimand. I must take steps to make you and our reluctant parishioners understand how necessary the changes are for the Church's life and mission. You must overcome your fear. Nostalgia has no place in the great march forward.'

'Nostalgia? It's surely too early to be talking about nostalgia.'

Jos did not hear from Fr. de Jonge before the council closed in December. The enthusiastic liturgist was evidently too preoccupied with the triumph of his faction and appealing to his fellow priests to discern where the council's spirit was leading them to think about the nuisance priest thousands of miles away. It gave Jos the time to answer Femke's letter. But the break from De Jonge's haranguing did not relieve him of the periodic flashbacks of the dark nights of bombing, the roar of aircraft, the orange explosions lighting the night sky and the Germans' anti-aircraft fire. He could not shake them. He wondered whether Femke experienced the same flashbacks. Nevertheless, he found the time to write between his duties and the flashbacks.

He did not abbreviate his shocked response to the document on the liturgy. He laid out his arguments in full to avoid the impression that emotion primarily drove him. He made the same appeal to Femke. Did she think he was too negative and too pessimistic? Did he see things clearly? He sometimes thought the dreadful experiences of the war affected his thinking. He remembered how single-minded he had been in guiding his charges out of Holland or carrying his messages to the underground amid the mayhem of war. It had been necessary to shut the war out. His survival and that of the people under his charge depended on it. Did it now affect his thinking?

'Are you writing a book or something?' said Tom, passing through the dining room, holding a glass of beer. It was Saturday afternoon, and Jos had sat at the dining room table to write his letter. He had a calming view of the front road activity, and he could spread out.

'I'm answering some questions about the council that Mother Augustinus sent me. She has worries about some aspects of the council's documents.'

'Some aspects of the documents? The whole bloody council is a worry. I should be happy I've got someone to explain it to me, but you just make it worse.'

'I'm sorry, Tom, but—'

'No need to be sorry, mate. Much of what you say makes sense, but don't let me bother you. I hope Mother whatshername benefits from your explanations.'

Jos watched Tom settle on the verandah. It was likely he would stay there the rest of the afternoon. His drinking had not worsened, but it was still concerning. He returned to his letter, now tackling Femke's thoughts on restructuring the female religious orders. The Decree on the Adaptation and Renewal of Religious Life (*Perfectae Caritatis*), she wrote, urged religious orders—male and female—to preserve the traditions and the spirit of the original foundation. Many aspects of the religious life were indeed repeated and recommended. The discussion of the evangelical counsels of poverty, chastity and obedience was particularly edifying. However, the exhortation to retain the traditions and foundational principles in female religious orders came up against Cardinal Schuermans' radical vision for women, contradicting the recommendation to preserve them.

The overriding principle was renewal and adaptation to modern ways and ideas. A spirit of renewal took precedence over all else. The constitution, the prayer books, and ceremonies had to be rewritten, and obsolete laws suppressed. All updating would be 'ineffectual unless animated by a renewal of spirit.' The 'criteria and principles of adaptation and renewal' governed the revision of all aspects of the community. All members of the order, as 'one class of sisters,' must contribute to the process of democratic reconstitution. Finally, the religious habit must be 'simple and modest' and suited to the apostolic circumstances. 'The habits of both men and women religious which do not conform to these norms must be changed.'

'I had the impression, Fr. Jos,' Femke wrote, 'that there was a tug of war between the traditionalists and the progressives. They were pulling this way and that, with the Schuermans faction prevailing. I cannot see anything but chaos ahead. My sisters are already well on the way to replacing our present habit. You could scarcely say some of the designs are habits at all. Some want to get rid of the habit altogether. Why need a habit if one's apostolic work is among the general community to whom we must adapt? I look forward to your response. As I asked before, am I too pessimistic? Have I not enough trust in my fellow sisters? The answer seems plain when considering the same questions you asked me.'

Jos had to agree about her fears of disintegration. Cardinal Schuermans' extreme views, more ideological than religious, were reflected in some of the papers she had sent and were visible in the decree. He had missed the democratic principles running through the cardinal's views, the decree, and much of the debate in his reading. He had been too preoccupied with the liturgy. But now he could see a preference for a democratic structure based on member election as opposed to an authority based traditional ways regulated by a hierarchy of management. Traditional government was a form of democratic government. After all, there was no fixed personal authority. Election and appointment came from the order's members, but differently from Schuermans' conception of democracy.

Such a democratic structure had echoes of the classic works of the Anglo-Saxon philosophers Thomas Hobbes and John Locke and their state of nature theories. Materialist metaphysics underpinned those theories, which was incompatible with the Thomistic metaphysics that underlay the Church's thinking on government issues—as reflected in the social encyclicals of Pope Leo XIII. A Lockean or Hobbesian democracy would destroy the Church. He ended with, 'Femke, I know I can't give my comfort. My thinking may appear even more bleak than yours. But I have attempted to state my reasons clearly. I encourage you to look further into the references I have given. You were on the right track in discerning an Enlightenment influence in the discourse. Let me know if you have any further questions. Keep me abreast of your thoughts—and well-being.'

IN FEBRUARY 1966, Fr. De Jonge seemed to remember he had unfinished business with Jos. He requested a report from Fr. Tom about the progress in his Lae parish. Fr. Tom made much of introducing the changes to which he appended a few sentences about Fr. Jos's reasons for providing the unchanged Mass to the older people.

'This will not do,' De Jonge wrote back. 'You have the order's direction to carry out the council's decrees. Please do it. You must submit to the majority's wishes, which I represent. We don't want our parishes left behind in the Church's progress to a new, enlightened age.'

'A new enlightened age?' said Jos. 'It seems I have heard that revolutionary language before.'

'Where?' said Tom, who could not hide his annoyance at the order.

'I'll write again to De Jonge,' said Jos, evading the question, 'and tell him I am entirely to blame. I am too fixed in my ways. I'm just obeying my conscience concerning our older parishioners.'

'Best of luck, mate.'

A reprimand came by return. If Fr. Jos understood the proper notion of conscience, he would note that a properly formed conscience dictated that he implement the council's decisions. He must obey the legitimate direction of the order. And the older people must follow. Jos did not bother to reply and continued with the unchanged Mass. Another reprimand would turn up, he expected. A rebuke did not come, at least not immediately. Instead, a succession of bulletins arrived about the most radical change so far proposed. Priests would be required to turn around and face the congregation. The laypeople, as the people of God, must play a full active role in the services. Prepare for it. In April 1967, the Vatican formally instructed priests to face the people. The instructions for more cuts and changes kept coming.

'It seems you were right all along,' said Tom, who had become bewildered by the rate of change.

'I take no satisfaction. It was no guess. It was there in the discourse of the liturgists in Germany, France, and Holland. Fr. de Jonge's boast was not idle. Our order has been at the forefront of the changes. You can expect more.'

'Good God, no. What else can they do?'

'If they treat the Mass essentially as a celebratory meal, what do you think?'

'I dare not think.' Tom hesitated. 'I can't help wondering whether I became a priest for this.'

'That's a dangerous thought. And unlike you.'

Late in 1967, Fr. de Jonge requested an update about the progress in Lae. Tom's report was the same as the last. He had followed instructions, but Fr. Jos still said the traditional Mass. The charge of wilful disobedience thundered in De Jonge's reply. The council had changed nothing about obedience to properly elected authority. Fr. van Engelen was breaking the solemn vow he had taken at ordination. Did his vow of obedience mean nothing? He was obliged to confess this grave sin with a genuine spirit of repentance. His disobedience, however, was one thing. The implementation of the Mass was another. Fr. de Jonge would fly to New Guinea to oversee the implementation of all aspects of the new Catholic service. If there is no full compliance after that, the provincial had no choice but to suspend those refusing to comply.

'This moment had to come,' said Tom. 'What will you do?'

'I don't know. We'll see.'

'You're a stubborn man, Jos. It's obvious you think there's something dramatically wrong. You know, and I know, that the Church, in the person of the pope, is authorised to make changes.'

'Yes, that's correct. But the pope is not authorised to make changes to the faith that we're here to spread.'

'He's not doing that, is he?

'I'm saying in principle. No, that's not my first concern. There's no overt heresy in the Mass changes. The chaotic road on which the order of the Wounded Heart of Jesus is travelling is the problem.'

'It's becoming all too much for me,' said Tom, sighing and running his hand over his brow, a gesture that had become a habit during the last two years. The cheerful, relaxed manner of the former building professional had gone. Frans and Marijke's Christmas letter, to which Jos had looked forward, was all about the changes to the Church and its liturgy. The Church in Holland was polarising, with Frans and Marijke stuck on the conservative side. Frans, who had trouble containing his scorn, declared that the country had gone mad. And it was not the Church convulsions alone with its garrulous, gifted theologians who dominated the pages of the newspapers, courtesy of a shameless bunch of supportive journalists.

The youth had decided their parents were a bunch of grandmas and grandpas whose views of the world were moribund. They—the young people—had to take the lead and gently put the old folk out to pasture. The students at the government-funded universities and schools of higher education took the lead in the revolt. But there was no gentleness about their tactics. The scandalous stink-bombing of Crown Princess Beatrix's wedding in 1966 to her mild-mannered German fiancé Claus was an outrage. Are we to put up with this? said Frans. Is the government to sit on its hands?

The only news outside the Church and Dutch society was about Anneke and Joop and their studies. Anneke was already in her second year at university in Amsterdam, majoring in English language and literature, while Joop was in his final school year. The two younger brothers were going about their business, unconscious of the social and religious storm around them. There was no mention of Truus van den Donker, Cees, or Gerda, who was in her final university year. Indeed, there had been little news about the Van den Donkers in the last two years, only that Cees was often away from Middelburg on business, and Gerda's Companions of Creation had closed. Jos was disappointed.

In the meantime, a letter arrived from Femke acknowledging his reply. She thanked him for his explanation and advice. For the moment, however, she was embroiled in the fuss caused by the implementation of the council's decree on religious life. She would write when she had more time. That also disappointed Jos. He missed the intellectual connection with someone who thought like him.

February 1968 came, and Fr. de Jonge had still not carried out his threat to fly to Lae to bring his recalcitrant priest into line. His continual elevation, now to assistant provincial in the Sydney house, meant that more weighty tasks consumed his days. Jos would keep. Tom continued to lament that the steady flow of bulletins about the new liturgy showed how right Jos was in his predictions. A few months later, the news that the same cultural group of two years before was back in Lae and arranging another expedition deep into the hills took Jos's attention away from his disappointments and the zeal of the swollen, upbeat bulletins.

'All the same people?' said Jos to the tour operator after Sunday Mass.

'As far as I can gather,' said Sam Robertson. 'I haven't seen them, just heard from the young fellows who couldn't wait to boast about such a daring tour.'

'Isn't it strange these non-academic people are interested in the old native customs?'

'Strange? What do you call strange? People are increasingly interested in Papua New Guinea's history, but not many as reckless as this group, though. It's a growing market.'

'As reckless?'

'Yes, you wouldn't catch me wandering deep into those hills with just a tour operator's clipboard.'

That afternoon, Jos took a stroll to the native market, where he lingered for some time. As he was leaving, he saw Cees van Donker with the same woman on his arm, approaching with the remaining group bunched a few paces behind. Now there was an addition. An overweight young woman dressed in bohemian style and taking a keen interest in the indigenous environment strolled beside Cees. As they came closer, he recognised Gerda, his daughter. He hastened out of view, and as soon as the group was busy talking to the same vendor with the wooden carvings, he hurried back to the presbytery. The following Saturday afternoon, it was his turn in the confessional. About midway through the session, a penitent entered the confessional but said nothing. Jos glanced through the grille and made out the top of a head.

'Can I help you?' he said, looking directly into the shaded cubicle. The person appeared to be crouching out of view. 'Shall I mention some sins or omissions ...?' There was no answer. 'I can't help you if you don't tell me what you're here for.'

'I'm going to kill you,' said a native voice after a long silence. 'I'm sorry. Very sorry.'

'Do you realise that murder is a very grave sin?'

There was no answer. The door of the confessional opened, and without delay, another penitent knelt to confess. The same considerations about the confessional seal occupied Jos for the next day, after which he came to the same conclusion. He must not break the seal. In the past, such strange occultist predictions had not bothered him too much. There had been a retreat from the animism that had governed the native's social and religious life, but it had not wholly disappeared. That realisation and, more importantly, the attempt to poison him put him on his guard.

At the same time, a change in his routine must never give the appearance that he was acting on information heard in the confessional. The confessional seal was sacred and inviolable. The only observable change was his extra care about his food, but that did not spark Tom's interest or the cook's. Tom was occupied with adjusting to the changes the bulletins regularly mandated, and the cook accepted whatever the priests did. As nothing happened over the next few months, and life went on as usual, Jos relaxed a little.

Chapter 25

Of Human Life

AFTER ALL THE trouble over access to the document on the liturgy, it was a surprise that a package arrived without warning from Sydney in June containing the council's major documents. They were the four constitutions, including the Constitution on the Sacred Liturgy.

'What are we supposed to do with these?' said Tom, handing the opened package to Jos.

'Are there no instructions?'

'No, just the documents.'

'I imagine we're supposed to read them,' said Jos, taking out the documents and examining them.

'It's surprising De Jonge hasn't taken the opportunity to give us another earbashing.'

'Perhaps he has made do with his bulletins.'

'Or perhaps someone has sent them without his knowledge,' Tom volunteered with a nonchalant shrug.

Jos thought a moment. 'Yes, you could be right. If that is so, we are not the only ones with doubts.'

'You mean you. I don't know what I am supposed to think.'

'Don't deceive yourself, Tom. At the very least, you're not comfortable, just like whoever sent the documents.'

'Perhaps so. But would they, like you, have the courage to confront De Jonge?'

'One would hope so if they felt strongly.'

'Anyhow,' said Tom with a dismissive wave, 'you summarise them for me again. And go easy on the shock.'

Two days later, Jos was ready to give Tom his summary.

'Wait, I need a beer to fortify me. You grab one, too, Jos.'

'Well, I have good news for you,' said Jos, hoping Tom would not insist.

'That's a change.'

'I'll be brief. The dogmatic constitutions on Revelation, *Dei Verbum*, and the Church, *Lumen Gentium*, are fine—apart from an odd distinction in the document on the Church—'

'What distinction? What's odd about it?' said Tom. 'Explain.'

'Well, I have to think about it some more, but it looks like the sort of fine distinction theorists make to confuse people who aren't theorists. Let's leave it. It's not important for my summary.'

'All right, go on,' said Tom, waving his hand and taking a sip of beer.

They, *Dei Verbum* and *Lumen Gentium*, merely repeat the dogma you and I are familiar with. I hardly know why a great big council was needed to restate it all. Now, the Pastoral Constitution on the Church in the Modern World, *Gaudium et Spes*, is different—

'Here we go. Hit me with it.'

'No, no, it's fine, too ... no, better than fine. It's impressive. The purpose of the council shines in it. It looks at the state of the modern world and outlines ways the Church can deal with it—pastorally. The Church's enduring views on such critical matters as abortion and euthanasia are restated. Leo's social teaching is restated. The divine and natural laws underwrite everything. If read in its entirety, as a pastoral document, in line with tradition, I can't see how anyone could object—'

'That's a relief.'

'Unless, of course, it did not suit someone's agenda.'

'Yes, that's a point—someone's agenda. Who could you be thinking of, I wonder? What about the fourth document?

'That's on the liturgy—The Constitution on the Sacred Liturgy. Unfortunately, it outlines the agenda De Jonge is following, the agenda we've had the painful experience of. But there's no heresy.'

'Three cheers.'

'But it could lead to sacrilege. Prepare yourself.'

'Sacrilege! No, Jos, stop there. I don't want to hear about it.'

'All right, but let me suggest we make time to read through the first three constitutions together so we understand more about the council. Maybe De Jonge's agenda will make more sense.'

Jos was relieved Tom did not want to hear his full analysis of the document on the liturgy. It would be too shocking. What's more, the uncertainty of his extreme conclusions still plagued him, just like his conclusions about Muller's and Van Rossem's motivations and their possible hand in Albers's and Bart's execution. No, it was too outrageous to contemplate. The majority of council fathers could not be so blind. They must see what he saw. But then, who was he to set himself up against the world's bishops? At least three of the council's documents reassured Tom. The reassurance would be short-lived.

ON 30 July 1968, Frs. Tom and Jos woke to the sensational news that Pope Paul VI had overnight issued a blockbuster encyclical, *Humanae Vitae*, which covered the love between husband and wife and their responsibilities as parents. From the morning's radio and newspaper reports, Jos quickly understood that the papal letter had exploded across the world for one reason. The pope had reasserted the Church's traditional teaching on birth control against the advice of the Pontifical Commission purposely set up to study the matter. He had also defied the world's gifted theologians. The marriage act must always be open to life. To artificially frustrate the natural God-given order of the married state was a grave sin.

Over the next few days, Jos and Tom collected the international newspapers available in Lae to gauge the world's response. The reporting of Catholic and secular commentators was practically uniform in their condemnation and scorn. What had possessed the pope? Why had he defied the advice of his own special commission? The same gifted theologians paraded through the media, enlightening the world's audience with their authoritative opinions, the one more outspoken than the other. American bull theologian Fr. Corky Cullen, a leader in the council debates, said such an outrageous, unprofessional decision did not bind him, nor should it bind the faithful. The pope was a prisoner of the ignorant, hidebound conservatives still controlling the Vatican.

'I'm afraid to ask what you think of this,' said Tom, sitting with a glass of beer in front of the newspapers spread over the dining room table.

'I am rather afraid of the next Sydney bulletin,' said Jos, increasingly worried about Tom's beer consumption.

'Well, what do you think?'

'The pope had no choice.'

'These jokers in the newspapers thought he had.'

'They're wrong.'

'As simple as that?'

'Yes, in a word.'

'I wish I had your confidence, Jos.'

'Look, Tom, think about it. It is not deep. The prohibition of artificial birth control based on the natural law has been the Church's constant teaching. The pope had no authority to change it, whatever the dissenters' subtle, refined arguments.'

'Dissenters? Is this another new word?'

'Tom, I don't want to load you with more worry, but I can see from the reactions in the newspapers that this will develop into a question of authority, not of Church teaching.'

'What on earth do you mean now?'

'The teaching of the ages is clear. The Church's theologians are acting as a faction, a political faction. They will place their authority over and against the pope's and the Vatican's curia.'

'No, Jos, stop. Please stop. I don't want to hear anymore. I can't bear it. Leave me to my beer in peace.'

'Tom, be at least reassured that the Pastoral Constitution on the Church in the Modern World condemns contraception—in two places, no less. The dissenters' own council speaks against them. I suspect it will not be the only contradiction they fall into.'

Fr. de Jonge's bulletin arrived two days later.

'I don't want to read it,' said Tom. 'Summarise it for me, will you.'

It was no more than Jos had expected. De Jonge regurgitated the opinions of the most scathing of the theologians. Corky Cullen collected the signatures of 200 theologians and submitted a collective analysis to the *New York Times*. The pope's faults of reasoning, ignorance of Church, and basic theology were legion. Jos thought there was rather a lot of question-begging and unargued claims thrown around in the piece. De Jonge humbly submitted this analysis to the honest scrutiny of his fellow priests. They could not fail to be convinced of the error of the Vatican on this matter. Really? In quoting Fr. Hilarius de Koning, he said the Vatican's unfeeling directive would torment married couples, but they should follow their consciences in the end. One theologian, said De Jonge triumphantly, found the encyclical 'intellectually, emotionally and spiritually repugnant.'

'If you want a summary, Tom, it's the same as the reactions in the newspapers. Total condemnation.'

'What are we to say to the people in the pews?'

'You must decide what authority you obey.'

'That's what you'll do?'

'Of course.'

'Need I ask who you choose?'

'No.'

'You are in for it again, Jos, you realise.'

'Let it come.'

'I'm with you, I suppose.'

A week later, a formal letter arrived to announce Fr. de Jonge would fly to Papua New Guinea to discuss recent events and settle the question of the new Mass once and for all. Fathers Connolly and Van Engelen should clear their appointment books and hold themselves ready. There was no need to pick him up from the airport. He would take a taxi to the hotel and arrange a meeting from there. De Jonge did as he said and rang from the hotel to say he would arrive at the presbytery at 9 a.m. sharp. At the stipulated time, a taxi pulled up, out of which stepped Frs. Muller and De Jonge dressed in civilian clothes—slacks, business shirt, and necktie. De Jonge was spotless in a tastefully chosen combination, while Muller was dressed like an elderly man without a wife.

'Who's that?' said Tom.

'Fr. Muller, the deputy superior general. What on earth is he doing here?'

'And what's with the clothes?'

'Prepare yourself, Tom. We're about to hear some major changes.'

Fr. Muller settled his subordinates at one side of the dining room table and stood at the other.

'I have a lot to get through,' he said, laying a manila folder on the table and flipping it open. 'Please remain attentive. First, I formally introduce Fr. de Jonge as the new provincial of your area. Father's outstanding work during and after the council has rightly earned his election by his priestly brothers to this distinction. Respect his directives. Second, I am the new superior general. Fr. van Rossem has retired, and our brothers in the community have given me this honour. With that out of the way, let me move to important matters within our priestly community.

'In brief, our order of teaching and missionary priests has been at the forefront of implementing the spirit of the Second Vatican Council. We are proud of this distinction. Now, in line with the council's pastoral and ecumenical emphasis, we have taken steps to bring ourselves closer to the people we serve and to engage with the ministers of other denominations—our separated brethren.

'The seminary in Noord-Brabant was closed at the end of the 1966 academic year. The junior seminarians were sent home to attend their local high school. Premises were purchased in Amsterdam, to which the priests of the motherhouse and the senior seminarians have been sent. The senior seminarians will continue their training among ordinary folk. The fraternity has done away with the religious habit to ensure nothing stands in the way of this pastoral agenda. Religious habits are a sign of separation and unhealthy rigidity. Henceforth, there will be no such signs. You are to follow, that is, dress accordingly. Any questions?'

Jos glanced at Tom, who stared at the new superior general, blinking and open-mouthed.

'What distinguishes us then as a religious order?' said Jos. 'What happened to the saying, we are in the world but not of the world?'

'Precisely our pastoral and ecumenical objectives. Haven't you been listening?'

'I have been listening to the dismantling of an old and venerable order of priests.'

'You are not improving, are you, Fr. van Engelen?'

'I don't know what you mean by that.'

'Only this, Father: your perversity is an obstacle to our community's pastoral plans. I am not going to stand here arguing with you. The die has been cast. It is for you to obey. Now, on this question of obedience to the community's licit requests, you must take steps to say the Mass that puts us closer to the people. No arguments, no discussions; you are to do what every other priest of our community has done. Above all, you are to satisfy your vow of obedience.'

'I cannot do that. I will not do it.'

'As I said, I'm not going to argue about it. Just do it. Now, on a fundamental pastoral matter, I must talk to you about the pope's unfortunate letter on birth control. No, Fr. van Engelen, I am not discussing it. Just sit quietly and listen.' He wagged his finger. 'We must minister to those many couples who will be in torment and confusion about the pope's irrational and insensitive decision. Compassion and understanding are what must guide us. We must emphasise that their decision, in the long run, is for them a question of conscience.'

'And the confusion of forcing them to choose between the dissenters and the pope?'

'You have developed a very objectionable way of expressing yourself, Fr. van Engelen. I asked you to keep quiet and listen.' Muller turned to the papers before him. 'Please respect my authority.'

'And the authority of the great council?'

'I beg your pardon,' said Muller, looking up from the papers.

'Should I follow the authority of the council?'

'Now, Fr. van Engelen, I have trouble following the wanderings of your mind. Of course, you should follow the authority of the council—whose directives my senior confreres and I pronounce.'

The council condemns contraception, as the Church always has.'

'It certainly does not,' said Muller, a frown revealing surprise and uncertainty.

'In the Pastoral Constitution on the Church in the Modern World.'

'I am afraid you have been misinformed.'

'In paragraphs 51 and 87. I can show it to you if you like.'

'Do you have a copy of the document?'

'Yes, of course. We received the four constitutions from the Sydney house.'

'Is this right?' said Muller, turning to De Jonge.

'Not on my authority,' said De Jonge, squirming.

Muller glared at De Jonge. 'We'll talk about that later.' He turned back to Jos. 'This is just the very problem we have been guarding against. You must leave the interpretation of the council documents to those with the authority and capacity to interpret them under the guidance of the council's spirit. Now, Fr. van Engelen, for the very last time, I require you to be silent and listen.'

'As you wish,' said Jos, seeing he would only antagonise Muller further if he continued.

'Thank you. And I want a cooperative spirit instead of those stubborn, offensive looks. Now, let us discuss strategies to deal with the confusion the pope has engendered. Remember, compassion must guide us.'

Jos and Tom sat back and listened to the new superior general expatiating on the new regime's practical aspects of compassion and understanding. Gone were the sneer and sarcasm of the subordinate who imagined he could always do better. Now was the exercise of power, and the last thing Muller expected was his subordinates' divided attention. Jos could not help glancing at De Jonge, who sat in his sartorial magnificence, only breaking his attention to brush an imagined speck from his slacks and shirt. Muller's catalogue of directions took the meeting through to noon.

'We will break for lunch now,' said Muller, 'but as a final instruction, a very important instruction, I inform you that our community in the Netherlands introduced communion in the hand three years ago. We delayed its introduction in the Oceania region because it was clear the Australian people were not ready for it. The processes of maturity have been slower there than in Holland. But our progress cannot be retarded any longer. From this Sunday, you will give communion in the hand and not on the tongue. Communion on the tongue is simply another of those archaic signs of separation and the sad history of clericalism. We are one folk in the one faith.'

'What?' said Tom, sitting up.

'The old ghost of clericalism,' said Jos, unable to stop himself.

'Fr. van Engelen, I won't say it again. I will suspend you if I have one more incident of sneering disrespect.'

'Sneering disrespect?' said Jos. 'I wonder where I could have seen that example.' Seeing Muller had no idea of the allusion, he continued, 'Well, if you think my comment was a sneer, I apologise, but—'

'Your apology is accepted. Now, Fr. Connolly, I know this is new to you, but you must make an effort to break old attitudes for the sake of legitimate progress. The pain of change will be rewarded. We will meet again after lunch. There is much still to discuss. Fr. de Jonge and I will return to our hotel.'

'Did you know about the change in Holland?' said Tom when Muller and De Jonge had left them. 'I mean, communion in the hand.'

'Yes. I didn't mention it because, well, because I hoped the Vatican would succeed in stopping it. Holland was among the first. There appears to have been an unchecked stampede in Holland to what they call progress.'

'But it's sacrilege. It overturns everything our theological supervisors taught about the Eucharist, the ordained priesthood, and the real presence.'

'Of course, it does.'

'What will you do?'

'I told you. I won't do it.'

'He'll suspend you.'

'I don't know what he means by suspension. What from? From duties that will fall on your shoulders? He's not making sense. There has been a big change in Muller. Shows what a little power will do to the disgruntled.'

'You know him better than I do,' said Tom, gazing, glazed-eyed, through the window at the commercial activity in the street.

'I surely do.'

Frs. Muller and De Jonge did not return after lunch. They sent a message saying they would familiarise themselves with the town and its people in preparation for their pastoral announcements at Sunday Mass. Their pastoral familiarisation took them through to Saturday, which included much tourist activity and the purchase of various items, to which the many parcels taken back to their hotel testified. The appearance of new clothes hinted at the contents of some parcels.

On Saturday, Fr. de Jonge sported a bright, floral tropical shirt about which he showed no self-consciousness. Fr. Muller's new clothes still displayed the lack of a wife's tactful supervision. The Saturday meeting was more of the same, with the added announcement that Muller and De Jonge would depart on Monday. Tom and Jos were relieved the meeting ended before afternoon tea. Before leaving, Muller repeated the strict instructions for Mass the following morning.

'I want this to be a flawless communal ceremony. I want this to be the standard-bearer of the new pastoral approach our community of priests has adopted.'

Not expecting a reply or comment, he left the presbytery with De Jonge in his wake.

'De Jonge is like a dutiful handmaiden,' said Jos.

'I haven't noticed. All this new stuff has filled my brain. I can't compute anything else.'

'Don't let it get you down, Tom.'

'I didn't become a priest for all this rubbish.'

'Be careful, Tom. They are dangerous thoughts.'

Jos said his usual 8 o'clock Mass on the following morning. Fr. Muller was waiting in the sacristy when Jos and his altar server left the sanctuary.

'Stubbornness and perversity,' said Muller, 'I have never experienced anything like it.'

'I told you I would not do it, and you don't have the authority to force me. The Vatican has not approved communion in the hand.'

'But the council has—the spirit of the council. The Vatican must obey the prescriptions of the Second Vatican Council.'

'Obey a competing authority, you mean, an alternative Magisterium.'

'Once again, Fr. van Engelen, I must tell you there's no discussion. Your duty is to obey your legitimate authority.'

'Exactly.'

Muller stood staring at Jos, frustrated and undecided. 'This has reached a serious point of disruption. Suspension hangs over you. I will see you after 10 o'clock Mass.'

Frs. Tom and Jos sat in the back pew while Fr. Muller said Mass, assisted by Fr. de Jonge. Movement and murmur spread through the congregation at the announcement of communion in the hand. No more than half went up to receive it.

'People here are not as eager as the Dutch, apparently,' said Jos while he and Tom waited at the front of the church, dressed in their religious habit.

'Apparently not.'

They were kept busy for the next half-hour speaking to the parishioners, half of whom enthusiastically approved while the rest remained undecided. A small number were vociferous in their objections. What was next, they said? Muller and De Jonge appeared after most parishioners had departed.

'It was not a great success,' said Jos before Muller could speak.

'It will take time, but they will accept it in the end. That is our experience. The process has started, and you can do nothing about it.'

'Then why would you suspend me—whatever that means?'

'That means you will be removed from this parish, that is, if my management team and I in Sydney decide on such radical action. There is still time for you to reconsider. No, no more talk about it, Fr. van Engelen. Just listen to what I have to say. You are both in religious habits. You have two weeks to make the change. I will set up a parish council to assist you in your work. They will report on such matters.'

'We already have an auxiliary parish group.'

'I want a council according to my wishes.'

At that moment, Gerhard Bann approached them. 'Good morning, Fathers,' he said, 'I hope I'm not interrupting—

Fr. Muller, turning to face him, blanched.

'No, you're not interrupting,' said Jos, noticing the reaction.

Herr Bann fixed his gaze on Muller. Muller shifted.

'Fr. Muller, do you remember me?'

'Yes, Major Bann, I remember you.' He stopped. 'I am rather surprised to see you here, evidently on familiar terms with Frs. van Engelen and Connolly. Or is it just Fr. van Engelen?'

'Well, I hope I am on familiar terms with both priests. They have been very welcoming.'

'I suspect Fr. van Engelen was the initial contact.'

'Correct.'

'There's a story behind that, no doubt.'

'There is, but I leave Fr. van Engelen to tell as much as he wants.'

'I seem to remember a lack of enthusiasm in chasing down the third spy,' said Muller after some hesitation.

'And I seem to remember your insistence on finding him.'

Muller hesitated again. 'You do not see it correctly, Major. I wanted the matter cleared up as quickly as possible. I wanted to know where Fr. van Engelen had got to.'

'That was it, was it?'

'Yes, but I will not carry on this useless discussion over something that happened long ago and is now dead and buried—or should be.'

'As you wish, Fr. Muller, though you initiated the subject.'

'I will rely on Fr. van Engelen to fill me in later about the relationship between a Nazi soldier and himself.'

'I was a German soldier. I am now a German businessman. Gerhard Bann.' He handed his business card to Muller.

Muller looked at the card and frowned. 'I have nothing more to say. I will leave you and Fr. van Engelen to talk about your mutual interests. Good morning, Herr Bann.'

They watched as Muller, with De Jonge following, marched off towards the town centre.

'I presume your business visits are meeting with success, Herr Bann,' said Jos.

'Indeed, we have a contract for some traffic engineering here and in Goroka in the highlands. I am here with a few colleagues, making final arrangements. We would like to invite you to dine with us during the week if that's all right with Fr. Connolly. I am sure my colleagues who do not speak English very well would enjoy your company. We would also like to take advantage of your knowledge of Lae and its people.'

'Of course, Jos, go and enjoy yourself,' said Tom. 'You need a break from this council business. It's eating you up.'

Chapter 26

The assault

FOUR DAYS LATER, after Muller and De Jonge had left Lae, Jos joined the four German businessmen in the first-class restaurant of Lae's most expensive international hotel. As he expected, the men were friendly but polite and formal, asking many questions about the town and the region. Towards the end of dinner, Jos posed the question in his mind.

'If I may ask, Herr Bann, what was Fr. Muller's role in the search? You had not mentioned any contact with him.'

'I had hardly any. It was indirect. The commandant dealt with Van Rossem and Muller. I was present a few times and later heard about the discussions. As I said, Muller was keen to find you. He showed signs of impatience about the lack of success.'

'That was risky, wasn't it?'

'Not really. He projected an attitude of cooperation, a willingness to ensure the seminary did nothing to upset the German command in Breda. He was impatient for us. The commandant seemed to appreciate that.'

'Perhaps there was another motivation?'

'No "perhaps" about it, in my view. He must have known you would be executed if found. Why would he want you out of the way?'

'That's the big question, Herr Bann, and it has to do with the reasons the superior general brought me back from the missions.' He related Fr. Albers's concerns.

'That makes sense of the whole affair. Something didn't add up about the suddenness of the raid and the information that led to it. It seemed too neat and too easy. Usually, a series of events raised suspicion. We worked through the suspicion until we had convincing proof of enemy action. Then, we would carry out a military raid. Interrogation would follow.

There was no lead-up this time, and execution immediately followed without any interrogation. It was unusual, especially seeing the Gestapo had no objections. The Gestapo just loved the chance to exercise their special interrogation skills.'

'Did you see anything of Fr. de Jonge at the time? He and his friends were rather thick with Muller.'

'No. The commandant only dealt with Van Rossem and Muller.'

'What about the SS officer?'

Bann thought for a moment.

'Oh, I see where you're going with this.'

'Well, what do you think?'

'It was only a rumour about the SS officer and someone in the seminary. There's nothing substantial to work on.'

'You've given me a lot to consider, Herr Bann. It's been something of a breakthrough.'

'How sure are you of the motivation you suspect?'

'I've thought long about that. If someone, whether Muller or someone else, wanted me out of the way, the reason would seem to be to safeguard the program of Marxist or other ideological influence. A future program of subversion would depend on it. The pieces are falling into place.'

'Have you thought you might still be in danger—as I've already suggested?'

'No, surely not. That was all finished with the death of Fr. Albers. I'm an irritation to Muller, but I am no danger now to his regime.'

'I wouldn't count on it. Fr. van Engelen, I had a career in the military. I am familiar with tactical warfare.'

'Warfare? I have nothing to fear from Muller except embarrassment at his choice of clothes.'

'I'm glad you can joke about it.' He paused. 'How confident are you that your native parishioners have given up their animism and the sorcery that goes with it?'

'Very confident, as I've said. Our native parishioners are devout, some an example of piety and devotion. Why, what's the connection?'

'They could be used to get at you.'

'No, no, I can't accept that,' said Jos, waving such a suggestion aside. 'How?'

'Someone could stir up suspicions about someone with an evil influence.'

'That sort of sorcery is now found way out in the hills, not among my parishioners.'

Herr Bann glanced at his colleagues, who were closely following the exchange. One nodded at Bann.

'Fr. van Engelen, we heard a rumour in Goroka that a priest in Lae is responsible for some harm suffered by someone somewhere. It was all very vague. One of the natives, a technical person acting for us, mentioned it. He had heard a whisper among the natives when organising a working party. As I say, it was nothing more than an unsubstantiated rumour. It may be nothing. But if a sorcerer is involved, it could be a threat. I hope you and Fr. Connolly are mindful of such things.'

'Of course, Herr Bann, but I have full confidence in our parishioners. It was probably just idle talk, some idle boasting.'

'We hope you are right.'

When Jos left the hotel to walk to the presbytery, Herr Bann offered to accompany him.

'There are few lights at places along the route. It could present an opportunity for someone wishing to resolve the sorcerer's spells.'

'No, I'm fine. No need. Thank you. I've walked the route many times.'

Herr Bann accompanied him to the roadside entrance before wishing him a good evening. When Jos turned after walking some distance, Bann was still at the roadside, staring at him in the glow of the hotel lights. Further on, some figures were huddled among the bushes a little way in from the road. He looked back again. Gerhard Bann's colleagues had joined him. They were looking at him without speaking. He thought that odd. Then, he had that same feeling when walking Amsterdam's dark streets after Marlies's exorcism. Some evil was bending over him.

As he turned into a side street leading to the presbytery, he heard the rushing of feet and the rustling of clothing. Before he could turn, a crushing blow across his back and head sent him rolling over the ground. He caught glimpses of shadowy, robed figures accompanied by dull flickering lights and chanting while he bore the crippling pain of repeated blows to his back and legs. He felt the slashing of a knife. A roar and a burst of shouting stopped the chanting, the blows, and the slashing. The candles went flying, and robes were torn at, followed by the trampling of feet. Men speaking German bent over him, one calling for an ambulance. Jos came briefly to his senses in Lae hospital's intensive care ward. He was trussed up like a pig prepared for sacrifice. But such feelings were hazy. The pain of his injuries overwhelmed all else.

'Where am I?' he said, indistinctly aware of someone by his bedside.

'In the hospital in Port Moresby,' said the nurse. 'You're safe. Just relax.'

'How did I get here?'

'Please, Fr. van Engelen, don't worry about that for the moment,' said the doctor, materialising from behind the nurse. 'We need to get you fit for the trip to Sydney, where you will receive specialist treatment.'

'Where am I?' said Jos, looking around. He had a faint recollection that he had already asked that question.

'You're still in Port Moresby hospital,' said the nurse.

'How long have I been here?'

'Five days. Just relax and let us care for you.'

He opened his eyes to see a doctor beside him.

'How bad is it?'

'It's quite bad, but you'll live. You will need specialist treatment. We'll send you to Sydney as soon as we are confident you can fly.'

'My injuries?'

'You suffered broken bones, but we'll discuss your condition when you're up to it. You're loaded with antibiotics and painkillers.'

'How did I get here?'

'You have a very generous friend who had you flown here from Lae.'

'Herr Bann, I imagine.'

'Yes. He will explain when he comes to visit in a few days.'

Jos's conscious moments became more frequent. He opened his eyes to find Herr Bann sitting beside his bed.

'Herr Bann, I believe I have you to thank for being here. Why?'

'Fr. van Engelen, if you are inclined to ignore the danger you're in, I'm not. Fr. Connolly told me of the attempt to poison you.'

'Did he just?'

'Do you have any idea what's behind this latest attempt? It shows all the signs of sorcery and the occult. I mean, besides what we've already discussed.'

'I have nothing to say, Herr Bann.'

Bann hesitated. 'The seal of confession?' Jos shook his head. 'Okay, that confirms it. You're still in danger. We must get you out of here as soon as possible.'

'Surely you exaggerate.'

'No, Father, I had a chat with Fr. Connolly. A threat has dogged you over the years. It is not only possible that someone in your order wants you eliminated. This latest attack suggests another source of hostility. You know. Tell me.'

Jos related his clash with Cees van den Donker and his visits to Lae. 'I can't believe that fellow's animosity is so great that he would try to kill me.'

'No, this runs deep. There are things you're not telling me.'

Jos closed his eyes. 'I'm sorry, Herr Bann, I can't think about it anymore.'

'I'm sorry, Father. I'll come again when you're better able to concentrate.'

The hospital shifted Jos from the intensive care department to a private room where he came under constant supervision.

'Who's paying for all this?' he said to the doctor during one of his many visits.

'Your German friend.'

'I can't have you paying for all this, Herr Bann,' he said on the next visit a week later.

'You can't do much about it now, can you?' said the German with a smile. 'Relax, I can afford it. You're almost ready to fly to Sydney.'

'Is that really necessary? Surely, the hospital here can handle it.'

'You know your attackers tried to castrate you, don't you?'

'I suspected. Didn't they know I was a priest?'

'I'm glad you can joke about it in your discomfort. That is a good sign. They failed but made a bit of a mess. So, you need specialist reconstructive surgery for your future health and comfort. Sorry to be so blunt about it. And you need to get out of this place.'

'I'm in your hands, I suppose.' He closed his eyes. 'What have my superiors said about this?'

Herr Bann had been in contact with Fr. Muller, who at first objected to outside interference. When Bann explained Jos's danger and where the threat might be, he backed off. Herr Bann could organise Fr. van Engelen's hospital care so long as what seemed an enormous, unnecessary expense did not burden the order. Bann said he would send a letter freeing the order from all costs and liability. The day before Jos was to fly to Sydney accompanied by a nurse, Fr. Tom turned up dressed in slacks and an open-neck shirt.

'You're a sight,' said Tom.

'So are you in your new outfit. It's an improvement on Muller's tastes.'

'I had a lot of builders' labourers as an example of bad taste.' He took the chair beside Jos's bed. 'I find it hard to get my head around all this, Jos. All these changes, and now it looks like someone has it in for you. At least, that's what Gerhard Bann says. What's his role in all this, anyhow, this former German soldier?'

'I don't know, Tom. I am too tired to think about it. I suppose he wants to help me. As you say, he has concluded someone is after me.'

'What am I going to do without you, without your support? Muller's council is already pushing me around, particularly a couple of women who fancy themselves as experts on the council.'

'Don't let them. You're the parish priest.'

'Muller says I am a sort of coordinator of a consultative body. The trouble is, he's chosen people I don't agree with. I don't know what's going to happen. I didn't become a priest to be a sort of political functionary.'

'No, indeed. But my brain is not up to thinking about it. I am sorry, Tom. You'll have to manage your way through it without me—at least for the moment. I will keep in touch. I'm told I'll recover.'

'Please do. Don't forget me.'

'God bless you, Tom.'

Fr. Jos waited in the hospital reception hall, glad to have Gerhard Bann's nurse at his side. He was in no way able to manage by himself. His right leg was in plaster, his ribs braced, his arms and groin bandaged, and his face full of healing scratches. And he barely had the energy to stand by himself.

'You're still groggy from the sedatives and painkillers,' said the doctor when he came for his final consultation. 'We would not normally allow a patient to travel in your condition. Your friend, however, has been persuasive. And he evidently has the money to provide adequate care.'

'I trust him, Doctor.'

'I'm glad you do. Now, I have given Bann and the nurse the necessary instructions. Relax and enjoy the trip.'

'Why are you doing all this, Herr Bann? I have to ask again.' said Jos when seated in the plane between him and the nurse.

'Let us say I don't want your courage to be pointless. I am a tool of Providence.'

'What can I say to that?'

'Besides, why can't I make some reparation for my many sins?'

'Again, what can I say? You know your faith, ex-Nazi.'

'Forget my motivations. You are in no condition to saddle yourself with unnecessary worries. You must give your mind and body time to heal.'

'You could have been a priest, Herr Bann.'

A taxi was waiting for them at Sydney airport. It took Jos and his two carers directly to the hospital, where the following morning, he underwent surgery.

'The surgery went well,' said Bann two days later. 'It was delicate adjustment work, but the surgeon, outstanding in his field, is satisfied he could do no better. Your bodily functions should operate as normal—except perhaps for some limitation which should not bother you.'

'That's what the surgeon said. Thank you for being a little more delicate.'

'You know castration is an ancient form of punishment and humiliation?'

'My mind had not stretched that far, but I understand.'

'I'll be gone for a few weeks for some business negotiations, but I will return. Your task is to recuperate.'

'Really, Herr Bann, I can't take up any more of your time and money. You have done enough, surely. More than enough. And what about this caring and competent young woman here? Is she still necessary?'

'Yes, Fr. Jos, absolutely. Jeannie is a first-class nurse. She will look after your medical needs and act as a guard.'

'Act as a guard?'

'The evidence puts Fr. Muller squarely in the process of betrayal. Others almost certainly played a role. They wanted you out of the way for whatever reason. The evidence also suggests some sort of occultism at play. Are they connected? That is a central question. You don't seem to understand that you are vulnerable in your present state.'

'All right, Herr Bann, I'll do as you say. I don't have the energy to protest.'

'It's not just physical energy. Your mind is down, too.'

The days flowed by, filled with a steady routine of medical care from the surgeon, the ward doctor, and Jeannie, the nurse. Jos was thankful they did not bother him too much with conversation. They seemed to understand his disinclination to chat. How right Bann was about his mental state. He was so flat that he had trouble concentrating on his standard prayers. He had requested his breviary, but it lay unopened on his bedside cabinet. A week later, Fr. Muller strolled into his room.

'I hear you're recovering well, Fr. van Engelen. That is good to see. I haven't been before this because the doctor said you were not up to having visitors.'

'I wasn't aware ... I suppose I'm not so talkative at the moment.'

'I'm told you need time to recover. So take all the time you want. You'll come to the monastery when you are ready to be discharged. Herr Bann has suggested a room where the nurse will have access without bothering the monastery's routine. That's arranged.' Muller gave Jos a questioning look.

'Thank you, Father,' said Jos, disinclined to explain Bann's action.

'What's the connection between you and this former Nazi?'

Jos was not so exhausted as to drop his guard.

'Fr. Timmermans and I came across him when we followed the people fleeing Breda. He let us through.'

'Is that all? Is that the explanation for this extraordinary intervention in the affairs of a priest—and the extraordinary cost?'

'Herr Bann is a successful businessman. He says he can afford it. I have no reason to doubt him.'

'The more important question is why.'

'I suppose he felt sorry for my predicament—I mean, after the assault.'

Jos could see in Muller's eyes that he did not accept his explanation. He could also see that Muller knew he saw it.

'He has gone to all this expense because he felt sorry for a priest he had passing contact with?'

'Herr Bann is Catholic. He was obeying the law of charity.'

'Exemplary behaviour,' said Muller, the old sneer and sarcasm returning. He raised an eyebrow. 'You have never explained what you did and who you did it with during your disappearance.'

'I don't see the connection,' said Jos, understanding Muller was deliberately needling him.

'I think you do.'

'You'll have to talk to Herr Bann. Forgive me if I have no wish to return to that painful time.' Jos would not play Muller's game. Muller seemed not to understand what he was revealing about his actions.

'All right, I'll let you rest, but I will come back to this matter simply because you have not satisfactorily explained your relationship with a Nazi you had dealings with during the war.'

Jos would not rise to the bait. 'As you wish.'

Three days after Fr. Muller returned to Holland without further pestering Jos, Fr. de Jonge appeared in the doorway.

'May I come in?'

'Yes, of course.'

'You're feeling better? Fr. Muller said you were not quite your old self,' said De Jonge, glancing at Jeannie, who rose to leave the room as she did when Muller visited.

'Yes, I should be discharged shortly,' said Jos, wondering about De Jonge's rather tentative manner.

'We're ready to receive you—you and your nurse. Fr. Muller said you have all the time you want to recuperate. Perhaps you would like to return to Holland for a time?'

'I had not thought about it?' said Jos, suspecting De Jonge wanted him anywhere but in Sydney.

'It's something to consider before you take up duties.'

'Has there been any information about my assault? I assume the police have investigated.'

'No, no, nothing final. The police seem to think it was robbery.'

'Really?'

'Yes, well, we'll hear eventually.'

'Not that it matters too much. I won't be returning to Lae, I assume.'

'No, no, you'll be assigned here in Australia after you have sufficiently recovered.'

That was a nothing visit, thought Jos, after De Jonge had left. It was nothing more than a perfunctory inquiry about his health and a lot of uneasiness when De Jonge was usually self-assured. Not even a mention of his favourite subject. De Jonge's changed manner did not long occupy his thoughts. Jos sank back into that vagueness of thought amid the physical lethargy. He was suspended in time, doing nothing but staring at the ceiling of his hospital room. One advantage of his lethargy was the disappearance of his war flashbacks—no more booming explosions and clouds of orange smoke. The doctor snapped him out of it by permitting his discharge.

A lay brother fetched him and took him and Jeannie to the monastery. The brother helped Jos struggle with his plastered leg and braced ribs to his room, where he flopped on the bed. Jeannie came each morning and stayed until the afternoon to help him wash, supervise his meals, and change his dressings. When Jos was sure he could manage, he thanked Jeannie and said she was no longer required. Jeannie objected, citing her instructions from Herr Bann, but did not persist when it became clear Jos was determined.

'You've been rebellious, I hear,' said Bann when he came two days later.

'It was not proper for a young woman to be here so often. Besides, I thought I could manage by myself. Changing the dressing was not too difficult. I enjoy your company, Herr Bann, but perhaps it is no longer necessary for you to be here so often. Surely you have to return to Germany.'

'No, don't worry about me. I have work here in Sydney. It's good to see you improving.'

'Yes, I think I am.'

Fr. de Jonge appeared in the doorway. Seeing Bann, he stopped and seemed on the point of excusing himself.

'No, come in,' said Bann, 'I'm about to leave.'

'It's nothing really,' said De Jonge, coming no further into the room. 'I'm just checking on Fr. van Engelen—to see how he is feeling.'

'I'm fine. Thank you.'

'Fr. de Jonge,' said Bann, 'do you remember that SS officer who used to visit the seminary?'

De Jonge grasped the door frame. 'I remember a group of German soldiers visiting the seminary,' he said, shifting. 'I can't specify.'

'You are sure you don't remember the SS officer?'

'No. Should I?'

'I'm just trying to think of his name.'

'How do you expect me to remember if you don't?'

'I thought you might. I was chatting recently to former comrades, and we could not remember his name. We remembered he accompanied the commandant to the seminary.'

'I can't help you. I'm sorry.'

'You put him on the spot,' said Jos when De Jonge had left them. 'He seemed uncomfortable. Do you suspect him?'

'I noticed his obsequious manner in the presence of Muller.'

'Yes, I noticed, too. He acted like Muller's secretary.'

'It may mean nothing,' said Bann. 'But keep an eye on him.'

'What, do you think he or someone else could do something here?'

'Whoever it was at the seminary, they were trying to get you killed. Do not forget that. That is why I wanted Jeannie with you. She's more than a nurse.'

'Oh, don't tell me. She's on staff.'

'Yes, a valuable member of staff.'

'German?'

'Correct. She's a very competent young lady. Part of her upbringing was in London, and she's a trained nurse. I was so impressed with her treatment of my dying father that I offered her a job. Since joining my company, she has had other training. So you can have complete confidence in her. Now, Fr. Jos, I am returning to Germany tomorrow. Jeannie will remain in Sydney as my business contact. If you need anything, contact her.' He put Jeannie's business card on his bedside cabinet. 'Keep it hidden, please.'

'You overwhelm me, Herr Ban. You've been so kind.'

'Don't upset yourself, Father. I told you, it's reparation for my sins. Besides, I like you. We are on the same side in Church matters.'

'Why is that not a surprise?'

'Good. Now, relax and rest. I will see you in around a month. And don't forget to contact Jeannie if you need anything. Anything at all.'

Jos thought he could manage the change of dressing, and for a week or so, the wound seemed to be healing. But then it began to grow red and ooze. He rang Jeannie, who immediately came.

'There's something wrong here,' she said after an examination. 'It should be healing. Where are your dressings?' Jos pointed to his cabinet. 'They seem all right, but I will replace them. No, I'll come each day and do it myself with my dressings.'

She came each day, and the infection receded.

'What did I do wrong?' said Jos.

'I don't know. It could be anything. But don't worry. It seems to be recovering. Please do not touch anything. Let me do it. Be careful of any source of bacteria. I will wipe everything around you with disinfectant.'

Jos improved a little in mind and body. He felt inclined to take over the dressing again, but Jeannie remained firm. It was better to wait until there was no risk of infection. She had been in contact with Herr Bann, and he insisted on her supervision.

'He told me to tell you not to be foolish.'

'All right, I'll behave myself. When will he be back?'

'I'm not sure. He's still in Germany.'

That afternoon, De Jonge came to tell Jos an international phone call had been booked for 8 p.m. Australian time.

'What's happened, Frans?' said Jos, sitting in De Jonge's office with De Jonge looking on.

'Pappa is gravely ill. If you can, you should come immediately. He has asked for you.'

Fr. de Jonge was all solicitousness, encouraging Jos to prepare at once. He would arrange the bookings. But all flights were booked for the next few days. It was a busy time for international travel. Jos rang Jeannie. Jeannie rang back within a half-hour, saying bookings had been made for the next morning, direct to Amsterdam from Sydney.

'Bookings?'

'Yes, I will accompany you. Be ready for the taxi at 6 a.m.'

Jos asked De Jonge to send a telegram to Frans with arrival details, which De Jonge carried out with a surfeit of willingness and good wishes.

'Go with our blessings and prayers,' he said, 'and don't hurry back. Stay as long as you want.'

Chapter 27

Final confrontation

'GOOD LORD, what's happened to you?' said Frans when Jeannie wheeled Jos from customs.

'It's a long story, Frans. I was assaulted in New Guinea. Jeannie is my nurse. She speaks German and English. I will tell you more about it later. Let's go home. I'm worn out.'

'Welcome, Miss. English would be better.'

Once on the road to Zeeland, Jeannie gave an account of Jos's injuries, their causes, and her place in the proceedings.

'Why didn't you say anything, Jos?' said Frans in Dutch.

'I didn't want to worry Mamma and Pappa.'

'What's the connection between you and this German businessman?'

'Not now, Frans. I will tell you about it later.'

'Your brother has been very ill, Mr. van Engelen,' said Jeannie. 'I don't think he realises how ill. He will need to rest before he returns to Australia. Please call me Jeannie.'

'Thank you, Jeannie. Will you be with him in Middelburg?'

'I have instructions to stay with Fr. van Engelen while there's still a risk of infection.'

'Instructions? Infection?'

'No, Frans, not at the moment, please.'

'Yes, brother,' said Frans, looking over his shoulder at Jeannie, who maintained her businesslike expression.

'How is Pappa?'

'Very bad. He's sinking fast. No particular illness, just old age. His heart is giving out. He's conscious, though talking is too much for him. He will be overjoyed to see you. He's in the hospital. The doctor says he could go at any time. We can visit him directly.'

'Good. Take me straight to him. And please don't say much to Mamma about my condition.'

JEANNIE found a wheelchair at the hospital and took Jos to his father, where his mother, Marijke, and sisters crowded around the bed. Their mouths fell open.

'Not now. I'll tell you all about it later,' he said, rising from the wheelchair and hugging his mother. 'Will you all let me talk to Pappa alone for a moment? Just a little distance from the bed.'

His mother, Marijke, and the sisters moved away from the bed while Jeannie helped him to the bedside chair. She retreated behind the family, keeping her eye on the priest. Fr. Jos bent over his father and took his hand. The family watched him whispering into his father's ear for some time while his father moved his head and lips now and then. Gradually, Fr. Jos bent forward until he had his head and arms over the bed. He remained that way for a minute, with the family looking on apprehensively. Then, raising his head, he made the sign of the cross. Still holding his father's hand, he beckoned the family. His mother put her arm around him and clasped her husband's hand. Simon van Engelen drifted away peacefully. The doctor came to confirm his passing.

'I think he waited until you arrived,' said Jos's mother with her arms still around him. 'He desperately wanted to see you before he passed from this world. I'm so thankful you're here.' She looked him up and down. 'What's happened to you, *lieverd*?'

'Yes, Fr. Jos, what's happened?' said Marijke.

'Can I talk about it later?'

'Fr. Jos was assaulted in New Guinea,' said Frans. 'I can tell you more about it, but not now. Jeannie is his nurse. He needs some attention to stab wounds.'

'Stab wounds? What in heaven's name has happened?'

'Later, Mamma, please.'

Jeannie helped Jos to bed when they arrived home. She briefly explained the New Guinea assault, leaving many questions unanswered for a bewildered family. She apologised she could not say more, but it was essential to understand that Fr. Jos was very sick, much more than his appearance would suggest. The next day, the family's doctor, now quite old, examined him. He confirmed Jeannie's diagnosis.

'Fr. Jos has suffered a serious assault. He has a broken leg, some fractured ribs, and several stab wounds in the groin that are open to infection. I can assure you he has a very competent nurse looking after him. I am afraid I cannot give you any information about the assault. That will be for Fr. Jos to provide when he feels well enough to talk. As you know, he suffered terrible deprivation during the war, weakening his constitution. You will have to be patient. It will take him time to recover from this present condition.'

'How much do you know about this?' said Marijke when she and Frans were alone. 'It seems strange.'

'I know little more except that a German businessman is paying for Jos's care.'

'A German businessman? What's going on there? Why not his order?'

'I have no idea. Jeannie says Meneer Bann will come. When, she doesn't know. Perhaps we'll get an explanation from him.'

'What's your brother got himself mixed up in?'

The family did not bother Jos before the funeral. He was too tired to talk, spending most of the time sitting silently in an armchair or lying on his bed. Mevrouw van Engelen made Jeannie welcome, setting her up in the bedroom next to Jos. Anneke arrived from Amsterdam and, not much younger than Jeannie, struck up a friendly rapport with her. Her favourable opinion of Jeannie put the family at ease. The funeral took place four days later. Anneke helped Jeannie prepare Jos and took charge of the wheelchair. Simon van Engelen requested that Jos say Mass and preside over the burial ceremonies. Jos had to resign himself to letting Fr. Matthijs say Mass, but he insisted on the graveside ceremony. Several times, he tottered before Jeannie and Anneke held him upright. After the ceremony, they took him back to his parents' house and at once to his room. He did not move from there. Jeannie attended to him day and night.

'Will he be all right?' said Marijke. 'He's not moving. He seems to be worsening. It's like he's in a coma.'

'It doesn't look good,' said Frans, who came daily.

'I can only say that he is frail, but otherwise, there's little wrong with him physically,' said Jeannie. 'The infection is under control with antibiotics, and the painkillers are coping with the fractures.'

'Perhaps we should call the doctor again.'

The doctor came and again confirmed Jeannie's opinion.

'It seems to me he's exhausted physically and mentally. He needs time and rest. Perhaps you should again question his continuing in the priesthood.'

'Again?' said Frans.

'Yes, I have repeatedly recommended that Fr. Jos accept laicization. In my view, the brutal treatment of the war rendered him unfit for the burdens of a missionary priest.'

'I don't wonder he said nothing about it to the family,' said Frans. 'He would die rather than give up his vocation.'

'That may be the choice,' said the doctor. 'There's no way of knowing, but his heart must have taken a fearful pounding through the years. Too much pressure, and it may give up.'

Gerhard Bann arrived a couple of weeks later. After he visited Jos, who could barely acknowledge and thank him, he recounted his meeting with Jos during the war and his suspicions that he was betrayed.

'That explains a lot,' said Frans.

'Explains a lot of what?' said Marijke. 'I don't think the rest of us have ever heard anything about this.'

'Jos was not keen to talk about it.'

'Fr. Jos is a courageous and modest man,' said Bann. 'After the war, I was interested enough to find out if he survived. I found him in Papua New Guinea, where my company has business interests. I learned the full story. I also learned that someone or some people were still after him. The assault in Lae was not robbery. That's why I intervened and got him out of there as soon as possible.'

'Who do you think is after him?' said Frans.

'There are two forces that may be connected. It seems almost certain, at least to me, that someone in his religious order betrayed him to the German command in Breda. They wanted him out of the way. He was an obstacle to their plans. Fr. Jos can tell you more about that. Second, someone or some people connected with the occult want him dead. There was a clear occultist element in the Lae attack. Whether the two are connected, I cannot say for sure. It seems impossible, but there is surely some linkage between the attacks. Perhaps it is the occult.'

'Cees and Gerda van den Donker,' said Marijke. 'Frans and Fr. Jos have tangled with Meneer van den Donker. His strict reformed community expelled him for his belligerence and outrageous religious opinions.'

'Yes,' said Frans. 'Later, it became known that both father and daughter were dabbling in what's called New Age philosophy, but what others simply call the occult.'

'Meneer van Donker has an ungovernable hatred of Catholics, especially our family,' said Marijke.

'There's a candidate, indeed,' said Bann. 'Fr. Jos mentioned him.'

A few days later, Bann and Jeannie were enjoying a coffee on Marktplein. It was market day.

'Herr van den Donker,' Bann called.

About to enter a row of stalls, Cees van den Donker turned to see from where the summons came.

'Do you have a minute?' said Bann in English without moving from his chair.

'Well, what do you want, German?' said Cees, approaching.

'It's Gerhard Bann, businessman, successful businessman. I believe you were recently in Lae in New Guinea investigating the animism of the natives there?'

Cees frowned. 'What's that got to do with you?' he said in a heavy accent.

'Fr. van Engelen almost died in an attack in Lae, which appears to have its origin in sorcery, something I believe you dabble in.'

'It's a pity that bit of fascist rubbish survived. But so what?'

'I was in the German army during the war. I was a major, responsible for many operations during which many died.'

'So, Nazi?'

'I met Fr. van Engelen during the war. I found him a man of great courage and manly virtue.'

'Manly virtue, that slimy celibate?' Cees laughed.

'I think the balance between Fr. van Engelen and those who want him dead or out of the way is unfair. I intend to even the scales up a bit by adding my weight to Fr. Jos's side.'

'Good for you,' Cees said, shifting.

'Fr. van Engelen wouldn't hurt a fly. But I would.'

'Good for you, Nazi.' He looked at Jeannie. 'Who's this, your girl-friend?'

'You mean like the woman you took to New Guinea?'

'Your stinking Nazi jackboots are still in our country. Take them back to Naziland.'

'You are warned, Herr van den Donker. I'll come after anyone who attempts to harm Fr. van Engelen.'

'Another fascist Catholic, no doubt. You people stick together, don't you?'

'You had better believe it.'

Later that same day, Truus van den Donker came across Marijke at the market.

'I thought I might see you,' said Marijke when Truus approached her. 'You want to hear about Fr. van Engelen, don't you? Well, I don't think I can give you more information than you have likely heard. Fr. Jos is not well. He suffered a terrible assault in New Guinea. He can't leave his bed.'

'Oh no,' said Truus, her hand instinctively raised, 'is he really in such a bad way?'

'Yes, our doctor says it will take some time for him to recover.'

'Oh, I'm sorry. Will you ... will you pass on my best wishes? Will you tell him he's in my prayers?'

'Of course, Truus. He will know he's in your prayers.'

'Do you think so?'

'Of course. He knows how strong your faith is.'

'Thank you, Marijke.'

'No thanks necessary. Fr. Jos knows those who have affection for him.'

'Oh, does he?'

'Of course, Truus. He will appreciate your concern.'

Gerhard Bann stayed a week in Middelburg. Each day, he visited Jos but did not stay long because Jos was not up to much conversation.

'I'm sorry, Herr Bann, I just don't have the energy.'

'Nothing to be sorry for, Fr. Jos. I know what you have been through. You need your rest. You'll get better. You just have to get over this hump.'

'Thank you, Herr Bann, thank you for everything you've done. Thanks to Jeannie, too. She has been so kind. I'll keep you in my prayers.'

'No thanks necessary. Just get well. I'll keep in touch.'

The doctor assured Bann that Jos only needed rest. His family would look after him. He would monitor his wounds, which were now healing well. Jeannie had done outstanding work, but her services and expense were no longer needed. He would keep an eye on Jos's condition. Jeannie left Middelburg with Bann. Jos continued to improve. In time, the doctor removed the bandages from around his ribs and the plaster on his leg. The wounds healed. Marijke and Frans came frequently, but Jos was still quiet, only conversing out of politeness. His mother was worried.

'You've got to snap out of it, Jos,' said Frans.

'Snap out of what?'

'Well, whatever is keeping your mouth shut.'

'I don't know what's keeping my mouth shut, as you put it.'

'Something is. Do you want to talk about it?'

'I don't know what to talk about, Frans. I feel so worn out. My mind is a blank. A big blank.'

'Mamma is worried about you?'

'I'm aware. I can't help it.'

Marijke came with Frans on the next visit, but there was no change. Jos was just as unresponsive.

'Did I tell you that Truus van den Donker said she would keep you in her prayers?' said Marijke.

'No, at least I don't remember,' said Jos, looking up.

'Yes, she asks after you whenever I see her.'

'Does she? Thank her for me, will you please?'

'Did you see how Jos sparked up at the mention of Truus van den Donker?' said Marijke later.

'Yes, I did. Curious.'

'Do you think a visit would help his frame of mind?'

'I'm not sure,' said Frans. 'I was a little surprised at his reaction. Her name was the only thing that has brought some life to him.'

'That's what I thought.'

'It would be risky,' said Frans. 'What that brute would do if he found out is anybody's guess.'

'It's worth a try. Jos does not sleep well. Your mother says he lies with the bedside lamp on for long periods before he goes to sleep. Perhaps if we sneak Truus in late?'

'It's full of risk, not only about Cees but the gossip mill if anyone sees her entering the house. But it's worth a try. We must do something to break him out of his depression.'

Frans and Marijke waited for a cloudy night with the moon on the wane. Frans collected Truus at the farm in Vrouwedijk and brought her to the family home in Middelburg. She draped a shawl over her head before alighting from the car. Frans escorted her to the front door, shielding her as best he could. After greeting Frans's mother and leaving her waiting in the lounge, they took Truus to Jos's room. Marijke knocked lightly and opened the door. Jos was lying on the bed, still dressed and propped up against pillows.

'We have someone who asked to see you,' said Marijke, leading Truus into the room.

'Oh,' said Jos, straightening himself.

'Truus wanted to see how you were.'

'Hello, Truus. It's kind of you to come, but isn't it a little late?'

'No, no, not at all. I had to be careful,' said Truus, with the thin shawl still draped over her head like a veil.

'Yes, I understand.'

'I am so sorry to see you're not well again. It seems so unfair.' She came nearer to the bed.

'We are sent these trials. I'll rise above it eventually—with time.'

'You spoke to me about suffering—what it meant. Do you remember?'

'Yes, I should counsel myself with my own words, shouldn't I?'

Truus came closer to the bed.

'Do you remember all those years ago in Amsterdam when you saved me from death?'

'Of course.'

'Do you remember that you held my hand and said a prayer with me? To comfort me?'

Jos nodded.

'Can I say a prayer with you now?'

Without waiting for an answer, she knelt beside the bed, bowed her head, and took Jos's hand.

'O, Lord Jesus, bring comfort to Fr. Jos as he brought comfort to me. Fill him with your spirit. Help him to bear his suffering.'

She bent over and brought Jos's hand to her lips. Jos leaned forward and put his hand on her head. She pulled the shawl away so his hand rested on her bare head. They remained that way for a while, and then Jos made the sign of the cross over her.

'Come on,' whispered Marijke, leading a bemused Frans out of the room. 'Give them some privacy.' She wiped her eyes.

Less than a minute later, Truus emerged from the room.

'Thank you for bringing me. I appreciate it more than I can express. Would you kindly take me home, Meneer van Engelen?'

Marijke did not enter Jos's room but waited with Frans's mother until Frans returned.

'She asked me to keep the meeting private,' said Frans. 'She assured me she understood Jos's commitment as a priest. Of course, I said I would.'

'I hope it does some good,' said his mother, 'though it seems a lot of trouble.'

'It seems you were right,' said Frans as they drove away.

'I did not realise how much. What a heart-wrenching scene.'

'Did you speak to him?'

'No. When I returned to his room and slightly opened the door, he was kneeling beside his bed, his head in his hands. I closed the door quietly and left him. He turned the light off shortly after.'

The following morning, Frans arrived to find Jos sitting in an armchair in the lounge room.

'Feeling better?'

'Well, I had enough energy to get dressed and come and sit here while Mamma brought me breakfast and fussed over me.'

'That's an improvement.'

'I suppose so. Frans, you will keep what you witnessed last night private, won't you?'

'Of course, Jos, you don't have to ask.'

'I know, but I had to mention it. It changes nothing, you know.'

'I know.'

Their mother entered the lounge room carrying a tray with a pot of coffee, cups and saucers, and a plate of biscuits.

'Your brother seems in better spirits,' she said, pouring coffee for Frans.

'So I see.'

'Was it Mevrouw van den Donker's visit? It seems strange. She's still Strict Reformed, isn't she?'

'As far as I'm aware,' said Frans.

'Poor thing, for that charming, handsome woman to have such a frightful husband. It was very kind of her to visit you, Jos, wasn't it?'

'Yes, Mamma, it was very kind.'

'Strange that a strict reformed woman should have such consideration for a Catholic priest, don't you think?'

'Truus van den Donker is a special woman, Mamma,' said Frans.

'Indeed.'

Jos's state of mind gradually improved. Truus's reference to his counselling about suffering was a jolt. How could he have forgotten? But then, Truus herself, her pure heart, and her kindness under the load she had to bear—that was a model to snap him out of his self-pity. He feared Cees would somehow find out about their late-night assignation and be on the warpath. But, no, nothing happened. No bluster and abuse anywhere. It was all quiet on the war front. Nor was there any gossip about the German and his assistant. He had half-expected rumours about the young woman and the former Nazi officer. But nothing. Herr Bann had charmed everyone. Frans again became his consolation as he took him for walks around his favourite parts of Walcheren.

'It's time for me to go,' said Jos two months later while walking along the dunes near Oostkappelle on the northern side of the former island.

'I had a feeling your mind had turned in that direction.'

'I must get back to my duties. It's time to put it all behind me.' He stopped, leaned on his walking stick, and looked at the castle that had risen before them. 'That castle will forever be connected with Cees van den Donker and Truus.' He was silent for a time. 'Have you seen her?'

'No. Nor has Marijke. She seems to have gone to ground. I haven't seen Van den Donker, either. He's usually prowling around the town, snarling at people.'

'That's the signal for my departure.'

Jos wrote to Fr. Muller, telling him he wished to return to duties in Australia. Muller was all kindness and cooperation, not wasting any time preparing plane tickets and documentation. He had sent instructions to Fr. de Jonge about his duties, which, he promised, would not be onerous, given his condition. Jos wrote to Gerhard Bann about his plans and once again thanked him for his care. He could not help wondering yet again about his motivations. Was it, as he said, just kindness and admiration? What else could it be? He had nothing to offer Bann except the sacraments. He should not be so distrustful, he told himself.

Jeannie rang him to say Bann was in America but would contact him in due course. He wished him the very best in this new phase of his life. How did he know it was a new phase? He spent his last days with his mother, Frans, and Marijke, thanking them, too, for their care. Nothing was said about Truus's night visit, which was a relief. Two days before his departure, Anneke unexpectedly turned up to have a chat with him. She was on a week's visit to her parents. It was fine weather, so Jos took her to the back garden for their chat. The next day, Frans and Marijke drove him to Schiphol for his KLM flight to Sydney.

Chapter 28

Return to Sydney

FR. DE JONGE was all smiles and pretended cooperation. He allocated the same out-of-the-way room Jos had occupied after discharge from the hospital. Fr. Jos would have peace there. Jos did not care if De Jonge's purpose was to get him out of the way of his fellow priests and the regime implemented in accordance with the spirit of the council. He wanted peace and solitude as much as De Jonge wanted it for him.

'You'll have reduced duties,' said De Jonge, 'while you recover.'

'I'm pretty well right now. I had a rest in Holland.'

'You've said that before. Fr. Muller wants to ensure there is no repeat collapse.'

The brutal Lae bashing was hardly a case of collapse, but Jos held his tongue, curious about what De Jonge had in store for him.

'Perhaps pastoral work with older people,' he said. 'I'm sure many are still confused about the recent changes.'

'We'll see, Fr. van Engelen. We must set out a program if you want to do pastoral work.'

'I think it's unwise to pressure older people.'

'As I say, we'll look at that in due course.' De Jonge's smiles weakened to show a little irritation. 'Now, about your Masses, Fr. Muller shows you admirable forbearance. He will allow you to say the old Mass in consideration of your condition. But it will be for a limited time. When you are completely fit, you'll change to the New Mass that the pope will officially promulgate shortly.'

'I assume with adjustments ... I mean, your adjustments.'

'Our adjustments, Fr. van Englen,' De Jonge stressed, wagging his finger. 'We are still members of the same community. However, there are aspects of the new Mass, I admit, that lag behind the spirit. We'll talk about those in due course. It is to be hoped that Pope Paul makes the adjustments liturgical experts have recommended. But, returning to Fr. Muller's generous allowance, you will be permitted to say the Old Mass so long as it's in private. You'll have one of the church's side altars. And it will be at 10.30 each morning.'

Jos thanked the provincial. He was all generous consideration.

'All right, that's settled then,' De Jonge continued, ignoring Jos's helpless sarcasm. 'But there is just one more item to deal with. As you know, the order has done away with the unpastoral religious habit. We must break down the barriers between us religious and ordinary people. We are all the people of God. There is to be no sign of separation. No more clericalism. You are to cease wearing the religious habit as instructed.'

'You want us all to go around looking like refugees from a charity shop?'

'I will endeavour to ignore your objectionable remarks in consideration of your condition.'

'Am I wrong? Have a look around you.'

'I admit some of our confreres lack taste in clothing, but it is early days while we all adjust to the new circumstances. You are required to obey the rules and procedures the community has collectively agreed upon.'

Jos had nothing more to say. In stubborn contravention of the new democratic order so lauded by De Jonge, he continued to wear his habit. De Jonge evidently thought it wise not to fight him over it for the moment. He had weightier matters on his mind. Jos's refusal to give up his habit caused friction between him and the rest of the community, many of whom he was not acquainted with. He accepted it. It was a small price to pay for sticking to what was proper for a priest. As time passed and he mixed more, he understood there was more than one cause of the friction.

A majority embraced the post-council regime with enthusiasm and exploited the new freedom. They wandered in and out of the monastery at will. It was not only the priests. The junior seminary at Ringbark Park had been closed, and the senior seminarians in priestly training were now at the city monastery, attending the nearby university. They, too, wandered about the place. The beer they were free to drink in their rooms encouraged the wandering. Worse, the wandering and drinking kept some out late at night. Guzzling beer and wandering who knows where, that was all fine, thought Jos, but wearing the habit of two centuries—oh, no, that was not on. The wandering priests and seminarians frowned at Jos and made comments behind their hands. The minority, still unsure about the changes, were peeved that Jos, and not they, had the gumption to resist. Jos noticed something else about the seminarians—two in particular.

They were the youngest seminarians, hardly out of school, it seemed. Their fresh faces, fair hair, and slim build turned out to be deceptive. They often had the attention of De Jonge, who showed indiscreet favouritism towards them. Nat and Denny, as they called themselves, acted innocently to De Jonge's attention, smiling and simpering unashamedly. But Jos sometimes caught them with far less innocent expressions, often after De Jonge's attention was elsewhere. Thinking nobody was watching, certainly not the crippled priest thought out of sight, they would exchange sly smiles and raise eyebrows. Their two-faced behaviour, though justly making a fool of De Jonge, disgusted Jos. One afternoon in the community room, Jos caught their attention. They made a cup of tea and wandered over to where he sat. After a polite greeting, Denny spoke.

'We've been to Holland, Father. We were there for about six months.'

'We loved it,' added Nat. 'Where do you come from, Father?'

'From Middelburg in Zeeland.'

'Yes, we know Middelburg,' said Denny. 'We spent two days there—such a beautiful old medieval town.'

'But we were mostly in Amsterdam,' said Nat. 'We had many friends there.'

'Is that how you came into contact with the order of the Wounded Heart of Jesus?' said Jos.

'Yes,' continued Nat, showing surprise, 'we got to know some seminarians there.'

'And they influenced your decision to join the religious life?'

'You could say so,' said Denny, the bright, innocent look fading.

Jos did not speak. He looked from one to the other. Nat shifted, and Denny frowned.

'Are you sure you have both given it enough thought?' said Jos.

The young men blinked, their eyes fixed on Jos's penetrating expression. Denny stood up, cup in hand.

'That's none of your business.'

Nat, his uncertainty about Jos's meaning cleared away, also rose.

'A vocation to the priesthood is not something to exploit,' said Jos.

'I know now why they say your injuries have not just crippled your body,' said Denny, raising his chin. 'We have a vocation. That's all you need to know.'

'It would be better in the long run if you did not carry on your fraud,' said Jos, ignoring the insolence and disrespect.

'You're the only one who thinks it a fraud,' said Nat, his anger dissolving into a smile. 'Come on, Denny darling. Let's return to our rooms.'

Jos watched them mockingly mince from the common room.

'The order has always been strict about the characteristics necessary for the priesthood,' said Jos when he caught the sociable, impeccably attired provincial on his own. 'Are the standards still being followed?'

'Yes, why? Not that it is any of your business, Father.'

'I've seen a few seminarians who would have raised questions in the past.'

'Who and what?'

'Too much drink.'

'We have to exercise patience, Fr. van Engelen, and show a little charity. We must allow them the time to mature and embrace the pastoral exigencies of their vocations.'

'Pastoral exigences? If they haven't been able to control their drinking by now, there are other impulses they might not control in their pastoral rounds.'

De Jonge looked hard at Jos, his eyes narrowing. 'Fr. Muller has remarked on the objectionable manner you have developed in expressing yourself. When you came to the seminary, you were quiet and cooperative. That has changed.'

'The seminary has changed.'

'Fr. Muller thinks your wartime experiences have disturbed you. I do, too. That's why we have been tolerant—at least until now.'

'The drink was a minor point I wished to make. The behaviour of some seminarians should have raised flags.'

'What behaviour? What are you talking about now?'

'Some are altogether too familiar with each other.'

De Jonge seemed not to understand at first. 'How dare you,' he said, raising his finger. 'The law of charity seems to have deserted you, Father. I will not stand here and listen to such foul imputations. I mean very foul character imputations. Each seminarian must be free to discover himself and his vocation free from prejudice, just as you did.'

'There is the more important question of self-control.'

'Are you listening, Fr. van Engelen?' said the provincial, whose face had reddened to apoplexy.

'I am thinking of the regulations of the past.'

'This distasteful conversation will end with the request that you reflect on your attitudes. The tolerance we have shown you is not inexhaustible. Now, I have meetings to attend.'

Jos watched the provincial march along the cloisters to his office, dressed in a navy-blue business suit, white shirt, and black tie. He went to the common room, made himself a cup of tea, and sat near a group of older priests dressed like slobs, unshaven, and hair unkempt.

'Come and join us, Jos,' said one of the priests. 'Not all of us want to ignore you.'

'Thank you,' said Jos, 'I'm not sure what everyone thinks of my stand on the liturgy. I have caused enough trouble.'

'Yes, well, some of us are still shell-shocked by the changes,' said Fr. Ray Williams, who Jos knew as a professor of theology, 'but don't want to stand in the way of progress, as our provincial puts it.'

Despite the gesture of friendship, Jos quickly saw that the group did not want yet another conversation about the council and its changes.

'Where are Fathers Johnson, Donaldson, and Gallagher? I haven't seen them.' Jos had spent some time with them on his visits to Sydney after finding mutual philosophical interests.

There was a pause while the priests looked at each other.

'Johnson and Donaldson have been laicised, and Gallagher simply shot through,' said Williams.

'You surprise me. What happened?'

'Did you know about the new policy of bringing male and female religious into contact with each other?'

'No, I have been a little out of touch.'

'Well, the priests and nuns were certainly in touch. All three priests found nuns they liked, and the nuns liked them, so they left. Gallagher was so in love that he could not wait for laicization. A bouncing baby boy appeared six months later. They're all married with young families. It's a delightful family scene when they turn up to Mass.'

'Good heavens.'

'You might well say that. Others among us don't have the power to attract a nice nun or resolve to go out into the big bad world.'

With each word, Williams's manner became so cynical that Jos excused himself and retreated to his room. It was something else to work on his mind. Frequently, he could not sleep because of it all. When his restlessness became too much, he would go for a walk outside the monastery grounds. He did not go far because his leg still bothered him. He would sit on the bench of a bus stop shelter and watch the traffic and the comings and goings of students from the nearby university. In this way, he was able to negotiate his way through the monastery community without causing problems for himself and others.

One evening in January, three months after his return from Holland, a car drew to a stop outside the monastery entrance, not far from where he sat. Nat and Denny got out and, seeing him, gave a friendly wave before strolling through the entrance. Not long after the car drove off, a second car drifted to a stop. A young woman was at the wheel, and a young man was in the passenger seat. They clasped each other passionately and sank out of sight for a while. After righting themselves, the young man hopped out and, with a wave, disappeared into the monastery. Some days later, a commotion sounded from De Jonge's office, so loud that members of the community, including Jos, came from the common room. A man appeared in the corridor, yelling and pointing at the provincial.

'I don't care what you say about young people having to experience life. I won't have one of your disgusting seminarians screwing my daughter. If she must behave like a slut, I prefer she did it with someone who did not intend to take a vow of chastity. At least she would then have some prospects of commitment.'

De Jonge appealed to the man, his hands raised, but the angry father fluttered a hand in his face and stomped off. De Jonge became aware of the audience in the corridor and, with a frustrated wave, retreated to his office. Jos wondered whether he would publicly discipline the seminarian.

'Have you taken action against the seminarian?' he said after hearing nothing more about the incident. 'In truth, the seminarian should be dismissed, not just disciplined.'

'I'll thank you to mind your business,' said De Jonge. 'These are sensitive matters.'

'The father's right. It's stupid for a seminarian to engage in sexual activity when he intends to take a vow of chastity—or at least be a priest.'

'Stupid? You are showing once again, Fr. van Engelen, how deeply you are stuck in the past. There are new ways of dealing with the maturing processes of young people. Besides, the celibate life of the clergy is under question. But, really, none of this is your business.'

'I would be appalled if you did not expel that seminarian.'

'Well, you're free to be appalled. Just don't interfere. And I might add that you're running close to the wind once again. Expulsion might be an option, but not for the seminarian.'

It seemed not to occur to De Jonge that his expulsion might cause scandal beyond the monastery. Jos saw it was pointless to discuss the matter and desisted. Why bother wasting his energy? He resolved to ignore these pointless irritations. He could not, however, ignore everything. Indeed, signs of disintegration came one after the other. Before classes started in February 1969, Fr. Toon Achterkamp, the seminarian with whom De Jonge had surveilled the Vos farmhouse, appeared in the common room early one morning. Jos thought it strange that Achterkamp's unannounced appearance hardly sparked an interest.

'Hello, Fr. Achterkamp,' said Jos, approaching him while he made a cup of coffee. 'I have not seen you since the seminary days.' Achterkamp still radiated the fastidiousness of that time.

'I have been in Australia.'

'Teaching?'

'At the colleges run by the order,' said Achterkamp, giving the impression he was not interested in a conversation.

'Between assignments?'

'No, I'm returning to Holland.'

'I suppose you will be happy to be back home in Holland.'

'Not really. Now, if you will excuse me, Fr. van Engelen, I have a meeting with Hans ... Fr. de Jonge.'

Jos watched Achterkamp exit the common room with cup in hand. Seeing Fr. Williams sitting close by, he said, 'Fr. Achterkamp appears unhappy about returning to Holland.'

'About being returned to Holland, you mean,' said Williams with a mischievous smile.

'Returned to Holland? Disciplinary action?'

'You could say that.'

'What for, if I may ask?'

'You may ask,' said Williams, lounging back with his mischievous smile unchanged, 'but I'm not saying anything. If you want to know more, you had better speak to Fr. de Jonge.'

'Then, it's serious, I take it, presumably about his conduct as a teacher.'

'Ho, ho,' said Williams, holding up his hands and shaking his head, 'I didn't hear that.'

Enough said, thought Jos. For the rest of the day, he caught glimpses of Achterkamp deep in conversation with De Jonge. At times, he appeared to be appealing to the provincial. At one point, De Jonge put his hand on Achterkamp's shoulder and shook his head as if nothing else was to be said. The following morning, Achterkamp was nowhere to be seen, and no word was uttered about him. Again, Jos resolved to ignore the goings-on at the monastery. He was helpless to do anything about it. Sometime later, Williams, holding a book and looking around furtively, cornered him in the common room.

'There's nobody here,' he whispered, 'so we can talk. Make yourself a tea and join me. I have something for you.'

Jos, wondering about Williams's furtive manner, did as requested.

'Look, Jos, I don't say anything about the council—it's pointless, anyhow—but I'm in much agreement with your stand. The council was hijacked—'

'Hijacked? What exactly do you mean?' He said, understanding, but could not suppress his surprise at the stark image.

'I mean that a powerful faction at the council had long planned to steer the Church in the direction of their ideology. The council provided the opportunity. They succeeded, as you know. It was a takeover. Of course, much of this I have learned after the fact. Indeed, few people could have envisaged what the council unleashed.'

'Certain radical ideas about the Church and its liturgy existed before the council,' said Jos, 'but how can you be sure there was a definite organised plan to manipulate the council as you claim?'

'You ask the right question. Here, the evidence is in this book.' He handed the book to Jos. 'Now, keep it out of sight and don't show it to anyone here. It's banned—by De Jonge. He will be furious with me if he learns I gave it to you. His ideological mates will be, too. It is written by an

American priest who ran a news service at the council. You have a firsthand witness. Take it to your room at once. We can talk about it later if you wish.'

Jos took the book and his tea to his room. Two hours of reading was enough. The cardinals and bishops of the so-called Northern Alliance, the countries of Northern Europe, were indeed well-organised and prepared for the council. Most bishops had little idea of their plans or even understood their progressive ideas and motivations. The progressives steamrolled the conservatives, leaving them dismayed and shell-shocked in the first phase. He finished the book the following day. The only difference in the story was that some traditional bishops rallied and fought back. The book confirmed Jos's impression of the council from his limited reading of the documents and the reports. The council was as much a political contest as it was about the pastoral goals of the Church in the modern world. It was urgent to complete his reading of the documents.

'You are right, Ray,' said Jos when he met Williams in the common room. 'The book provides strong empirical evidence that the progressives manipulated the council. My reading of the documents is limited. There is no heresy in the four constitutions, but there are grounds in the document on the liturgy for the present liturgical chaos.'

'Exactly. You won't find out-and-out heresy in the rest of the documents, but you will find a basis for what they call the 'spirit' of the council. The spirit of the council is destroying the Church as you and I knew it.'

'Well, why don't you do something? Why do you sit back, if you don't mind me saying so, and regard the world with cynicism?'

'I suppose I deserve a serving of your Dutch forthrightness. But, Jos, what can I do?' Williams held up his hands in an appeal. 'I'm old and tired. I don't have the strength to fight De Jonge and his mates. It's useless for me to try. I'll just make myself a nuisance. I resign myself to rot here until the good Lord has mercy on me and takes me away.'

Jos understood his feelings of helplessness—when everything seemed to go against you. He had just been through it himself.

'You've got to pull yourself out of it, Ray. Don't give up completely. There are things you can do for yourself. If you don't want to wear the habit, at least make an effort to groom and dress neatly. It's for your self-respect. You're a highly qualified theologian. If you don't have an audience in our fraternity, you might find one outside. There are theological periodicals and magazines you can submit non-controversial articles to.'

'Another serve of Dutch forthrightness,' Ray said with a helpless smile. 'I deserve it, I suppose. Thanks, anyhow, Jos. I wish I had the same spirit as you. I would say the old Mass if De Jonge didn't jump on me from a great height.'

'You make the same stand. We can stand together.'

'No, that's going too far. Let me begin with not looking like a ragbag.'

ON PRECISELY the subject of the Mass, it was a growing problem he could not ignore. The monastery's church was a sandstone building with origins in Australia's colonial period. It had long ceased to be a parish church. Until the council, some people in the vicinity had preferred it to the local church. Now, with the end of the council, a small number attended the regular new Mass offered at the main altar by the monastery's priests. The provincial's generous permission for Jos to say the old Mass at an obscured side altar at the inconvenient time of 10.30 in the morning was begrudging rather than generous.

Jos did not expect anyone to attend, and he did not care. Nothing mattered except the opportunity to say the traditional Mass. He said the Mass by himself, struggling on his walking stick with the server tasks. In the following weeks, a few people turned up. A retired man volunteered to serve Mass and relieve him of his dependence on the walking stick. More and more people came, mostly older people. By February 1969, a small congregation attended Jos's Masses. De Jonge found out.

'This was never the intention,' he said, accosting Jos after Mass. 'I have permitted you to say Mass alone, not secretly start a private rebellion against the council's decrees.'

'I'm not starting anything, and it's not secret. The people come of their own accord. You speak to them or close the church at 10.30.'

Drawn up to his full sartorial magnificence in his natty navy-blue suit, pristine white shirt, and black tie, Fr. de Jonge addressed the people after the next Mass. He informed them that Fr. van Engelen's Mass was private, not open to the general congregation. It was the New Mass that they were required to attend. The old people were unimpressed. They kept coming, and the group kept growing. De Jonge closed the church but had to reopen it when the people shouted and hit the front doors with their walking sticks. He addressed them again and said the church would be closed. If they insisted on rowdy activity, he had no alternative but to call the police. The next day, an official from the archbishop's office rang to ask whether it was true some silly person at the monastery had foolishly threatened to call the police on old people who just wanted to attend Mass.

'I want you to pack your bags,' said De Jonge between gritted teeth two days later. 'You will take the plane to Melbourne this afternoon. You will stay overnight at the Melbourne house. The next day, you will be taken to the country town of Binawarra, where we have a church without a priest. That will be your parish. You are to keep expenses low, just what is necessary to keep the parish running. Not many Catholics are in the area, so you will not be overburdened.'

Fr. Ray Williams caught Jos as he was about to step into the taxi. 'You're an uncompromising fellow, Jos, but I must admire you. I'll do my best to pull my socks up. I wish you all the best.' He held out his hand.

'Thanks, Ray,' said Jos, taking his outstretched hand. 'All the best. You will be in my prayers.'

'I'll need them.'

Chapter 29

Peace at last

THE SENIOR seminarian took Jos's provisions into St Philomena's presbytery in Binawarra while Jos, supported on his walking stick, looked around the town square of the small country town about 100 miles northwest of Melbourne. The town was in Victoria's 19th-century gold rush district, sporting beautiful sandstone colonial buildings. An aura of tranquillity pervaded the place. It relaxed him. The seminarian left him after ensuring the presbytery was clean, fully equipped, and ready for service. There was nothing to complain about. De Jonge had organised everything in advance of his expulsion. Very prompt of him. No doubt arrangements had been made for his meals, laundry, and cleaning. He had to give credit where it was due. Late in the afternoon, he received a knock on the door.

'Welcome, Fr. van Engelen,' said a big man with a big voice and a florid complexion. 'Welcome to our little town. Bill Huckerby, principal of the town's high school.' He took Jos's hand and shook it vigorously.

'Thank you, Mr. Huckerby,' said Jos, somewhat overwhelmed.

'Hey, none of that mister stuff. It's Bill. Okay?'

'Yes, Bill, thank you for the warm welcome. Will you be one of my congregation?'

'No, no, none that, too. I'm yet to cross the Tiber. Anglican, on the high side.'

'Oh,' said Jos, wondering why he was the first to greet him.

'The mayor received a call from your people,' said Bill, as if reading Jos's thoughts, 'asking for help preparing your living arrangements. He handed the matter to me. I do these sorts of things here, you know. You've got someone for the cleaning, meals, and laundry. Give me a call if you need anything else. I'll drop by tomorrow.'

A small group attended Mass the following Sunday. They had heard they now had a resident priest who would offer Mass every Sunday. They were surprised, and most were pleased that it was the traditional Mass. Only a few were critical, citing the spirit of the council. Why had Father not said the new Mass? Where was the renewal and the ecumenical spirit? Despite the complaints, the congregation grew each Sunday until the small church was almost full. Jos did not have to appoint a parish council. People came forward straightaway.

Two months later, he could only wonder at the change. Some beautiful young families, one in particular, were his great consolation. They were warm, devout, and ever ready to assist him. They made him feel like family. Bill Huckerby, despite the first impressions of a rather jolly clownish character, turned out to be well organised, competent, and ready to help in Jos's administrative matters. He was also a man driven by kindness and an unaffected Christian charity. He and his wife, Joanne, were now good friends. Jos wrote to his mother and Frans and Marijke that he had not been so content in a long time. Indeed, he could not be more content. Marijke wrote to say how pleased they were with the news. They had been so worried about him. Jos looked for news about Truus. He was not disappointed.

'Within a week of your departure,' wrote Marijke, 'I met Truus on market day. It has become our meeting day, by the way. Anyhow, she had a comely blush on her youthful cheeks when she saw me. We had a chat and a coffee. She seemed at ease, which suggested that Cees was away. She had that same sadness in her eyes, but her manner showed she was at peace. I waited for her to bring up that evening, but she didn't. She asked how you were. I could only tell her you were back in Sydney and we had not heard from you yet. We did not expect a letter for a while.'

'When we received your letter, I phoned her with the news. She asked to see me on the next market day rather than talk on the phone. We met at our usual cafe, and I showed her your letter. I hope you don't mind. There was nothing private, I thought—just an account of your circumstances. She clutched it so long that I thought she must have read it several times. She smiled (she has such a lovely smile) and gave it back to me, saying she was glad you were happy. Please tell me if you prefer I didn't share your letters with her.'

As he had always done with news about Truus, Jos read and reread the letter until he put it away with the rest of the letters in his shoebox. He wrote to Marijke that he did not mind her sharing the last letter. Truus should know his circumstances, but perhaps it would be better if there were no virtual correspondence between them. They would be false to each other. Marijke understood. Fr. de Jonge phoned to ask how he had settled in. He was effusive when Jos said everything was running well, and he was content.

'I'm glad to hear that, Fr. van Engelen. You needed to be on your own to reflect on the future and how you would go forward to meet the great blessings of the council.'

'I assure you, Father, I am thinking about the council every day.'

'That's the spirit. It is hard to leave the old and redundant behind. It is hard to resist sinking into a mire of nostalgia, but we must resolve to engage with the modern world for the sake of the future Church. I will leave you alone to attend your small congregation. Don't hesitate to contact us if you need anything.'

Opposite St Philomena's presbytery was a lush, extended park that formed part of the town square. From the day of his arrival, Jos went each morning to sit on one of the park benches, where he relaxed and watched the busy shopping centre. It had now become a habit. Many people came to talk to him there. They found approaching him on his bench easier than in the presbytery. Several months later, Jos was watching the people descending from the Melbourne bus when he started and pulled himself to his feet. He waved his walking stick.

'Hello, Jos, mate. I bet you weren't expecting me,' said Tom Connolly, dressed roughly and carrying a rucksack.

'What has happened, Tom?'

'What do you think? I shot through.'

'What, did you speak to De Jonge about it?' said Jos, knowing the answer.

'No, I'm not speaking to that fancy boy. It'd be pointless.'

'Do you think it is wise to burn bridges?'

'There were already burnt—blasted, bombed, and burnt. Everything about my religious life collapsed before my eyes. The last straw was that bunch of ignorant jerks who paraded as the enforcers of another religion.

It was one thing to cop it from Muller and De Jonge. By hell, I wasn't going to cop it from that bunch of new-age clowns.'

'What are you going to do?'

'Go back into the building trade. But not in Brisbane. Don't want to face the gossip. I've come to Melbourne to look around. I'm pretty confident about finding work. I have a good track record. But I would like to spend a week or two here, Jos, if you don't mind. I need your advice. I'm totally lost—in my head, I mean.'

'Of course you can, Tom. I've got a couple of spare rooms.'

'Are you sure? I'm happy to stay at the local hotel.'

'You're staying with me. No arguments.'

Jos spoke long with Tom about his decision. He talked about his determination to stick with the Church of the ages. There would be a cost. He knew that. The martyrs knew it, too. Tom listened without saying much. Jos understood. Tom needed time to process it all. He went on walks in the fields and hills surrounding Binawarra. He met up with one of the men who came to Mass every morning and was also a keen bushwalker. On most afternoons, they set out together, Tom returning with a healthy flush to replace the drawn cheeks. On the day before his departure, he and Jos were sitting in the park when a luxury car parked outside St. Philomena's. Out stepped Gerhard Bann.

'Well, what do you know?' said Tom.

'Indeed,' said Jos.

'Hello, Fathers,' said Bann, dressed smartly but casually. 'I'm glad to find you both here.'

'You can forget the "father" tag,' said Tom.

'Oh, so it's happened to you, too? I can't say I'm surprised. Priests everywhere are walking out.'

'Are they?' said Jos. 'Is it so bad?'

'Yes, Fr. Jos. You've been too isolated by sickness and circumstances to be fully aware of what's happening. The religious orders, male and female, are bleeding members. It's been a pyrrhic victory for the German and Dutch contingents who led the council assault.'

'It's tragic, but what are you doing here, Herr Bann? I'm delighted to see you, of course.'

'I've come to see how you were. I'll just overnight. I have business in Melbourne.'

'That turns out well. Tom is returning to Melbourne tomorrow.'

'Then you must come with me, Tom, if I may call you Tom. And you both must call me Gerhard. We are in Australia, after all. It will, of course, remain Fr. Jos.'

'Thank you, Gerhard. I'd appreciate a lift.'

'Tom's looking for work in Melbourne,' said Jos. 'He's in the building trade.'

'Then, I might be able to help. Well seen, Fr. Jos.'

Tom took advantage of the extra time to join his new friend Charles on a final bushwalk, leaving Gerhard and Jos alone in the afternoon. They chatted about developments in the Church in Holland and Germany, Jos showing surprise at how much he had missed.

'It's the same in both countries,' said Gerhard, 'with the collapse more serious in Holland. Of course, the council people don't see it that way. The turmoil is the price for the brilliant new age ahead for the Church.'

'I tremble for the future.'

'Actually, Fr. Jos, there's another reason I came. I have some news. I have been in contact with a former officer whom I could not previously find. He learned from one of the others that I was asking about the SS officer who visited the seminary with the commandant.'

'From your expression, I see it's significant,' said Jos, sitting up.

'Yes, but not conclusive. The officer had the information from the SS officer's valet. The valet was convinced his superior had an interest in the seminary—interest in someone. But he never dared to comment or ask questions.'

'De Jonge.'

'That's where it points.'

'But it is not one hundred per cent conclusive.'

'No, but it seems enough,' said Gerhard. 'I think you should keep his betrayal in mind.'

'That does not exonerate Muller and Van Rossem.'

'No, it's only to say De Jonge played a role. However, I'm inclined to think Muller was the leader, which raises questions about the relationship between De Jonge and Muller.'

'I think it's just superior and subordinate,' said Jos after a little consideration, 'an obsequious, manipulated subordinate.'

'Perhaps. Anyhow, it's De Jonge, as your provincial, you should be careful of.'

'What would be the point now, Gerhard?'

'I can't see into the future, but a person like that ... You don't know what he's capable of.'

'As Oceania's Provincial, he's playing the role of the council's champion. He would not want to jeopardise that, would he?'

'Perhaps not. But temptation ...'

Jos was silent for a while.

'How is Jeannie?'

'Very well. She's hard at work in Germany,' Gerhard said, glancing at Jos. 'She's a valued member of my executive team. Nothing else if you're wondering.'

'I'm sorry if I appear intrusive.'

'Don't worry. I understand people might wonder. But, no, I have not gone with the sexual revolution. I'm married and monogamous, and that's the way it will stay.'

'Sexual revolution?'

'Prepare yourself, Fr. Jos. When you catch up with events, you will understand the push behind the furore over the pope's encyclical.'

'I hardly dare think about it if the turmoil in the order is a sign.'

'It is a sign, and I dare say more will unfold in your community.'

'You seem to know a lot about this business when I have the impression most in the general community have little idea—and could not care less. I include Catholics.'

Gerhard hesitated. 'I'm aware you've been wondering about my motivations. I understand.' They were in the front parlour. The German stood and walked to the window overlooking the park. 'It's the outcome of the war. When I came across you that night outside Breda— by the way, you were lucky the sergeant did not shoot you. Anyhow, I was already experiencing creeping doubts. Chasing all those poor people down jolted me. By the war's end, I was more worried about keeping my soldiers alive than shooting the enemy.

'After the war, I suffered through a painful period of reassessment: the extermination camps, the destruction of so much, the shocking Dresden bombings. I once saw an American propaganda film. It said you couldn't trust a single German. I do not blame the Americans, but, really, most

Germans were like most Americans. The German people let Hitler and the Nazis seduce them. The fear of communism was all around the West. Rightly so. But Hitler exploited that fear. Perhaps the Germans were more susceptible. I don't know. When I saw you that night, I saw a person utterly committed to his beliefs. I see now the same commitment in your stand against your superiors. It has nearly cost you your life. I stood by you because, if for nothing else, I don't like bullying. That's it.'

'I'm sorry if I've shown some unease. It's insulting considering all you've done.'

'Fr. Jos, it has not ended. We will keep in touch.'

When Gerhard and Tom were on the point of leaving, Jos asked Gerhard if he could have a minute, no more, with Tom.

'Tom, I hope our conversations have done some good.'

'They have, Jos. You have reduced the muddle.'

'Please don't make any precipitous decisions. Give yourself a chance. You were a good priest. You know, you can always leave our order and apply for a diocesan position. Think about it.'

'I can't think about it, Jos. But I promise I won't make a decision without contacting you.'

Jos accompanied Tom to Gerhard's car.

'Goodbye, Tom. Gerhard, farewell. I bless you and your family.'

'Thank you, Father.'

Fr. Jos waved the car off and hobbled to his bench in the park. He looked around the park, green and lush, and listened to the peaceful murmur of the shopping centre. He could not imagine what was ahead of him, but he would be happy if his future were in Binawarra. He only ever wanted to be a parish priest. His thoughts turned to that soft-hearted woman alone on her farm outside Vrouwekerke. 'Blessed are the clean of heart, for they shall see God,' he whispered. Three months later, the other woman appeared near the end of winter. Alone at the wheel, Femke parked her small old-model sedan in front of St. Philomena's church and alighted. She was not in her habit but was well-groomed and dressed neatly and modestly. There was no makeup.

'I should be surprised to see you here,' he said when Femke joined him on the park bench, 'but somehow, I'm not. I am ready for a long, detailed explanation.'

'I'll give a short explanation first. That's probably all that is necessary,' she said with her familiar smile.

'Before you start, Femke, I would lack hospitality if I did not offer lunch, especially after your long drive. I presume you have driven up from Melbourne. Now, I cannot make lunch myself, and it would not be proper to entertain a single woman in the presbytery. But there is a cosy old-fashioned tea shop on the square. If you will accompany me, Femke dear,' he said, standing awkwardly. 'You'll have to walk at my pace, though.'

'Take my arm, Jos,' she said, offering her arm while contemplating him. 'You bring me to tears. After all ...' she bowed, unable to complete her thought.

'No need,' he said, taking her offered arm. 'I'm as happy as I could be here.'

'Well, Cardinal Schuermans' vision for religious life, specifically for female religious, has prevailed in most female orders in Holland,' she said after they were served. 'The changes were abrupt in many communities. In our order, they were steady but insistent until last year, when the democratic reorganisation was accomplished. As I could not go along with the new regime, I resigned from all executive positions. It was proper to allow the new executive committee to conduct themselves without me looking over their shoulders. I did not, however, want to leave the religious life. So, I asked for leave to further my studies. The Decree specifically encourages further studies for female religious. It was granted. I am enrolled in postgraduate studies at John Batman University in Melbourne. I have a small flat close to the university. Any questions?' She smiled warmly and patted his arm.

'I have one question,' said Jos. 'What do you see for the future?'

'I don't know, Jos. I really don't know. The council has turned everything on its head. I don't think that was the intention. I'll wait and see. For now, I will attend to my studies and continue to live the life of a religious. I can't let that go. I hope you'll allow me to visit you now and again.'

'Of course, Femke, you are always welcome.'

They lingered over lunch and talked long about their time together during the war.

'Do you mind, Sister?' said Jos, taking her hand after they had finished lunch, and the plates and cups were cleared away.

'No, Brother Jos.'

They fell silent and gazed around the square, at the lush park and the country folk going about their business.

'I can't wish for more than this,' Jos said, letting go of her hand. For a moment, his thoughts returned to Middelburg.

END

Common Dutch words or phrases

Goedemorgen – Good morning (formal)
Goeiemorgen – Good morning (everyday)
Goedemiddag – Good Afternoon (formal)
Goeiemiddag – Good afternoon (everyday)
Plein – square
Lieverd – darling or dear
Schat – dear darling (literally treasure)
Goede hemel – good heavens (an exclamation)
Allemachtig – lit. almighty (an exclamation like 'my goodness' or 'good lord')
Kasteel Zaligheid – Castle Bliss or Castle of Heavenly Bliss
Meneer – Mr. or sir
Mevrouw – Mrs. or madam
Juffrouw – Miss
Mof – a pejorative word for the Germans during World War 2
Papegaai – Parrot
Stroopwafel – Sweet syrupy cookie or biscuit
Bolus – a syrupy pastry, specialty of Zeeland

Notes on spelling and pronunciation
Dutch spelling deviates in some respects from English. The 'ee' in the name 'Cees' is a pure vowel sound and approximates the 'a' in 'case', without the diphthong slide; 'c' is usually pronounced as 's' but in the case of the name 'Cees' it is pronounced as a 'k'. Cees is thus roughly pronounced as 'Kayse' without the diphthong slide; the 'ij' that appears in Marijke (and many other Dutch words) is equivalent to the diphthong 'ay' in English, thus

with a diphthong slide; 'v' is usually pronounced as an 'f'; 'j' is pronounced as a 'y'; 'w' is pronounced like 'v'. Here are some of the main Dutch names in the story, spelt *roughly* the English way:

Cees van den Donker: Kayse fun den donker
Zeeland: Zayland
Jos van Engelen: Yos fun Engelen
Anneke: Ann-e-ke
Marijke: Maray-ke ('ke' is short)
Lodewijk: Lo-de-vayk

Select Bibliography

For background reading on the occult and goddess worship, the author relied primarily on these titles:

Goddess Unmasked: The Rise of Neopagan Feminist Spirituality, Philip G. Davis, Spence Publishing Company, 1998

Occult Feminism: The Secret Story of Women's Liberation, Rachel Wilson 2021

The Inner Goddess, Josephine Robinson, Gracewing, 1998

Women: Why Are You Weeping? Margaret E. Mills, News Weekly Books, 1997

Awakening Your Goddess, Liz Simpson, Barron's, 2001

Also By Gerard Charles Wilson

FICTION

Sixties Series

Times of Distress (Book 1)
In This Vale of Tears (Book 2)
Counterculture Dreams (Book 3) 2024
The Counterculture Goddess (Book 4) 2025
Love in the Counterculture (Book 5) due 2026
Dreams to Nightmare (Book 6) due 2026
The Castle of Heavenly Bliss (Book 7)
A Sense of Loss (Book 8) due 2027

Editing Constancy: A Jane Austen Story
Seeking the Divine Spark: A Satire in the Style of Evelyn Waugh

NON-FICTION

Social History Series

Prison Hulk to Redemption (Part 1)
War Depression War (Part 2)
Me 'n' Pete: Recalling a Fifties' Childhood (Part 3)
Communists, Billycarts and Two-Wheelers (Part 4) due 2027□

Politics and Media Series

Tony Abbott and the Times of Revolution
The Media of the Republic: Who Killed Diana?
The Telecard Affair: Diary of a Media Lynching 2nd Edition 2024